THE REAL OSAMU DAZAI

A Life in Twenty Short Stories

Translated and Introduced by
James O'Brien

TUTTLE Publishing

Tokyo | Rutland, Vermont | Singapore

Contents

Introduction

WHO WAS THE REAL OSAMU DAZAI?

Osamu Dazai had tried to take his own life on a number of occasions, two of these attempts assuming the form of *joshi*, the traditional Japanese suicide pact entered into by a pair of lovers. But when he disappeared with his mistress on a rainy night in mid-June of 1948, the signs that he was thoroughly prepared to die were unmistakable. Dazai and his companion, Tomie Yamazaki, left behind a series of farewell notes to friends and kin, the author conscientiously composing a last will and testament for his wife, Michiko. Photographs of Dazai and Tomie stood next to one another in Tomie's lodging in the Tokyo suburb of Mitaka, along with the traditional water offering to the deceased. Also nearby was a small pile of ashes, all that remained of the incense that the lovers had lit before departing.

After the police began an intensive search for the couple's whereabouts, they eventually found a suspicious-looking place along the Tamagawa Canal, midway between Dazai's own home and Tomie's residence. A strip of wet grass lay flattened from the top to the bottom of the bank, as if something heavy had slid down into the water. The ground nearby was strewn with several objects—a small bottle or two, a glass plate, a pair of scissors and a compact. A little ways downstream, two pairs of wooden clogs were found against the lock of a dam. Despite these ominous signs, an intensive search along the canal failed to turn up anything more. It was almost a week later—on July 19, the author's thirty-ninth birthday—that a passerby happened to notice two waterlogged corpses in the canal tied together with a red cord. This discovery occurred less than a mile from where the couple had evidently entered the water.

During the period that Dazai had gone missing and before his body was found, a few of his friends reportedly entertained hopes that he was merely in hiding. After all, they could remember those earlier occasions when Dazai had gone away to commit double suicide only to return safe and sound. Perhaps, they reasoned, he would hesitate, or miscalculate before again taking the fatal step—not merely to survive but, as usually happened, to write about his experience. In any event, given this history of abortive attempts upon his own life, it is only natural that certain friends might have held out hope even as they felt the deepest misgivings.

This life of desperation and tragedy seems wholly out of keeping with the favorable circumstances of Dazai's birth. His family had risen to a position of wealth and authority in the northern prefecture of Aomori through land acquisition and moneylending during the three generations preceding his own. By the time Dazai was born in 1909, his father owned the bank in Kanagi, the village where Dazai grew up, which was located on the Tsugaru Plain. Eventually Dazai's father would move into national politics, occupying a seat in each of the houses of the Japanese Diet at different times in his career.

Quite early in his life, however, Dazai began to see himself as a child of misfortune. The tenth of eleven children, he was more or less ignored by his frail mother. And the aunt and the nursemaid who did attend to him both went away while Dazai was still a child.

As the most intelligent of the family sons, Dazai did occupy the center of attention during most of his years of schooling. In the end, though, his intelligence proved to be detrimental, at least by his own estimation. Pressured to excel at school in order to uphold the family honor, Dazai came to hate his studies. After compiling an exemplary record in the local elementary school, he lapsed into mediocrity in the upper grades, and, shortly after enrolling at Tokyo University, he gave up altogether on his formal education. As schoolwork gradually became secondary, Dazai interested himself in the activities of radical students and worked at becoming a writer. His family became understandably upset by this turn of events, for their status and wealth were rooted in traditional social arrangements. One can readily imagine the family's indignation when Dazai published a tale called "A Landlord's Life," evoking the cruelty and indifference of a landlord toward his tenant farmers, the landlord being a thinly disguised version of the author's father, already deceased at the time.

Even after Dazai left his home region in 1930 to enter university, he continued to plague his family. He insisted on marrying a low-class geisha, and he accepted a substantial monthly allowance from his family on the pretext that he was still attending the university and working toward his degree, a deception bound to have severe repercussions once it was discovered. Subsequently, Dazai was formally disowned by his oldest brother, who had succeeded his father as the head of the household. The emotional shock of this action was compounded a few years later when the allowance he had continued to receive was terminated, leaving him in desperate financial straits. Dazai had a taste for personal extravagance, and he was generous too in subsidizing his radical friends, many of whom lived in poverty. His early years in Tokyo were wild ones, with lots of drinking and, for a time, even drug addiction to contend with. Such a life could only exacerbate the propensity for tuberculosis that Dazai shared with other family members.

Having fallen on hard times, Dazai resolved to change his ways. Separated from his first wife, he made overtures toward a reconciliation with his family back in Aomori. Eventually a second marriage was arranged for him through the good offices of the novelist Ibuse Masuji, one that the family privately sanctioned. Following the wedding in January 1939, Dazai settled down to a stable life with his bride, Ishihara Michiko. Several months after the marriage, he and Michiko moved to Tokyo. A daughter was born in 1941, the first of three children.

During the years of World War II, Dazai gradually established his reputation as a leading writer of the time. He thereby achieved a degree of financial independence, and, just as important, he could now hope that the family might overlook his academic failure and even his youthful radicalism. Dazai openly cultivated the goodwill of his family, returning to his Tsugaru birthplace several times during the war. When his house in Tokyo was severely damaged in a bombing raid, he went back to his hometown with his wife and children, and there he remained until November of 1946.

Returning to Tokyo, he soon became lionized as the writer who best expressed the desperation of a society in chaos. Exhausted by illness and besieged by everyone from opportunistic editors to maternalistic women, Dazai was simply unable to cope. It was almost inevitable that he would revert to his earlier life of dissipation. At the time of his death he was writing a comic novel about a bon vivant who tries to rid himself of a whole stable of mistresses. Critics of Dazai occasionally suggest that the author was expressing his own wish to rid himself of Tomie Yamazaki, whose insistent efforts to lure him into that final suicide pact are well documented.

Dazai's popular fame rests mainly on two novels he wrote during his final three years. They are *The Setting Sun* (1947) and *No Longer Human* (1948), both of which reflect the social and moral chaos in Japan following the Second World War. The novels achieved this wide effect by evoking the chaos in the lives of several individuals. These fictional characters exist as projections of the author himself. That is why the works are still avidly read eighty years after they first appeared.

To what extent do the stories in this collection reflect the life of "the real Osamu Dazai"? Dazai's postwar collapse recalls his troubled life of the 1930s. However, the writings from his early period differ strikingly from his postwar ones. The work he did during the relatively stable time in between these periods clearly made him a different writer. To cite just one example of the change, the major postwar writings move away from an explicitly autobiographical manner. The late novels reflect the younger Dazai's personal experience, but do not focus on specific events from his life.

The best of Dazai's writings from before the war's end are shorter than the novels. They are also less well known to the general reader. Here is a summary of the shorter works from throughout Dazai's career which are translated in this book. The summary attempts to place the works in loosely defined categories.

Overtly autobiographical writings constitute the largest category. "Homecoming" (1943) faithfully narrates a sequence of episodes involving his family, while "My Older Brothers" (1940) and "Memories" (1933) provide more freely organized accounts of Dazai's familial relations. "Eight Views of Tokyo" (1941) focuses mostly on Dazai's life in the city, while "Putting Granny Out to Die" (1938) gives a somewhat questionable account of a failed double suicide. Other writings which also seem to reflect phases of Dazai's life include "Das Gemeine" (lit., "The Common Herd," 1935) and "On the Question of Apparel" (1941).

Given these autobiographical tendencies, it might seem surprising how readily Dazai used extant literature as a source for his writing. "Heed My Plea" (1940) is based on the New Testament, while "Run, Melos!" (1940) gets its plot from the 1799 German poem "Die Bürgschaft" (The Hostage) by Friedrich Schiller. This practice became more common with Dazai during the war, when he elaborated on story plots from traditional Japanese tales. His sources were an extensive body of medieval tales known as *Otogi Zoshi*, and the work of Edo period comic writer, Ihara Saikaku. In 1947 he wrote a tale suggestive of the plot of the play, *The Love Suicides of Amijima* by Chikamatsu Monzaemon (1653–1725), regarded as one of Japan's greatest dramatists. Titled "Osan," the very plot of the story speaks to Dazai's marital infidelity at the time of its writing. Indeed, his retellings of the *Otogi Zoshi* tales too suggest Dazai's presence, in this case through language that only he could have written.

The remaining six of the twenty stories translated here come mainly, if not entirely, from the author's imagination. Scattered over the course of his career, these stories encompass both third and first-person narration. Several of the latter are women, the most amusing of whom is a one hundred yen currency note who observes the shenanigans of the postwar black market in "Currency" (1946). The distance between her and the aristocratic narrator of *The Setting Sun* from the same period is symbolic of a fact easy to overlook. Despite the intense focus on himself, Osamu Dazai was quite interested in the wider doings of Japanese society.

Though self-obsessed, Dazai wrote on a wide range of subjects. Even in dealing with himself, he did so in a variety of ways. Often he wrote, or seemed to write, quite directly of himself. At other times, he was more roundabout, or even devious, about himself. How he managed this task can only be intimated at in this introduction.

The early work entitled "Toys" (1935) embodies the author's self-persona in the most radical possible manner. The young narrator, who has the unmistakable marks of a stand-in for Dazai, talks to the reader as if to a listener within the narrative itself. He beguiles this person with a series of amusing anecdotes and an offer to have a drink together. What listener could resist hearing the narrator's infant memoir, one which begins with age three, moves back to ages two and one, and ends with the memory of his birth? Presently the narrator leaves his listener out of the picture and proceeds to the final revelation of "Toys," a direct and chilling encounter with death.

"Toys" demonstrates what Dazai can accomplish when free of plot constraints. On the other hand, a story from two years earlier shows equal agility with a tightly conceived plot. This story, "Undine," begins with an accidental death that occurs in a peaceful natural setting and ends with a suicide that is both a contrast to and amalgamation with this earlier death. There is no intrusive narrator manipulating the plot, let alone one who takes part in the action. The events of the story occur as if on their own. "Undine" (1933) is an extraordinarily moving tale. Why Dazai did not try his hand often at such writing raises a puzzle well worth pondering.

The self-absorption more common to Dazai takes various forms in his writings. Certain common references will momentarily call up a sense of his presence. If a character of any name vacations at his home in Aomori or lives in the village of Mitaka near Tokyo or is the son of a landlord, the reader can safely assume that the author is gesturing toward himself. If a character named "Dazai Osamu" appears out of the blue, expect a joke or two at his expense. More often the language itself indicates an authorial intrusion. If a monkey speaks with droll humor, the practiced reader of Dazai will recognize where the voice comes from.

As a person with suicidal tendencies, Dazai readily conjures up scenes of death. Given his skill with comedy, death readily comes up in the context of the comic. "The Flower of Buffoonery" is a long story not included in these translations. It is worth mention for the conspicuous comic dialogue that occurs in a hospital room occupied by Oba Yozo, the namesake of the main character of *No Longer Human*. The comedy takes place as Yozo recovers from an abortive suicide attempt in which his woman companion lost her life. Nothing close to that appears in this book. However, the reader might read "Putting Granny Out to Die" for its use of farce to evoke another attempt at double suicide.

Readers of *No Longer Human* will realize that comedy in Dazai can have a serious purpose. That same Yozo repeatedly tells how he used his gift for comedy to hide his sense of alienation from society. Although comedy and its role are prominently mentioned in the novel, comic actions themselves add up to no more than several briefly mentioned pranks. *The Setting Sun* too is longer on talk about comedy than actual demonstrations of it. The novel's protagonist Kazuko ends her narration of events by calling the drunken novelist with whom she has an ill-fated love affair as M. C.—"My Comedian." If Dazai had written only these two somber novels, he would seldom if ever be cited for his comedic gift.

Over most of his career, however, Osamu Dazai indulged this gift to the full. Some might complain that he obscured the tragic side of his life by turning too often to comedy. Others could object that the comic and the tragic become so intertwined even in the same work that the reader cannot even untangle them.

The comic in Dazai excels at both hiding and revealing

himself at the same time. The reader who has learned how to spot Dazai in the "planted" references to his life and the language characteristic of him willingly takes part in the game. That reader regards this fellow as a "will of the wisp" sort. And knows not to consider any one figment as the whole. It's a matter of playing along with Dazai rather than trying to pin him down. That at least is the Dazai who emerges from the stories and sketches collected in this volume. And that is the real Osamu Dazai surely embodied in the words he left behind.

James O'Brien
April, 2024

MEMORIES

I

I was standing by our front gate as twilight fell. My aunt was there too in a quilted wrap, the kind a nursemaid often wears when carrying an infant strapped to her back. The road before our house had grown dim and everything was hushed. I have never forgotten that moment.

She was speaking of the emperor, and I can still remember bits and snatches of what she said—*His Majesty . . . gone into seclusion . . . a true living god*. Filled with wonder, I repeated certain words—*A . . . true . . . god . . .*

Then I must have said the wrong thing. *No*, my aunt scolded, you should say, *Gone into seclusion*. I knew exactly where the emperor had gone, but I asked about it anyway. I still remember how she laughed at that.

Emperor Meiji had been on the throne forty-two years when I was born. When he passed away, I was only three.

I guess it was about then that my aunt took me to visit some relatives. Their village was about five miles away, near a broad waterfall in the mountains. I remember how white the water looked against the green moss as it cascaded down the cliff. I didn't know the man who held me on his shoulders to watch. When he showed me the votive pictures in the shrine below the falls, I became very lonely. Eventually I broke into tears and called out, "Auntie! Auntie!"

In a hollow some distance off, my relatives and my aunt had spread rugs on the ground. They were making lots of noise when I cried out, but my aunt heard and jumped up immediately. She must have slipped just then, however, for she stumbled, as though making a bow. The others couldn't resist teasing her. "Look!" they cried, "she's already drunk." As I watched these things occurring far down in the hollow, I felt so ashamed that I finally began screaming at the top of my lungs.

While still a child, I dreamed one evening that my aunt was going away and leaving me behind. I saw her standing in our front entranceway, totally occupying it with her bulk. Her breasts seemed large and red, and perspiration trickled down her skin. *I can't stand you*, she hissed, prompting me to run over and press my cheek to her breasts. No, I begged, please don't leave. Sobbing, I pleaded with her again and again. When my aunt shook me awake, I hugged her right there in bed and kept on crying. Even after I was fully aware, I wept quietly for a long time. Afterward I didn't tell anyone of my dream, not even my aunt. I remember plenty of things about my aunt from those early days. But I don't remember anyone else, even though there were surely many people in the house besides my father and mother. That's because our family included my great-grandmother and grandmother, my three older brothers and four older sisters and my younger brother too. Then there was my aunt and her four daughters. Except for my aunt, however, I was hardly aware of anyone. Not at least until I was four or five years old.

We must have had five or six tall apple trees in our big garden out back. I remember a cloudy day when some girls were climbing about in those trees. The garden had a chrysanthemum patch, and I vaguely recall a crowd of girls gazing at the flowers in full bloom. They were standing in the rain with umbrellas. I suppose they were sisters and cousins of mine.

From the time I was five or six years old, my memories become quite definite. Around that time a maid named Také taught me how to read. She really wanted me to learn, and we read all kinds of books together. Since I was a sickly child, I often read in bed. When we ran out of books, Také would bring back an armful from places like the village Sunday school and have me read them. I learned to read silently too. That's why I could finish one book after another without getting tired.

Také also taught me about right and wrong. Often we went to a temple where she would show me Buddhist hell paintings and explain the punishments they depicted. Sinners condemned to hell for arson carried flaming red baskets upon their backs, while those who had kept mistresses writhed in the grip of a green snake with two heads. The paintings depicted a lake of blood and a mountain of spikes, as well as a bottomless pit called "The Abyss" that gave off white smoke. Thin, pale wretches, wailing through barely opened mouths, were strewn over all these regions. "Tell a lie," Také said, "and you'd end up the same way—a sinner in hell with your tongue plucked out by devils." Hearing this, I screamed in terror.

The temple graveyard was on a small hill out back, with requiem posts clustered along the hedge-rose border. Besides the usual prayers in brush writing, each of the posts carried a dark, metal wheel. Fastened in a slot high on the post, each wheel seemed to me then about the size of the full moon. "Spin the wheel once," Také explained, "and if it clatters round and round and comes to a stop without turning back, then you'll go to heaven. But," she warned, "if the wheel starts back, you'll end up in hell."

Také would give a push and the wheel would spin smoothly until it slowed to a complete stop. When I tried, however, the wheel sometimes turned back. I think it was in the autumn that I went alone to the temple to test my luck. The wheels seemed to be in league with one another, for they all turned back regardless of which one I pushed. Though tired and angry, I kept myself under control and stubbornly pushed them time after time. As dusk fell, I finally gave up and left the graveyard in despair.

My parents must have been living in Tokyo about that time, and I was taken by my aunt for a visit. I'm told we were there a long while, but I don't remember much about my stay. I do remember an old lady who came to the house every so often. I couldn't stand her, and cried each time she showed up. Once she brought along a toy postal truck painted red, but it merely bored me.

Then I started going to the village grade school, and that left me with different memories altogether. Suddenly Také was no longer around. I learned that she had gone off to marry someone from a fishing village. She left without telling me this, apparently out of fear that I might follow her. It must have been the next year that Také came to visit us during Obon, the Festival of the Dead. She seemed rather cold toward me, however, and when she asked how I was doing at school, I didn't answer. I suppose someone else told her. She didn't really compliment me. She just said, "Don't get too big for your britches."

At about the same time, certain events led to my aunt's departure as well. Having no son to carry on the family name, she decided that her oldest daughter would marry a dentist who would be adopted to continue the family line. Her second daughter got married and left, while the third died while still young. Taking along her oldest daughter and the new husband, as well as her fourth daughter, my aunt established a separate branch of the family in a distant town. The move occurred in the winter, and I was to go along. As the time to leave drew near, I crouched in a corner of the sleigh next to my aunt. That's when my next-older brother came up and slapped my rump right where it pressed against the lower end of the hood. "Hey there, little bridegroom!" he sneered, thumping me time and again. Gritting my teeth, I put up with his insolence. Indeed I thought my aunt was adopting me as well as the dentist. But when school began once again, I was sent back to my village.

I ceased being a child soon after entering grade school. It was then that my younger brother's nurse taught me something that took my breath away. It was a beautiful summer day, and the grass by the vacant house out back had grown tall and dense. I must have been about seven, and my brother's nurse could not have been more than thirteen or fourteen. My brother was three years younger than I, and the nurse shooed him off. She said, "Go get some leaf-grass"—that's our word for clover back home. Then she added, "And make sure it's got four leaves too." After he left, she put her arms around me, and we started rolling around in the tall grass.

Thereafter we would play our secret little game in one of the closets. My younger brother was always in our way. He even started howling one day when we left him outside the closet, an event that put my next-older brother on to us. Having found out from my little brother what the trouble was, my older brother opened the closet door. The nurse did not get upset; she merely said that we were looking for a lost coin.

I was always telling fibs too. On the Girls' Festival day of my second or third year in grade school, I told the teacher my family wanted me home early to help arrange the doll display. Having lied my way out of class, I went home and told everyone school was out for the festival. My assistance wasn't needed, but I got the dolls from their boxes all the same.

Another thing I enjoyed was collecting bird eggs. There were always plenty of sparrow eggs right under the tiles of our storehouse roof. But starlings and crows didn't nest there, and I had to turn to my classmates for these eggs. (The crow eggs were green and seemed to glow, while the starling eggs were covered with strange speckles.) In return for the eggs, I would hand over a bunch of my books. Wrapped in cotton, the eggs in my collection eventually filled an entire drawer of my desk.

My next-older brother must have suspected something. One evening he asked to borrow two books, a volume of Western fairy tales and a work whose title I've forgotten. My brother did this from spite, and I hated him for it. The books were gone, for I had traded them both for eggs. If I admitted this, my brother would have gone to reclaim them. So I told him the books were around somewhere and I would look for them. Lamp in hand, I searched my own room and then went all over the house. My brother laughed as he followed me about. He kept saying, "They're not here, are they?" And I kept insisting, "They are too." I even climbed up to the highest kitchen shelf for a look. Finally my brother told me to forget it.

The compositions I wrote for school were mostly hokum. I tried to portray myself as a model boy, for I believed people would applaud me for that. I even plagiarized. The essay entitled "My Younger Brother's Silhouette" was a masterpiece according to my teacher, but I actually lifted it word for word from a selection of prize stories in a magazine for youngsters. The teacher had me make a clean copy with a brush and enter the work in a contest. When a bookish classmate found out what I had done, I prayed that he would die.

"Autumn Evening," composed about the same time, was also praised by my teacher. I began this sketch by mentioning a headache I got from studying, and then went on to describe how I went out on the veranda and looked at the garden. I gazed entranced upon the quiet scene, the moon shining brightly, the goldfish and the carp swimming about in the pond. When a burst of laughter came from a nearby room where my mother and some other people were gathered, I snapped out of the reverie and my headache was suddenly gone—that's how the sketch ended.

There wasn't a word of truth to this. I took the description of the garden from my older sister's composition notebook. Above all, I don't remember studying enough to get a headache. I hated school and never read a textbook. I only read entertaining books. My family thought I was studying as long as I was reading something or other.

But when I put down the truth, things always went wrong. When I wrote that Father and Mother didn't love me, the assistant disciplinarian called me into the teachers' room for a scolding. Assigned the topic, "What If a War Breaks Out?" I wrote how frightening war could be—worse even than an earthquake, lightning, fire or one's own father. That's why I said that I would flee to the hills, at the same time urging my teacher to join me. After all, my teacher was only human, and war would scare him just like it would me.

This time the assistant disciplinarian and the school principal both questioned me. When asked what prompted these words, I took a gamble and said I was only joking. The assistant disciplinarian made a note in his book—*Full of mischief!* Then a brief battle of wits ensued between the two of us. "Did I believe," he asked, "that all men were equal?" After all, the assistant disciplinarian went on, I had written that my teacher was only human too. I hesitated before replying that yes, I thought so. Really, I was slow with my tongue.

"If," the assistant disciplinarian continued, "he himself was equal to the principal, why didn't they get the same salary?" I thought about that awhile and said, "Isn't it because your work is different?"

His thin face set off by the wire frames of his spectacles, the assistant disciplinarian immediately recorded my answer in his book. And then this man whom I had long admired asked whether or not he and I were equal to my own father. That one I just couldn't answer.

A busy man, my father was seldom at home. Even when he

was, he usually didn't bother about his children. I once wanted a fountain pen like his, but was too afraid to ask for one. After wrestling with the problem, I fell back on pretending to talk in my sleep. Lying in bed one evening, I kept murmuring, Fountain pen . . . fountain pen . . . Father was talking with a guest in the next room, and my words were meant for him. Needless to say, they never reached his ear, let alone his heart.

Once my younger brother and I were playing in the large family storehouse piled high with sacks of rice when Father planted himself in the doorway and shouted, "Get out of here! Get out, you monkeys!" With the sunlight at his back, father loomed there like a dark shadow. My stomach turns even now when I recall how frightened I was.

I didn't feel close to Mother, either. I was first raised by a nursemaid, then by my aunt. Until the second or third year of grade school, I didn't really get to know my mother. Some years later, as she lay on her futon next to mine, Mother noticed how my blanket was moving about. "What are you up to?" she asked suspiciously. Well, two of the menservants had taught me something, and Mother's question put me on the spot. I managed to say that my hip was sore, however, and that I was rubbing it. "You needn't be so rough about it," Mother replied. Her voice sounded drowsy. I massaged my hip awhile, without saying anything.

My memories of Mother are mostly dismal ones. There was the time I got my older brother's suit from the storehouse and put it on. Then, strolling among the flower beds in the garden out back, I hummed a mournful tune I had made up and then shed a few tears besides. Suddenly I felt that, while wearing this particular outfit, I might try fooling around with the student who did our household accounts. So I sent a maid to call him. He didn't come though, even though I waited a long time. In my anxiety I ran the tip of my shoe along the bamboo fence. Finally my patience gave way and, with both fists thrust into my pockets, I let out a wail. When Mother found me, she got me out of that suit and, for some reason or other, gave me a good spanking. I felt utterly ashamed.

Even as a child I wanted to be well dressed. My shirts had to be made of white flannel and have buttons on the cuffs, or I wouldn't wear them. My undershirt collar, which I let show an inch or two above my shirt collar, also had to be white. During the Full Moon Festival the students in the village all dressed up in their Sunday best for school. I always chose my flannel kimono with the wide brown stripes for this occasion. Arriving at school, I would glide along the corridor with tiny steps, just like a girl. I made sure no one was around, since I didn't want people knowing what a fop I was.

Everyone kept saying that I was the ugliest boy in the family. And if they had known how fussy I was about clothes, they would surely have had a good laugh at my expense. I pretended not to care about my appearance, and this seemed to do the trick. I gave the impression of being dull and uncouth, no doubt about it. At mealtimes my brothers and I sat on the floor, a tray before each of us. Grandmother and Mother were also present. It was awful hearing them remark over and over how ugly I was.

Actually I was quite proud of myself. I'd go down to the maids' quarters and ask offhandedly who was the best boy in the family. The girls usually said that my oldest brother was. Then they added that Shucha—that's me—was second best. I resented being second, but blushed to hear it all the same. Indeed, I wanted them to say I was better than my oldest brother.

It wasn't just my looks that displeased Grandmother. I was clumsy as well. At every meal she cautioned me about holding my chopsticks properly. She even said that the way I bowed made my rump stick out indecently. I had to sit properly in front of her and make one bow after another. No matter how often I tried, she never once complimented me.

Grandmother was a headache for me in other ways too. When a theater troupe came from Tokyo to celebrate the opening of our village playhouse, I went to every performance without fail. My father had built the playhouse, so I always had a good seat for nothing. Each day when I got home from school, I hurriedly changed into a soft kimono. Then I ran off to the playhouse, a narrow chain dangling from my sash with a pencil attached to the end. That's how I first got to know about Kabuki. While watching the performances, I would shed one tear after another.

Even before this time, I had been something of a performer myself. I really enjoyed calling the menservants and maids together and telling old stories or else showing films and slides. After the Tokyo troupe had left, I rounded up my younger brother and my cousins to put on my own show. I arranged two comic *kyogen* pieces for the program—*Yamanaka Shikanosuke, The House of the Dove* and a comic dance known as *kappore*. The first had a teahouse scene set in a valley, during which Shikanosuke gains a follower named Hayakawa Ayunosuke. Adapting the scene from a text in a young peoples' magazine, I took infinite pains to cast the words in Kabuki rhythms: "Your humble servant / A man known to the world as / Shikanosuke." From *The House of the Dove*, a long novel that I had read over and over (and never without crying), I selected an especially pathetic section to render as a two-act play. Since the Tokyo troupe always ended its program with the entire cast performing a kappore dance, I decided to do that too.

With five or six days of rehearsing over, we scheduled our first performance for that evening. We had set up the stage on the wide veranda before the library room, with a small curtain suspended in front. It was still broad daylight when Grandmother came by, but she didn't notice the curtain wire. When her jaw got caught on it, she cried out, "You pack of river bums! Stop it! That wire could've killed me."

Despite this incident, we gathered ten or so menservants and maids for the evening performance. The memory of Grandmother's words weighed heavily upon me. While performing the title role in *Yamanaka Shikanosuke* and that of the boy in *The House of the Dove*, and even while dancing kappore, I felt isolated and completely listless. After that night, I would eventually I put on other plays, such as *The Rustler*, *The Mansion of the Plates* and *Shuntoku Maru*, but Grandmother always looked disgusted.

Though I didn't much care for Grandmother, I was grateful to her on sleepless nights all the same. From the third or fourth year of grade school, I had suffered from insomnia. Midnight would be long past, and I would still be lying awake in bed. Since I cried so often at night, the family tried to come up with remedies for my sleeplessness. Lick sugar before bed, I was told, or else count the ticking of the clock. I tried other suggestions, like cooling my feet in a pan of water or placing a leaf from the "sleeping tree" under my pillow. But nothing seemed to work. A bundle of nerves, I would anxiously turn over one thing after another in my mind. This only made falling asleep more difficult. I had a succession of bad nights after secretly playing with Father's pince-nez and cracking the lens.

The notions shop two doors away handled several kinds of books and magazines. One day I was looking at the illustrations inside the front cover of a ladies' journal, one of them a watercolor of a yellow mermaid. I wanted this illustration so badly that I decided to steal it. I had quietly torn the page out when the young manager sharply called out my boyhood name, "Osako! Osako!" I flung the magazine to the floor and rushed home. Blunders such as this one kept me awake for nights on end.

Sometimes I'd lie in bed needlessly worrying that a fire might break out. I'd wonder, "What if the house burned down?" and after that I couldn't sleep at all.

One evening I was heading for the toilet just before bed-time. The room where the family accounts were kept was right across the hallway from my destination. The room was dark, and the student who kept the accounts was running a movie projector. The picture on the sliding door he was using as a screen hardly seemed bigger than a matchbox, but I could make out a polar bear about to plunge off an ice floe into the sea. Observing this, I sensed something unbearably sad about the student. Back in bed, I thought about the movie scene and reflected as well on the life of this student, my heart pounding all the while. I wondered what would I do if the nitrate film in the projector caught fire. Beset by this worry, I couldn't get to sleep until almost dawn. On nights such as this, I would feel especially grateful to my grandmother.

Around eight o'clock in the evening, a maid would come to my room and lie next to me until I fell asleep. Since I felt sorry for her, I would lie still with my eyes closed. As soon as she left, I'd start praying that I could fall asleep. I would toss and turn until almost ten o'clock, then break into a whimper and get up. By that time the whole family other than Grand-mother would be in bed.

Grandmother would still be in the kitchen by the large hearth, sitting across from the night watchman. Ensconced between them in my quilted pajamas, I would dejectedly listen to their inevitable gossip about people in the village. Late one night, as I leaned over to hear, the beat of a great drum echoed from far away. People were still up, celebrating the Insect-Ex-pulsion Festival, an occasion when farmers try various means of ridding their fields of harmful pests. I have not forgotten how reassuring it was to know that others were still awake.

Thinking of that far-off drumbeat brings back other mem-ories. My oldest brother was at a university in Tokyo around then and whenever he came back for summer vacation, he brought word of the latest trends in music and literature. My brother studied drama, and he even published a one-act play in a local magazine. Called *The Struggle*, it was much discussed by the young people hereabouts. Along with my other brothers and sisters, I had listened to him recite the play just after he had finished the manuscript. Everyone had complained that it didn't make sense. I alone understood, even down to the poetic curtain line, "Ah, how dark the night is!" But I did think the title should be *The Thistle* rather than *The Struggle*. And in tiny letters I wrote this opinion in a corner of some used manuscript paper. Perhaps my brother didn't notice, for he published the play without changing the title.

My brother's large collection of phonograph records had both Japanese and Western melodies. I already knew the Japanese melodies because of the geisha who came to our house. Whenever he gave a party, my father would send word to a city some distance away to request their services. I remember being hugged by these geisha from the age of four or five. I recall watching them dance too, and listening to their songs, "Once Upon a Time" and "The Tangerine Boat from Ki Province."

As I lay in bed one night, a fine melody filtered out of my brother's room. I lifted my head from the pillow, listening closely. The next morning I got up early and went over. I selected one record after another and played every one on my brother's phonograph. At last I found the melody that had so excited me last night, a shamisen ballad about the ill-fated drummer Rancho.

But I felt much closer to my second-oldest brother. After graduating with honors from a Tokyo business school, he had come back to work in the family bank. This brother was treated callously, just like I was. Mother and Father said he was the worst boy in the family (after me, of course), so I figured looks were the problem with him too. He'd sometimes say to me, "I don't need anything now—but if only I'd been born good-looking." Then he'd ask teasingly, "What do you think of that, Shu?"

Despite such bantering, I never thought my brother so ill-favored. I regarded him as one of the smarter boys in the family, too. He seemed to drink every day and then quarrel with Grandmother. Each time this happened, I felt a secret hatred for her.

With my third brother, the one just older than me, I was always feuding. He knew many of my secrets, and that made me uneasy. He looked quite a bit like my little brother, and everyone remarked how handsome he was. I was, so to speak, being squeezed from above and below, and I could hardly bear it. When this older brother went off to higher school in Tokyo, I breathed a sigh of relief.

My little brother was the family baby. He had a gentle look as well, and this endeared him to Father and Mother. I was always jealous and would hit him now and then. Mother would scold me, and then I'd resent her too. I must have been about nine or ten when the problem with the lice occurred. They were all over me, scattered like sesame seeds on the seams of my underwear and my shirt. When my brother grinned about this, I just knocked him down—I really did. His head began swelling in several places, and that worried me. I got hold of some ointment labeled "For External Use Only" and applied it to his bruises.

I had four older sisters, all of them fond of me. The oldest one died, however, and the next one left to get married. The two youngest sisters went off to school, each to a different town. Whenever their vacation came to an end, the two of them had to go seven or eight miles from our village to reach the nearest train station. During the summer they could take our horse-drawn carriage. When hail was blowing about in the fall, however, or snow melting in the spring, they had no choice except to walk. They might have gone by sleigh during the winter, but the sleigh happened to make them both sick. That's why they ended up walking then too. Whenever they were due back in the winter, I'd go to the edge of our village where lumber was piled up. Even after the sun went down, the road remained bright in the snow. When the flickering lamps that my sisters carried finally emerged from the woods of the next village, I would throw up my arms and let out a whoop.

The school of the older sister happened to be in a smaller town. Because of that, the souvenirs she brought back could not compare with the younger sister's. Once she took from her basket five or six packets of incense-sparklers and handed them to me. "I'm so sorry," she said, a blush upon her cheeks. At that moment I felt my breast constrict. According to my family, this sister too was homely.

She had lived in a separate room with my great-grand-mother until she went away to school, so how could I avoid thinking of her as the old lady's daughter? Then, around about the same time as I was finishing grade school, my great-grand-mother passed away. I caught a glimpse of the small, rigid body dressed in a white kimono as it was being placed in the cof-fin. I fretted about what to do if this scene kept haunting me.

I graduated from grade school in due course, but I was too frail for higher school. My family decided to send me to a spe-cial intermediate school for one year to see if I got stronger. If I did, Father would send me to higher school here in the province. My older brothers had all studied in Tokyo, but that would be bad for my health. I didn't care much about going to higher school, anyhow. But I did get some sympathy from my teachers by writing about how frail I was.

The intermediate school belonged to the county, a new unit of government back then. Five or six villages and towns had gotten together and put up the building in a pine grove more than a mile from my home. Many bright students from grade schools throughout the area were enrolled, and I had to main-tain the honor of the grade school I had come from against this competition. I had to strive to be the best, even though I would often be absent because of my health.

Nonetheless, I didn't study there either. To one headed for higher school, the place seemed dirty and unpleasant. I spent most of every class drawing a manga serial. During recess I would explain the characters to my classmates and even give impersonations of them. I filled four or five notebooks with such manga.

With my elbow braced on the desk and my chin resting in my palm, I would gaze outside for a whole hour. My seat was near a window where a fly once got smashed. Glimpsed from the side, the look of the dead fly struck me time and again. It almost seemed to be a large pheasant or a mountain dove.

I would play hooky with five or six friends and together we would head for the marsh just beyond the pine grove. While loitering at the edge of the water, we would gossip about the girls in our class, then roll up our kimono skirts to stare at each other's fuzz. It was great fun to compare how we were all doing.

I kept my distance from every girl at school though. I was so easily aroused that I had to watch myself. Two or three of the girls had a crush on me, but I was a coward and pretended not to notice.

I would go into Father's library and take down the volume of paintings from the Imperial Art Exhibition. As I gazed at a nude painting buried somewhere among the pages, my cheeks would begin to glow. Another thing I would do is put my pair of pet rabbits in the same cage, my heart pounding as the male climbed on and hunched its back. By doing these things I kept my own urges from getting out of hand.

I was really a prig and didn't tell anyone about the pleasurable massaging I'd discovered. When I read how harmful it was, I decided to stop. But nothing seemed to work.

Since I walked all the way to school and back each day, my body grew stronger. At the same time little pimples came out on my forehead like millet grains, much to my embarrassment. I would paint them with a red ointment.

That same year, my oldest brother got married. On the evening of the wedding, my younger brother and I tiptoed up to the bride's room and peeked in. She was having her hair done, with her back to the door. I caught a glimpse of the pale, white face in the mirror, then fled with my younger brother in tow.

"What's so great about her?" I swaggered. Ashamed of my forehead and the red ointment, I reacted all the more violently.

As winter drew near I had to start studying for the entrance exam to higher school. I looked over the book ads in the magazines, then ordered various reference works from Tokyo. I arranged them on my shelves, but didn't do any reading. The higher school of my choice, located in the province's largest city, would attract two or three times more applicants than it could admit. Now and then I was overcome with fear; I had to get down to studying or else I would fail the exam. A week of hard work would restore my confidence. During these bouts of study I would stay up until midnight and usually get up at four the next morning. A maid named Tami stayed by me. I'd have her keep the charcoal fire going and make the tea. No matter how late she stayed up, Tami always came to wake me at four o'clock the next morning. While I puzzled over an arithmetic problem involving a mouse and the number of her offspring, Tami sat quietly nearby reading a novel. Presently she was replaced by a fat, elderly maid. When I heard that Mother was behind this change and thought of what her motive might be, I could only frown.

Early the following spring, while the snow was still deep, my father coughed up blood in a Tokyo hospital and died. The local paper published his obituary in a special edition, an event that affected me more than the death itself. My own name appeared in the paper's list of surviving kin.

Father's body was brought home one night in a great coffin mounted upon a sleigh. I went along with a large crowd to meet the hearse near the next village. Eventually a long procession of sleighs glided from the woods. The hood of each vehicle re-flected the moonlight, creating a lovely scene.

The next day our family gathered in the shrine room where the coffin rested. When the lid was opened, everyone burst into tears. Father seemed to be asleep, his prominent nose looking very straight and pale. Enticed by the weeping, I too shed some tears.

For the next month the house was in such chaos that one might have thought a fire had occurred. I forgot about my stud-ies altogether. And, when the time for the final exam arrived, I could only give haphazard answers. The examiner knew about my family, though, and I was graded third highest among the group. I suspected that my memory was starting to weaken. For the first time ever, I felt I could not handle an exam with-out preparing for it.

II

Although my scores were low, I also managed to pass the en-trance exam for higher school that spring. The school was in a small town on the coast and, when the time came, I had to leave my own village. I dressed quite stylishly for the trip—new *hakama* formal pants, dark stockings and laced boots. Rather than wrapping myself in the usual blanket to keep warm, I threw a woolen cloak over my shoulders and deliberately left it unbuttoned. When I reached my destination, a dry-goods store with an old tattered *noren* curtain hanging in the front entrance, I took off this outfit. The shop was run by distant relatives with whom I would lodge, and to whom I became deeply indebted over time.

There are people who get suddenly worked up over any-thing whatever, and I'm one of them. Now that I was in higher school, I'd put on my student cap and new hakama just to go to the public bathhouse. Catching my reflection in the shop windows along the way, I'd even nod my head and smile.

I couldn't get excited about school, however. Not that the place wasn't nice enough. The building was situated at the edge of town, with a park behind extending to the Tsugaru Strait. It was painted white outside, and inside there were wide hallways and classrooms with high ceilings. During class one could hear the hiss of the waves and the sough of the pines.

But the teachers in that school were always persecuting me. As early as orientation day, the gymnastics instructor called me a smart aleck and started hitting me. That really hurt, since he was the very person who had been so gentle with me on the oral examination. Knowing that my father had passed away, he had understood why I wasn't prepared for the entrance exam. When he had mentioned this, I had hung my head for his benefit.

Then the other instructors started hitting me. They gave all sorts of reasons for dishing out such punishment. I was yawning, grinning or whatever. My unrestrained yawning apparently became a subject of conversation in the teachers' room. It amused me to think what dumb things they talked about there.

One day a student from my own village called me over to the sand dune in the schoolyard. "You're bound to flunk," he warned, "as long as they keep hitting you like that. And," he added, "you really do act like a smart aleck." I was dumbfounded. That afternoon after class, I hurriedly set out for home along the beach. With no one else around, I sighed as the waves licked against my shoes. I raised my arm, wiping the sweat from my brow with my shirt sleeve. A gray sail, astonishingly large, wavered past my very eyes.

I was a petal quivering in the slightest breeze, about to fall any moment. Even the slightest insult made me think of dying. Believing I would amount to something before long, I stood up for my honor so firmly that I could not allow even an adult to make light of me. That's why failing at school would have been a disaster. From that time on I became tense in the classroom, so anxious was I to pay attention. During every lesson I believed myself in a room with a hundred invisible foes. I could not let my guard down in the least. Every morning before setting out for school, I turned up a playing card on the desk in search of my daily fortune. A heart was lucky, a diamond promising; a club was foreboding, while a spade meant certain disaster. At this time of my life, spades turned up day after day.

With an exam coming soon, I memorized every word of my natural history, geography and ethics textbooks. I was finicky, and for me the exam was a matter of do or die. But my method turned out to be faulty. Inexorably I felt hemmed in and unable to adapt to the exam. Certain questions I answered almost to perfection. In other cases, however, I tripped over the words and phrases in my confusion and ended up soiling the test booklet with mere gibberish.

Nonetheless, my marks that first term were the third highest in the class. Even in deportment I received an A. I seized my report card in one hand and, holding my shoes in the other, dashed out to the beach. Having been tormented by the prospect of failing, now I was absolutely elated.

With the term over, I made preparations to go home for my first vacation from higher school. My younger brother and his friends would hear of my brief experience in glowing terms. I stuffed everything I had acquired into the trunk, going so far as to include even some sitting cushions.

Tossed about in the carriage, we came out of the woods of the neighboring village. The rich green of the rice paddies spread out like the sea, and the familiar roof of my own home, with its red tiles, rose conspicuously in the distance. I gazed toward home as though I had been away for ten years.

Never have I been so elated as during the month of that vacation. To my younger brother I boasted of the school as something one might dream of. In my telling, even the small coastal town seemed part of a vision.

I was supposed to paint five watercolors and collect ten rare insects for my homework. I spent the whole month wandering through the fields and the river valleys, sketching the landscape and looking for insects. I took my younger brother along for help. He could hold the collector's kit, with the tweezers and jar of poison, while I carried the net on my shoulder. I chased after locusts and cabbage butterflies all day long. When night fell, I would get a crackling fire going in the park and, as the insects flew by, flail away at them with a net or a broom.

My next-older brother was enrolled in the sculpture division at art school. He was making a bust of my next-older sister, who had just graduated from a girls' school. While he fiddled with clay beneath the chestnut tree in the garden, I stood nearby sketching her portrait time and again.

She may have taken her posing quite seriously, but my brother and I merely poked fun at each other's work. My sister was usually more impressed with my work, yet my brother only ridiculed my talent. When you're young, he claimed, everyone says you're gifted. He dismissed my writing too, calling it grade-schoolish. In return I was openly contemptuous of his abilities.

One evening this brother came over to where I slept and whispered, "Osa! I've got a bug for you!" Squatting on the floor, he slid a tissue wrapping beneath the edge of the mosquito net. He knew I was collecting rare insects. And when I heard the scratching noise inside the tissue as the insect struggled to get out, I realized what kinship meant. I undid the paper roughly, and my brother gasped, "He'll get away! Look! Look!" I could see it was only a stag beetle, but I put it down as "sheathed and winged," one of my ten types, and handed it in.

I was depressed to see the vacation end. Returning all alone to my second-floor room at the dry-goods store, I opened my trunk and almost burst into tears. At such times I always sought refuge in a bookstore. There was one close by, and I hurried there then. Just to see all the books lining the shelves would lighten my mood as if by magic. This particular store had one corner containing a half dozen volumes that I couldn't buy even though I wanted to. Now and then I would linger there and peek inside the covers. I would try to act casual, but my knees would be shaking. Of course, I didn't go to bookstores just to read the articles on human anatomy that these books contained. I went because any book gave me comfort and solace at the time.

My schoolwork, however, became more and more boring. Nothing was worse than coloring in mountain ranges, harbors and rivers on an outline map. But I was a stickler for doing things properly, so I would spend three or four hours at this. In history and certain other classes the teachers told us to take notes on the main points of the lectures. Listening to a lecture was like reading a textbook, so the students merely copied sentences straight from the book. Being attached to grades, I worked away at such tasks day after day.

In the fall there were various athletic events for the higher-school students in town. Out in the countryside we had never played baseball, so I only knew such terms as "center field," "deep short," and "bases loaded" from books. Eventually I learned how to watch a game, but I didn't get worked up about it. Whenever my own school competed in tennis, judo or even baseball, I had to join the cheering section. This made me dislike higher school all the more.

Our head cheerleader would look purposely shabby as he climbed the knoll in the schoolyard corner and, holding a fan with the rising sun insignia, gave us a pep talk. Reacting to him, the students would cry out with glee, "Slob! You slob!" When a match took place, this cheerleader leaped up during every break in the action and started waving his fan. "ALL STAND UP!" he'd shout in his funny English. And we would get up, our tiny purple banners flapping in unison, and sing the fight song: "Our Foe is Worthy, But . . ." It was quite embarrassing. When I spied an opportunity, I'd slip away from the cheering section and go home.

Not that I myself never played sports. My complexion had a faint darkness, which I blamed on that massaging habit of mine. I got flustered when people mentioned my face, for they seemed to be indicating my secret vice. Somehow or other I felt I must improve my color. That's why I took up sports.

I had long fretted about my complexion. As early as my fourth or fifth year of elementary school, my next-older brother had already spoken to me of democratic ideas. Then I heard certain complaints, even from Mother. She once told visitors to our home that democracy had meant much higher taxes and that most of the family harvest now went to the government. I was quite confused by the various things I heard. At the same, I tried to be democratic toward our family's servants. In the summer I lent a hand to the men mowing the lawn, and in the winter I helped shovel snow from the roof. Eventually I discovered that my help wasn't welcome. It even seems the men had to redo the part of the lawn that I had tried to mow. To tell the truth, I was actually trying to improve my color. But even hard work didn't do any good.

During higher school I got into sports because of my complexion. On the way home from school in the summer, I always took a dip in the ocean. I liked to use the breast stroke, keeping my legs wide apart, just as a frog might. With my head sticking straight out of the water, I could observe various things even as I swam—the delicate shading of the waves, the fresh leaves on shore, the drifting clouds. I kept my head stretched out like a turtle. If I could bring my face even a bit closer to the sun, I'd get a tan that much quicker.

There was a large graveyard behind the house where I lived. I laid out a hundred-meter course for myself and took up sprinting in earnest. The graveyard was surrounded by a dense row of poplars and I would loiter within the grounds and examine one gravestone inscription after another whenever I got tired. I read some unforgettable phrases—"Moonlight Penetrates the Pool Bottom," for example, or "Three Worlds, One Purpose."

One day, on a dark, moist gravestone covered with liverwort, I made out some writing that said, "The Deceased, Jakusho Seiryo." Ascribed to the dead man in accord with Buddhist practice, the name evoked the solitude and quiet of the grave. Disturbed by this discovery, I made up several lines of verse and wrote them down on the white paper that had recently been folded like a lotus leaf and left before the grave. Intended to suggest a certain French poet, the lines read: "I am in the ground now, together with the maggots." With my index finger I traced the words in mud as delicately as a ghost might have done.

The next evening I went to the grave before I did my sprinting. The words of the ghost had washed away in the rain that morning, so none of the bereaved kin would have been offended by seeing them on a visit to the grave. The white lotus leaves had torn in places.

Even as I fooled around like this, I got better at running. My leg muscles began to bulge too, but my complexion remained the same as ever. Beneath the deep tan on my face a pale, dirty color still lingered. It was quite unsavory.

I was very intrigued by my face. When weary of reading, I would take out a hand mirror and gaze at myself. Smiling, frowning, looking contemplative with my cheek resting on my palm, I never got bored. I mastered certain expressions guaranteed to make people laugh. Wrinkling my nose, pursing my mouth and squinting, I would turn myself into a charming bear cub. I chose that particular look when I was puzzled or dissatisfied.

Around this time, my next-older sister was in the local hospital because of an illness. If I showed her my bear-cub face, she would roll about in bed laughing hard and holding her stomach. My sister had a middle-aged maid from home for company, but she was still lonely. That's why my visits meant a lot to her. My slow footsteps in the hospital corridor echoed louder than those of other people, so my sister could hear me approaching her room. By the time I got there, she would be elated.

If I didn't visit her for a week, my sister would send the maid to fetch me. With a solemn look the maid would say, "You'd better come or your sister's temperature will go up. She'll be worse off then."

I was now fourteen or fifteen, and veins had become faintly visible on the back of my hand. I felt something strange and momentous taking place within me. I was secretly in love with a classmate, a short fellow with dark skin. We always walked home together after school, blushing when our little fingers merely grazed one another. Once, as we were heading along the back road after school, my friend noticed a lizard swimming right in a ditch where parsley and chickweed grew wild. Without a word he scooped up the lizard and gave it to me. I couldn't stand such creatures, but I pretended to be overjoyed as I wrapped this one in my handkerchief. Back home, I released the lizard in the garden pool where it swam around, its tiny head wavering. I looked in the pool the next morning, but the lizard was gone.

Stuck on myself, I never considered telling my companion how I felt. I usually didn't say much to him, anyway. With the skinny girl from next door, it was even worse. She was a student too, and I was quite aware of her. Even when I came toward her on the street, though, I quickly looked away as if in contempt.

One night in autumn, a fire broke out near our house. Along with the others I got up to watch the flames shooting from the darkness of the neighborhood shrine and the sparks scattering all around. A grove of dark cedars loomed above the flames, and small birds darted through the air like innumerable fluttering leaves. I knew perfectly well that the girl was standing in her white pajamas by the gate next door and looking at me. I kept gazing toward the fire, though, with the side of my face toward her. I figured the glare of the flames would make my profile glitter and look splendid.

Being this way, I couldn't initiate anything on my own, neither with this classmate nor with the girl next door. When alone, though, I would act bold. I'd close one eye and laugh at myself in the mirror, or carve a thin mouth in the desktop with a knife and press my lips to it. When I colored it with red ink afterward, the mouth turned so dark and ugly I gouged it out with my knife.

One spring morning, when I was a third-year student, I was on my way to school when I stopped on a bridge and leaned against the vermilion-painted railing. A wide stream flowed below, just like the Sumida River, and I drifted into a reverie the like of which I had never known. I felt as though someone was behind me, and that I myself was always assuming some pose or other. I would comment on my every gesture, no matter how slight, as if I were standing beside my own self. Now he's perplexed and is just looking at his palm—that's what I would say. Or maybe—He muttered something now while scratching behind his ear. Because of this habit, I could no longer act on the spur of the moment, as one less aware of himself would. When I came out of that reverie on the bridge, I trembled in my loneliness. And, while still in this mood, I thought of my past and my future. I went on across the bridge, various memories coming to mind, my footgear clattering on the floorboards. Again, I fell to dreaming. And I finally let out a sigh. Could I really become someone?

That's when I started getting fretful. Since I couldn't be satisfied with anything, I kept writhing about in vain. Masks in one layer after another—as many as ten or twenty—had fastened themselves upon me, and I could no longer tell how sad any one of them really was. In the end I found a dreary way out of my dilemma—I would be a writer. There were many others who were subject to this same sort of incomprehensible agitation, and all of them would be my confederates.

My younger brother had started higher school by then, and the two of us shared a room. After talking over the matter, we got together with five or six friends and began a little magazine. A large printing shop stood just down the street on the other side, and I easily arranged to have our magazine produced there. I had the shop use a pretty lithograph for the front cover too. When everything was ready, we distributed copies to our classmates

Thereafter I published something in each monthly issue. At first I wrote philosophic stories on ethical questions. I proved adept at composing a few lines in the style of the fragmentary essay. We kept the magazine going for about a year, but I got into trouble with my oldest brother about it.

Anxious about this mania for writing, my brother sent me a long letter from home. "Chemistry uses equations," he wrote, "while geometry depends on theorems. With literature, however, there isn't anything equivalent to these equations or theorems that help clarify matters. That's why genuine understanding of literature comes only with age and the right circumstances."

My brother had written in a formal and stiff manner, and I agreed with what he said. In fact, he had set down my very qualifications. Responding immediately, I said I was truly fortunate to have such a splendid older brother. His letter was right on the mark. But I had to point out that my interest in literature didn't hamper my studies. Indeed, I worked all the harder because of it. I let my brother know exactly where I stood, mixing in some exaggerated feeling here and there.

More than anything, I felt I had to stand out from the crowd. The very thought kept me at my books, and, from the third year of higher school, I was always at the top of the class. For someone who doesn't want to be thought a drudge, that's quite an accomplishment. Instead of my classmates jeering at me, I actually brought *them* to heel, including the judo champ we had nicknamed Octopus. In one corner of the room there was a large jar for wastepaper. Sometimes I would point to it and wonder out loud if an octopus could fit inside. The champ would stick his head in the jar and let out a strange, reverberating laugh.

The good-looking fellows in class were devoted to me as well. Even when I cut out triangular, hexagonal and flower-shaped plasters and pasted them over my pimples, no one joked about it.

The pimples were distressing all the same, especially when they kept on spreading. Each morning when I awoke, I would run my hand over my face to see how things were. I bought all sorts of ointments, but nothing seemed to work. Before going to the drugstore, I'd write down the name of the ointment. "Do you have any of this?" I would ask, showing the scrap of paper with the writing. I had to make it seem I was doing someone else a favor.

I was horny—that's what the pimples really showed. The mere thought made me dizzy with shame. Actually, I'd be better off dead. My face attained its greatest notoriety within my family just about then. My oldest sister, who had gone to live with her husband's household, supposedly said that no woman would come to our own house as my bride. Informed of this, I applied even more ointment.

My younger brother worried about my pimples too. Time after time he went to buy medicine in my stead. As children, my brother and I had never gotten along; when he took the entrance exam for higher school, I prayed that he would fail. After we began living together away from home though, I gradually came to appreciate my brother's even temper. As he grew up, he turned quiet and shy. Occasionally he submitted an essay to the magazine, but his writing was flat. His grades didn't look good next to mine either, and this troubled him. I would be sympathetic, and then he'd get even more discouraged. His hair came down in a widow's peak over his forehead, something he detested as effeminate. He sincerely believed that his narrow forehead had made him a dunce.

When I was with someone during this period of my life, I would either reveal everything about myself or else conceal it. To be honest, the only one I really confided in was this brother of mine. He told me everything about himself and I did the same.

One dark night in early autumn we went out to the harbor wharf. A breeze was blowing in from the strait as we talked about the red string my Japanese-language teacher had once described. The teacher had said that each boy in the class had such a string tied to the baby toe of his right foot, but no one could see it. The other end was always attached to a girl's baby toe. The string was very long, and it wouldn't break even when the boy and girl were far apart. It wouldn't tangle either, even if the two of them met right on the street. And, our teacher said, this string meant that the boy and girl were destined to marry each other.

When I first heard this story, I was so excited that I rushed home to tell my younger brother. And that evening on the wharf, listening to the waves and the cry of the sea gulls, we spoke of the red string once again.

"What's your wife-to-be doing right now?" I asked.

My brother shook the wharf railing two or three times with both hands. Then, somewhat awkwardly, he said, "She's walking in a garden."

That was just like my brother. Yes, a young girl in large

wooden clogs, walking in a garden with her fan and gazing at the primroses—how perfect for him.

Now it was my turn. Gazing out at the dark sea, I said, "Mine's wearing a red sash." And then I closed my mouth tight. A ferry boat heading across the strait seemed to float along the horizon, its windows entirely lit up as though the boat were actually a large inn.

One thing I had kept from my brother. When I came back for the vacation that summer, a new maid was working in the house. Wearing a red sash over her *yukata* cotton kimono, this petite girl had been very abrupt in helping me out of my shirt and trousers. Her name, I had learned, was Miyo.

Whenever I went to bed, I would secretly light up a cigarette and think of various ways to begin a story. At some point Miyo must have detected this habit. One evening, after laying out the futons, she placed a tobacco tray right beside my pillow. When she came in the next morning to straighten up, I told her that I smoked on the sly and she should not bring me the tray. "All right," she said, a sullen look on her face.

When a troupe of storytellers and musicians came to our village that summer, the household servants were allowed to see a performance. "You go too," my brother and I were told. But at that period of our lives, we only made fun of such provincial amusements. Instead of the theater, we headed for the rice paddies to catch fireflies. We had gone almost as far as the woods of the neighboring village, but the dew was so heavy we came back with only twenty or so fireflies in our cage.

Presently the servants came wandering in from the theater. I had Miyo spread the futons and hang up the mosquito net. Then my brother and I turned out the light and released the fireflies inside the net. As they glided back and forth, Miyo stood outside the net watching. I sprawled out on the futon alongside my brother, more aware of Miyo's dim figure than of the faint glowing of the fireflies.

"Was the performance interesting?" I asked, a little awkwardly. Until then, I had never talked to a maid about anything other than her household chores.

"No," Miyo answered softly.

I burst out laughing. But my younger brother remained silent as he waved his fan at a firefly caught on the edge of the net. Somehow or other I felt very odd. After that, I became quite conscious of Miyo. Whenever the red string was mentioned, it was her image that came to mind.

III

I was in the fourth year of higher school now, and several classmates came over to visit almost every day. I would serve cuttlefish and wine, then tell them all sorts of nonsense. "A book's just come out," I once said. "It tells how to light charcoal." Another time I showed them my copy of *The Brute Machine*, a novel by an up-and-coming writer. I had smeared oil over the cover, so that I could exclaim, "Here's how they're selling things nowadays. A strange binding job, isn't it?" I astonished them again with a work entitled *My Lovely Friend*. I had cut out certain parts and arranged for a printer I knew to insert some outrageous paragraphs of my own. "This book," I told my friends, "is truly a rare specimen."

Miyo began to fade from memory. Anyway, I had this odd feeling of guilt over two people falling in love in the same household. Besides, I never had anything good to say about girls. I'd think of Miyo for only a moment, but still I'd get angry with myself. So I didn't say anything about her to my friends, let alone to my brother.

Then I read a well-known novel by a Russian author that gave me pause. The work tells of a woman who gets sent to prison. Her downfall begins when her employer's nephew, a university student from the nobility, manages to seduce her.

I lost track of the general sense of the novel, but I did put a bookmark of pressed leaves at the page where they kiss for the first time beneath a wildly blooming lilac. For me, a great novel wasn't about other people; I couldn't avoid seeing myself and Miyo in this couple. If only I were bolder, I'd act like that student. Just thinking about these things plunged me into despair. Timid and provincial, I had led a totally dull life. I would prefer instead to be a glorious martyr.

I told my younger brother these thoughts one evening after we went to bed. I'd meant to be serious, but the pose I assumed got in the way. I ended up acting flippant: patting my neck, rubbing my hands together and speaking without any elegance whatever. How pathetic that habit made me act this way.

My younger brother listened in bed, his tongue flicking across his thin lower lip. He didn't turn toward me. "Will you marry her?" he asked. It seemed a difficult question to ask.

For some reason or other I was taken aback.

"Who knows," I shrugged, "if that's even possible?" I tried to sound disheartened.

My brother suggested that such a marriage wasn't very likely. He sounded surprisingly circumspect and grown-up.

Listening to him, I realized how I truly felt. I was offended and angry. Sitting up on the futon, I lowered my voice and insisted, "That's why I'm going to carry on this fight."

My younger brother twisted about under his calico blanket, as if he were going to say something. He glanced at me and smiled slightly. I too broke out laughing and said, "Well then, since I'll be leaving . . ." Then I extended my hand toward him.

My brother stuck his right hand out from the blanket. I shook his limp fingers several times, laughing softly.

It was easier to convince my friends. They pretended to rack their brains as they heard me out, but that was merely for effect, as I well knew. They would accept my plan in the end. And that's exactly what did happen.

During the summer vacation of that fourth year, I virtually dragged two of these friends home with me, insisting that the three of us prepare for our college entrance exam together. I also wanted to show off Miyo to them, but this I kept to myself. I prayed that neither of my friends would seem disreputable in the eyes of my family. The friends of my older brothers were all from well-known families in the region and wore jackets with many buttons. My friends wore cheaper jackets with only two buttons.

At that time a large chicken coop stood near the vacant house out back. There was also a caretaker's shed where the three of us could spend the morning studying. The outside of this shed was painted green and white, while the inside had a wood floor about four tatami mats large and a new table and chairs, the furniture varnished and arranged in an orderly manner. There were two wide doors, one to the north and the other to the east, along with a casement window facing south. When someone opened the window and doors, the wind always blew in and riffled the pages of our books. Outside a flock of yellow chicks ran in and out of the grass that grew as thickly as ever around the shed.

The three of us would look forward to lunchtime, eagerly trying to guess which of the maids would come to fetch us. If it was someone other than Miyo, we would make a fuss by pounding on the table and clicking our tongues. When Miyo came, we would fall silent, only to burst out laughing when she left. One fine morning my younger brother joined us to study. As noon approached, we began our usual guessing game. My brother kept to himself, however, pacing back and forth near the window as he memorized English words from his vocabulary cards. The rest of us made all sorts of jokes; we threw books at one another and stomped on the floor. I also went so far as to get personal with my brother. Anxious to draw him into the fun, I said, "You're pretty damned quiet today. What's the matter with you?" Then, chewing lightly on my own lip, I glared at him.

"Shut up!" he yelled. His right arm whirled about, and several vocabulary cards flew from his hand. I turned away in amazement. And suddenly I made an unpleasant decision. From now on, I'd give up on Miyo. Within a few minutes I was doubling over with laughter, as though nothing had happened.

Luckily someone other than Miyo came to announce lunch. We went back in single file to the main house, taking the narrow path that ran through the bean field. I lingered behind, whooping it up as I tore off one round leaf after another.

I never figured I'd be the victim in this affair. I did feel disgusted all the same. The white lilacs I treasured had been soiled in mud. And the prankster who did this was my own flesh and blood.

For two or three days thereafter, I fretted over all sorts of things. Wasn't it Miyo herself who had been walking in the garden, just as my brother said? After I confided in him, he had been almost embarrassed to shake my hand in congratulation. To be blunt about this matter, I had been taken for a dolt. And nothing was more humiliating to me than that.

During this period one misfortune followed another. My friends, my brother and I were all seated at the table one day as Miyo served lunch. Even while doing this, she crisply waved a round fan with a monkey's face painted in red. I would watch her carefully, to see which one of us she fanned the most. When I realized that she favored my brother, I gave way to despair and let my fork clatter onto the plate.

Everyone was banding together to torment me. I rashly suspected my friends of knowing all along. I'd better just forget about Miyo—that's what I told myself.

Several days thereafter I went out to the shed in the morning while neglecting to remove the package with five or six cigarettes by my pillow. Later, realizing my mistake, I rushed back only to find the room made up and the cigarettes gone. Now I was in for it. I called Miyo and asked reproachfully, "What happened to the cigarettes? Did someone find out?"

She looked gravely at me and shook her head. The next moment she stood on her tiptoes, reached behind the upper wall panel and brought out the small green package with its sketch of two flying golden bats.

This episode restored my courage a hundredfold and revived my earlier determination. All the same I felt disheartened over my brother's role in the affair. I was uncomfortable with him because of this; and, in the company of my friends too, I stopped making a fuss about Miyo. From now on I wouldn't try to entice her. Instead, I would wait for her to make the next move. I was able to give her lots of opportunities too. I often summoned her to my room and told her to do useless chores. Whenever she came in, I somehow managed to assume a relaxed and carefree pose.

In order to attract Miyo, I paid close attention to my face. The pimples had now disappeared, but I maintained the treatments out of habit. Among my possessions was a compact, a beautiful silvery thing with a lid carved entirely in the pattern of a long, twisting vine. I gave myself an occasional facial, putting a little of my heart in the task each time.

I figured it was now up to Miyo—except that the right moment didn't come. Every so often I would slip out of the shed where we were studying and go back to the main house. Catching a glimpse of her flailing away with her broom, I would bite my lip.

The summer vacation finally came to an end, obliging me to leave home along with my younger brother and my friends. If only I could instill a small memory in Miyo, something to remember me by until the next vacation. But nothing ever happened.

When the day came to leave, we all piled into the family

carriage with its dark hood. Miyo was at the front door for the leave-taking, along with the other members of the household. She kept her eyes on the ground without looking at my brother or me. The light green cord that usually held up the sleeves of her kimono was untied; she kept fumbling with it as though it was a rosary, even as the carriage pulled away. I left home on that occasion filled with regret.

In the autumn I went with my younger brother to a hot-spring village on the coast, a trip that took about thirty minutes by train from the school town. Our youngest sister had been ill and she had come to this village to take the waters. I lived there awhile, in a house Mother was renting, just to prepare for my college entrance exam. Since there was no escaping my reputation as a bright student, I had to demonstrate that I could graduate from higher school and go on to college. I came to hate school more and more, but something drove me to study with all my might.

I would stay overnight with my mother and sister at the rented house, commuting back and forth to school each day by train. My friends came to the village every Sunday for a visit. By then, Miyo was only a distant memory to all of us. We would go out for a picnic, selecting a large flat rock by the sea upon which to have our beef stew and wine. My brother had a beautiful voice and knew lots of new songs. He would teach us some of them, and we'd sing together. When we finally got tired of this, we would lie down on the rock and take a nap. By the time we awoke, the tide would be in, cutting off the rock from the shore. For a moment we still seemed to be dreaming.

I saw these friends during the week too. I'd get depressed if even a day went by without them.

One autumn day when a brisk wind was blowing, one of my teachers struck me on both cheeks in class. It was an arbitrary punishment for some gallant deed of mine, and my friends were livid. After school, the entire fourth-year class gathered in the natural history room and talked about getting the teacher fired. There were even students who clamored, "Strike! A strike!" I was quite upset by all this. "If you're going on strike just for my sake, please stop it," I begged. "I don't hate the teacher. It's not important, not really." I went among them making this plea.

"Coward! Egotist!" That's what my friends called me. Gasping for breath, I hurried from the room and went all the way back to our rented house. When I arrived, I headed straight for the bathhouse. There was a plantain tree in a corner of the garden just outside the window. The wind had stripped it bare, except for a few leaves that remained to cast a greenish shadow onto the bathwater. I sat on the edge of the pool, sinking into a reverie like someone already half-dead.

When haunted by a shameful memory, I would try to get rid of it by going off alone and mumbling, "Oh well . . ." I pictured myself wandering among the students and murmuring, "It's not important, not really." I scooped water from the pool and let it trickle back over and over. And I kept repeating the words, "Oh well . . . Oh well . . ."

The next day the teacher apologized to the class. The strike never happened, and things were patched up between the students and me. Nonetheless, the mishap cast a pall over my life. Miyo was often in my thoughts after that. Without her, I might well have gone to pieces.

My sister's treatment had ended, and she was supposed to depart with Mother the coming Saturday. I decided to go along, on the pretext of seeing them safely home. I kept the trip secret from my friends, and I didn't tell my brother why I was really going home. I thought he would know anyhow.

I set out from the village with my mother, sister and brother, the latter accompanying us only as far as the school town. There we all paid a courtesy visit to the people at the dry-goods store who were helping my brother and me, then headed for the station and the trip home. As the train for home was about to pull out of the station, my brother stood on the platform and pressed his pale forehead with its widow's peak to the window. "Don't give up!"—that's all he said.

"Not on your life," I blithely replied. I was certainly in a good humor.

Yet by the time we had passed the last village and the family carriage was drawing close to home, I was very much on edge. Night had fallen, and both the sky and surrounding hills were pitch dark. Listening to the rice fields rustle in the autumn wind, I was suddenly terror-stricken. I kept my eyes on the darkness outside the window, my head jerking back in surprise whenever a pale clump of pampas grass loomed up from the roadside.

Virtually the entire household was crowded under the dim entry lamp to greet us. As the carriage halted, Miyo herself came bustling out, her shoulders hunched against the cold.

That evening, lying in bed in a second-floor room, I thought of something depressing. I was tormented by the idea of mediocrity. Hadn't I been a fool in this affair? Anyone could fall for a woman. And yet, I told myself, with me it was different. I couldn't put it into words. There simply wasn't anything vulgar involved, that's all. I mean vulgar in every sense too. But wouldn't any man in love make the same claim? Still, I mused, sticking to my guns even as I choked on my cigarette smoke, in my case there's a philosophy at stake.

During the night, while pondering the family quarrel that would surely erupt over my marriage plans, I attained an almost chilling sort of courage. I would never do anything mediocre—of that I was convinced. And I would definitely make my mark in the world. Thinking over these things, I became quite lonely—without knowing why, either. I couldn't get to sleep, so I gave myself a massage. During that time I put Miyo out of my mind. I would not defile her along with myself.

When I awoke early the next morning, the sky was bright and clear—perfect autumn weather. I got up immediately in order to gather some grapes in our arbor. I had Miyo come too, with a large bamboo basket. In giving her instructions, I tried my best to sound nonchalant, so that no one would get suspicious.

The arbor, which was in the southeast part of the field across from our home, covered an area roughly equal to twenty tatami mats. As the grapes ripened, a reed screen was normally set up about the arbor. We opened the little wicket gate in one corner and went into the enclosure. A few yellow bees were buzzing about in the warm enveloping air. Sunlight filtered through the screen and the grape leaves, casting Miyo in a pale green light.

On the way over I had devised one plan after another, my mouth twisting in a villainous smile. It felt so awkward to be alone with her, however, that I almost got irritated. Upon entering the enclosure, I had purposely left the wicket gate open.

Since I was tall, I didn't need a stool to reach the grapes. I began snipping off the clusters with my garden shears and handing them to Miyo one by one. She would quickly wipe the dew with her clean apron and put each cluster into the basket below. For what seemed a long time neither of us spoke. I was getting quite resentful when Miyo, reaching for the last cluster, quickly drew back her hand.

I shoved the grapes at her and shouted, "What're you doing!" My tongue clicked in disapproval.

Groaning, Miyo seized her right wrist with her left hand.

"You got stung?" I asked.

"Yes," she replied, her eyes squinting, as if dazzled by something.

"Fool!" I scolded.

She smiled and didn't say anything.

I couldn't remain there any longer. I'll get some ointment

for it, I said, and hurried toward the gate. Having taken her back to the main house, I looked for the ammonia in our medicine cabinet. When I spotted the purple tinted glass, I seized the bottle and shoved it toward her as roughly as possible. I wouldn't treat the sting myself.

A bus with a gray tarpaulin roof had just started running to our village and back. Tossed about in this humble vehicle, I departed that very afternoon. Everyone urged me to take the family carriage, but I felt that its shimmering black finish and its coat of arms were far too aristocratic for me. Holding in my lap the basket of grapes that Miyo and I had gathered, I gazed with profound feeling upon the fallen leaves that covered the country road. I had done by best to make her remember me, and I was content. Miyo was mine now. I could relax.

The vacation that winter was my last as a higher-school student. As the day drew near for going home, my younger brother and I felt a certain awkwardness toward one another.

Arriving at home, we went over to the kitchen hearth and sat down. We were on the floor, directly across from one another, with our legs crossed. As we glanced around anxiously, our eyes met two or three times. Miyo was nowhere about.

After dinner, my second-oldest brother invited us to his room. We sat around the charcoal brazier to play cards, but every card in the deck seemed blank to me. While conversing with my older brother, I seized an opportunity to ask, "Isn't one of the maids missing?" I tried to sound casual, keeping my face hidden behind the five or six cards in my hand as though truly absorbed in the game. It was fortunate that my younger brother was present. If pressed by my older brother, I'd make a clean breast of everything.

My older brother cocked his head this way and that. While deciding which card to play next, he mumbled, "You mean Miyo? She had a quarrel with Granny and went home. An obstinate bitch, if ever there was one."

He threw down a card. I played one of mine and my younger brother, without a word, played his.

Four or five days later I went out to the caretaker's shed by the chicken coop. The young caretaker, who liked to read novels, filled me in on what had really occurred. Miyo had been defiled by a manservant. It had happened only once; but when the other maids found out, she could not bear to stay on. The manservant had done other mischief too and had already been sent away. But the caretaker had to spill the entire story, including the manservant's boast of how Miyo had murmured, but only after the deed, "Stop! Stop it now!"

With New Year's Day past and the winter vacation nearly gone, my younger brother and I went into the family library to look at various books and scroll paintings. As the snow fluttered down on the skylight, I gazed around eagerly. Since Father's death, my oldest brother had been making changes as the new head of the family. I could see something different each time I visited—from the selection of books and paintings to the newly decorated rooms. I unrolled a painting that my oldest brother must have recently acquired. It was a depiction of yellow rose petals scattered on water.

My younger brother brought over a large box of photographs and started going through the collection quickly, warming his fingertips now and then with his white breath. After a time he showed me a newly mounted print. Miyo must have gone to my aunt's house with Mother, for the print showed all three women. Mother sat by herself on a low couch while Miyo and my aunt, who were the same height, stood behind. The garden was in the background, with roses blooming in abundance.

My brother and I sat next to one another and gazed momentarily upon this print. In my own heart I had long ago made peace with my brother. I had hesitated to tell him of this other business concerning Miyo, and so he still didn't know about it.

I could now look at the photo with a show of equanimity. Miyo must have moved slightly, blurring the outline of her head and shoulders. My aunt, her hands folded upon her sash, was squinting. They even look like one another, I thought.

MY OLDER BROTHERS

My oldest brother was twenty-five the year Father died, my next-oldest brother twenty-three and my third-oldest twenty. I was fourteen. My older brothers were so kind and grown-up that I did not feel my father's loss at all. To me my oldest brother was a father and my second oldest a caring uncle. I was always playing up to them. I would say the cheekiest things, and they would forgive me with a smile. They let me behave as I pleased and never set me straight on any matter.

They must have had worries well beyond me. No doubt they struggled behind the scenes to protect both the family estate and the varied political interests of their father. They had no older uncle they could depend upon either. My brother of twenty-five and my brother of twenty-three could manage things only by working together. My oldest brother was already the town's mayor at twenty-five. With a bit of political experience behind him, he became a provincial assemblyman at thirty-one. He seems to have been the youngest assemblyman in the nation, and the newspapers called him "the Prince Konoe of A Prefecture." He appeared in the comics and became exceptionally popular.

Nevertheless, his aspirations were not along these lines, and he always appeared to be somber. His bookshelves were crammed with the complete works of Wilde and Ibsen, as well as works by various Japanese playwrights. He wrote plays himself. And he occasionally gathered his brothers and sisters together and read them his work. The genuine delight he felt on these occasions was evident in his face. I was young and did not understand him very well, but I sensed the sorrow of fortune was his main theme. From among his repertoire I vividly recall a long play entitled *The Struggle*, even down to the facial expressions of the characters.

When my oldest brother was thirty, the entire family started a little magazine with the quaint title of *Bluets*. My third brother, who was studying plastic arts at a college, did the editorial work. He had dreamed up the title himself and was quite taken with it. He ended up designing the magazine cover. With its haphazard, surreal look and heavy sprinkling of silver dust, the picture on the cover was incomprehensible.

For the first issue my oldest brother dictated to me an informal essay called "Eating." I can recall his very words even now. Hands folded behind his back, he walked about our second-floor Western-style room and gazed at the ceiling.

"You're ready, then? Ready? I'll begin."

"Yes," I answered.

"I will be thirty years old this year. Confucius said that he stood firm at thirty. But I have no place to stand. I might collapse at any moment. The intense feeling that life is worth living has disappeared. Forcibly put, I'm no longer living except when I eat. Here I mean by eating neither some universal activity nor a general craving for life. I mean a heaping bowl of rice itself, that feeling the moment you chew . . . beastly pleasure . . . a coarse story . . ."

Even though I was only a middle-school student, I felt unbearable sorrow for this brother as I hurriedly wrote down his outpourings. Prince Konoe of A Prefecture was utterly lonely. Despite the ballyhoo about him, no one knew that.

My second brother didn't publish anything in this first issue. He did admire Tanizaki Junichiro's fiction from the earliest period on and doted upon the personality of the poet Yoshii Isamu. He had that openhearted magnanimity of someone-in-charge, as well as a zest for sake. Drinking never got the better of him, however; he was a modest person who looked after things earnestly and served constantly as an adviser to his older brother. He seemed as well to cherish the lively gallantry expressed in Yoshii Isamu's lines:

> The sort of man
> Who goes to the Licensed Quarter
> And never comes back,
> Thus I fancy my real self.

When he published his essay on doves in the prefectural paper, a recent portrait appeared as well. "How about that? Shows a bit of the man of letters in me, right? You can tell the resemblance to Yoshii Isamu." He joked even as he proudly showed off the photo. In fact, his was a splendid face, quite in the manner of the famous Kabuki actor Sadanji. My oldest brother's face too, with its narrow lines like those of the equally renowned Shocho, was also notable within the family. The two of them were sensitive to these traits and, when deep in their cups, they might imitate how both actors performed in such plays as *The Love Suicides at Mount Toribe* and *The Mansion of the Plates*.

My third brother sneered at these recitations. He would recline on the sofa of our Western-style room and listen at a distance to his older brothers. This brother was enrolled in art school, but his health was so poor that he devoted scant energy to modeling his clay figures. He absorbed himself in novels instead and, with help from his literary friends, he published a little magazine entitled *Crossroads*. He drew his own cover design and wrote feeble stories with such titles as "It All Ends in a Bitter Smile." For his pen name he selected two pairs of kanji characters with the reading "Yumekawa Riichi." Though his older brothers and sisters laughed and said it was a terrible name, he went ahead and had the printer make up cards in English letters, one of which he offered to me with a mildly pompous air. Even I turned rigid when I read the surname "Umekawa." I asked my brother whether it wasn't "Yumekawa." Had he deliberately changed the printing of the name?

"Damn! I'm not Umekawa." And his face turned red.

He had already distributed the name cards to friends and teachers as well as to his favorite coffee shops. It appeared that my brother had specified "Umekawa," and the printer was not at fault. After all, a Japanese might write a *u* anywhere in a word, thinking that it would be read as *yu*. The episode became a huge joke in our house, and thereafter everyone started speaking of Professor Umekawa and Doctor Chubei (referring to the play by Chikamatsu, *The Courier for Hell*, in which postal courier Chubei falls in love with the prostitute Umegawa). As I said, my brother's health was poor, and he passed away ten years ago when he was just twenty-seven. A marvel of beauty, his face always brought to mind a certain slim girl with large eyes. She was portrayed by the artist Fukiya Koji and appeared each month on the cover of a girls' magazine read by my sisters. I could gaze idly at my brother, not with envy but with a feeling of almost ticklish pleasure.

Serious by nature, this brother harbored a genuine sense of integrity. But he also seemed influenced by an interest he had in the rakishness and satanism once practiced in France. He could sneer recklessly at people or feign a proud indifference. My oldest brother was already married and had an infant daughter. When summer arrived, the child's young uncles and aunts came back from schools in Tokyo, or other cities. Everyone would assemble in one room and compete noisily for the child's attention. My third brother would stand slightly apart and poke fun at her. "What! She's still got that pink skin . . . Gives me the creeps . . ." But finally, as if he could no longer restrain himself, he too would stretch out his arms and call out, "Come to your uncle from France."

At suppertime, each family member sat on the floor in designated order facing a tray: on one side, my grandmother, mother, my first, second and third brothers and me; and on the opposite side, the family clerk, my sister-in-law and my sisters. Even on the hottest days of summer, my two oldest brothers would stick with sake as their beverage. Each had a large towel placed at his side and used it to wipe away the pouring sweat while downing cup after cup of the warmed drink. Between them they consumed more than a magnum bottle every evening, but they were such strong drinkers that their posture never slackened.

My third brother never joined in. He sat in his own place ignoring his older brothers as he poured wine into his elegant glass and sipped it. The meal itself he finished hurriedly. Thereafter he rose slowly and gave a solemn bow. Then he went off as though he were effacing himself. It was certainly a magnificent performance.

The first editor of *Bluets*, this brother had me collect manuscripts from the entire family. These he would read with his usual sneer. I was slightly elated, though, when I presented "Eating," the essay which my oldest brother had dictated to me. The editor sneered the moment he read it. "Sounds like he's giving orders. *Confucius said* . . . What nonsense." Even though he understood the loneliness of his oldest brother, my third brother was relentless, owing to his satanic habits.

He condemned the efforts of others, but his own writings were dreary affairs. For the first issue of this quaintly titled magazine, the editor exercised caution by printing two short poems of his rather than a story. No matter how much I think about it now, they don't seem noteworthy. It's truly regrettable that my brother of all people would publish them. It's not easy for me to acknowledge poems of this sort, but here they are. "The Red Canna" comes first:

> There is a red canna flower
> It resembles my own heart. Etc., etc. . . .

The second is "The Pretty Petals of the Cornflower":

> The pretty petals of the cornflower,
> One, two, three,
> I put them in my sleeve. Etc. . . .

What sort of poems are these? Wouldn't my stylish brother have better served his reputation by leaving them carefully buried in his memento box? That's what I now believe. But at the time I respected his deep interest in the burlesque and his affiliation with the coterie that published the rather well-known Tokyo journal *Crossroads*. He seemed quite proud of the poems and recited the red canna bit in a strange cadence while proofreading at the printer's. I was smitten by what seemed a masterpiece. I have other fond memories of the journal *Bluets*, many of them. But I can't be bothered with them now. I will take leave instead by describing the circumstances surrounding this third brother's death.

During his last few years, with tuberculosis spreading through his body, my brother was constantly in and out of bed. He remained full of energy, however, refusing to be hospitalized or even to return to the family home. He rented an entire house near Toyamagahara in Tokyo, let one of the rooms to a married couple from our area and lived freely by himself in the rest of the dwelling. From the time I entered higher school I did not return home for vacations. I usually visited my brother's place and walked about the city with him. "Look," he exclaimed in a hushed voice as we walked along the Ginza, "It's Kikuchi Kan!" He looked so earnest as he pointed toward an elderly corpulent gentleman that I could hardly doubt him. We were drinking tea at the Fujiya Confectionery on the Ginza when he nudged me with his elbow and whispered, "Sasaki Mosaku! At the table right behind you!" Some years later I met both Mr. Kikuchi and Mr. Sasaki and realized that my brother had been telling me fibs.

This brother owned a volume of stories by Kawabata Yasunari, *Adornment with Emotion*, the title page of which bore the inscription: *To Mr. Yumekawa Riichi, from the Author*. According to my brother, Mr. Kawabata had given him the book when they met at a hot-spring resort in Izu. I wonder about that one too, and I'll inquire of Mr. Kawabata the next time we meet. I'll be relieved if my brother was telling the truth. Unfortunately, there seems to be a slight variation in the calligraphic style between the letters I've received from Mr. Kawabata and the inscription on the book as I remember it.

My brother constantly played harmless tricks of this sort on people. With him, you couldn't let your guard down for a moment. Fooling others was evidently a pastime of the French satanists, and he could not fight off this vice of theirs.

My brother died in early summer of the year I entered the university. On New Year's Day he had a hanging scroll with his own calligraphy placed in the parlor alcove. Visitors to the home burst into laughter when they read his words running down one side of the scroll:

> My mind this spring
> Is at one with the Buddha.
> I shall enjoy
> Neither wine nor appetizers.

My brother let out a grin, but not from his usual impulse to trick people. This time he was serious. Yet, since he was always playing tricks on them, his visitors simply laughed. It did not even occur to them to worry. Eventually he contrived to go around with a small rosary about his wrist and call himself the Foolish Monk. The words "Foolish Monk, Foolish Monk" he intoned so somberly that all his friends went around imitating him. This gave rise to a momentary fad.

My brother did not do this as a mere joke. He knew in his heart that the moment of his extinction was drawing near, but that satanic streak kept him from giving into grief. Working hard on comedy, he grandly fingered his beads and made his companions laugh. It was shameful, he said, for a foolish monk to be still agitated over a certain woman, but it proved nevertheless that he wasn't quite withered yet.

Once he invited several of us to join him as he strolled off toward a coffee shop at Takadanobaba. Along the way he suddenly realized he had forgotten to wear his ring. The Foolish Monk was quite stylish and whirled about without a moment's hesitation to head back home. When he returned with the ring on his finger, he nonchalantly thanked us for waiting.

Having enrolled at Tokyo University, I moved into a boardinghouse near my brother's place. But we saw each other just once or twice a week, so hesitant were we to interrupt our studies. We always headed for the vaudeville theater or walked around to the teahouses when we did meet. My brother would fancy a certain waitress, but his rakishness made him affected and left the girl unmoved. During this period he was secretly in love with a girl at a Takadanobaba coffee shop, yet distressed by his dim chances. Thanks to his lofty pride, he never glared at her nor made any vulgar jests. He merely continued to drop by, drink his cup of coffee and quietly leave.

One evening the two of us entered the coffee shop together. Again the prospects looked unfavorable, and we left after drinking our coffee. On the way back, my brother stopped at a florist's and ordered a large, expensive bouquet of carnations and roses. He came out of the shop and stood there fidgeting with the bouquet in his arms. I understood fully what he was going through. Flinging myself into action, I snatched the bouquet away and sped down the road like a jackrabbit. At the coffee shop, I called the girl from behind the front door. "You know Uncle, don't you? (That's what I called my older brother.) These are from him. And don't forget." She merely gazed even as I blurted out these words and handed over the bouquet. I could have thrashed her on the spot. I wandered back to my brother's place utterly depressed. He had crawled into bed and sullenly buried himself under a blanket. My older brother was twenty-eight at the time; I was twenty-two, just six years younger.

In April, my brother started to work on his sculptures with a special passion. He had engaged a model, apparently to fashion a large torso. I did not wish to annoy him, so I mostly stayed away from his place. When I did drop by one evening, I again found him buried in bed, his cheeks somewhat flushed. "I'm giving up on the name Yumekawa Riichi. From now on I'll simply be Tsushima Keiji." It seemed strange to hear my brother stop jesting and say his real name so gravely that I suddenly felt like crying.

Two months later, before he could finish the torso, my brother passed away. The couple who lived in the house had said that he didn't look right and I thought so too. I was overwhelmed when the physician we consulted calmly declared it was a matter of only four or five days. I immediately sent a telegram to our oldest brother back home, then stayed by my ailing brother removing with my own finger the coils of phlegm that gathered in his throat. When our oldest brother arrived two nights later, a nurse was called in and various friends began to come by. I felt reassured by their presence, especially after those two nights of lonely vigil which even now seem like a time passed in hell.

As he lay beneath the dim light, my brother had me open one chest drawer after another. A variety of letters and notebooks were found and I was instructed to throw them away. My brother watched with a strange look as I tore apart his mementos and wept out loud. I felt in those moments that only the two of us existed in the entire world.

Surrounded by friends and his older brother, Keiji was about to breathe his last when I called out to him. He responded in a firm voice, telling me I could have his diamond tie pin and platinum chain. He was lying, albeit on pure instinct. The taste for style was unforsaken; he would confound me even on death's door. I knew that my brother did not have a diamond tie pin or whatever, and thus I wept all the more over his pathetic dandyism. My older brother, a splendid artist who created nothing to bequeath; my older brother, the handsomest man around but unloved by a sole woman.

I had planned to write of events following directly upon his death. But I suddenly realized this melancholy was not mine alone, but something everyone feels with a death in the family. To write so grandly would amount to a special claim in my case, and I quailed at the thought of offending my readers.

My oldest brother was composing a telegram for back home. At the words, "Keiji died at four o'clock this morning," this thirty-three year old man imagined something or other and began to weep uncontrollably. Even now the scene sends a shudder over my wasted body. No matter how much wealth they command, I pity my brothers for having lost their father so early.

ON THE
QUESTION OF APPAREL

I was fascinated for only a short time—fascinated with apparel. While a freshman at Hirosaki Higher School, I would wear a stiff sash over my striped kimono—whether I was heading for the house of a certain lady for lessons in ballad-chanting or merely out for a stroll. This caper lasted just one year. When it was over, I threw away my stylish clothes in disgust. Not on principle, mind you, not at all. But something happened during freshman year that made me change my ways. On a visit to Tokyo for the winter recess, I flung aside the entrance curtain to an *odenya* bar one evening and walked in dressed to the hilt. With the nonchalant assurance of a man-about-town, I told the waitress, "Make it a hot flagon. Mind you, make it hot, now."

It was hot all right, but I still managed to swallow the sake. Then, having gotten my tongue untied, I let go with every bit of bluster I had memorized for the occasion. And when I had uttered my final sentence—something like, "What the hell're you talking about?"—the waitress smiled brightly and asked in total innocence, "So you're from Tohoku?"

She probably meant it as a compliment, but this reminder of my provincial speech quite sobered me. I'm not an utter fool. In disgust I gave up on stylish clothes right then, and thereafter I tried my best to wear ordinary things. But I'm tall for a Japanese and I stand out even when walking down the street. (I've been measured at five feet seven inches, but I don't believe it. I'm actually five six and a half.)

Even when I got to the university, I tried to dress normally. But my friends kept up their warnings, claiming that high rubber boots were out of place—no doubt about it. But I found them convenient. You don't need any socks; you simply put the boots on over your bare feet or you wear *tabi*, and no one can tell which it is. Generally, I wore mine without socks, and they kept my feet plenty warm. When you leave the house, there's no need to squat at the front door and fiddle around forever tying up the laces. You shove one leg into a boot, then the other and off you go. And when it's time to remove the boots, you needn't bother taking your hands from your pockets. Give a kick and your boot comes right off. While they're on, you can go through a puddle or along a muddy lane without a care. They're real treasures, these rubber boots of mine, so why shouldn't I walk about in them?

But, my solicitous friends replied, the boots were strange and I had better give them up. They claimed that wearing such boots in perfect weather seemed eccentric. So they must have thought that I wore the boots just to be stylish—a terrible mistake on their part. Ever since that freshman year when I learned to my sorrow that I wouldn't qualify as a man-about-town, I had cherished simplicity and economy in matters of food, dress and shelter. But I was taller than most men, and my features—my nose, for example, or my entire face—were larger than average. Somehow this seemed to offend people. I would put on a sports cap in total innocence, only to hear all sorts of advice from my concerned friends. "What! You've really come up with something there!" "Hardly suits you . . ." "It's strange, so you'd better get rid of it."

So what was I to do? Evidently a man must discipline himself in proportion to his size. I would have gone quietly into hiding, but people would not permit it.

In desperation I considered growing a full beard in the manner of our prime minister a few years back, His Excellency Hayashi Senjuro; but the sight of a big, bearded fellow prowling in and out of the three rooms of my small house would be strange indeed, so I had to give up the idea.

Once a friend of mine looked at me seriously and said, "You know, if George Bernard Shaw had been born in Japan, he wouldn't have made it as a writer." Equally serious myself, I pondered the extent of literary realism in Japan and then replied—"Yes, you're right. Our approach to writing is quite different here." I was going to mention several more ideas when the friend laughed and said—"No, that's not what I mean. Isn't Shaw seven feet tall? A writer like that couldn't manage in Japan."

He was quite offhand and took me in utterly. I couldn't really laugh off his innocent joke, either. Indeed, there was something quite chilling about it. If I had been just a foot taller . . . ! That was too close for comfort.

Having surmised in that freshman year how evanescent fashion could be, I gave up on choosing my garb. Instead, I put on whatever was at hand and acted as though I were dressed like any ordinary person. My friends kept finding something or other to criticize all the same. I was momentarily unnerved by their comments and began to fret over my appearance. I kept these worries to myself, however. And, after hearing time and again how uncouth I was, I gave up on wearing a particular garment or ordering a *haori* jacket of antique cloth tailored just for me. No, the craving for style was gone now, and so I docilely put on whatever had been given to me.

I'm not sure why, but I'm very stingy about clothes and geta clogs. Spending money on such things cuts me to the quick—that's really how I feel about it. I'll set out to buy a new pair of geta with five yen in my pocket, only to pace back and forth in front of the shoe store. When I'm completely bewildered, I make a determined rush into the beer hall next door to spend every sen. I must be set against wasting my own money on clothes.

Until three or four years ago, Mother would send me clothes and other things from home for every season. But we hadn't seen one another for over ten years, and I could tell from her choice of gaudy patterns that she didn't realize I was now a man of taste who sported a mustache. A certain kimono of flecked cloth, loose-fitting and unlined, made me seem like a sumo wrestler of low rank, while the nightshirt dyed all over with peach blossoms transformed me into a doddering actor of the modern stage. This simply wouldn't do. And yet, since it was my policy to meekly wear whatever was given to me, I did so regardless of how appalled I really was. Friends who dropped in could hardly keep from laughing when they saw me sitting gravely on folded legs in the middle of my room and puffing on a cigarette. I was hardly amused, however, so I eventually took the offending clothes to the storehouse.

I can't even have Mother send me one kimono any more. Instead I must buy whatever clothes I need from my own income as a writer. I'm so stingy that I've bought just two kimonos the last three or four years: an unlined, flecked garment in the Kurume style and a white summer kimono, also flecked. When I need something else, I withdraw one of Mother's selections from the storehouse. For summer wear I've another flecked kimono with a white background, and as autumn draws near, I alternate between two unlined kimonos—one of a patterned fabric, the other of silk. At home I always wear two kimono: a light *yukata* underneath a padded *tanzen*.

When I walk about in the silk kimono, the hem of the skirt rustles pleasantly. Unfortunately it always rains if I go out in that garment, a warning perhaps from my dead father-in-law who once owned it. I've encountered veritable floods in that kimono, once in southern Izu and again at Yoshida, next to Mount Fuji. The Izu incident occurred in the early part of July, when a rampaging stream almost swept away the tiny inn where I was staying. I was drawn into the incident at Fuji-Yoshida because of the Fire Festival in late August. When a friend from the area invited me for a visit, I replied, "It's too hot now, but I'll come once the weather cools down." My friend's response to this was rather testy. "The Fire Festival occurs just once a year," he wrote, "and the weather's plenty cool already here in Yoshida. By next month it'll be too cold."

I hastily got ready to leave. As I left home, my wife found fault with my appearance. "You'll run into a flood again if you keep wearing that same kimono," she said. Her words gave me a sense of foreboding.

The weather was fine as far as Hachioji. But from the moment I boarded the train at Otsuki for Yoshida, the rain came down in buckets. The passengers on their way for sightseeing or mountain-climbing were so packed in they could barely move. Hearing each and every one of them grumble about the rain, I was so overcome with guilt for having worn my late father-in-law's kimono that I couldn't even look up. Since the rain was even worse at Yoshida, I scurried along with the friend who met me into a nearby restaurant. My friend seemed to feel sorry for me, but I was the one to really feel contrite, knowing as I did the real cause of the storm. I couldn't confess, though, for my sin was too terrible.

The Fire Festival was a shambles.

On the day the trails up Mount Fuji close for the winter, each household in Yoshida heaps up kindling at the front gate, hoping to start a blaze greater than all the others. The spectacle was in honor of Konohanasakuya, the princess who underwent a trial by fire to prove to her consort Ninigi that the triplets she bore following their one night of love were truly his. I had never seen the festival and was anxious to be there. But the downpour had ruined the preparations, so my friend and I just stayed in the restaurant and drank as we waited for the rain to slacken. As the wind picked up in the evening, a waitress opened the shutter slightly and murmured, "Ah, there's a small fire out there."

My friend and I stood up and observed the glow in the southern sky. Even in the midst of this raging storm, at least one person had managed to light a beacon for the princess. But I couldn't help being depressed, knowing as I did that my own kimono had brought on this terrible storm. If I so much as hinted to the waitress that the man standing before her had come brazenly down here from Tokyo on no special errand and ruined one of the few annual pleasures enjoyed by all Yoshida residents—young and old, men and women—I would probably end up getting thrashed by the townspeople. And so, ever a blackguard, I told neither the waitress nor my friend about this crime.

When the rain eased up late that evening, my friend and I left the restaurant to spend the night at a large inn near the lake. By the next morning the weather had cleared, so I said goodbye and boarded the bus that ran to Kofu through the Misaka Pass. The bus had gone by Lake Kawaguchi and must have been starting its climb up the pass some twenty minutes later when it came to a halt. Seeing the huge avalanche that blocked the road, we fifteen or so passengers got off, hitched up our kimono skirts and started picking our way over the avalanche in groups of two or three. Finding the road again, we kept on walking, determined to get through the pass. No matter how far we went, there seemed no way of getting to Kofu. Finally we gave up and returned despondent to our own bus.

All of this came about because of that cursed silk kimono of mine. The next time I hear even a rumor about a drought, I'll put on the kimono and set out for the affected area. I'll just take a stroll, and the rain will come down in torrents—an unexpected service from someone so generally incompetent.

In addition to the rainmaker, I still own the first kimono I ever bought with payment for one of my manuscripts, an unlined garment in the Kurume style. I take good care of this article, wearing it only when I go out on special occasions. I consider it a first-class garment, yet other people don't give it much attention. Whatever business discussions I have while wearing this kimono turn out rather poorly. I'm treated off-handedly, and that means the kimono must seem like ordinary apparel in the eyes of others. Feeling defiant as I head for home, I hit upon the example of my fellow Tsugaru writer, Kasai Zenzo, a careless dresser if there ever was one. That's when I swear firmly never to give up my unlined kimono.

The period during which I change from unlined to lined clothing is a difficult one. For about ten days, from late September through early October, I'm totally alone with my miseries. I have two lined kimonos sent by Mother, one of a patterned fabric, the other of some kind of silk. The designs of both are so delicate and the colors so subdued that I keep them at home, without depositing them at a storehouse in some obscure corner of town. However, I'm not the sort to turn out in a silk kimono and felt sandals, twirling a cane as I stroll along. In fact I've worn the silk kimono only twice in the last year or so—to celebrate the New Year at my wife's home in Kofu and to assist a friend at a meeting with a prospective bride. In both instances I had misgivings about the kimono, and a cane and felt sandals were simply out of the question. I dressed instead in *hakama* formal trousers and a new pair of "single-block" geta.

I'm not trying to act barbarian by disliking sandals. After

all, sandals look elegant and they don't make a racket like geta. So you needn't leave them at the cloakroom when entering a quiet place like a theater or library. But when I tried wearing a pair of them, the soles of my feet seemed to be slipping on a straw mat. It was irritating and unbearable. I felt far more weary than when I wear geta and since then I've never put on a pair of felt sandals.

To walk about twirling a cane gives one a feeling of importance, and that's not bad at all. But as I'm a bit taller than most people, and canes are always too short for me. I've got to bend somewhat to make sure the tip strikes the ground. I must look like an old lady on her way to visit a grave as I go along hunched over, my cane tapping at every step. Five or six years ago I came across a long, narrow *pickel*, as the Germans call it, and started using it as a cane, but quickly gave it up when a friend grumbled about my poor taste. It wasn't a question of taste, however. Since the typical short cane wouldn't let me walk resolutely, I soon became irritated with it. For one with my physique, a long, sturdy pickel was a necessity.

I've also been instructed to hold the cane so that it doesn't strike the ground. It gets to be luggage then, and that's something I can't tolerate. When I go on a trip, I figure out how to board the train empty-handed. Life itself is bound to be dreary if you carry a lot of baggage about. The less the better. After spending the thirty-one years of my life more or less weighed down, why should I carry an onerous piece of luggage even while walking?

Whenever I go out with something, I try to stuff the article inside the front opening of my kimono, regardless of how unsightly it looks. I certainly can't do that with a cane, though. A cane's got to rest on the shoulder or hang from the hand, a bother in either case. Besides, a dog might well mistake a cane for some barbaric weapon and begin barking furiously. There's nothing good about carrying a cane. Regardless of how I think about it, I'm just unfit for a silk kimono, felt sandals, white *tabi* socks and a cane. Maybe it's just the pauper in me.

While I'm on this subject, I should mention that I haven't worn foreign clothes in the seven or eight years since I quit school. It's not that I dislike them, far from it. Since they're light and convenient, I'm always yearning for such clothes. Mother never sent me any from home, though, and I can hardly wear what I don't own.

Since I'm five feet six and a half inches tall, a suit ready-made in Japan wouldn't fit. And to have a tailor make one would surely cost more than a hundred yen, with the shoes, shirt and other required accessories. I'm stingy about my needs; I'd rather hurl myself from a cliff into the raging sea than throw away over a hundred yen on a suit of clothes.

On one occasion I had to attend a celebration in honor of a friend's new book. With nothing to wear other than a *tanzen* padded kimono, I had to borrow from another friend. Clad in a foreign outfit—jacket, shirt, necktie, shoes and socks—I showed up with a craven smile on my lips. My reputation suffered again, for my friends did not seem impressed with my appearance. I heard all kinds of remarks—"So you're wearing a suit for a change . . ." "Well, it's hardly an improvement . . ." "Nope, it doesn't agree with you . . ." "What? Again!"

Finally the friend who had lent the clothes whispered to me in the corner. "Thanks to you, that suit of mine's already notorious. I don't think I'll be wearing it to go out anymore."

That's what happened the one time I tried wearing foreign clothes. Since I'm not about to waste a hundred yen on a tailor, it will probably be a long time before I try again.

For now, I have no choice but to go around in the Japanese clothes I have on hand. As I said earlier, I have two lined kimonos, but I don't like the silk one. I prefer my patterned kimono. Anyway I'm comfortable in the poorest kimono, the sort a student might wear, and I would gladly spend the rest of my life living as a student. When I have a meeting scheduled for the next day, I fold my patterned kimono and place it under my mattress for the night. I feel somewhat edgy, as though I were about to take the college entrance exam, but at least the kimono will appear to be pressed. It's a fine garment, one for special occasions. As autumn deepens and I can begin going proudly about in this kimono, I breathe a sigh of relief.

It's the time between seasons that's really troublesome—especially between summer and autumn. Any transition annoys a feckless person like myself, and I can't make up my mind between my unlined summer garment and my lined autumn one. To tell the truth, I want to wear my lined kimono with its flecked pattern right away, but the days are still too warm. So I stick to my unlined garment, and that makes me feel cold and desolate. No wonder that I go about hunched over and shivering in the wind—or that criticisms about "advertising my penury" or "acting from spite" or "menacing people like some beggar" start all over again. In fact, I long to dress properly, without upsetting people by looking like Han Shan and Sheh Teh, those two beggars who appear in the Zen paintings. The trouble is, I don't have a serge kimono, and that's what I need most.

Actually, I do sort of have one. It's a kimono with pale red stripes running both down and across that I bought on the sly during my fashionable days as a higher-school student. When I awoke from the spell of fashion, I realized a fellow like me couldn't wear such a garment. It obviously belonged on a woman.

I must have been insane. The kimono was so gaudy that words can hardly describe it. Remembering how I used to put on this garment and stroll aimlessly and languidly about, I can only hide my face and groan. I never should have worn it. I can't stand the sight of that kimono, and I've left it in storage a long time now.

Last autumn I tried to arrange the clothes, blankets and books I had left in the storehouse. I sold off the useless items and brought the rest back home. My wife was present as I opened the large cloth bundle. Needless to say, I was nervous and embarrassed to reveal before her very eyes how slovenly I had been before our marriage. A filthy yukata cotton kimono had been left in the storehouse, and a rolled-up tanzen padded kimono with a tear in the backside had not been repaired. Nothing that came out of the bundle was presentable. Dirt, mold, garments with strange, gaudy patterns—that's all there was. This was not the legacy of a solid citizen, and I cringed in self-contempt as I unpacked the bundle.

"Sheer decadence!" I declared. "But I suppose we can sell the stuff to some rag-picker."

"Oh no!" my wife shot back. She inspected each article, ignoring the filth. "Look! This one's pure wool! Let's remake it."

The serge kimono! I almost fled in horror. What was it doing here? It should have remained in storage. I had picked up the wrong article at some point. Blunderer!

"I wore it years ago. Rather flashy, wouldn't you say?"

I hid my embarrassment and spoke calmly.

"What luck! You don't have a single serge kimono, and now you can wear this."

I couldn't. During the ten years in storage, the kimono fabric had turned a strange color, something on the order of bean jelly, while the red stripes had faded to an unhealthy persimmon color. It was an old woman's kimono, and I turned away from it in disgust.

This past autumn I leaped out of bed early one morning, knowing that I had to finish a story that very day for a certain publisher. An unfamiliar kimono lay neatly folded alongside my pillow. It proved to be the serge kimono itself, just right for the cool weather already in the air. Washed and re-sewn, the garment was more presentable than before, but there was no mistaking the bean-jelly fabric and the persimmon-colored stripes. With work to be done, however, I couldn't bother about my appearance. I dressed in silence and started writing without any breakfast. I finished slightly past noon and was just breathing a sigh of relief when an old friend unexpectedly dropped in.

His timing was perfect. We ate lunch, talked over various matters and went out for a walk. Only as we were entering the woods at Inokashira Park did I realize how strange I looked. I came to a halt and groaned, "Oh no, I shouldn't be out like this."

My friend stared at me, his brows knit in a worried expression. "What's the trouble?" he asked. "Is it your stomach . . . ?"

"No, nothing like that." I forced a smile. "It's an odd kimono, don't you agree?"

"Well . . ." His tone was somber. "It seems a bit flashy."

"I bought it ten years ago," I mentioned, moving forward a step or two. "It seems more suitable for a woman, and the color's changed too . . ." I couldn't go any further.

"Calm down," my friend counseled, "It's not so noticeable."

"You think so?" I was already feeling better.

We came out of the woods, descended the stone steps and strolled around the pond.

But the thing kept bothering me. I was a big, hirsute fellow, thirty-one years old, with some experience of hardship. Yet here I was wandering through the park in a pair of worn-out geta clogs and a tasteless kimono. A stranger might take me for some filthy neighborhood bum, and friends would become all the more contemptuous of me. There he goes again, they would exclaim, it's about time he grew up. That's how misunderstood I've been all these years.

"How about going to Shinjuku?" my friend proposed.

"Are you kidding? If someone sees me around Shinjuku in this outfit . . ." I shook my head.

"No one will think the worse of you."

"Count me out," I stubbornly insisted. "Let's stop at the teahouse instead."

"I need a real drink. C'mon, let's get out of here and head for town."

"They serve beer at the teahouse."

I didn't feel like heading for town—not in this kimono. Besides, my story needed revision, and that made me uneasy.

"It's too chilly at the teahouse," my companion countered. "I want to relax with a drink."

I had heard he was having a bad time of it recently.

"Well," I conceded, "Asagaya maybe. But not Shinjuku."

"You've an interesting place in mind?"

It wasn't especially interesting, but the tavern at Asagaya had its advantages. I had been there occasionally, and whenever I was a bit short, my credit was good until the next visit. Since they knew me, this strange outfit would not arouse suspicion, either. I needn't worry about how I looked. After all, the tavern didn't employ any hostesses.

Dusk was settling when we left the train at Asagaya and started to walk down the street. I could hardly bear to see my reflection in the store windows, just like some Han Shan or Sheh Teh in those Zen paintings. Since the kimono was bright red, it reminded me of how an old man puts on a colorful undergarment to celebrate his eighty-eighth birthday.

These were difficult times, and there was nothing I could do about it. My writing had gone unrecognized. The last ten years seemed to have passed as one day while I loitered about Asagaya in a pair of worn-out geta. And I was back again today, decked out in the red kimono as well. Always I seemed to be on the losing end.

"Things don't change no matter how old you get. I've tried my best, and yet . . ." As we walked along, I began to let my grievances against life come tumbling out. "Maybe that's what writing's all about," I went on. "But there's something wrong with me. Imagine, walking about in an outfit like this one."

My friend looked at me sympathetically. "That's right, you've got to dress properly. Now I've suffered plenty of setbacks at the office . . ."

He worked for a company in Fukugawa, but he wasn't the sort to spend money on clothes.

"It's not just how you dress," I tried to argue. "It goes deeper. I didn't get the right sort of education. Now take Verlaine's case, for example . . ."

What did Verlaine have to do with my red kimono? An abrupt shift of thought even for me, and I felt quite sheepish about the remark. Whenever I'm feeling down and out, though, I remember Verlaine's doleful countenance, and it helps. The very weakness of the man gives me the strength to pull myself together and keep going. I firmly believe that true glory can emerge only after the most timid introspection. In any event I want to live on, to have a life bereft of means but filled with pride.

"Was I stretching things with that Verlaine business?" I asked. "Well, regardless of what I say, this kimono is out of the question."

I was at my wits' end, but my friend merely chuckled as the street lights came on. "Forget it," he counseled.

That evening at the tavern I struck my friend in the face—an awful blunder. For this, the kimono was surely to blame. Of late I had disciplined myself to laugh off just about anything, and even violence, up to a certain point at least, did not affect me. But that night I acted. I believe the red kimono was entirely at fault, a good example of the frightening influence clothes can exercise over a man.

I was so depressed when we entered that I took a seat in the darkest corner, abjectly ignoring the tavernkeeper as I drank my sake. My friend, for some reason or other, was in very good spirits. He denounced all artists—ancient and modern, Eastern and Western—and ended up lashing out at the tavernkeeper. Now the latter, I knew, had a temper. On one occasion a young fellow had gotten out of hand, just like my friend was doing, and begun to shout at the other patrons. The tavernkeeper had suddenly looked stern, as if he were a different person. "What's the matter with you?" he had scolded. "Don't you realize what the country's going through?" He had then ordered the young-ster off the premises, with a warning never to return.

Tonight it was my friend who was defying this formidable tavernkeeper, and I shuddered at the thought that both of us might be thrown out at any moment. Normally I would have added my own bombast to his, and to hell with the ignominy of getting tossed out of a tavern. But I was too embarrassed about my appearance. "Psst! Psst!" I quietly hissed, keeping an eye on the tavernkeeper. Sharper and sharper became my friend's tongue until we were just one step away from getting kicked out. Then a desperate course of action occurred to me—the precedent of Ataka Barrier and the blow that Benkei delivered to save Yoshitsune's life in the famous old story. Having made this decision, I slapped my friend twice on the cheek—taking care not to hurt him while making the sharpest possible sound.

"Calm down! You don't usually act like this. What's the matter with you tonight? Calm down!" I shouted loud enough for the tavernkeeper to hear and was just sighing with relief that we would not be thrown out when Yoshitsune arose and came at Benkei.

"What's the big idea, hitting me like that? You won't get away with it!" he screamed.

The plot had gone awry. Poor Benkei stood up, utterly be-fuddled as he dodged blows left and right, and hoped that someone would come to his rescue.

Finally the tavernkeeper came straight over to where I was and said, "You're bothering the other customers. Would you mind leaving?"

But why was he asking *me* to leave? Come to think of it, I was the one who had started the fracas. And how could someone else realize that I was only playing the role of Benkei and not really chastising anyone? To all appearances I was definitely the aggressor.

Filled with chagrin, I left my friend drunk and raving in the tavern. Once again, my appearance had failed me. If I had been properly dressed, the tavernkeeper would have recognized my character to some extent and he would not have humiliated me like that. Thus did Benkei, now expelled from the tavern and trudging with his shoulders hunched through the Asagaya quarter, reason to himself. I want a serge kimono, he thought, I want something in which I can stroll about without a care. But I'm so stingy about buying clothes that I'll have all sorts of trouble from here on out as well.

Assignment: How about a citizen's uniform?

TOYS

Something will turn up. I pass each day hoping that something will. But there are times when nothing does. That's when I drift back home, like a kite when the string breaks. Still in my everyday clothes, with no hat, and arms folded, I quietly enter my parents' home five hundred miles from Tokyo. I slide the parlor door open, then stand immobile upon the threshold.

Magnifying glass in hand, Father reads the political news in a murmur while Mother sits alongside with her sewing. Their facial expressions change. They both rise and sometimes Mother lets out a brief cry as if tearing silk. They gaze at me a few moments. And once they see my pimples and legs still in place and realize I'm no ghost, Father turns into a raging demon and Mother collapses in tears.

The moment I leave Tokyo, I habitually act as one dead to the world. Regardless of how much Father rails or Mother pleads, I respond with an enigmatic smile and nothing more. People refer to the pain of "sitting on a mat of needles." But I'm in a reverie, like someone who "rests on fog and clouds."

The same thing happened again this summer. I needed three hundred yen, two hundred fifty yen to be precise. I can't stand being poor. As long as I'm alive, I want to treat people to a meal and wear fancy clothes. My parents wouldn't have even fifty yen in cash. But stashed away in a far corner of the family storehouse were twenty or thirty valuable objects. I had already pulled off three thefts, and this summer would be my fourth.

Of the writing so far I'm unshakably confident. The problem is with my pose from here. Do I assume an impeccable pose for this story called "Toys"? Or, do I provide a pattern of feeling? I must be discreet, though, about putting things abstractly. Let one word of theory escape and there's no end to it. You chase on and on after a previous remark, with nothing in hand finally but footnotes by the thousand. You're stuck too with a headache and fever, along with the reproachful feeling that you've made an ass of yourself. That's when you thrash about as if to keep from drowning in a jar of night soil. Take my word for it.

Just now I'm thinking about this sort of story. A fellow called I, by means hardly worth mention, brings back memories from when he was three, two and one. I describe these memories of three, two and one not exactly as a bizarre tale. In fact I take measured delight in the puzzle of an infant. Fastening on that alone, I spread open the manuscript paper to record the very guts of the tale, the memories of a certain man from ages three, two and one. Nothing more.

"As I recall, I was three when . . ." I write hurriedly on to ages two and one, and end with the memory of my birth. That should take care of it. So I lay my brush aside very deliberately.

But the earlier problem is back already. Assume an impeccable pose? Or provide a pattern of feeling? The impeccable pose is, of course, mere artifice. I move the tale forward by soothing, coaxing and by occasionally bullying the reader. When the time is ripe, I quickly dismiss my image with a word of seeming profundity. Oh, not that I wholly dismiss it. The image merely slips behind a sliding door. And when the smiling face innocently reappears, the reader's exactly in the place I chose. Such are the ways of artifice, the object of each writer's diligence. I'm not averse to artifice of this kind. Indeed, I was counting on a skillful use of it for my infant-memoir.

Well, this house of cards is about to collapse, so I had better decide on my outlook.

I made a pretense of gradually withdrawing from my impeccable pose. But I piled up one precaution after another so I might attempt to return at some moment. With the earlier language still in place, you should have figured that out. To bind the reader thus with a golden chain of unshakable conceit is no mean feat.

To be honest, I actually did plan to return.

Why did this fellow briefly described at the start wish to revive memories from three, two and one? How would he do this? And what happened to him once he did? With all these matters in hand, I would deal with the before and after of the memoir, crafting a tale thereby of impeccable pose and a pattern of feeling.

You can drop your guard now. I don't feel like writing anymore.

Shall I write? Well, if you're agreeable to memories from my infancy—just five or six lines per day. And you alone to closely peruse them. Okay, let's get on with it.

How about a quiet drink, just the two of us. We'll celebrate this roguish tale beginning we know not when. Then, down to business.

I remember the first time I ever stood on the ground—the sky clear after a shower, the soil still wet and dark, plum blossoms . . . Yes, the garden out back. A woman's soft arms had carried me there and put me gently down. I had taken two or three fearless steps when I suddenly noticed the ground spreading to infinity. The soles of my feet felt the endless depth of the earth, my body froze and down I plopped. I broke out howling, as though set on fire. The hunger was unbearable.

I'm making it all up. All I remember is a faint line of rainbow after the sky had cleared.

If something is properly named, one understands without even listening. My skin does the listening. I gaze distractedly at an object and the word for it goes tickling over me. Thistle, for example. Wicked words, however, have no such effect. Certain of them you can't take in, no matter how often you hear them. Person, for example.

The winter I was two years old, I once went crazy. Fireworks no larger than adzuki beans seemed to burst within my head, and I instinctively placed both hands over my ears. The sound disappeared that instant. All I heard then was water flowing occasionally from far away. The tears kept coming, and eventually my eyes were smarting. Colors around me changed gradually, and I wondered if a piece of tinted glass had gotten in my eye. I picked at the eyelid again and again.

Actually I was gazing at flames in the hearth as a woman held me to her bosom. Turning dark, the flames suddenly became a wondrous thicket of kelp on an ocean floor. There were green ribbon-like flames as well as palatial yellow ones. Finally I noticed a flame white as milk and I almost forgot myself. I recall someone grumbling, "Oh, he's done it again. He trembles like that whenever he's wet." It tickled me to command attention. My breast swelled and I tasted a kingly joy. I figured I was in the clear, that no one realized I was aware of them. I wasn't being disdainful either.

Something similar occurred a second time. It was late one night with a fierce wind blowing, and I was talking to the toys as I did on occasion.

I asked the doll on my pillow, "Daruma, you're not cold, are you?"

The daruma replied, "I'm not cold."

I asked again, "Really, you're not cold?"

The daruma said, "I'm not cold."

"You're sure?"

"I'm not cold."

Someone dozing nearby looked up at us and laughed. "The child loves his daruma. He keeps staring at it without uttering a word."

I knew that once all the grown-ups were sound asleep, forty or fifty mice would start scampering about the house. Sometimes four or five garden snakes crawled upon the tatami mats. The grown-ups, breathing heavily in their sleep, were oblivious to the scene. They remained unaware even when the mice and snakes crawled into their beds. I was wide awake throughout the night. During the day I would sleep a bit while everyone watched.

No one realized that I had become insane; when I recovered, nobody could tell the difference.

There is something from an even earlier time, a memory that comes back whenever I see undulating grain in a field of barley. I was watching two horses deep in the grain—a red one and a black one. They were certainly energetic. Aware of their power, I had no chance to resent how rude they were leaving me nearby and utterly to myself.

I saw another red mare—or perhaps it was the same one. The mare seemed to be sewing something. After a while she stood up and brushed the front of her kimono, evidently removing bits of thread. Then, twisting about, she pricked my cheek with a sewing needle. "Does it hurt, little fellow? Does it?"

It certainly did.

When I try in various ways to calculate on my fingers the date of Grandmother's death, I always arrive at the eighth month after my birth. Memory alone renders parts of the day with clarity—the mist broken in a triangular patch, allowing a glimpse of the prized complexion of the midday sky . . .

Everything about my grandmother was small—her figure,

her face, even the arrangement of her hair. As she held me in her arms that day, she wore a crepe kimono with a pattern of scattered cherry petals the size of sesame seeds. I inhaled her strong perfume while watching the birds quarrel in the sky. Suddenly Grandmother shrieked and threw me to the tatami. I saw her face as I tumbled down. The skin beneath her jaw quivered; the white teeth clicked together two or three times. Then she fell flat on her back. People came running up and crowded about her. Then they began lamenting together in the faint tones of the bell cricket.

I lay next to Grandmother silently inspecting the face of a corpse. Tiny wrinkles arose on both temples and spread in waves over the entire area of the pale, refined countenance. When people die, their wrinkles start to move and keep moving as if they possess a life of their own. That's all I have to say.

Eventually an unbearable odor crept from her body.

Even now my ear is caressed by the lullabies Grandmother sang—"The wedding of a fox, the bridegroom away . . ." Oh, spare me the rest!

Das Gemeine

I. Magic Lanterns

At the time, each day was my last.

I was in love—for absolutely the first time. I used to be anxious about my manhood and would display only my left facial profile. If the woman hesitated even a moment, I pirouetted instantly about and was off like the wind. But now I was done in. I could no longer maintain the wise, almost invulnerable manner that once held fast to me. I was, if I may say so, openly and utterly in love. A quiet voice spoke the whole truth: love is blind, I could do nothing about it.

Twenty-five years old. I was newly born. I was alive. Truly alive. And involved. Love is blind, I could do nothing about that. Mine, however, seemed unwelcome from the start. I was about to reach a bodily understanding of that old-fashioned notion, Double Suicide by Coercion, when I was soundly repulsed. The matter ended with that. My woman simply faded away.

Friends call me Sanojirozaemon, Sanojiro for short. It's an old, historical name.

"Sa-no-ji-ro, you say? Well, that will help. With a name like that, you'll cut a neat figure. Getting on after being jilted shows that you've been spoiled from the start. Just relax."

I'll never forget it was Baba who said this. Even so, it was surely Baba himself who started calling me Sanojiro and other things. Baba's the fellow I first met at the sweet-sake stand in Ueno Park. That's the small stand near Kiyomizu Temple with coverings of red cloth on its two benches.

Between lectures I would stroll into the park through the rear gate of the university. I sometimes went as far as the sweet-sake stand because of the waitress. Kiku was seventeen; she was also diminutive, bright-eyed and alert. Her features were quite similar to those of my love and, since it took a bit of cash to meet with the latter, I would content myself when penniless by gazing upon Kiku as I sat on a bench sipping my cup of sweet sake.

Early this spring I noticed a bizarre looking man at the sake stand. It was a beautiful Saturday and, when the lecture on French lyric poetry ended around noon, I devised a stupid verse and melody of my own and made my way through the park humming and crooning. Are the plums blooming? Are cherries hardly in bud? My version was utterly different from the French poem I had just learned.

I was taken aback by the lone customer. There was something about him that was simply out of place. He was of average height, though extremely thin, and wore an ordinary jacket of black serge. But the overcoat hanging over his jacket was weird. I couldn't tell the style, but it seemed at first glance the sort of coat Schiller might have worn—an unspeakably baggy thing of beautiful gray velvet with numerous buttons.

Now for the face. A fox trying to disguise itself as Schubert, if you'll permit an offhand expression. A forehead of incredible prominence, small steel rim glasses, wild curly hair, a pointed jaw, the stubble of a three-day beard. There was no luster whatever to the skin, and one might with only partial exaggeration invoke as a comparable example the tarnished green of a warbler feather. The man remained seated in the center of a bench with his legs crossed and pompously sipped his tea from a large cup. But didn't he raise his arm just now and wave me over? So, feigning a smile pointless even to me, I sat down on the edge of his bench.

"It's because of the tough cuttlefish I ate for breakfast." The voice was soft and husky, as if he were trying deliberately to quash it. "This back molar on the right side—I can't bear the pain. Nothing confounds a person like a toothache, don't you agree? If I took aspirin, it would clear up right away . . . Say, did I call you over here? Sorry, but I'm . . ." He glanced toward me, a slight grin at the corner of his mouth. "I can't tell one person from another. I'm blind. No I'm not. I'm just mediocre. It's all for show. Just a bad habit. Whenever I meet someone for the first time, I can't keep myself from putting on this silly act. You know the old saying: give him enough rope and he'll hang himself. Stop it! I'm simply ill! How about yourself? Literature? You'll graduate this year?"

"No, I've got another year. I flunked once."

"Ah, a writer." He raised his cup without smiling and sipped the sweet sake. "I've spent almost eight years in the music school across the way. I can't graduate—no doubt about it. Because I haven't taken an exam even once. You know, of course, how gravely rude it would be for one person to judge another's talent."

"Of course I do."

"I was only trying out that speech on you. To tell the truth, I'm stupid. I often sit myself down here and watch the people flow by. I couldn't endure it at first—all those people and everyone of them ignorant of me, paying no attention at all. And when I realized that . . . Oh, what the hell. You don't have to agree with me so heartily. I've only been trying to humor you all along. Right now I'm quite content with things. Indeed, I feel fine—as if a clear stream is flowing beneath my pillow.

This is not resignation. It's a prince's gratification for sure." He gulped down his drink and shoved the cup toward me.

"You see the words on this cup? *The white horse is too proud to gallop.* I should stop. This is too embarrassing. Tell you what, you can have this cup. I paid an antique dealer in Asakusa plenty for it and I keep it here just for myself. You know, I like that face of yours. Deep color to the eyes, a look one yearns for. You can use this cup if I die. And I'll probably be dead tomorrow."

Thereafter we would often run into each other at the sake stand. Baba certainly did not die. He got a bit chubby instead, his dark cheeks swelling like peaches. He called it alcoholic fat, adding in a whisper how risky this was for one's health. We got along better from day to day and I wondered why I didn't flee rather than become so close to him. Was it because I admired his talent? Joseph Szigeti, the celebrated violinist from Budapest, came last fall to give three recitals in Hibiya Hall. Angered over the poor response to each recital, this proud and solitary genius of middle age wrote a letter to the *Asahi Shimbun* newspaper saying that the Japanese ear for music was no better than that of a donkey. However, he appended a poem-like refrain which exempted a certain young man from this scathing attack on the native audience. Apparently, the identity of this person was intensely debated in the music circles of that day. In fact, the youth was Baba.

Baba was in a well-known Ginza bar when he noticed in a corner beneath a potted tree the large, reddish dome of Szigeti's head. Szigeti had been humiliated for the third time that evening at Hibiya Hall. World famous but unappreciated in Japan, he smiled with feigned indifference as he sipped his beer. Without a moment's hesitation, Baba walked straight to the table next to Szigeti's. Things fell into place right away and, before the evening was over, they had hit the best cafés from one end to the other of the Ginza. Szigeti not only picked up the tab, he remained a perfect gentleman no matter how much he drank. His dark bow tie stayed firmly in place, and he never touched a waitress the entire time.

Art unrelated to analytical intelligence was of no interest—that's how he put it. As for literature, his favorites were Thomas Mann and André Gide, the latter name rendered by him as "Chitto." After mentioning these writers, he began biting the nail of his right thumb in a joyless manner.

The two friends took leave of one another by the lotus pond in the front garden of the Imperial Hotel. It was already dawn as they limply shook hands, their faces turned away from one another. Then they swiftly parted. Later that day Szigeti boarded the *Empress of Canada* in Yokohama and sailed to America for his next engagement. His letter with the refrain appeared in the *Asahi* the following day.

Listening to Baba relate this exploit—his eyes blinking rapidly in understandable embarrassment, his mood turning peevish toward the end—I could not avoid feeling suspicious. Did he know languages well enough to keep talking with a foreigner throughout the night? From that first doubt an endless train of others followed. What was his theory of music? How well did he play the violin? What sort of compositions did he write? I knew nothing even of these matters. Occasionally Baba came walking by with a shiny black violin case under his left arm, but there was never anything inside. According to him, the cold, empty case symbolized the present condition of humankind. At such times I wondered whether the fellow had ever taken a violin in hand. Regardless of whether I believed in his talent or not, there was no way to measure his skill.

I too considered the case more important than the violin inside. So perhaps it was Baba's appearance and joviality that attracted me, rather than his abilities and character. He would turn up in all kinds of different outfits. Besides business suits of various kinds, he might wear a student uniform or a pair of overalls. On one occasion he made me blush with embarrassment by showing up in white *tabi* socks and with a stiff sash about his waist. He told me without batting an eye that he changed clothes regularly to keep people from having a definite impression of him.

I forgot to mention that Baba lived on the outskirts of Tokyo in Mitaka Village and came to the city every day without fail. His father was a landlord or something with lots of money, and that's why Baba had all those clothes to change into. He was yet another example of a rich man's pampered son. That's what I thought, so it was hardly his appearance that attracted me.

Was it his ready cash then? I don't like to mention this, but he would pay the entire bill whenever we went around together, even if that meant knocking me aside to reach the cashier. A supremely delicate interaction between money and affection existed between us; no doubt his wealth had a certain charm for me. From the beginning our relationship was one of lord and retainer, a tale which ended with me being always led around.

Ah, the cat's out of the bag now. I had no will of my own in those days. Baba was a goldfish and I was his turd. The goldfish would swim off and I would unsteadily follow. That was certainly how Baba and I remained together. On the eighty-eighth day, or last day of spring, for example . . . You know, it was a funny thing with Baba. He was acutely aware of the calendar and would wistfully mention it was Buddha's Death Day or that we had entered the zone of the Elder Brother of Metal. Then he'd go on about the Boy's Festival or The Darkness Celebration or other business I scarcely understood.

Anyway, on that final day of spring, I was at the sake stand in Ueno Park absorbing the mellow warmth of the cherry tree leaves and caterwauling cats, showers of falling blossoms and hordes of woolly worms. I had been drinking a beer all alone when I suddenly became aware of Baba. He was sitting right behind me in a bright green suit and likely about to murmur in the husky voice I had come to know that today was the last day of spring. But he stood up abruptly as if he were embarrassed and vigorously swung his shoulders around. And so, having determined for no particular reason to commemorate this final spring evening, we set out with a laugh for Asakusa. We visited five or six cafés that evening, and I quickly found an inseparable friend in Baba.

He spoke interminably of the quarrel between Dr. Prague and the Japanese musical world, as if he wished to chew the matter up and spit it out. Prague was a great man, and Baba would tell me why. As he mumbled the reasons to himself, I became restless for my woman. I invited him along.

"Let's go see the magic lanterns," I whispered. He didn't know what I meant about magic lanterns. "All right, all right, I'll be boss just for the day. I'll take you since it's the final day of spring." Covering my embarrassment with such banter, I shoved Baba into a taxi while he continued to mutter about Prague. Hurry! Hurry! Oh, the unvarying thrill as I cross the river and enter the District of Magic Lanterns. It's a spider's web of identical lanes conveniently radiating from the center, a row of houses on each side of the lane, a young woman gaily laughing at each tiny window. One step into this area and the weight on my shoulders immediately lightens. Here one can leave his manners behind, a sinner in refuge.

It seemed to be Baba's first time. But he showed little surprise as he strolled slightly apart from me through the district, inspecting one by one the face in each window. In one alley and out, turn in one alley and come to a stop. Here I gently nudge Baba in the ribs. "Over there," I whisper, "she's my favorite. Been that for some time now." My love moved her thin lower lip to the left and gazed unblinkingly as I whispered to Baba. He had stopped in his tracks, his arms hanging limp. Face thrust forward, he had begun to scrutinize my woman.

Eventually he turned about and almost shouted, "Ya! Just like her! Exactly like her!"

I winced almost at once and came up with a forced reply. "Oh no, she doesn't come close to Kiku."

Baba seemed mildly perplexed. "I'm not into comparing," he replied laughing. The next moment he was frowning. "You don't compare things. That's just a stupid tendency." He mumbled these words slowly as if he were trying to convince himself. Then he walked away.

The next morning Baba and I remained silent in our taxi. One wrong word and we might get into a fight. The tension subsided as the car eased its way through the milling crowds of Asakusa. Only then did we feel at home.

Baba spoke first in a solemn voice. "That woman last night," he began, "she taught me something. Even the life we lead here is not so easy as it looks. That's how she put it."

I tried to laugh as best I could. Baba smiled with unwonted cheerfulness and patted me on the shoulder. "That's the best district in Japan. Every one of them holds her head high. What a surprise to find they're not ashamed. They live to the hilt each day."

Thereafter Baba became like a close relative. I had gained a friend for the first time in my life. But the moment I gained a friend, I lost my love. I was abandoned so ignominiously that I couldn't speak about it. I gained a certain notoriety—and this absurd name of Sanojiro as well. It's okay to talk about it now, but it wasn't a joke then. I even thought of dying. With the disease I had caught in the district getting no better, I might become a cripple any moment. I could not fathom why a person must go on living. When summer vacation arrived, I returned to my home in the mountains two hundred miles north of Tokyo. I passed the days sprawled in a chair beneath the chestnut tree in the garden. And mindlessly puffed on seventy cigarettes a day.

Baba sent a letter. "My Dear Friend," it began. "Won't you

delay this business of dying? If you take your life because of me, I'll fancy I'm the cause of your spite. If that's all right with you, go ahead and die. I was never thrilled about living, either before and even less so now. But I won't take my own life. I can't endure one who makes something of himself. I'll wait for an illness or a catastrophe. For the time being, though, my only illnesses are a toothache and hemorrhoids. It doesn't seem I'll die naturally very soon, and catastrophes seldom happen. I once passed an entire night at an open bedroom window waiting for a robber's attack, but the only creatures to steal in were moths and winged ants, some beetles and a host of mosquitoes. (You're probably telling yourself we're two of a kind.) Say, shouldn't we publish a book together? I'll pay off all my debts with the profit, then I'll try to have a good sleep for three days and nights on end. Debt's the very marrow of my unsettled self. A blank hole of debt lies darkly within my breast. Publishing a book will might expand it further. But that will be all right. I'm only looking for a way out.

"The book will be called *The Pirate*.

"We'll talk about the details later, but I plan to publish it first as a magazine to send abroad. France will make a good partner. You certainly look like an outstanding linguist, so you'll put the manuscript into French. Maybe we can send a copy for André Gide to critique. We 'll get a straightforward dispute going with Valéry. And shouldn't we try to confound the somnolent Proust? I can hear you sighing, Too bad but Proust is already dead. Cocteau is still alive though. I say, if Radiguet were still kicking . . . Shall we delight Professor Decouvre with a copy? I pity that man.

"Isn't this a captivating dream? And not so hard to bring about. (The words dry as I write. The style peculiar to composing letters. Not exactly narration, nor dialogue, nor description, but a pointless style that stands on its own. Oh, what a silly remark.)

"I spent the entire night doing calculations. Three hundred yen and we can put out a splendid volume. I can manage a sum like that on my own. Why don't you write a poem to send Paul Fort?

"I'm thinking of a symphony in four movements entitled *The Pirate*. Perhaps I'll publish it in the magazine just to upset Ravel. As I keep saying, getting things done isn't difficult—not as long as you've got the cash. What's with this excuse that it can't be done? You too should fill your breast with bright fantasies. How about it? (Why must we Japanese end our letters with a wish for the recipient's health? There's an uncanny tale around of a man who was dumb, illiterate and clumsy at story-telling. But he was skillful at writing letters.) But, how about my letter? Is it good? Or is it bad? Be seeing you."

To: Mr. Sanojirozaemon
From: Baba Kazuma

II. The Pirate

See Naples and die.

When I reminded him that the term "pirate" had a shabby meaning in the world of publishing, Baba immediately replied, "So much the better." We decided to use French for the title, and thus our magazine became *Le Pirate*. There were any number of models—*La Basoche* of Mallarmé and Verlaine, *La Jeune Belgique* of the school of Verhaeren, *La Semaine* and *La Type*, all of them periodicals in which young artists of an earlier day first addressed the world—red roses blooming in the garden of international art, so to speak. Baba's "pirate fever" became more and more intense after I hastened back to Tokyo following the summer vacation. Eventually I too caught his enthusiasm and whenever we were together we spoke of our wonderful vision for . . . no, I mean our detailed plans for the magazine.

Four issues a year, one per season. Sixty pages in octavo

and glossy paper throughout. Each member of the group to wear a pirate outfit, with the flower of the season in his lapel. A number of mottoes. Never swear to anything. Happiness is . . . ? Render no judgments. See Naples and die. Etc. . . . The membership to be composed exclusively of handsome fellows in their twenties. The finest techniques in each area of the arts. Taking a cue from *The Yellow Book*, we would find a gifted painter to rival Beardsley and provide the illustrations. We would display our talents abroad without the benefit of an International Cultural Exhibition. As for capital, Baba had two hundred yen, and I had a hundred. The plan was to squeeze two hundred out of the other fellows.

About those other fellows—well, Baba would first introduce me to Satake Rokuro, a relative of sorts who was studying at the Tokyo School of Fine Arts. I arrived at Kiku's sweet-sake stand at four o'clock one day, just as I had promised. Baba awaited me as he rested upon the bench with its covering of red cloth. He had dressed for the occasion in the style of the Meiji period: *hakama* formal pants in striped Kokura fabric and an unlined kimono of dark blue and splashes of white. Crouching before him with a lacquered serving tray and gazing up to his face was Kiku. Her kimono had a leaf-patterned sash of red hemp, and a white flower was pinned to her hair. She remained utterly still.

The fading sunlight brightened Baba's dusky countenance while the evening mist rising about the two figures gave the scene an air of strange enchantment. I drew near and roared at Baba. Kiku leaped up startled, then turned and greeted me with a smile. But as her full cheeks turned red, I grew slightly confused and the words "Was that wrong of me?" slipped out unexpectedly. Kiku gave me a strangely serious look, then pivoted about and scurried inside with the tray hiding her face.

It amounted to nothing. I felt as though I had watched a marionette perform, and saw her off with uncertain thoughts.

As I sat down with doubts in my mind, Baba grinned and said, "She's a true believer. That posture of hers was just right."

Perhaps embarrassed by the white horse inscription, Baba had long ago abandoned his special cup. He now used the simple porcelain cup of an ordinary customer. Taking a sip of plain tea, he resumed: "She asked how many days it took to grow this beard. I said two. 'Take a close look,' I told her with a straight face, 'you can see it grow ever so slightly.' Didn't you see her crouching there and staring at my jaw with those big saucer eyes? Unbelievable. Does she believe out of ignorance? Or is it cleverness? Shall we write a novel on the subject of believing? A trusts B. Enter C, D, E, F, G, H and lots of other characters one after another. With the plot shifting, B gets maligned in various ways. Yet A trusts B all the same. Does not doubt . . . never doubted from the start. Feels reassured. A's a woman, B's a man. A dull novel, wouldn't you agree . . . Ah, that's it . . ."

I merely listened to his strange jocularity and quickly pretended I could not detect what was going on within. "Sounds like an interesting story. Shall we have a go at it?" I spoke as eagerly as I could, my eyes vaguely gazing at the great bronze statue of Saigo Takamori before us.

Baba seemed relieved, his face slipping back into its usual sullen expression. "But," he added, "I can't write a novel. You like ghost stories, don't you?"

"Yes, I do. Ghost stories seem to excite my imagination like nothing else."

"How about this one?" Baba licked his lower lip, then carried on. "There's such a thing as Ultimate Knowledge. It's a Bottomless Pit that makes your hair stand on end. One glance and that's it; you turn speechless. Even with a brush in hand, you can only scribble a self-portrait in the corner of your manuscript. Not a single letter, though. Nevertheless, our man stealthily plots a single novel frightening even to the worldly.

The moment he does this, all other novels become hollow and monotonous. It's a truly frightening novel. Take the issue of self-consciousness—how to wear your hat for example. You push it back on your head and it becomes bothersome; tilt it forward and you can't relax; try finally to just doff it, that's all the more strange. Vis-à-vis this general question of where to anchor self-awareness, this novel offers a solution sharp as a stone rapped on a *go* board. A sharp solution? That's not so. Unruffled? Cut glass. White bone. A clean-looking something. No, that's not the case. No description will do. It's a solution, pure and simple. Doubtless there is such a novel. But from the day the author conceives it, won't he become markedly debilitated and end up crazy, suicidal or mute? You realize that Radiguet committed suicide. Cocteau's evidently pretty far gone too and spends his entire day with opium. Valéry's been dead already for ten years. Even in Japan there was a time that many were done in by a single book. As a matter of fact . . ."

"Hey . . . hey . . ." a husky voice called, interrupting Baba's tale. I turned around, quite startled. To Baba's right a diminutive figure in a student's blue uniform stood unmoving.

"You're late," Baba growled as though he were angry. "This fellow here with me," he went on, "Is a Tokyo University student. We call him Sanojirozaemon. And this guy," he went on, pointing to the newcomer, "Is Satake Rokuro. He's the art student I spoke of earlier." Satake and I both smiled wryly as we nodded to one another. To me his smooth, delicate face gave the impression of a milk-white, highly polished Noh mask. The pupils of the eyes seemed like tinted glass, with no definite focus. His nose was knife-like, a cold ivory miniature, his eyebrows long and narrow like willow leaves, his thin lips strawberry red . . . For someone with such a striking face, his arms and legs were surprisingly meager. He was barely five feet tall, with the small, shriveled palms of a lizard. He remained standing and began speaking to me in the soft, dead voice of an old man. "I've heard about you from Baba. Had a tough time of it, haven't you."

He was already getting under my skin. I took another look at his shiny, white face. It had no more expression than a box.

Baba clicked his tongue loudly. "Look here, Satake, you can stop that teasing. Teasing so calmly is a sign of sheer meanness. If you want to abuse a person, do it with a vengeance."

"I wasn't teasing, y'know," Satake gently replied. He took a purple handkerchief from his breast pocket and slowly wiped the sweat from around his neck.

Baba let out a great sigh and rolled over on the bench. "Can't you say anything without adding on a 'y'know' at the end? It gives me such an icky feeling."

I felt the same way.

Satake carefully folded the handkerchief and slid it into his breast pocket. Then he remarked offhandedly, "Next thing you'll give me that nasty remark about my 'morning glory' face. Isn't that so?"

Baba slowly rose and spoke more firmly. "I'm not arguing with the likes of you. Not here, at least. We'd just play to the audience, wouldn't we?" There was something between him and Satake that I didn't know about.

With a show of his porcelain-like teeth, Satake managed to grin. "Well, I guess you don't need me any more, then?"

Baba deliberately looked away and let out a slow yawn. "That's right."

"Well, if you'll excuse me . . ." Satake stared at his gold-plated watch a long time, as if he were thinking things over. "I'm going to hear a new symphony at Hibiya Hall. That fellow Konoe is really good at selling tickets. This young foreign lady's been sitting next to me every time. I like that."

He scurried away nimble as a mouse.

"I'll be damned! Hey, Kiku, your lover just left. Bring me a beer. How about having one yourself, Sanojiro? I've brought a bore into the club. He's like a piece of seaweed. Even if I knock him down, I lose. Doesn't put up any resistance, just clings to every punch you throw at him." Baba's voice suddenly dropped to a whisper. "That fellow held Kiku's hand, cool as you please. Guys like that make easy sport of somebody's wife. But maybe he's impotent. We're not related by blood either. I don't want to argue with the likes of him in front of Kiku. I can't stand competing. I'm telling you, that pride of his makes me shudder." Still holding his glass of beer, he gave a deep sigh. "You've got to admit it, though, the guy's a real painter."

I had fallen into a reverie. As dusk fell, all sorts of lights had come on, casting a spectrum of colors over Ueno Park. Baba's monologue seemed to drift away as I gazed down at the crowd in the Hirokoji district. A commonplace sentiment overwhelmed me—a sentiment contained in the mere words, *Ah, Tokyo.*

Five or six days later the newspaper carried an article about a pair of tapirs the Ueno Park Zoo had recently bought for mating. Immediately I wanted to see them, and after my last class I headed for the park. It was near the great fenced enclosure for waterfowl that I saw Satake seated upon a bench and drawing in a sketchbook. Reluctantly I went over and tapped him on the shoulder.

He groaned slightly, then looked up toward me. "So, it's you. You surprised me for a moment there. Have a seat. I'm in a hurry to finish this, but I've got something to tell you. You can wait a few minutes, can't you?" He spoke in a strange, aloof manner. Finally, taking up his pencil, he turned away and went on sketching. I stood behind him hesitating, then sat resolutely down and peeked at the sketch.

Satake seemed to know I was watching. "Pelicans," he mumbled as the pencil continued rapidly sketching a variety of poses in bold strokes. "Twenty yen apiece, and there's a man who will buy any number." He grinned complacently. "You know, I can't stand to spout nonsense the way Baba does. Has he gotten to 'The Moon Over the Ruined Castle' yet?"

"'The Moon Over the Ruined Castle'?" I didn't get his point.

"Not yet, eh?" He was making a large sketch in the corner of the paper—a pelican looking behind itself. "Baba composed the melody for 'The Moon Over the Ruined Castle' some time ago. He used the name Taki Rentaro and sold the entire rights for it to Yamada Kosaku for three thousand yen."

"You mean the famous song?" My heart was soaring.

"The whole thing's a lie." A sudden breeze riffled the pages, giving a glimpse of flower sketches and nude women. "Baba's famous for his nonsense. You see, he's quite clever at it, and he can fool anyone at first. You've heard about Joseph Szigeti?"

"I'm afraid so," I replied. This was quite the letdown.

"And his letter with the refrain?" He put the question wearily, then closed his sketchbook. "Thanks for waiting. Let's take a walk. There's something I want to tell you."

Let's give up on the tapir mates for today. And lend an ear instead to this tale from Satake, himself a creature more bizarre than any tapir.

We had gone past the waterfowl enclosure and the seal pond and were approaching the cage holding a brown bear as large as a knoll. When Satake began to speak, he seemed to be reciting something told time after time already. The words, which would have conveyed a certain ardor if written, merely gurgled by when conveyed in Satake's hoarse, somber voice.

"Baba is no good. Does there exist a musician who knows nothing of music? I have never once heard the man carry on a discussion of the subject. I have never seen him hold a violin. Does he compose? I doubt whether he can read a note. He's the cause of much grief in his home. It's not even certain whether he's enrolled in music school. A while back by the way, he wished to become a novelist and studied with that in mind. But he says he read so many books he could no longer write. Ridiculous. Lately he's learned about self-consciousness and goes about parroting the term without the least embarrassment. I can't talk in fancy terms, but I know what self-consciousness is all about. Several hundred coeds, for example, line up on both sides of the street. I happen to come by all alone and try slipping nonchalantly through. Things turn awkward then, I don't know how to hold my head nor where to look, and I start whirling about at my wits' end. Self-consciousness of this sort, if that's what's involved, is truly excruciating, and you don't go around simply babbling about it. Don't you find it strange the way Baba talks so casually about publishing a magazine? Pirate! What's the meaning of that? He just likes the carefree sound. There will be problems if you put too much faith in Baba. I predict trouble and my predictions always come true."

"But . . ."

"What do you mean, but?"

"I really trust Baba."

"Is that right?" He dismissed my heartfelt words, a look of blankness on his face. "I don't believe a word Baba says even about this new magazine. He'll tell me to put up fifty yen—nonsense! He just wants to raise a fuss. Not an ounce of sincerity in the guy. You probably don't know it yet, but three of us are coming to your boardinghouse the day after tomorrow. There's Baba and me. And also a fellow Baba knows through a certain professor at his music school. He's a young writer named Dazai Osamu, and the three of us will be drawing up final plans for the magazine. How about that? Shouldn't we look as bored as we can? And pour water on any discussion? No matter how fine a magazine we produce, we won't look high class. Regardless of how far we get, we'll be tossed aside. I'm no Beardsley, and I really don't care. I'll work hard on my paintings, sell them for plenty, and have fun. That's enough for me."

We were before the mountain-lion cage as he finished. The lion had arched its back, and the glittering green eyes were fixed upon us. Satake slowly stretched out his arm and crushed his partially smoked cigarette right on the lion's nose. His posture at that moment seemed to me as natural as a rock.

III. The Gateway to Eminence

Beyond this point the shellfish are cheaper.

"By hook or by crook, then . . . the magazine to end all magazines . . ."

"No, just a pamphlet."

"There you go again. I've heard plenty about you, and I've got your number. Imagine, a magazine that'll put Gide and Valéry to shame."

"Did you come here just for laughs?"

In the brief time I was downstairs, it appeared that Baba and Dazai had already begun to quarrel. When I entered the room with the tea utensils, Baba was slouched over the desk in one corner, an arm propped against his cheek. The fellow named Dazai sat in the corner diagonally across, his back leaning against the wall, his two legs with their long, hairy shins flung out upon the floor. The eyes of both were half-closed and drowsy, and their speech was slow and laborious. But even I could tell from the lethal anger simmering within those eyes and the fragmented words that flickered forth like a snake's tongue, that the duel between them was a dangerous one. Satake lay sprawled out next to Dazai, a bored look on his face, a cigarette in his mouth, his eyes roaming the room.

The entire business was doomed from the start.

That morning Baba had invaded my room at the boarding-house while I was still sleeping. He was neatly dressed in his student uniform, with a bulky yellow raincoat pulled over it. The coat was drenched, but Baba did not remove it. Instead he hurriedly paced around the room while grumbling to himself.

"My nerves must be shot. I'll go crazy in this rain. Get up, get up. My weight's already down just brooding about *The Pirate*. Get up. I met this fellow named Dazai just the other day. My senior classmate introduced him as a brilliant novelist. But the fates have been cruel and now we're stuck with him. I'm telling you, he's a dreadful case, this Dazai. Yes, an absolutely dreadful case. I seem to be physically repelled by such a man. He crops his hair to the scalp, as though he were a deeply pious monk. Vulgar taste. Yes, that's it. He decorates himself all over in vulgar taste. I guess all these so-called novelists are like that. They ask themselves, now where did I mislay my thinking, learning and passion? Dime-store novelists all from the word go. He's got a big, sallow face glistening with oil. And his nose—I tell you I've read of a nose like that in Régnier. A supremely precarious nose, with deep wrinkles alongside that barely keep it from collapsing like a dumpling. Exactly! Régnier's got it just right. The eyebrows are short, thick and dark. And shaggy enough to almost conceal his small fidgety eyes. The forehead seems stubbornly narrow with two visibly carved wrinkles. A really sad case. He's got a thick neck too, and hairline with a dunce-like feel to it. On his neck just below the jaw I noticed three red pimple scars. I'd figure him to be about five foot seven and a hundred twenty pounds. A size eleven sock and still in his late twenties. Oh, I forgot to mention something important. He's got amazingly stooped shoulders—a virtual hunchback. Now, close your eyes a moment and picture him . . .

"Never mind, it's a sham. A complete sham. He's just pretending. No doubt about it. Make-believe from beginning to end. There's nothing deranged about these piercing eyes of mine. He's got a sparse unkempt beard. No, he can't keep anything unkempt. He grows that beard deliberately. Ah, I can't figure out just who it is I'm describing. Have a look: now he's acting like this, now like that. Can't move a finger or clear his throat without a point by point debriefing. Utterly revolting! The guy's got a face as smooth as an egg—no eyes, no mouth, no eyebrows. Or, having painted on the eyebrows and glued on the nose and eyes, he make a show of indifference. And the ART he makes of doing it! Christ! The first time I looked at him, I felt as if someone was licking me with devil's tongue. Consider the awesome gang we've brought together: Satake, Dazai, Sanojiro, Baba. An epochal event if the four of us merely stood silently in a row. Yes, I'll go ahead with it! It's fate. And can't even disagreeable companions be fun? My life ends this year, and I'm waging everything on *Le Pirate*. Will I become another Byron? Or a bum? The lord will grant us five pence. Satake can stuff his rebellion."

All of a sudden he lowered his voice. "Time to rise. I'll open the shutters. The others will be here soon, and I'm looking to advance plans for *The Pirate* today in this very room."

Baba's enthusiasm was infectious, and I began to stir underneath the covers. Then I leaped up, kicked the bedding aside and helped him with the rotting, creaky shutters. They opened on the roofs of the Hongo district which looked blurred in the rain.

Satake arrived around noon. He wore a jacket of light blue wool over his velvet slacks. He had neither a raincoat nor hat, and the cheeks of his rain-drenched face had a wondrous, moon-like luster to them. Without a word of greeting, he sank like a dying glowworm into a corner of the room. Finally he said, "Please excuse me. I'm worn out."

Moments later the door slid open, and Dazai moved indolently into the room. One look at him and I turned away in consternation. This would never do. From Baba's description I had drawn two images, a favorable and a negative one; the real Dazai fit the negative one to a T. To make things worse, wasn't he decked out in precisely the sort of costume Baba most abhorred? A tie-dyed sash and brightly colored Oshima-style flecked kimono, his sports cap a bold, checkered pattern, his under-kimono composed of pale yellow silk just long enough to give a glimpse of the hem. Dazai gently raised the hem as he sat down and pretended to look out the window. "The rain falls on the town," he intoned, his voice thin and reedy as a woman's. The sentence concluded, he turned toward us, narrowed his muddy bloodshot eyes to a thread's width and displayed a smile that wrinkled his entire face.

I fled the room and headed downstairs. When I returned with the tea utensils and the iron pot with the hot water, Baba and Dazai were already arguing. Dazai, his hands clasped behind his sheared head, was speaking. "The words don't count," he said, "It's whether we're really for it, don't you think?"

"For what?"

"The magazine. If we do it, we do it together."

"What did you come here for?"

"Maybe the wind blew me in."

"We can talk about it. But we give up the prophecies, the epigrams and the jokes at least. And maybe you could drop that grin of yours into the bargain."

"Well, let me ask you something. Why did you invite me?"

"You come whenever someone calls then?"

"Yes, I suppose. I say to myself I have to."

"A man's calling has top priority. Don't you agree?"

"As you please."

"My, what a gift for banter. You don't give a damn. Ah, sorry to bow out of joining in with you, I mean. You get my point, so now it's your turn to strike. Oh, the hell with this."

"You or me, it's all joking from the start. If you don't deliver a punch line, you don't get one in return."

"Here I am, with a huge pair of hanging balls. What to make of it? That's the feeling. I'm behind the eight ball, right?"

"Your words don't add up, if I can put it like that. What's

the matter with you? It's as though you and your friends know about the artistic life, but nothing whatever of the work."

"Is that supposed to be a critique? Or the presentation of your research? An exam answer maybe? And I'm told to grade it?"

"Merely a slur."

"If I may put it this way, my words never add up. That's a specialty of mine, a rare kind of specialty too."

"A placard for never adding up."

"So, that's it for skepticism. Let it be. I don't care much for comic dialogues."

"You seem unaware of the piercing sorrow that comes when you expose your tenderly nursed works in the marketplace. And the emptiness of heart that comes after praying to the Harvest God. Indeed, you've only passed under the first gate to his shrine."

"Oh hell, you're still into prophecy? I haven't read your novels, but I have the feeling they're mostly cheap jokes. Take away the sentiment, the wit, the humor and the posing and there's nothing left. I sense the worldliness in you, but not the spirit—the human stomach, but not the artist's refinement."

"I see that, but I've got to survive. I have this feeling that artistic works bow down before society and beg for help. So I think about making my way in the world. I don't write as a hobby. If it were a matter of having proper status and writing for pleasure, I would never have begun. Once I start writing nowadays, I realize the whole thing will turn out well. Beforehand, though, I wonder at length whether I should get on with it. I consider from every angle whether the effort is worth it, decide it's not, and end up doing nothing."

"And in spite of those sentiments, you said—what were the words?—Yes, Let's do it together, all of us."

"So you're delving into me now? Well, I just felt like getting angry. Anything would have done. I was just longing for some shouting."

"Ah, I get it. You take a stance wielding a shield then. You can't even try putting up a fight."

"I like you. I still don't have my own shield. They're all borrowed from someone else. If only I had my own, no matter how ragged."

"You do!" I interrupted. "Imitation!"

"That's right. Score one for Sanojiro. A once-in-his-lifetime feat, that's for sure. Dazai, a silver-plated shield with a mustache pattern fits you exactly. Yes, Dazai calmly takes up his shield already. We alone are left utterly naked."

"This may seem an odd question," Dazai ventured, "But do you take more pride in strawberries decked out for the market or the naked ones in nature? The Gateway to Fortune's the Entrance to Hell and it sends people straight into the marketplace. I know the sadness of decked-out strawberries, however. And lately I've begun to respect them. I won't flee. I'll go to where it takes me." His mouth twisted in a painful grin and he added, "And when I awaken on the way . . ."

"Stop. Not one more word." Baba limply waved his left hand before his nose to interrupt Dazai. "If you wake up, the rest of us won't survive. Hey, Sanojiro, lay off. This is getting to be a bore. I'm sorry for this my friend, but I quit. I don't want to become somebody's fodder. You can look around and find some fried bean curd to feed Dazai. Dazai, *The Pirate* is suspended on opening day. And in its place . . ." Baba stood up, walked straight over to Dazai. "You spook!" he cried.

Dazai's right cheek got loudly slapped with an open palm. For a moment his face seemed that of an infant about to weep. But, drawing his dark lips tight, he looked up proudly. I suddenly took a fancy to his face. Satake pretended to drowse nearby, his eyes tightly closed.

The rain did not stop even as evening fell. By then Baba and I were drinking sake in a dusky *oden* bar. At first we drank in silence; but after an hour or two, Baba began to slowly open up.

"Satake has already won over Dazai, no doubt about it. They came together right up to the boardinghouse. He's that much of a go-getter. I'm on to things. Hasn't Satake talked with you on the sly?"

"He has." I poured a drink for Baba. Somehow or other I wanted to help.

"Satake tried getting you away from me. For no particular reason either. There's a strange vengeful streak in him. He outdoes me. No, perhaps I just don't get it. No, maybe he's a commoner pure and simple. That's it—what the world calls a regular guy. But, that'll do. We drop the magazine, I feel relieved. Tonight I'll prop my pillow high and sleep without a care. You know, I'm about to be disinherited anyway, and I'll wake up one morning to find myself a penniless beggar. My heart was never in the magazine, not even from the start. I like you and didn't want to leave you, so I tossed out this idea of *The Pirate* for your sake. Your heart expanded with visions of *The Pirate* and tears welled in your eyes as we discussed various plans. I had lived till now just to see those eyes—that's what I believed. You taught me the real meaning of love—that's how I feel now. You're open—and pure. A handsome youth as well. I sense within your eyes the ultimate in flexibility. It's not me, not Dazai, not Satake who sees into the depths of Wisdom's Well, it's you. You of all people! Damn, why do I carry on like this? Frivolity. Fury. One remains silent about real love until death. It was Kiku who taught me that. I've got big news for you by the way. And you can't do anything about it. Kiku's in love with you. She said, 'How could I say it to that nice Sano-jiro even if I die? Because I love him so much I could die.' She blurted out that paradox, broke a bottle of cider over my head and shrieked as if she were mad.

"But, really now, who do you like best? Is it Dazai? Eh? Satake then? Surely? So . . . Me . . ."

"I'm . . ." I decided to make a clean breast of things. "I can't stand any of you. It's Kiku alone I like. I feel I've been seeing her longer than the woman across the river."

"All right, that will do." Baba assumed a faint smile, but suddenly put his left hand over his face and began sobbing. "I'm not crying," he pronounced, his rhythm reminiscent of the stage. "Fake tears. Crocodile tears. Damn! It's okay if everyone says that and laughs. I'll still carrying on this farce from my birth until I die. I'm a ghost. Ah, please don't forget me. I have my qualities. Who composed 'The Moon over the Ruined Castle'? There are fellows who say I'm not Taki Rentaro. MUST they be so skeptical? If it's a lie, so be it. No, it's not a lie. And we've got to speak truly about what's true. It's not a lie, that's for sure."

Rain was falling as I staggered from the bar all alone. *The rain falls on the town.* Weren't those the words Dazai mumbled earlier? Yes, I must be tired. Please forgive me. Ah, that sounds just like Satake. A-ah, Baba's turn now, with the click of his tongue for good measure.

In these moments a forlorn doubt began to overwhelm me. I felt a shudder as I wondered just who I was. I had been taken away by a shadow of myself. What's this Ultimate in Flexibility business! I began running straight ahead. A dentist's. An aviary. Chestnut vendor. A bakery. Florist. A roadside tree. The used bookseller. A Western-style building . . . I became aware as I ran of my low muttering—"A tram, hurry. Hurry, Sanojiro. Hurry, a tram." To an erratic rhythm I chanted over and over. "Ah, my creation, my one and only poem. What a mess! Done in from stupidity. Done in from a mess. Done in from a mess. Headlight. Explosion. Star. Leaf. Signal. Wind. Aah—"

IV.

"Satake, have you heard that Sanojiro was struck by a tram last night and killed?

"Yes, I heard it on the morning news."

"He sure pulled off that accident well. It won't end for me unless there's a noose around my neck."

"And you'll be the one who lives longest. Oh no, my predictions always work out. Look at this . . ."

"What is it?"

"It's two hundred yen. I sold some pelican sketches. I wanted to have some fun with Sanojiro, so I worked hard on them."

"Give it to me."

"All right."

"Kiku. You know Sanojiro was killed. Ah, he's gone. Can't find him wherever you look. No tears now."

"I'll try," she said.

"Here's a hundred yen. If you buy yourself a nice kimono and sash, you'll surely forget about him. Water takes the shape of the vessel. Satake, let's you and me be friends, at least for tonight. I'll take you to an interesting place, the best in Japan. Somehow I'm getting sentimental over our mutual survival."

"We all die, whoever we are."

EIGHT VIEWS OF TOKYO

For One Who Has Suffered

A mere village in the southern part of Izu, with only a hot spring to recommend it. About thirty households, one might surmise. With only a trifling sum to spare, I settled on this desolate place knowing it would be cheap. July 3, 1940.

At the time I had a bit of cash to spare. The future, however, seemed quite dark. Probably I wouldn't be able to write at all. If I couldn't come up with a story in the next two months, I would be penniless as usual. Small comfort when you think about it, but for me this was the first breathing spell of any kind in a decade. When I settled in Tokyo in 1930, I was living with a woman named H. My oldest brother sent us enough money each month from the country, but H and I were fools; though warning each other against extravagance, we had to pawn an article or two at the end of each month.

I finally parted from H after six years. I had nothing except my bedding, a desk and lamp, a wicker trunk—and some ominous debts. Two years later a conventional marriage was arranged for me through the help of a certain mentor. And two years after that, I was able to breathe once again. Nearly ten volumes of my mediocre writings had been published, and even without a definite commission, I felt that I could peddle two of every three pieces if I really tried. From now on I would skip the charm and do adult work, write what I only wanted to write.

Though lonely and subject to anxiety, I was happy from the depths of my heart. For a month I could write freely without troubling over money. My life for the time seemed like fiction. But with ecstasy and worry both churning within, I could not get to my writing. That was the unbearable part.

Eight Views of Tokyo. There's the short piece I wanted to write some day, write slowly and painstakingly. I would describe my ten years in the city, guided by scenes from various periods of my life. This year I turned thirty-two, which meant in the Japanese outlook that I was entering middle age. And, whether I considered my body or my emotions, I could not alas deny this. I told myself to remember. Youth is over, old fellow. Look the part of a thirty year old. Eight Views of Tokyo. I wished to write my farewell to youth without flattering a soul.

The guy's gotten to be a Philistine, hasn't he. That sort of malicious rumor reached me along with the breeze. I firmly replied in my heart that I've always been a Philistine. You just didn't notice. You've got things backward. When I determined to make literature my life's work, you fools readily took me for an ally. I smile faintly. Perpetual youths live on the stage, not in literature.

Eight Views of Tokyo. I've got to write about that—during this very moment. I've no pressing commitments for a while and more than a hundred yen on hand. This is not the time to pace around in a tiny room and let out sighs of ecstasy and worry. I must keep moving on.

After buying a large map of the city at Tokyo Station, I boarded a train for Yonehara. This is not a vacation, I repeatedly told myself. I will spare no effort fashioning this precious monument to a single life. At Atami I changed trains for Ito, and from Ito I took the bus to Shimoda. For three hours the bus jostled me about as it headed south along the eastern shore of the Izu Peninsula. When I got off at this forlorn village of thirty households, I figured a night's lodging would cost me no more than thirty yen. There were just four inns standing in a row, all of them pathetically small and primitive. The one called F seemed a trifle better than the others, so I chose it. When the slovenly, ill-tempered maid had led me upstairs and shown me the room, I felt like weeping in spite of my age. I remembered the single room I had rented at a boardinghouse in Ogikubo three years earlier. The boardinghouse was low class even for Ogikubo, but my room there was not so cheap and gloomy as this six-mat affair next to the futon closet.

"You don't have anything else?" I inquired.

"No, everything is taken. Anyway, it's cool here."

"Oh?"

She seemed to be trifling with me, perhaps because I looked so shabby.

"The rate's either three yen fifty sen or else four yen a night. And lunch is extra. So . . . ?"

"I'll settle for three yen fifty sen. And let you know when I want lunch. I'll be here about ten days. I want to get some studying done."

"Just a moment." She went downstairs and returned shortly. "Er . . . if you're staying awhile, we collect before you move in."

"I see. How much do you need?"

She mumbled that any sum would do.

"Shall we make it fifty yen?"

"Okay."

I laid the bills out on top of the desk. Then I could no longer contain myself.

"Here, take all of it—ninety yen. I'll keep just enough in my own purse for cigarettes." I wondered why I had come to such a place.

"Thank you. I'll look after it."

The maid left the room. I had important work to do and I must not get irritated. I told myself firmly that I could hardly expect a better reception in my present straits, then took from the trunk my pen, ink and manuscript paper.

A breathing space ten years in the making had come to this. But the sadness of it had been ordained by fate. Telling myself this plain truth, I stiffened my will and set about my business. I had not come for fun, but for hard work. That evening I spread the large map of Tokyo across my desk under a dim lamp. How many years had passed since I first spread open such a map? When I first arrived in the city ten years ago, I shied away from even buying one. Afraid of being ridiculed as a country bumpkin, I hesitated over and over. I finally bought the map using a deliberately rough tone of self-derision. With the map secure inside my kimono, I stalked back to the boardinghouse. Later that night, having shut the door and the windows, I stealthily unfolded it. Wonderful patterns of red, green and yellow appeared. I ceased breathing even as I gazed. The River Sumida . . . Asakusa . . . Ushigome . . . Akasaka . . . They were all there, and I could go anytime I felt like it. I seemed to be witnessing a miracle.

As I gaze at the map now, the city appears like a mulberry leaf eaten away by silkworms, and all I think of are the distinct lives of people living there. They all push into this monotonous plain from the entire country, dripping with sweat as they jostle one another, fight for a scrap of land and taste some joy in the midst of these trials. They glare at one another and they quarrel. The women call to the men, and the men merely walk about half-crazed. Suddenly and without reason, I remember a forlorn passage from a novel entitled *Lignite*—"Love? To dream of beauty and to do what's squalid." The words in the book had no direct bearing on the subject of Tokyo.

Totsuka, where I first settled. My next-older brother had

rented a house in the area and was studying sculpture. I had graduated from Hirosaki Higher School in 1930 and enrolled in the French department of Tokyo Imperial University. I couldn't read a word of French, but I was in awe of Professor Tatsuno Yutaka and wanted to hear his lectures on French literature. I rented a back room in a newly constructed boardinghouse about three blocks from my brother's place. There was between us a tacit awareness that misfortune could occur when two brothers, no matter how well disposed, live under the same roof away from home. And so, without exchanging a word, we understood that I would live in same neighborhood but three blocks apart.

Just three months thereafter my brother fell ill and died. He was twenty-six. I remained at the boardinghouse in Totsuka after his death, and from the second semester I ceased going to school almost entirely. Without troubling much about it, I had begun to assist in the shady activities of the political movement society fears above all else. I had nothing but scorn for the literature that styled itself as a wing of that movement, albeit with a certain exaggeration. For the time being I was an unspoiled man of politics.

That autumn the woman named H, whom I mentioned earlier, came to the city at my request. I had known her back home from autumn of the year I entered higher school. She was a geisha, the innocent kind, and we had enjoyed knowing each other for three years. We had not yet become intimate, so I rented a room for her on the second floor of a carpenter's house in the Higashi Komagata area of Honjo Ward. My father had been dead seven years, and it was my oldest brother who eventually came from home to inquire about the woman. We two orphaned brothers met in the somber room of my Totsuka lodging. When he saw how brutish I had suddenly become, my brother wept. I handed her over to his care only on the condition that we would eventually marry. Without a doubt the older brother who agreed to do this suffered far more than the younger brother who proposed it.

The night before handing her over, I took the woman into my arms for the first time. Then my brother accompanied her back home for the time being. The woman was merely listless. A dutiful note that she had arrived home safely, and thereafter not a word. She seemed to be quite content. To me that was not fair. The struggle I had waged upset my entire family and gave my mother a taste of hell. How shameful of this woman to lounge about in blind self-content. I thought she should write every day. She must love me more and more. But she was the sort who didn't like to write. I gave way to despair.

Morning and night I hurried about doing the usual political business. I never refused a request to help out. Yet, my limitations in this line of endeavor gradually became apparent, and I despaired a second time. It was a bar girl from a Ginza backstreet who fell for me. Each and everyone of us goes through a stage of being liked—a squalid stage. I persuaded her to leap with me into the sea at Kamakura. You should die when you're worn out, I felt. And I was worn out by that unholy work. My body could not endure it. I had undertaken it simply from fear of being called a coward.

H thought only of her own happiness. You weren't really a woman, I thought. You didn't notice how I suffered, so this is what you get. Serves you right. The hardest part for me was being alienated from my entire family. More than anything else, I tried to drown myself knowing how shocked my mother, my older brothers and my aunt were over the affair with H. The bar girl died and I survived. The episode left a black mark on my life, and I've written of it a number of times already. I was held in detention, but avoided prosecution after an investigation. This was near the end of 1930.

My older brothers treated their brother who had attempted suicide with consideration. The oldest, faithful to his word,

paid off H's contract and sent her to me in February. She arrived with a casual expression on her face. We rented a house
in Gotanda for thirty yen a month. It had been built on land
subdivided from Prince Shimazu's estate. H bustled around
performing the household chores. I was twenty-three at the
time and H was twenty.

Gotanda was an idiotic phase in my life. I had no willpower
whatever, no desire for a fresh start. I lived merely to humor
the friends who occasionally dropped in for a visit. Instead
of shame, I felt toward my sorry criminal record a touch of
pride. Seldom attending school and loathe to exert myself in
any way, I passed the time gazing unconcernedly at H. Stupid.
I did nothing. Gradually I slipped back into the movement,
but the old enthusiasm wasn't there. The nihilism of an idler.
That was me during the days I first occupied a house in a corner of Tokyo.

We moved in the summer to Dobocho in Kanda. As the
end of autumn approached, we proceeded to Izumicho, again
in Kanda. By early spring we were at Kashiwagi in Yodobashi.
Nothing worth mentioning occurred. I concentrated on writing
haiku under the pseudonym of Shurindo, as if I were an old
man. Thrown into jail twice for that other activity of mine, I
took the advice of friends and moved my domicile each time
I got out. I felt neither enthusiasm nor hatred. If told something was for the good of all, I would sluggishly agree to go
along with it. We passed the time, H and I, living like a pair of
animals in our lair. H was full of life. She would scream at me
two or three times each day, then turn serenely to her English
lessons. I had devised a study schedule for H, but her memory
didn't seem up to it. She had just gotten the alphabet down
when she gave up. She was hardly up to writing a letter and
would not even attempt it on her own, so I made rough drafts
for her. She fancied herself playing the role of a gangster's
mistress, so she hardly got upset when the police hauled me

off. On certain days she took delight in seeing the movement as a form of chivalry. Dobocho, Izumicho, Kashiwagi. In the meantime I turned twenty-three.

Late in the spring I had to move once more. The police were about to call me in when I bolted. Things were a bit complicated this time. But, thanks to a cock-and-bull story I fed my brother, H and I had a two month's allowance on hand as we pulled out of Kashiwagi. The furniture was placed in the safekeeping of various friends, and with only our smallest possessions, we moved into an eight-mat room on the second floor of a lumber dealer in Hatchobori, Nihonbashi. I passed myself off as Ochiai Kazuo from the island of Hokkaido. It was an austere time, and we watched our money carefully. I put my anxiety to rest in the vague hope that things would somehow improve. I gave no thought to the future; I could do nothing. Occasionally I went to the university and napped for hours on the grass in front of the lecture hall.

One day I was told a disagreeable tale from a student in the economics department who had graduated from my higher school. It seemed as though I were swallowing boiling water. I couldn't believe it, and I loathed the student for telling me. Mindful that H alone could clear up the matter, I hurried home to our room over the lumber dealer, but I found it difficult to speak up. It was a late afternoon in early summer, and the setting sun was pouring its heat into the room. I sent H out to buy a bottle of Oraga Beer, just twenty-five sen at the time. I drank the bottle, but when I told her to get me another, she exploded. Thereupon my spirits rose. In a voice as offhand as I could manage, I told her what I had heard that day from the student. She grumbled in our country dialect that it was nonsense, then quickly frowned as if she were angry. When she went on with her sewing with no sign of guilt, I thought her innocent.

That evening I read the wrong book—Rousseau's *Confessions*. I came upon the passage where the author learns how bitter life can taste by discovering his wife's past. I couldn't bear it anymore and ceased to believe that H was innocent. That night I got it out of her. Everything I had heard from the student was so. And the truth was even worse. There seemed to be no end as I probed on and on. So I called a halt midway.

Of course, I was hardly qualified to criticize anyone on THAT score. How about my own incident at Kamakura? I nevertheless spent the night seething in anger. Till now I had cherished H as though she were a veritable jewel. Proud of my woman, I had managed to survive for her sake alone. I had rescued her while she was still innocent—or so I thought—and, like a hero of old, I had believed her every word. I even boasted to friends that I had taken her in because she was so steadfast. No words can describe my innocence. I was stupid as they come, with no comprehension of women. I did not despise H for her deceit. On the contrary her confession was so touching that I wanted to pat her on the back. It was just too bad and that's all there was to it. I could grind my life into powder, so disgusted had I become. I turned myself in to the police.

The prosecutor's investigation was suspended, and I returned still alive to walk the streets of Tokyo. There was no place to go other than H's room, and I hastened to her. It was a dreary reunion. We smiled abjectly at one another and exchanged a limp handshake. We left Hatchobori and rented the one-room cottage of a mansion in Shirogane. My older brothers were running out of patience, but they secretly continued my allowance. H perked up as though nothing were amiss, while I awoke slowly from my stupidity. I put together a one-hundred-page manuscript, a last will and testament. Now regarded as my maiden work, "Memories" was to be an unvarnished account of vices going back to childhood. It was the autumn of my twenty-fourth year.

As I sat in our one-room cottage gazing upon a garden of wild grasses, I forgot utterly how to laugh. For the second time

I determined to die. If you call that pretense, then so it is. I felt content. I had come to regard life as a drama—or rather, to regard drama as life. Now I was no longer of use to anyone. My one and only H had been soiled by the hand of another, and my urge to live was gone. I was one of the fallen masses, a mere fool. I decided to die and thus carry out faithfully the role history had assigned me, the pathetic role of always losing to others.

But life is not a drama, and no one knows the second act. Some men come onstage in the role of the defeated, but never exit till the very end. I undertook this trivial confession of "Memories" for one purpose only—to show that such a squalid child as I had actually lived. Against all expectations, the testament began to prey on my mind, and a light began to glow dimly within my own emptiness. It was too soon to die, for I could not rest content with this one work. I had written part of my tale, and now I had to write the whole of it. I would make a clean breast of my entire life. There was plenty to write about, and I chose for my next attempt the incident at Kamakura. But something was missing, and so I wrote another work. Dissatisfied a second time, I let out a sigh and set to work again. I could punctuate my writing with commas, but I could not put a period to it. A demon would beckon, only to devour me. I was making no headway whatever.

It was 1933 and I turned twenty-four. By all means I had to graduate from the university this spring. But what were the chances of graduating when I didn't even take the examinations? Unaware of this, my brothers back home seemed to harbor an expectation. Their renegade brother was loyal enough to show he could graduate and atone for the stupid things he had done. But I betrayed them to the hilt. I had no intention of graduating.

To betray a trust is a maddening kind of hell, and during the next two years I lived in that hell. Give me one more year,

I pleaded with my oldest brother. I will graduate without a doubt. He did give me that year—and I betrayed him. The following year the same thing happened. A prey to fear and self-loathing, subject to suicidal reflections, I devoted myself to those egotistical works, my so-called last will and testament. If only I could bring this off . . . Perhaps my stuff was childish, affected and sentimental; but I was staking my life on that sentimentality. I placed each work I finished—the third, the fourth—in a large paper bag. The number slowly increased until finally I took up my brush and wrote on the bag *Final Years*. This deliberately chosen title meant that things would come to an end with these writings.

Early that spring there was talk of selling the house in Shiba, so we had to move again. Unable to graduate, I took a large cut in my allowance from home. We had to retrench. One of my friends, a solid citizen who worked for a newspaper, offered to rent us a single room in his house in Amanuma, a district of Suginami Ward. Again, I hadn't the least intention of graduating, and during the two years we lived in his house, I caused my friend much anxiety. In my desire to conclude the book, I was like one possessed. I avoided embarrassment by telling both H and my friend that I would graduate the following year. Once a week I donned a student uniform and left the house. I would go to the university library, randomly select a book and flip through it, take a nap, jot down rough drafts for my stories. In the evening I left the library and returned to Amanuma. Neither H nor my friend doubted me in the least. On the surface everything was fine; but within me a struggle was taking place. There wasn't a moment to waste. I must finish, I told myself, while the money was still coming. And the work was hard. I would write something, then tear it up. I was being devoured by that hideous demon to the very marrow of my bones.

A year went by and I failed to graduate. My older brothers

were furious, but I made my customary plea all the same. I was duping them again as I promised to graduate the following year, but there was no other way. I could hardly make my benefactors a party to the deception by telling the truth. Like the prodigal son, I preferred to go my own way. Surely I could not come straight out and say I needed another year to finish my last will and testament. They would think me a self-conceited, poetic dreamer and that would be the worst thing. Even if they wanted to send the money, they would be obliged to stop if I told them such a fantasy. Had they kept up the allowance while aware of the truth, they would eventually be regarded as accomplices. I didn't want that. I know this will sound like a crook's apology, but I had to be the cunning, cajoling younger brother deceiving his elders to the end.

Once a week I would continue to put on my uniform and head to school. H and my friend nobly believed I would graduate next year. I felt cornered as one dreary day followed another. I wasn't a criminal, and deceiving others was pure hell.

Presently the three of us left for another part of Amanuma. My friend had found the previous location inconvenient for getting to work, so he moved in the spring to a house near Ogikubo Station, just behind the marketplace. At his urging we rented a room on the second floor. Unable to sleep, I drank raw sake and coughed up phlegm. Probably I was ill, but I couldn't worry about that. I had to hurry and finish the works inside the paper bag. I know it sounds conceited, but I wished to bequeath them to everyone as my apology. Devoting my entire strength to the task, I managed to finish late in the fall. From the twenty or so works inside the bag, I chose fourteen. The rest I burned, along with the manuscript paper I had scribbled on. There was a whole trunkful. I took the load into the yard and burned it completely.

"Why did you burn them?" H asked that evening.

"Because I don't need them anymore," I replied, smiling.

"Why did you burn them?" she asked once more. There were tears in her eyes.

I began making the necessary arrangements. I returned borrowed books to my friends, sold my letters and notebooks to a trash dealer. Along with the works I slipped two letters into the bag labeled *Final Years*. Everything now seemed in order. It was frightening to be with H, so I went out every evening to drink cheap sake. In the meantime a classmate came to me and inquired about starting a journal. I was indifferent to the idea, but agreed to cooperate if the journal was called *Blue Flower*. This quip set the game in motion, and people came forward from every quarter to join. Two of them soon became close friends and helped me rekindle my earlier enthusiasm for the final time. It was all a mad dance the night before death. We got drunk together. We thrashed our duller classmates; we made friends with the coarsest women. The contents of H's chest of drawers disappeared even before she noticed. A collection of genuine belles lettres, *Blue Flower* appeared for the first and last time in December. By then, the other members of the group had gotten so fed up with our senseless antics that they scattered, leaving us behind. We became known as "the three fools." But we remained lifelong friends, and I learned plenty from those two.

It was now March and, with the day for graduation drawing near once again, I tried to appear lighthearted. I took an entrance exam for a newspaper company, amusing both H and myself by claiming that I would become a reporter and live a commonplace life the rest of my days. I would eventually be found out, but I wished to sustain our happiness, if only for another day or even a moment. More than anything else, I was afraid of shocking people and, when the occasion required it, I would tell desperate lies. It was always thus. Finally I would be cornered—and think of suicide. I could not get the wrenching truth out, even though delay simply meant that people would be all the more shocked and enraged. From moment to moment I fell further and further into this hell of desperation. Needless to say,, I had no intention of joining a newspaper company. I could hardly pass the exam anyway— or the university exam for that matter. My policy of deception had been flawless, but now it collapsed. I thought it was time to die. In the middle of March I went off alone to hang myself in the hills at Kamakura. It was 1935.

That was five years after I had caused an uproar by leaping into the sea at Kamakura. Since I could swim, drowning was beyond me. This time I chose hanging, a method said to be foolproof. I failed miserably and woke up still alive. Perhaps my neck was thicker than average. I returned absentmindedly to the house in Amanuma, my neck red and swollen.

I had failed to settle my own fate. When I arrived home, a strange unknown world opened up. H greeted me at the door and gave me a gentle pat. Others were sympathetic, saying over and over how good it was to have me back. I was dazed by the gentleness of life. My oldest brother hastened from the country. Despite the abuse he poured on me, I could not but think him fond and loving. You might say that I was experiencing certain marvelous feelings for the first time in my life.

An unexpected turn of fate soon took place. Just days after my return I was attacked by severe stomach pains. I endured a full day and night without sleep and applied a hot water bottle to the painful region. Only on the verge of fainting did I finally call a doctor. I was carried in my bedding to an ambulance and taken to the hospital, where an appendectomy was immediately performed. I had been tardy in calling the doctor, and the hot water bottle had been a mistake. The infection had spread to the peritoneum, and the operation proved difficult. Two days later my lungs took a turn for the worse, and I began vomiting blood. I was more dead than alive, and even my physician gave up hope. But a miscreant such as myself could hardly die. Gradually I began to recover and, within a month, the wound in my abdomen had healed.

Since my lung ailment was contagious, I was transferred to Kyodo Hospital in Setagaya Ward. During this period H never left my side. She told me with a smile how the doctor had said she must not kiss me. The hospital director was a friend of my oldest brother, and I therefore received special consideration. We rented two large sick rooms and moved in our furniture, setting up our own domicile right in the hospital.

May . . . June . . . July . . . The striped mosquitoes had arrived, and a white net had just been suspended in the room where we slept when the doctor recommended a move to Funabashi on the Chiba coast. H and I rented a new house on the edge of town. The change of scenery was to help me recuperate, but once again it didn't work. A hellish perturbation had begun instead. During those days at Asagaya Hospital, I had developed an odious dependence on narcotics. My dressings used to be changed morning and evening, and the doctor himself first used the drug to deaden the pain. Presently I was unable to sleep without the drug. I became so miserable that I appealed to the doctor night after night. He had already given up hope and so he kindly gave in every time. Even after I moved to the second hospital, I pleaded obstinately with my brother's friend, the director. He went along reluctantly once in every three tries. I no longer sought the medication for the pain, but merely to relieve the guilt and irritation. I didn't have the strength to endure loneliness. After moving to Funabashi, I got the drug from a local doctor by complaining of insomnia and toxic symptoms. Later I forced this coward to write a prescription allowing me to make the purchase directly from the pharmacist. Before I knew it, I had become a wretched addict, pinched for money. I was receiving ninety yen a month from my brother, and he refused to provide for any additional expense. That was only to be expected. I was merely toying with my own life, without repaying my brother's affection in any way.

From autumn of that year I began to appear occasionally on the streets of Tokyo. I was fully aware of the bedraggled, half-sane demeanor I bore at the time. I could hardly forget. I had become the coarsest youth in the entire country. I would set out for town to borrow ten or twenty yen. I even wept in front of a magazine editor. And was scolded by another for begging so persistently. During that period it seemed possible my manuscripts could earn a little money. I had still been in hospital when, thanks to the backing of friends, two or three stories from the paper bag titled *Final Years* were published in magazines of quality. The praise and the censure that met this work were too much for me; I turned dizzy with dismay and anxiety, and my need for drugs grew. Tormented more and more, I would set out for a magazine office seeking an interview with an editor or even the company president and pressing for an advance on my manuscript. In my distress I overlooked the simple truth that others too were struggling for all they were worth. Eventually every last one of the manuscripts in the paper bag were sold. There were none left to sell. I could not come up with a new work right away. My material had run out and that was it. Established critics pointed at me and declared, "Talent, but no virtue." I myself believed, "The seed of virtue, but no talent." After all, I only knew how to go crashing ahead. An utter lout. Scrupulous to a fault, I reacted in desperation against the moral obligations that came with one's bed and board. I was nothing but shameless. I was raised in a highly conservative home, and going into debt was the worst sin. Attempting to repay my debts, I simply created larger ones. To rid myself of the shame, I took the drugs more and more. The druggist's bill kept on rising. Sometimes I walked about the Ginza whimpering in broad daylight. I wanted money. I borrowed from nearly twenty people, almost as though I were fleecing them. I could not die. Only after I had paid them back completely could I do that.

People had begun to avoid me. In the fall of 1936, a year after we moved to Funabashi, I was placed in a car and driven to a certain hospital in Tokyo's Itabashi Ward. I slept through the night and awoke to find myself in a mental asylum.

I was released one fine afternoon about a month later. H had come to meet me, and I was alone with her in the car. Though separated for a time, we remained silent at first. After the car drove off, H spoke up.

"You're off the drugs, then?" She sounded peevish.

I said the one I thing had learned from the hospital. "I won't trust people after this."

"Yes." Ever the pragmatist, H apparently understood me to be speaking of money. She nodded fully and went on. "You just can't trust them."

"I don't trust you either."

H looked embarrassed.

The house in Funabashi had been given up during my hospital stay, and H was again living in a one-room apartment in Amanuma-sanchome. Two magazines had each commissioned a story from me, and I set to work that very evening. Having finished the stories and collected my payment, I went off to Atami and spent the entire month drinking. I had no idea what to do next. My oldest brother had given me a monthly allowance for three years, but the mountain of debt from before my hospital stay remained unchanged. I had planned writing a splendid novel at Atami and paying off with the earnings the most worrisome of the debts facing me. But I could hardly endure the desolation around me, let alone write a novel. All I did was drink. I was a good-for-nothing fellow, through and through. At Atami I ran up more debt. Whatever I did went wrong. I was done in utterly.

I returned to the apartment in Amanuma bereft of all hope

and let my bedraggled body slump to the floor. I was already twenty-nine, with nothing to show for it. I had one padded dressing gown and H had only the clothes on her back. I thought we had reached that so-called rock bottom. Clinging to my brother's monthly sum, I lived quietly as an insect.

But this was not rock bottom, not yet. Early that spring, a Western-style painter came to discuss something totally unexpected. He was a very close friend, and I felt suffocated as I listened. H had already committed the lamentable deed with him. I remembered suddenly how upset she appeared in the car at that philosophic declaration of mine upon leaving the cursed hospital. I had given H lots of trouble, but I intended to stay with her as long as I survived. Yet, so poorly did I express my feelings that neither H nor the painter knew that I loved her. Although he had come for my advice, I was at a loss. I did not want to hurt anyone. And, as I was the oldest one of us, I wished to stay calm and give superb guidance. Confused and upset by the gravity of the matter, I dithered. This left H and the man almost contemptuous of me. Still I could do nothing. In time the painter became more and more evasive. In spite of my own anguish, I felt pity for H. Already she seemed able and willing to die. When I couldn't take it any longer, I too thought of dying. Let's die together. Even the gods will forgive us. So, like a brother and sister on close terms, we set out for Minakami hot springs. The next evening the two of us went into the mountains to commit suicide. I thought to myself that she must not die—and struggled to that end. H survived. I used drugs on myself—and failed marvelously.

Finally we parted. I did not have the courage to keep her any longer. You might say that I abandoned her. Even though I put on a show of patience and humanitarian bluff, I could plainly see the ugly hell of days ahead for us. H returned to her mother's home in the country, and no one knows what happened to the painter. I remained alone in the apartment and began cooking my own meals. I remember drinking rotgut. My decaying teeth began to fall out, and my face grew ugly. I moved to a nearby boardinghouse. It was utterly squalid, the perfect place for me. I often drank alone in my room of four and a half mats. When drunk, I would go out and lean against the boardinghouse gate murmuring haphazard songs:

> Bidding the world farewell
> I stand by the gate.
> The pines stay in place
> While withered, moonlit fields
> Flit through my mind.

Except for two or three close friends, no one sought my company. Little by little I came to understand how others saw me. I was an ignorant blackguard, a crackpot, a cunning vulgar libertine, and a swindler. I would live off the fat of the land; then, in a pinch, I would intimidate my benefactors in the country by carrying out a mock suicide. I had abused my virtuous spouse and finally driven her away as if she were a dog or cat. There were other stories about me told by men of the world in indignation and scorn. I was treated as a cripple, as someone left for dead. When I realized this, I could not step out of the boardinghouse. Nights when the sake was gone, I found comfort in reading detective stories and munching on rice crackers. Neither the magazines nor the newspapers asked for manuscripts. I didn't feel like writing anything. I couldn't write. Although no one pressed me for payment, I agonized in my very dreams over the debts that had piled up during my addiction. I was now twenty-nine years old.

What was it that brought things around? That got me to think I had to live? Was it the misfortunes of my family back home that gave me the proper strength? My oldest brother was accused of election fraud right after winning a seat in the Diet.

I stood in awe of my brother's severe nature. Surely it must have been the evil men around him. My older sister died. My nephew died. A younger cousin also died. All this I learned from hearsay, for direct contact with home had ceased long ago.

This run of ill luck in the family slowly brought my sprawling body to a sitting position. I had felt embarrassed at the very immensity of our family home. And driven to desperation as a child encumbered by wealth. From early on, alarm over my undeserved good fortune had made me servile and pessimistic. I believed as any such child might that children of wealth would be cast into a great hell. To flee from this would be cowardly. So I worked at dying magnificently, as a very child of evil. One evening, however, it came to me that I was hardly a child of the rich; I was an indigent without even clothes to wear. My allowance from home would end this year, and I had already been removed from the family register. Moreover, this family in which I was born and raised had fallen to the depths of misfortune, and I no longer had privileges of birth for which I had to be grateful. On the contrary I was a minus. And with that discovery, I had to bring up another important fact. As I lay in my boardinghouse room, devoid of even the will to die, my body became noticeably more robust as if by magic. Any number of things might explain why one changes direction in life. There's age, war, a shift in historical views, disgust at idleness, humility about literature, a belief in God and much else. But they seem hollow. Though aiming for the utmost accuracy, such explanations let an odor of falsity through the cracks. That's because people probably don't choose a way after thinking of this and considering that. Mostly they end up at some point simply walking through a different field.

Early in the summer of my twenty-ninth year, I wanted to become a serious writer for the first time. A late awakening, when you think about it. Yet it got me writing industriously in my unfurnished room of four and a half mats. I worked late

into the night, sustaining myself with a snack from the leftover rice on my supper tray. I wasn't writing a last will and
testament anymore, I was writing in order to live. A mentor
gave me encouragement. Even when the others jeered, he kept
up his quiet support of me. I had to repay that precious trust.
Presently I finished a work entitled "Putting Granny Out to
Die," a candid account of how H and I had gone to Minakami
to commit suicide. It sold right away. An editor who had not
forgotten was waiting for such a work. I did not squander the
commission, but headed immediately to the pawnshop, re-
deemed my best set of clothes and left on a trip. With a fresh
outlook on life, I set about writing a long novel in the mountains of Koshu. I spent a full year there without completing
the book, but I did manage to publish over ten stories. Voices
of support sprang up on all sides. The literati proved receptive
and I thought a life in their company would be happy indeed.

In January of the next year, 1939, the same mentor arranged
a conventional marriage for me. Well, it wasn't all that conventional since I didn't even have a penny. My wife and I rented
a small, two-room house on the outskirts of Kofu City for six
yen fifty sen a month. I published two more volumes and, with
the small surplus after expenses, began to clear up those worrisome debts. It was a real struggle, all the same. Early that
autumn we moved to Mitaka Village. This was near Tokyo, but
still beyond it. A total break had occurred in my life from the
time I left the boardinghouse in Ogikubo with one suitcase.

I was now living by my pen. On an overnight trip I simply
wrote "Occupation, Writer" in the guest book. Even if I had
difficulties, I seldom spoke of them. They might be greater
than before, but I would merely smile. The fools said I had
become a Philistine. Well, the sun setting over Musashino is
always huge. And descends boiling upon the horizon. Sitting
cross-legged in the three-mat room which faces the sun, I
supped on our meager fare and said to my wife, "I'm the man

you see here. I won't be rich or famous. But I will protect this home somehow or other." That very moment the woodblock print series *Eight Views of Tokyo* came back to me. The past emerged as a revolving picture lantern.

Though beyond the city limits, Inokashira Park is considered one of the notable places in Tokyo. Since the park is close to my home, I could rightly include The Evening Sun over Musashino too among my Eight Views. To determine the other seven, I went through the album of memories in my own heart. In this case, however, it was not the scenes of Tokyo that made for art. It was myself in the midst of those scenes. Did art hoodwink me? Or did I hoodwink art? Neither, for art and I are one.

The Rainy Season at Totsuka. Twilight over Hongo. The Kanda Festival. First Snow at Kashiwagi. Fireworks over Hatchobori. The Fall Moon at Shiba. The Cicadas of Amanuma. Lightning over the Ginza. The Cosmos Flowers at Itabashi Asylum. Morning Mist in Ogikubo. The Evening Sun over Musashino. The dark flowers of memory dance and scatter, and one can hardly gather them. In any event, to arrange the whole in eight views would be obtuse.

That spring and summer, I came upon two more views. On April 4, I visited Mr. S in Koishikawa. An adviser of stature, he had been greatly alarmed by my illness five years ago. In the end I was severely scolded and banished from his presence. This New Year's I paid him a courtesy call and offered my greetings along with an apology. I didn't see him again until that April day. After he agreed to endorse a reception for the book of a good friend of mine, I questioned him about painting, and the writings of Akutagawa Ryunosuke. Then he said in his usual solemn way, "I might have dealt harshly with you, but everything seems fine now. I'm happy about that."

Then we took a taxi to the art museum in Ueno. We looked over an exhibit of Western-style, mostly tiresome paintings. I paused before one of them. Mr. S eventually came up and gazed at it closely. "Saccharine, isn't it?"

"Nothing to it," I declared.

It was H's painter.

After we left the museum, Mr. S took me to Kayabacho for a preview showing of the film *Conflict*. The pleasant day ended with tea on the Ginza. As evening came on, Mr. S announced that he would go home by bus from Shinbashi Station. I walked with him to the station, telling him along the way of my plan for "Eight Views of Tokyo."

"Indeed," he said, "the setting sun is huge over Musashino."

He paused on the pedestrian bridge before Shinbashi Station and motioned toward the bridge at the Ginza. "There's a picture for you,' he whispered.

"Yes." I stopped and gazed along with him.

"There's a picture for you." He repeated the words as if talking to himself.

More than the scene we were gazing upon, I would include among my Eight Views of Tokyo Mr. S and the derelict student he had once banished.

Two months later I encountered a scene even more cheerful. A special delivery letter had arrived for my wife. It was from her younger sister and said: "T will be leaving tomorrow. We'll be able to see him for just a moment at Shiba Park. Please come at nine and have my brother-in-law convey how I feel. I'm such a fool I haven't said a thing."

She was twenty-one and so small she seemed like a child. A marriage had been arranged for her last year; but shortly after the exchange of presents, T had been drafted into a Tokyo regiment. I had spoken to him once when he was in uniform. He was an alert, polished young man, and now he was apparently heading for the front. Within two hours a second letter arrived. "After some thought, I realized how bold my earlier request was. It's fine not to say anything to T. Just come and see him off." My wife and I both burst out laughing. Her younger sister had gone to the home of T's parents a few days ago, and we could readily imagine her whirling about.

We rose early the next morning and left for Shiba Park. A large crowd had gathered on the grounds of Zojoji Temple to see the men off. I caught hold of an old fellow in khaki who bustled about elbowing his way through the crowd and asked him about T's regiment. I was told they would approach the main gate, stop five minutes to rest and then depart. My wife and I were standing by the gate watching for the regiment when her sister arrived clutching a small flag. T's parents had also come along, and I met them for the first time. We were not yet definitely related, and I was awkward with people anyway. I merely nodded, without greeting them properly, and turned to the girl.

"How about it? You're not nervous?" I inquired.

"It's nothing." She replied and laughed gleefully.

"What's the meaning of that?" My wife said frowning. "Laughing out so loud."

Many people had gathered to see T off. A row of six large banners, each emblazoned with his name, stood by the gate. The men and woman who worked in the factory run by T's family had been given a holiday in order to be present. I stood toward the end of the gate, away from everyone. I felt out of place. Some of my teeth were missing, and I was dressed like a slob. I was an indigent man of letters, wearing neither proper trousers nor even a cap. T's wealthy parents were doubtlessly wondering about this sorry-looking relative of their son's fiancée. When my wife's sister came over to speak, I chased her away. I said, "You've got an important role today, so stay with your father."

There was no sign whatever of T's regiment. Ten o'clock passed, then eleven, then twelve. Still no sign. Groups of schoolgirls rode by in a number of sightseeing buses. A poster with the name of the school was posted to the door of each vehicle. The name of my hometown school also appeared. My oldest brother's daughter should be a student there and was probably on the bus. I thought how she might have noticed her foolish uncle loitering before the celebrated temple gate without realizing who he was. Each time the twenty or so buses passed by, the young guide in her uniform would point toward me and begin some explanation or other. At first I pretended to be indifferent, but in the end I would strike some sort of pose. I folded my arms in the composed manner of the Balzac statue. Thus did I myself become a famous sight of Tokyo.

One o'clock was drawing near when shouts arose. "They're here! They're here!" Soon trucks full of soldiers pulled up to the main temple gate. T knew how to drive a Datsun, so he himself was in the cab of his vehicle. I watched absentmindedly from the back of the crowd.

"Brother," my wife's sister whispered. She had made her way through the crowd and was shoving me forward. Aroused, I looked up and there was T already down from the truck. He seemed to have noticed me standing at the back of the crowd and was saluting toward me. Still doubtful, I hesitated a moment and looked all around. Yes, it was surely me he was saluting. I pushed decisively through the crowd together with the younger sister. When we were right in front of T, I said, "Don't worry about a thing. She may be foolish, but she's aware of a woman's main purpose. Don't worry in the least. We'll be responsible for her." I spoke without a trace of my usual smile, then looked at the girl. Her slightly raised face had a tense look. Blushing momentarily, T gave another salute.

"Don't you have anything more to say?" This time I smiled at the girl.

"Not anymore." She lowered her gaze.

Shortly thereafter the order came down for the men to depart. I tried to slip back into the crowd, but my wife's sister kept shoving from behind. This time I ended up right below the cab of the truck. T's parents were the only other persons standing there.

"Don't worry about anything while you're away," I called out to T.

His honored father abruptly turned toward me. The look of disgust that flashed in his eyes seemed to demand to know just who this meddling fool was. This time, however, I did not flinch. Wasn't I aware and able to affirm that the ultimate in human pride was rooted in suffering to the point of death? The draft board may have turned me down and I was a pauper to boot. But I wasn't going to hang back now. The celebrated sight of Tokyo let out another exclamation: "Don't you worry!" If some problem did arise with the marriage, I would be their final source of help as the outlaw who ignored public opinion.

With this scene from the main gate of Zojoji Temple, I feel that my story has the tautness of a bow drawn full as the moon. Days later I sallied forth with pen, ink, paper and that large map of Tokyo. What's occurred in the ten days since my arrival at this hot spring on the Izu Peninsula? I still seem to be at the inn, but what am I up to?

HOMECOMING

T he summer before last, I went home for the first time in ten years. And this autumn I finally completed and sent to the editors of a certain periodical a manuscript of forty-one pages describing the visit. Shortly thereafter, the two men who had arranged the visit home came to my humble house in Mitaka to announce that my mother was in a grave condition. I knew that she had grown feeble, but I had not expected to hear news such as this for another five or six years. One of the men, Mr. Kita, had actually accompanied me on that last visit.

My oldest brother, the head of the family by then, was away from home. I was able, however, to meet my second brother Eiji, my oldest brother's wife, my nephews and nieces, my grandmother and my mother. Mother was sixty-eight and growing senile. She didn't appear to be steady on her feet, but she was certainly not ill. I even imagined in my optimism at the time, that she might survive another ten years. Entitled "To Home and Back," my narrative represented an attempt to describe the visit as honestly as I could. For various reasons I had been able to remain only three or four hours, and as I concluded the sketch, I spoke of my wish to stay longer and see more. I had merely glanced at the area and still wanted to visit various other places. When would I again be able to view those streams and hills of my native region? If something did come up with my mother at some time or other, I might return and spend time looking about. But that thought was distressing, and I left off writing any more. Soon after dispatching the manuscript, the dreaded opportunity to return home had suddenly materialized.

Mr. Kita lives in Tokyo while my other benefactor, Mr. Nakabatake, runs a business in my native town. It was Mr. Kita, then, who declared somewhat tensely, "I'll go with you again. This time you'll need to bring your wife and child along."

The first time Mr. Kita had taken me alone. Now there would also be my wife and Sonoko, our infant girl of a year and a half. I have written in detail of Mr. Kita and Mr. Nakabatake in "To Home and Back." Mr. Kita is a tailor, while Mr. Nakabatake has a dry goods store. Both have long been on friendly terms with my family, and one might expect them to have a hostile view of me. I had erred five or six . . . no, the occasions were indeed beyond number. But even after my ties with the family were severed, these two men were the soul of kindness, offering assistance over the years and never once showing any dissatisfaction with me. Indeed, it was Mr. Kita and Mr. Nakabatake who, after some discussion, had decided to risk my oldest brother's wrath and work out a plan whereby I had manged to visit home after an absence of ten years.

"But will it work? I'll look like a fool if I get turned away with my wife and child." I expected the worst, as ever.

"That won't happen." Both men earnestly objected.

"What about last summer?" I asked. Evidently I was the sort of coward who looks before making the slightest leap. "You mean to tell me neither of you heard anything from my oldest brother Bunji after the visit? How about you?" I asked Mr. Kita.

"As the family head," Mr. Kita cautiously replied, "your brother must consider all your relatives. He can hardly welcome you with open arms. I think everything will be all right if I go along, though. When I met your brother in Tokyo after our visit, all he did was call me a rascal. He wasn't the least bit angry."

"How about you?" I turned to Mr. Nakabatake. "You haven't heard from my brother?"

"Not a word." Mr. Nakabatake looked up and went on. "Before he always had a sarcastic remark about any favor I did for you. This is the only time he hasn't said anything."

"You're sure then?" I felt a bit relieved. "If it's not too much trouble, I'd like to have you both along. Nothing should keep me from visiting Mother, and maybe I'll get to see Bunji this time. I'd be grateful if you both came. And how about my wife? Meeting the family for the first time will give her lots of trouble. There'll be complaints about needing a new kimono and whatnot. Could you talk to her for me, Mr. Kita? If I say anything, she's bound to grumble."

However, the problem was settled more easily than I expected. I called my wife into the room, and Mr Kita spoke to her of Mother's condition. When he mentioned that Mother should see her grandchild once, my wife placed her hands on the tatami mat and, with a bow, said to Mr. Kita, "Thank you for helping us."

Turning to me, Mr. Kita said, "When can you leave?"

We decided to leave in seven days, on October 27.

Even though her younger sister came to help, that week was a busy one for my wife. So many new things had to be purchased that I almost went broke. All the while Sonoko toddled about the house, oblivious to the fuss.

The express from Ueno Station left on the twenty-seventh at seven o'clock in the evening. It was so crowded we had to stand all the way to Haramachi, nearly five hours.

Along the way Mr. Kita showed me a telegram. CONDI-
TION WORSE. AWAIT DAZAI'S EARLIEST ARRIVAL. Mr.
Nakabatake, who had left shortly before, had sent the telegram
to Mr. Kita's house that morning.

We reached Aomori the next day at eight o'clock and transferred to the Ou Line. At Kawabe Station we caught the train
which ran between the apple orchards to Goshogawara. This
year's harvest seemed abundant, and my wife's sleepy eyes
widened as she marveled at the beauty of the apples. "How
pretty," she said. "I've wanted to see an orchard once when
the apples turn red."

The glistening fruit was so close you might pluck it by
reaching out.

By eleven o'clock the train arrived at Goshogawara. Mr.
Nakabatake's house was here, and his daughter was at the
station to greet us. We were to rest awhile at the house, allowing my wife and daughter an opportunity to change clothes.
Then we would proceed to my family home in Kanagi. Kanagi
was north of Goshogawara, about forty minutes away by the
Tsugaru Line.

As we ate our lunch, I heard the details of my mother's
condition from Mr. Nakabatake. It appeared that her death
was imminent.

"It's so good of you to come," he said, as if we had done
him a favor. "I kept worrying about when you would arrive," he
continued, "and now I can rest easy. Your mother hasn't said
anything, but she seems to be waiting anxiously."

The biblical tale of the prodigal son came to mind.

When we had finished our lunch, Mr Kita addressed me in
a somewhat firm voice. "You'd better leave your luggage here.
Don't you agree? If you show up carrying a suitcase when your
brother hasn't given his permission . . ."

"I see."

We decided to leave all the luggage behind. Mr Kita warned

us as well that it wasn't clear yet whether we would even be allowed to see my dying mother.

We boarded the train for Kanagi taking nothing but Sonoko's diaper bag. Mr. Kita was with us.

I grew more depressed by the moment. Everyone else was so good, not a wicked soul among them. Everything was awkward because of certain facts: I had done wrong in the past and was hardly upright even now. I was only an indigent writer of dubious repute.

"It's a beautiful place," my wife said as she gazed out the train window. "Brighter than I thought it would be."

"You think so?" The grain had been gathered and the paddy fields appeared cold and bare as far as the eye could see. "It doesn't look like that to me," I added. At the moment I felt no pride whatever toward the region of my birth. Only a trying pain. My earlier visit had not been like this, so enlivening had been the effect of viewing scenes from my youth after a ten-year absence.

"There's Mount Iwaki. They say it resembles Mount Fuji, so we call it Tsugaru Fuji." I was commenting with a forced smile and no enthusiasm whatever. "The low hills over there are called the Bonju Range. And there's Bald Horse Mountain." All in all, a lukewarm, haphazard performance on my part.

"This is my native village. And, if you go four or five lanes further . . ." Thus does Chubei, with a touch of elation, comment upon Ninokuchi Village in a pretty scene from the play *The Courier for Hell*. But, that's not the case with me. My Chubei felt a reckless anger.

"There's . . ." About to say "my house" as a red roof glinted beyond a paddy, I thought better of it. "My brother's house."

But it was a temple roof. "No, that's wrong. Ours is the slightly bigger roof also to the right." I was simply babbling.

We reached Kanagi Station. My little niece and a pretty young girl had come to meet us.

"Who's the young girl?" my wife whispered.

"Probably a maid. We don't have to greet her." The summer of last year I had mistaken a refined-looking maid for my brother's oldest daughter and had greeted her politely with a low bow. Since that had been quite awkward, I said we'd better be cautious this time.

The little niece was my brother's second daughter. She was seven years old, and I remembered her from the previous summer. "Shige-chan!" I called. The girl smiled without hesitation. I felt a trifle relieved. She at least did not know about my past.

When we arrived at the house, Mr. Kita and Mr. Nakabatake went right upstairs to my brother's room. I took my wife and daughter to the household Buddhist altar, where we offered a prayer to my ancestors. Then we withdrew to the "everyday room," which was set aside for the family and close friends and sat down in a corner. The wives of my oldest and second-oldest brother came to welcome us with warm smiles. Then my grandmother, eighty-five years old and leaning on the arm of a servant girl, came by. Her hearing seemed to be impaired, but she was cheerful all the same. My wife struggled to make Sonoko bow, but the girl absolutely refused. She tottered about the room instead, making everyone uneasy.

My oldest brother appeared, then went straight into the next room. His color was bad, and he looked shockingly thin. He also had a stern expression. A single guest who had come to inquire about Mother was in the room, and my brother spoke awhile with this person. Once the guest took leave, my brother entered the everyday room. Before I could utter a word, "Ah," he exclaimed and nodded. Then he gave a slight bow with his hands facing down.

"I've given you all sorts of trouble," I said. I felt rigid as I bowed in return. "My brother Bunji," I announced to my wife.

Before she began her bow, my brother turned and bowed to my wife. I almost panicked. Having finished his bow, my brother headed upstairs immediately.

I wondered what was going on. Something must have gone wrong. From before, my brother would act with this peculiar indifference and give a formal bow only when he was in a bad mood. Neither Mr. Kita nor Mr. Nakabatake had returned from upstairs. Had Kita blundered in some way? Suddenly I felt frightened and alone. My heart was beating rapidly when my sister-in-law entered the room smiling.

"Come along," she urged. I stood up, completely relieved. We would see Mother after all. Permission had been granted quite simply. What the devil! I must have worried a little too much about it.

As we crossed the hallway, my sister-in-law informed us that Mother had been anxiously "awaiting us for two or three days, really waiting for us."

Mother was lying in the ten-mat room that was annexed from the main house. She looked emaciated as a withered leaf in her huge bed. But her mind was clear. "Welcome home," she said.

As my wife greeted her for the first time, Mother raised her head and nodded. When I held Sonoko up and pressed the child's tiny hand against the shriveled palm, Mother's trembling fingers closed in a firm clasp. My aunt from Goshogawara wiped away her tears as she stood by the bed smiling.

In addition to my aunt, there were other people in the room, including two nurses, my oldest sister, my second-oldest brother's wife and several older women relatives. All of us went to the waiting room next door and greeted one another. They said things like, Shuji (that's me) hasn't changed a bit; he's a little chubby though; and he looks younger. Sonoko, less timid than I had feared, started smiling at everyone. The whole group gathered around the hibachi brazier and began to speak in hushed voices. Slowly the tension began to wane.

"Will you be staying longer this time?" someone asked.

"Well, I'm not sure. It will probably turn out to be two or

three hours, just like last summer. Mr. Kita said that would be long enough, and I'm going to do whatever he says."

"But you can hardly go straight back when Mother's so ill."

"Anyway, I'll have to talk to Mr. Kita about whether to stay or leave."

"But this doesn't involve Mr. Kita that much, does it?"

"Yes it does. Mr. Kita's been a great help to me up to now."

"Perhaps he has. But surely even Mr. Kita wouldn't . . ."

"No, that's why I'll talk to him about it. I won't go wrong if I follow his advice. He seems to be still upstairs talking to my brother. Maybe some problem or other has come up. After all, for the three of us just to walk in without permission . . ."

"You needn't worry about that. Didn't your brother Eiji send a special delivery letter telling you to come right away?"

"When was that? We didn't see anything."

"Oh, we thought you had come after reading the letter . . ."

"Good Lord! So the letter must have passed us on the way. What a shame. Mr. Kita looks like he's butting in." Now I understood everything. We had not been very lucky.

"What do you mean, a shame? Wasn't it better to get here a day early?"

I was disheartened all the same. How unfortunate that Mr. Kita had closed his business just to bring us here. And my brothers, who had planned to contact me when the time had come, were naturally upset. Everything had turned out completely wrong.

The young girl who had met us at the station entered the room and bowed toward me with a smile. I had blundered again. Blundered this time for being too cautious. She was no servant, but the daughter of my oldest sister. I had known her until she was six or seven as a tiny girl with dark skin. She had changed, though, and was now graceful and slender.

"This is Mitchan," my aunt said. "She's turned out really nice, wouldn't you say?"

"Really nice," I gravely replied. They all laughed as I added, "Her complexion's turned out fair too."

I had begun to relax slightly when I caught sight of my mother in the next room. Her mouth hung open, and she was breathing heavily, her shoulders shaking. Her thin hand wavered in the air, as though she meant to chase off a fly. Something was wrong. I stood up and went to her side. The others all gathered around her bed with worried looks.

"She seems to feel some pain now and then," the nurse whispered. Placing her hand underneath the quilt, she vigorously massaged Mother's body. I crouched by the pillow and asked, "Where does it hurt?" Mother barely managed to shake her head.

"You've got to hang on. You can't miss seeing Sonoko grow up." I held my embarrassment in check as I spoke.

Suddenly an older woman relative took my hand and placed it firmly in Mother's. I covered both of her hands in mine to warm the frigid skin. The relative buried her face in the quilt and wept. My aunt and sister-in-law were also crying. I twisted my mouth, trying to control my own feelings. After a time I could bear it no longer. I rose from Mother's side and went into the hallway. I walked down the hallway and entered the Western-style room. The room was cold and deserted. Two oil paintings—a poppy and a female nude—hung on the white wall. A poorly done wood carving stood alone on the mantelpiece. A leopard skin was draped over the sofa. The chairs, table and rug were the same as ever. I walked about the room telling myself over and over it would be a lie if I wept and struggled to hold back the tears. I said bravo for the dutiful son who slips into this isolated room to weep by himself. What a fake. Playacting pure and simple. Just a cheap movie. Turning into a soft Shuji at thirty-four, are you? You can drop this maudlin act right now. Too late for you to be the dutiful son. (Try to control this willful self-indulgence. Quit it!) You're faking if you cry. Quit it. The tears would be false. I walked around the room with folded arms talking to myself. I was at my wits' end and might break down at any moment. I smoked a cigarette, blew my nose, kept going with other expedient measures. In the end not a single tear fell from my eyes.

As it grew dark, I did not go back to Mother's sickroom. I remained silently resting on the sofa in the Western-style room. The room didn't seem to be used; nothing happened when I flipped the light switch. I remained alone in the cold darkness. Neither Mr. Kita nor Mr Nakabatake had come to the annex. What was going on? My wife and Sonoko seemed to be in Mother's room. Where would the three of us spend the night? Our original plan was in line with Mr. Kita's view: we would pay a brief visit, then depart from Kanagi to spend the night at my aunt's home in Goshogawara. But, wouldn't this hurried departure be awkward with my mother's condition so serious? In any event I wanted to meet with Mr Kita. But what the devil was keeping him? Was the discussion with my brother getting more and more involved? Perhaps, I mused, there was no place for me after all.

My wife came into the dark room. "What are you doing? You'll catch cold."

"And Sonoko?" I asked.

"She's asleep." My wife explained that the child had been put to bed in the room next to Mother's.

"Is that okay? You saw to it that she won't be cold?"

"Your aunt had a blanket for her."

"What do you think? They're good people, aren't they?"

"Yes." But then a look of doubt crept into her face. "What's going to happen? "

"Don't ask me."

"Where do we stay tonight?"

"Don't ask me. We're following Mr Kita's advice about everything. That's all there is to it. I've gotten used to that the last ten years. If we ignore him and talk directly to my brother, there'll be trouble. You don't see that? I don't have any rights here. I can't even bring in a suitcase."

"You sound a bit resentful of Mr. Kita."

"Nonsense! I know deep within how kind he's been. But relations with my brother get more complicated with Mr. Kita in the middle. There's not a single bad person out there, and I've got to protect Mr. Kita's reputation no matter what."

"That's for certain." Even my wife appeared to be catching on. "I felt it would be wrong to refuse Mr. Kita's offer to bring Sonoko and me along. It's put him in a bind, and I'm sorry for that."

"That's quite true. You shouldn't undertake to do favors lightheartedly. I'm a specially difficult case. I really sympathize with Mr. Kita this time. How awful to come all this way on purpose and no gratitude from my brothers or from us. We've got to figure out a way to rescue him, but we don't carry any weight here. If we start meddling, it'll just mess things up. We'll stay put and see what happens. You go back to the sickroom and rub Mother's feet. She's ill. Don't think of anything else."

But my wife made no attempt to leave. She remained in the dark, her head bowed. It would not do for us to be seen here, so I rose from the sofa and went into the hallway. This was the northern tip of Honshu and the cold was severe. Not a single star was visible as I looked through the glass doors. The sky was simply dark and imposing. I'm not sure why, but I wanted to get back to my work. Right! Get on with it. That's all I felt.

My sister-in-law came looking for us.

"What! Here of all the places!" Her voice sounded clear and astonished. Then she said, "It's time for dinner. Michiko, please join us." My sister-in-law did not seem at all wary. To me, this was an extremely hopeful sign. Perhaps I could avoid mistakes if I discussed with her any problem whatever.

We were taken to the room with the Buddhist altar in the

main house. The seating arrangements were for seven people: with their backs to the hanging scroll were the doctor from Goshogawara (who happened to be the adopted son of my aunt) along with Mr Kita and Mr. Nakabatake. Facing them were my oldest brother and my second oldest, myself and Michiko.

"The special delivery letter crossed us on the way." The words slipped out the moment I noticed my second brother. My brother nodded slightly.

Mr. Kita had a gloomy expression and was quite listless. He was lively at any party, so the gloomy expression that evening was notable. I was convinced something had come up.

The doctor on the other hand became cheerful after a cup or two. With that, the gathering lightened up. I stretched out my arm to pour sake for both brothers. I shouldn't worry any longer whether or not they forgave me. I didn't deserve forgiveness ever; indeed, I would abandon the syrupy, craven idea of begging for it. The only question was whether or not I loved my brothers. How fortunate are those who love. If I loved them, that was enough. I should rid myself of nostalgia and deep longing. Thus did I carry on this nonsensical monologue while I poured and drank myself silly.

That night Mr. Kita stayed at my aunt's home in Goshogawara. Perhaps he hesitated to stay at the Kanagi house with all the bustle over the sick woman. I accompanied him to the train station.

"Thank you for doing this. We're so grateful." I spoke from the heart. Parting from Mr Kita left me bereft. From here on there was no one to guide me. "Will they mind if we stay at Kanagi tonight like this?" I wanted to hear what he had to say.

"They probably won't mind." I might have been imagining it, but he sounded a little abrupt. "Anyway, since your mother is so ill . . ."

"Then, if they let us stay two or three days at the Kanagi house . . . Would that be too brazen?"

"It depends on your mother's condition. Anyway we'll discuss it on the phone tomorrow."

"You're . . . ?"

"I'm going back to Tokyo tomorrow."

"That's a shame. You went back right away last summer. This time we wanted to show you the hot springs near Aomori. We even made plans, but . . ."

"No. It's hardly the time for hot springs, with your mother so ill. She's much worse than I expected. By the way I'll figure out later what I owe for the ticket." Abruptly he mentioned the ticket. I was taken aback.

"C'mon now. I've got to pay for your return ticket too. Don't worry about such a thing."

"No, I'll figure it out exactly. And I'll talk to Mr. Nakabatake first thing tomorrow. He can send the luggage you left at his place over to Kanagi. That will take care of all my obligations." He marched on quickly into the dark. "The station's this way, isn't it? You don't have to see me off. This is enough, really."

"Mr. Kita!" I hurried a couple steps ahead to catch up. "Was it something my brother said?"

"No." He slowed down, then said gently, "You needn't worry about that anymore. I feel good this evening. When I saw Bunji, Eiji and you—three fine brothers every one of you—sitting together, I felt like crying I was so happy. I don't want anything more. I'm satisfied. From the very beginning I never hoped to get a penny from this. Even you must realize that. I only wished to have you three sitting alongside one another. It's a good feeling. I'm satisfied. You've got to hold your own, Shuji. It's time we old folks were leaving."

I saw Mr. Kita off and went back home. When I realized I could no longer depend on him and would have to deal directly with my brothers, I felt more frightened than happy. I was filled with a craven anxiety lest I commit a stupid impropriety and incur their wrath once again.

The house was crowded with visitors, so I went around to the kitchen and slipped through the door to avoid being seen. I was heading toward the sickroom in the annex when I glanced into the alcove next to the everyday room and saw my second brother sitting alone there. I crept up next to him as though drawn by a fearsome force and sat down. I felt a distinct tremor within as I asked, "Is this it for Mother?"

Even I felt awkward asking so abrupt a question. Eiji looked about for a moment with a wry smile, then replied, "It will be difficult this time."

At that moment my oldest brother suddenly came in. He seemed slightly confused as he walked around opening and closing closet doors, then sat down heavily next to our second brother.

Lowering his head, he pushed his glasses up on his brow and pressed a hand against his eyes. He said, "It looks bad this time, really bad."

I became aware at some point that my oldest sister had been quietly sitting behind me.

PUTTING GRANNY
OUT TO DIE

J ust then she intervened.

"Enough! I'll see it's done right. I've been ready for this from the start. There's no point going over . . . Not again." She complained in such a strange voice that I reacted.

"You can't! I know what you're up to. And you'll do it on your own. Will it be suicide? Or just giving way to despair? That's all it comes down to as I see it. When your parents are fit and you've still got a younger brother . . . Well, I can't just tell you that's how it is and be done with it, not when you're in this mood."

Even as he spoke these judicious sounding words, Kishichi himself suddenly felt like dying.

"Shall we die? Together? Even the gods are forgiving."

They began the preparations in earnest.

The wife had made love with another man, her husband having driven her to this by his own shattered life. By dying they would settle the matter. It was early spring, and they had fourteen or fifteen yen on hand, just enough to pay the bills for the month. Except for what they wore, the only clothes still unpawned were Kishichi's quilted dressing gown along with Kazue's lined kimono and two sashes. She wrapped these articles in cloth and cradled the entire bundle in her arms. Then, as seldom happened, the husband and wife went out side by side.

Kishichi did not have a coat. All he had to wear outside were his sports cap and blue silk muffler, the latter wrapped about the collar of his Kurume-style kimono. His geta clogs alone were new, and very clean looking. Kazue, who didn't have a coat either, wore a silk kimono and *haori* jacket, both with an arrow-fleck pattern. She also wore a pink shawl of foreign make, a shawl so large it hung to her waist.

They parted at noon a few doors before the pawnshop.

Kishichi waited in front of Ogikubo Station, silently smoking a cigarette as people slipped in and out of the building. Kazue returned, her eyes moving about in search of him. Suddenly she saw him and rushed forward almost stumbling.

"I've done it! He took everything!" She could barely contain herself. "He lent us fifteen yen, the fool."

She's not going to die. I won't let her. She's not crushed by life as I am. There's lots of strength in her, she won't die. She'll make amends just planning to die. That's enough. She'll be forgiven, which will be fine. I alone shall die.

"Good work!" He smiled and almost patted her shoulder. "Doesn't that make thirty yen altogether? Looks like we'll be taking quite a trip."

They bought tickets for Shinjuku.

After leaving the train, they rushed to a pharmacy and bought a large box of sleeping pills. Then they went to another pharmacy for a second large box of different sleeping pills. This time Kishichi went in smiling and all alone, so the clerk did not get suspicious. Afterward the two of them approached the pharmaceutical counter in the Mitsukoshi department store. Emboldened by the jostling crowd of shoppers, Kishichi asked for two large boxes. The saleslady had a thin, earnest face with dark eyes, and the faintest wrinkle of suspicion crossed her brow as she took the order. Kishichi found her so unpleasant that his show of joviality collapsed. The pills were handed over with indifference.

Aware that the saleslady was on her tiptoes watching, Kishichi deliberately pressed close to Kazue while they moved through the crowd. How unfortunate that people detected a strangeness in him even as he walked nonchalantly.

Kazue next bought a pair of white *tabi* socks at the Mitsukoshi bargain counter while Kishichi purchased a pack of the finest imported cigarettes. Then the couple left.

A taxi took them to Asakusa, where they entered a movie house to watch *The Moon over the Ruined Castle*. Kishichi was moved to tears when the roof and fence of the country school appeared, and the children's chorus broke into song.

"Let's pretend we're lovers," he quipped in the darkness. "They're supposed to hold hands at the movies, just like this."

He drew Kazue's tiny hand underneath his sports cap and held it tightly in his own. But it struck him as indecent for a husband and wife in their painful dilemma to be holding hands. In a panic he released hers.

Kazue laughed softly. She had been touched by the film's routine jokes, not by Kishichi's clumsy gesture.

A good simple woman who can enjoy a movie. It wasn't right for her to die. He couldn't do it.

"Shall we drop it?"

"If that's what you want." Absorbed by the movie, she answered firmly all the same. "I'll die by myself."

Kishichi sensed the wonders a woman might contain.

It was dark when they left. Kazue wanted some sushi, but Kishichi disliked the smell of raw fish. Anyway he wanted a fancier meal tonight.

"Not sushi," he declared.

"But I want some."

It was Kishichi himself who had long ago taught her the

virtue of selfishness. A merely submissive look, he insisted, showed mixed motives.

Everything came back to haunt him.

He drank a little sake at the sushi shop. Then he ordered fried oysters. He told himself this would be his last meal in Tokyo. The remark, as one might expect, brought with it a wry smile.

"How are they?" He was asking about Kazue's tuna fillets over rice.

"Awful," she said, as if truly disgusted. She took another mouthful and added, "Really awful."

Neither of them had much to say.

They left the sushi shop and headed for the vaudeville theater. It was so packed that no one could find a seat. The crowd just stood and watched while pushing and shoving from the very doors. Despite all this, a burst of laughter would arise now and again.

Jostled by the crowd, Kazue gradually became separated from Kishichi. She was petite and seemed a mere country girl struggling to see past the other spectators. Kishichi too was shoved about as he stood on his tiptoes and tried desperately to keep track of her. Indeed, he looked her way more than toward the stage. Kazue's head would move back and forth as she struggled to see the actors on stage; then she would quickly turn around looking for him. The boxes containing the pills were wrapped in a dark cloth and held tightly to her breast. Neither smiled when their eyes met, but they felt relieved to see one another.

I owe her plenty and won't forget it, he told himself. Everything's my fault. If people reject her, I'll do anything whatever to help. She's a good woman, that I know. I'm convinced of it.

And this business? Well, it won't do. It just won't. I can't laugh it off. No, it's the one thing I can't take in my stride . . . can't endure.

Forgive me. Just one last burst of egotism. I can manage the ethics of this, but I can't stand how it feels . . . can't take it at all.

A wave of laughter spread through the hall. Kishichi motioned to Kazue and they left.

"Let's go to Minakami," he said. "Okay?"

They had spent the last summer at Tanigawa, a hot spring resort nestled in the mountains an hour's walk from Minakami Station. Those had been trying days. But they had come through them, and the time spent there now seemed nostalgic as an old picture postcard. With mountains, streams and silvery evening showers, it seemed an appropriate place to die.

Kazue perked up the moment she heard the name Minakami. "I'll have to buy toasted chestnuts then. Last summer Auntie kept saying how she wanted some."

Kazue had been almost too kind and the mistress of the inn seemed genuinely fond of her. With just three rooms and no bath, the inn hardly seemed like a business. You went to the large inn next door to bathe. Otherwise, you clambered down to the open air pool in the river valley, taking along a lantern or candle at night and umbrella when it rained.

The couple who ran the inn lived alone and apparently had no children. Still, they had to bustle about when, as sometimes occurred, all three rooms were occupied. During such times Kazue helped out in the kitchen—or got in the way perhaps. The inn served salmon roe and miso rather than the usual fare.

Kishichi had felt at home during their stay. When Auntie came down with a bad toothache, he could not endure to watch and gave her aspirin. It was so effective she immediately fell sound asleep. Her ever-affectionate husband lingered in the room with such a worried look that Kazue could not help laughing.

Once Kishichi had been strolling by himself in a grassy field near the inn. Suddenly he looked up toward the entrance and saw Auntie. She was squatting on the floor in the dim hallway, just beneath the stairs and gazing at him. Kishichi had kept this memory to himself.

Auntie was younger than the word suggests, forty-three or four perhaps. She had a radiant look, and a manner that was composed and graceful. Her husband had evidently been adopted into the family. At Kishichi's urging, Kazue bought more chestnuts than she had intended.

Ueno Station had a provincial atmosphere, and Kishichi was ever fearful he might come across someone from his own locale. He was especially afraid he might be noticed that night, for there were shop clerks and maids from the provinces roaming about just then. Kazue purchased a magazine edition of Japanese detective stories, while Kishichi opted for a small bottle of whiskey. Then they boarded the ten-thirty for Niigata.

Once they were settled in opposite seats, they smiled faintly at one another.

"What do you think?" Kazue asked. "Won't this outfit seem strange to Auntie?"

"It doesn't matter. Tell her we went to a movie in Asakusa and your husband got drunk on the way back. Just tell her I said, 'Let's go to Auntie's place in Minakami.' I wouldn't listen to reason either, so we came. That'll do."

"Well . . . maybe . . ." Kazue seemed apathetic.

Then she went on, "Auntie will be surprised, won't she?" Apparently Kazue was anxious for the train to depart.

"Auntie will be pleased. That's for sure."

As the train pulled away, Kazue glanced fearfully at the platform. Her courage seemed to return with this, the last journey. She undid the cloth bundle in her lap, took out the magazine, and started to page through it. Kishichi felt his legs grow heavy and his breast tremble in discomfort. He took a swig from his bottle as though he were drinking a potion.

If they had the money, this woman would not have to die.

And, if that man of hers had been more forthright, things wouldn't have come to this. Kishichi couldn't bear to watch. The suicide of this woman was senseless.

"Hey, I'm a good fellow, don't you agree?" he suddenly blurted. "Am I the only one trying to be a good fellow?"

His voice was so loud that Kazue was taken aback. She frowned angrily at him. Kishichi grinned weakly in return.

"And yet . . ." Playing the fool now, he lowered his voice more than was necessary. "You're a normal woman, so you're not that unhappy. You're not bad and you're not good either. Indeed, you're a normal woman. But I'm different. A real jerk. No matter how you cut it, I'm below average."

The train had passed Akabane and Omiya. Now it ran steadily through the darkness. Enlivened by whiskey and the train's speed, Kishichi had turned loquacious.

"I know how disgraceful it looks when a man just trails behind a wife who's lost interest. That's absurd. I'm not that type anyway. I couldn't stand it. Let's pretend I'm a nice fellow who falls for a woman and can't give her up. I get dragged along until I'm dead. I won't go in for half-hearted sympathy either, with my artist friends calling me 'pure' and the worldly minded regarding me as a good weakling. No, I will die a victim of my own suffering. I'm not dying for you. There are plenty of things wrong with me. I'm overly dependent on people, I trust too much in their strength. I know that—and lots of other shameful things besides. Don't you understand even a little how I've striven to live like everyone else? I've come this far clinging to a straw. Regardless of my efforts, the straw will break with a bit more weight. You understand, don't you? It's not that I'm weak; the pain is too heavy. This sounds stupid I know—and bitter. But if I don't say this loud and clear, people will think I'm just brazen. They—and this includes you—will dismiss it as a pose, a mere gesture even when a fellow like me says he's really suffering."

Kazue was about to respond.

"Don't bother," he went on. "I'm not attacking you. You're a good person. You're always meek and believe what you're told. I wouldn't think of criticizing you. Even old friends of mine with far more education than you don't realize how I suffer. They don't trust in my affection either. That's no surprise. I'm just clumsy." He smiled wryly.

"I see, I see." Kazue was elated momentarily. "But that will do. What if the others overhear . . . ?"

"You don't see anything. To you I'm just a fool, right? Maybe inside I'm, you know, trying to be a good person. But I'm hiding it somewhere and that's what tortures me. We've been together these six or seven years now, but not once have you . . . no, I'm not trying to criticize you about this. It was only natural. Not your fault."

Kazue was not listening. She had already gone quietly back to her magazine. With a stern look on his face, Kishichi confronted the darkened window and carried on with his monologue.

"This is no joke. Why am I a good fellow? What is it people call me? Liar, idler, swellhead, squanderer, lecher—a bunch of worse names too. But I don't say a word. Or make even a single excuse. I had faith in myself, but I can't breathe a word of it. So it all comes to nothing. Anyway I've got a historical mission in mind. One can't live merely for personal happiness; I considered playing the role of villain in history. The gentle light of Christ is greater since the evil of Judas is strong. I thought myself one of those self-destructive types; my view of the world taught me that. I attempted a radical antithesis. I would propagate a self-destructive evil hoping that the coming light would spring back all the more. It was for that I prayed. I didn't care in the least what became of me. I wouldn't mind dying if my lawless role enhanced even a little the coming light.

"Anyone would laugh and say that probably won't happen. But I actually believed it. I was that much a fool. Probably I was mistaken. I must have gotten stuck on myself somewhere along the line. Life isn't a stage play, and this was no more than a soft-hearted dream. I will likely lose out and die soon, so urging that you be strong was probably a mistake. Not even a dog would touch the putrid meal left by a life that was thrown away. A person provided for is probably a nuisance. Unless I flourish along with others, there's probably no meaning in it."

The window did not respond.

Kishichi rose and stumbled toward the toilet. He entered, carefully closed the door, and hesitated a moment. He brought his palms closely together, a figure in prayer. It was not a pose.

When they reached Minakami, it was four o'clock and still dark. Most of the snow had melted, with just a few gray patches lying silently about the depot. Probably they could walk up the mountain to Tanigawa, but Kishichi played it safe and knocked on the window of a cab.

As the taxi made its way up the twisting road, the meadow alongside came into view. Here the snow was bright enough to light up the overhead darkness.

"Brrr . . . We didn't think it would be so cold. In Tokyo they're still going about in serge." Having explained their attire even to the driver, Kazue told him, "Turn to the right here!"

She grew more animated as they got closer. "I'll bet they're still sleeping," she exclaimed. Then she told the driver, "Just a bit further—"

"Stop right here," Kishichi interrupted. "We'll walk the rest of the way."

From there the road narrowed. Once they left the cab, both Kishichi and Kazue removed their tabi socks and sloshed barefoot in their geta clogs through a thin layer of melting snow. Kishichi was about to knock on the door when Kazue, who had fallen slightly behind, came rushing up.

"Let me knock. I can wake Auntie up." She seemed like a child competing for a prize. The couple who ran the inn were surprised, even a bit confused, by this unexpected arrival. Kishichi went directly upstairs to the room they had occupied the previous summer. Switching on the light, he heard Kazue's voice below.

"It's that . . . well, he wouldn't listen to reason. 'Let's go to Auntie's place' he said. You know how childish these writers are." She seemed quite cheerful, as if totally unaware of the fib she was telling. And then she started again on the serge clothing in Tokyo . . .

Auntie tiptoed upstairs. "We're happy to see you again," she remarked as she slowly pushed the rain shutters open. It had grown lighter outside, and the snowy mountain peak loomed close. Mist was rising from below, and one could see in the valley the dark line of a stream.

"It's terribly cold." Kishichi knew that was a lie, but he still said, "I'd like some sake."

"Are you all right?"

"Yes, I'm fine now. I've probably put on a little weight too."

At that moment Kazue appeared carrying a large brazier. "Ah, it's so heavy. Auntie, I borrowed this from Uncle. He said I could take it. I just can't bear this cold weather." She was having an odd bit of fun, with not even a glance toward Kishichi.

She turned grave the moment the two of them were alone. "I'm exhausted. I think I'll have a bath and go to bed."

"Can we make it to the outdoor bath down the road?" Kishichi asked.

"I guess so. They said they go everyday."

Wearing big straw boots, the innkeeper trampled down the newly fallen snow step by step. Kishichi and Kazue followed him down toward the valley stream in the dawn light. He had brought along a mat where the two of them could toss their clothes before sliding into the warm water. Kazue had grown plump, and one could barely imagine that she could die that very night.

Once they were alone, Kishichi nodded toward a white slope wreathed in heavy floating mist. "Up there maybe?"

"But can we climb it? The snow's quite deep."

"Better downstream maybe? The snow wasn't so bad toward the station."

When they returned to the inn, the bedding was already laid out. Kazue crawled in right away and began reading her magazine. A large foot warmer at the bottom of her futon seemed to provide relief from the cold. Kishichi rolled up the futon meant for him and sat before the table with his legs crossed. He drank sake while huddling about a small brazier. Dried mushrooms and canned crab were there as snacks. Some apples too.

"Shall we wait another night?"

"Okay," she replied without looking up. "Either way will do. But the money might not last."

"How much is there?" Even as he asked, Kishichi felt thoroughly ashamed.

Irresolution. The worst, most slovenly thing in the world. A tight spot for sure. Delaying like this gets us nowhere.

Perhaps he still lusted for her.

He felt stumped.

Alive, would he incline to stay on with her? What to do about those debts, those guilty debts? And the disgrace of his near insanity? And the pain of his illnesses, this pain which people did not accept. How about that? And his family . . .

"Look, you lost out to my family. That's for sure."

Kazue replied without looking up. "Right. I was certainly a bride they couldn't take.

"That's not the whole story. You didn't meet them halfway."

"That's enough! You've gone too far already!" She flung the magazine aside and went on. "Reasons, that's all you come up with. No wonder you're so disliked."

"Ah, so that's it," he responded and went on babbling . . . The sake already seemed to be affecting his speech.

Why don't I feel jealous, he wondered. Am I stuck on myself? There's no reason to dislike me. Am I sure of that? I'm not angry . . . Maybe it's that I'm so weak then? Or perhaps my way of taking things itself is arrogant? If so, my way of taking things is entirely wrong. My way of living till now wrong. Why can't I hate? Isn't such jealousy a humble, beautiful thing? Adding all these together, doesn't indignation become a highly gentle thing? Isn't sorrow in its purest form a man who goes off to die from the shock of being rejected by his wife? But what am I up to? All this about irresolution, respectability, hypocrisy, morality, debts, responsibility, assistance, opposition, historical duty, my family . . . no, it won't do!

Kishichi felt like waving a club about and smashing his skull. He told himself to have a nap, then be off. He must decide . . . must act . . . He flipped his quilt about and buried himself beneath it. Since he was dead drunk, he fell asleep quite readily.

He woke up drowsy just past noon. Unable to bear the misery, he jumped up. He was soon complaining of the cold to the person downstairs and asking for more sake. Then he went back to Kazue.

"C'mon, it's time to get going."

Even as she slept, Kazue opened her mouth slightly. Then her eyes flew open.

"It's time already?"

"No, it's just past noon. I couldn't stand the wait." He didn't want to think of anything; he wanted to die soon.

Things went quickly after that.

Kazue was told to say the two of them had long wanted to see the hot spring resorts hereabouts. They did not need a taxi either. The weather was perfect and they would take in the scenery as they wandered down the mountain. After walking a short distance from the inn, they turned around and saw Auntie running toward them.

"Look, there's Auntie." Kishichi was uneasy.

When she caught up with them, Auntie blushed and handed Kishichi a paper parcel. "Here. It's a silk cloth. I spun and wove it myself. It's nothing much, but . . ."

"Thank you," he said.

"Auntie, you shouldn't have taken so much trouble."

Both felt a sense of relief.

Kishichi strode off just as the two women were wishing one another well. Then he whirled around and came back. "Auntie, your hand."

She seemed embarrassed, then frightened as he gripped her hand tightly in his own.

"He's drunk," Kazue noted from alongside.

Drunk he was. Parting merrily from Auntie, he glided down the slope. As the snow thinned, revealing patches of ground, he began whispering to Kazue. "How about over there? Or maybe here?"

Kazue said that closer to the station would be better. There it wasn't so desolate. Eventually the town of Minakami appeared below in the dark.

"No more rain checks, okay?" Kishichi was now wearing his lighthearted manner.

"Yes," she solemnly replied.

Kishichi cautiously crept into a cedar grove to the left of the road. Kazue followed him. The snow had almost disappeared, and the ground was covered with a layer of sodden leaves. They marched ahead undaunted, then clambered up a steep slope. It took some doing even to die. They finally arrived at a grassy opening just large enough for the two of them. There was a little sunlight and a small spring.

"This will do." Kishichi was exhausted.

He laughed as Kazue spread out a handkerchief and sat

down. With hardly a word, she took one box after another from her cloth bundle and broke each seal.

As he picked up the boxes, Kishichi said, "I'll take care of the medicine. Let's see now. This'll do for you."

"That's not very many," she protested. "Will it be enough?"

"Enough for a beginner. I'm always gulping them, so it'll take ten times as many to kill me. If I survive, I won't be able to look anyone in the eye."

If he survived, it would be in jail. But, wouldn't it be a mean sort of revenge to let her survive alone? No way! Horrified at this parody of a dime-store novel, Kishichi scooped spring water with his palm and gulped the pills down. Kazue took hers at the same time with an unpracticed hand.

Then they embraced and lay down side by side. "So, this is farewell. May the survivor live well. Got it?"

Kishichi knew the sleeping pills alone would never kill him. Easing himself to the edge of the embankment, he undid his sash, looped one end about his neck and tied the other to a mulberry trunk. He would slide down as he fell asleep and be choked to death. The grassy field above the embankment had been specially chosen with this in mind. He fell asleep, faintly aware that he was sliding down.

He felt cold, his eyes opened. Total darkness, then moonlight filtering down. Where? he wondered . . . Suddenly he could tell. I'm still alive.

He reached for his throat. The sash was still wrapped about his neck and his rump was chilled. Then it came to him. His body had not fallen down the steep cliff; it had rolled sideways into a small hollow. Water trickling from the spring had collected there, chilling him to the bone.

I'm still here. I could not die. That was the stark truth. He had to see if Kazue had also survived. Let her live . . . let her live . . . With his weakened limbs, it would be a struggle even to sit up. This he managed only by exerting his entire strength.

She had to be alive . . . she had to be . . .

He untied the sash from the mulberry trunk and removed it from his neck. Then, sitting in the puddle with his legs crossed beneath him, he looked stealthily about. There was no sign of Kazue.

As he crawled about searching for her, Kishichi saw something dark below the cliff. It might have been taken for a small puppy. He slid down and went up close. It was Kazue. Her legs, when he took hold of them, were frigid. Was she dead? He gently touched her mouth to check her breath. Nothing. The fool! Done for, dammit! He was beside himself with rage. Thinks only of herself. He seized her wrist only to find the pulse beating softly, softly. She was alive then, alive. He thrust a hand inside her kimono and found her breast warm. What the devil. What a fool. So she pulled through. Well done, well done. She seemed very dear to him. A dose of that size could hardly have killed her. Ah, ah . . . Feeling somewhat relieved, he lay down beside her. Then he lost track of everything.

When he woke up again, Kazue was snoring loudly right next to him. He was almost embarrassed by the sound. She was a tough bird all right.

"Hey, Kazue! Pull yourself together. You're alive. And so am I." He shook her by the shoulder even as he tried to smile. Kazue remained peacefully asleep in spite of his efforts.

Mountain cedars rose straight overhead in the silent night, a cold moon hanging upon their sharp twigs. Tears welled up in Kishichi's eyes and he began sobbing. He was a child even now and wondered why a child must undergo such struggles.

"My chest, Auntie. It hurts so much," Kazue cried as she lay beside him. Her voice had a flute-like sound to it.

Kishichi froze. If someone happened to be passing on the road below and heard them, that wouldn't be good. "Kazue, we're not at the inn. Auntie's not here."

Unaware of what he was saying, she kept crying. At the

same time her body twisted as if in deep pain. She began to roll over and over down a gentle slope toward the road below. Kishichi forced himself to roll in pursuit.

A lone cedar had blocked the way, and he found her clinging about the trunk. "Auntie," she screamed, "It's so cold. Bring the brazier."

He saw in the moonlight that she was transformed. Her unraveled hair held a multitude of dead cedar leaves. It lay spread out and wild like the mane of a lion or the tresses of a shamaness.

Get hold of yourself . . . you at least . . . if you don't . . . He staggered to his feet, put his arms about Kazue and tried dragging her toward the center of the grove. Lunging and crawling, slipping, clinging to roots and clawing the dirt, he brought her closer and closer. How many hours passed as he struggled ant-like with his burden?

I've had it. She's too much for me. A good woman . . . but my strength is gone. Must I struggle for her my entire life? No way, there's just no way. I'll leave her. I've spent every last ounce of energy.

He made up his mind at that moment.

It won't work with her. I'll be relying on myself for good. I'll leave her, no matter what people say.

It was almost dawn, and the sky was growing light. Kazue had quieted down as a mist covered the grove. Kishichi told himself to be simple, to be direct. One should not snicker at that mere word "manly." There was no other way to live.

One by one he picked the cedar leaves from the hair of the woman sleeping at his side.

I love this woman. I love her so much I don't know what to do. She's the cause of all my troubles. But that's over with. I can leave her even as I love her. And somehow that gives me strength. I must sacrifice love in order to live. Well, isn't that the way things are? Everyone lives by acting like this. That's how you get by. There's no other way. I'm neither a genius nor a madman.

While Kazue slept soundly until slightly after noon, Kishichi managed to wobble around doing a number of chores. He took off his wet kimono to dry, then looked around for Kazue's geta. He buried the empty box of pills and wiped the dirt off Kazue's kimono with his handkerchief.

Kazue woke up and heard about last night from Kishichi. He laughed when she tilted her head and said, "I'm sorry, Daddy."

Kishichi was now able to walk normally, but Kazue could not move. For a while they merely sat discussing what to do next. Kishichi urged that they return to Tokyo with the nearly ten yen left over, but Kazue insisted that she could not board a train in her filthy kimono. Eventually they agreed that Kazue would return to the inn by taxi and claim that somehow she had stumbled in the mud while walking around another hot spring. She would rest there until Kishichi came back from Tokyo with money and a change of clothes.

Kishichi left to buy crackers, caramels and cider in Minakami. They were eating together back in the grove when Kazue took a sip of cider and immediately threw up.

They remained there until dusk. Kazue was barely able to walk when they slipped out of the grove. Kishichi sent her back to the inn by taxi, then took a train for Tokyo.

He made a clean breast of things to Kazue's uncle and asked that he see to everything. Taciturn as ever, the uncle merely said, "What a pity." How deep a pity resonated with his words. When he had brought Kazue back and taken her into his own home, he would also say, "There's something funny about that Kazue. She would spread her futon right between the innkeeper and his wife as if she were their daughter. She would sleep there calm as you please." Without another word, he would lower his head and chuckle.

A good man, he did not hesitate to go drinking with Kishi-chi even after the separation. Once in a while, he seemed to recall what had occurred and would sigh, "Poor Kazue!"

At such moments, Kishichi felt irresolute and ashamed.

CURRENCY

There are foreign languages that distinguish between masculine and feminine nouns. Words for currency are feminine.

I'm a one-hundred-yen note, number 77851. Take a quick look at the hundred-yen notes in your purse and perhaps you'll find me. I'm completely worn out, so I don't have the slightest idea who is caring for me now or whether I haven't been tossed into a trash bin. With modern-style bills now coming out, there's a rumor going around that we older bills are scheduled for burning. Rather than wonder if I'm alive or dead, I would prefer to be burned and have it done with. Whether I end up in heaven or hell is up to the gods. Probably it'll be in hell.

I was not born in this sad predicament by the way. In fact, at the time of my birth, the one hundred-yen note was queen of the currency. Only later did more welcome denominations like the two-hundred-yen or thousand-yen note emerge in abundance. The first time I passed through the teller's window of a large Tokyo bank, the customer received me with a slightly trembling hand. Yes, that's the truth. He was a young carpenter who slipped me unfolded into the front pocket of his overalls and walked out to the street, his left hand lightly held over the pocket as if he had a stomachache. All the way home from the bank, even while riding the tram, he kept the palm of his hand on the pocket. Inside the house he immediately placed me on the family shrine and offered a prayer. Such was my auspicious entry into life, and I would willingly have remained forever in the carpenter's house.

Unfortunately I could stay only a single night. The carpenter was in fine fettle that evening. With enough sake under his belt, he turned to the young, diminutive wife who was serving him and blustered, "I'm doing a man's work. Don't make fun of me." Now and then he stood up, took me from the shrine in both hands and made his young wife laugh with gestures of worship. Eventually, however, a quarrel arose between them, whereupon I was folded twice and placed in the wife's small purse. The next morning she took me to a pawnshop and exchanged me for ten of her kimonos.

The pawnshop vault was cold and damp, and I felt chilly from end to end. My stomach was giving me trouble when I was finally taken out into the light of day. This time I was exchanged for the microscope of a certain medical student, who proceeded to take me on a long journey. The lodging where he abandoned me was located on a small island in the Inland Sea. I remained inside a chest of drawers by the front desk for nearly a month. During this time I happened to hear the maids gossip about the student who left me here, then drowned himself in the sea.

"It's ridiculous to die alone. I'd die anytime with a handsome fellow like him." About forty years old and chubby, her face covered with pimples, the maid who spoke these words gave everyone a good laugh.

During the next five years I aged considerably as I wandered about Shikoku and Kyushu. People gradually lost their regard for me and, after six years away, I found myself drifting back to Tokyo. There my life changed drastically and I came to loathe myself. I was merely a female runner on the black market. But, if I had changed in my five or six years away, what about Tokyo itself? It was eight o'clock in the evening when I left the train station upon my arrival in the city. I was taken by a slightly intoxicated broker past Nihonbashi and Kyobashi, then walked up the Ginza to Shinbashi. It was so dark that we seemed to be in a forest. That no one went by was hardly surprising, and not a single kitten could be seen crossing the street. The area had the ominous look of a precinct of death.

Not long thereafter the usual hubbub and clamor started up. In the middle of the day-to-day confusion, I could not find a moment's rest. Like the baton in a relay I was passed from hand to hand at a dizzying pace. The result was not only this wrinkled look; odors of various kinds too permeated my body and drove me to desperation. Wasn't this a time when Japan itself became desperate? You will know what kind of people passed me from hand to hand and why they did this. You should know and are probably tired of hearing why they did this. I won't go into detail then, but merely say that the militarists or whoever weren't the only monsters around. This is a large issue for humankind, not just for the Japanese

You would think that people who might well die that night would forget entirely about greed and lust. But that doesn't seem to be the case. Lost in the blind alley of life, they cease to laugh together and greedily compete with one another. A person of real feeling cannot be happy so long as another is wretched. However, the general run of people, merely to obtain brief comfort for themselves or their families, will abuse, deceive and shove aside a neighbor. (Yes, dear reader, even you did that sort of thing once. It's all the more frightening that you do not realize this. You should be ashamed. If you're human, you should be ashamed. Shame is something you humans alone can feel.) A sorry, comic spectacle—that's what people make of themselves quarreling with one another like grappling demons. But even while serving as a lowly runner on the black market, I once or twice felt as though my birth was not a misfortune. Even now when I'm so old and decrepit that I don't know where I am, I cannot forget certain vaguely pleasant moments.

One of these goes back to the time I was taken by an old black-market crone to a town three or four hours by train from Tokyo. Here's a brief account of what happened. Till then I had gone from one black-market dealer to another, but somehow the women among them got twice more value from me than the men did. A woman's greed is appalling—far more extensive than a man's. The old crone was someone to be reckoned with. She had acquired me earlier from a man in exchange for a bottle of beer. Afterward she went to a wholesale dealer who usually sold wine for fifty or sixty yen a bottle. Advancing toward him on her knees, she bargained on and on in a whisper and smiled suggestively at certain moments. She finally received four bottles for me alone and easily carried them away on her back. Her skills in the black market had gotten her four bottles of wine for one of beer. By adding a little water, the wine could be made to fill almost twenty beer-size bottles. There's no end to a woman's greed, however. Without even the slightest look of pleasure, the old crone went away grumbling earnestly about how difficult the times were.

Deposited in the large purse of the black marketeer, I was dozing off when someone pulled me forth. This time I passed into the hands of an army captain in his late thirties, evidently an accomplice of the dealer. The transaction involved a hundred cigarettes, the brand called Glory that were usually reserved for servicemen. (The captain supposedly said a hundred, but the marketeer discovered later that the package contained only eighty-six cigarettes, whereupon he flew into a rage at that "swindling rascal," the captain.) Exchanged then for a package labeled "One Hundred Cigarettes," I was stuffed unceremoniously into the pants pocket of the captain and taken along that very evening to the second floor of a shabby restaurant at the edge of town. A heavy drinker, the captain sipped a some rare kind of brandy. He customarily got out of hand when drinking, and eventually he began to revile the serving lady.

"Nothin' but a fox—that's your face no matter how ya look at it. [He said 'fox' almost like 'fuchs,' and I wondered where he was from.] You'd better remember. A fox's got a pointed snout and whiskers—three on the right and four on the left. His fart's unbearable too, yellow smoke all over the place. A dog smelling it'll run around in circles and keel over. Nope, I'm not makin' this up. Your face is yellow too. Weird color. Your fart did it for sure. Phew!!! You're really cutting loose. No, you did do it. Don't you have any manners at all—farting right in front of a captain? Isn't it the most ridiculous . . . ? Even someone like me gets jumpy. Farted on right in front of my nose—and by a fox? I can't take that lying down."

The vulgar captain reviled the woman wholeheartedly. Then his ears picked up the sound of a baby crying on the first floor. "Noisy brat! Spoiling a good time. I'm a bundle of nerves, and I won't be made a laughing stock. Is that your kid? Strange, the fox's child wails like any ordinary urchin. What a surprise. Aren't you ashamed? In this business? With a child in your arms? Selfish. Japan's in a tough battle because you slummy women don't know your place. Half-wits, every one of you. That's why you think Japan is winning. Fools! You fools! No sense even talking about it. The fox and the dog. They go round and round and keel over. Win the war? That's why I drink every night and buy myself a woman. Anything wrong with that?"

"There certainly is." The serving woman's face turned pale as she responded. "What's all this grumbling about foxes? You needn't come if you don't like it here. No one can drink in Japan nowadays and tease women except you and your kind. And where does the money come from? Think about it. Most of what we women earn goes to His Majesty. And he passes it on so you can drink in a tavern. Don't poke fun at me. I'm a woman, so I can bear a child. You've no idea how horrible it is for a woman trying to nurse a child these days. There's not a drop of milk in our breasts anymore, and the child sucks in vain. Lately the children don't even have the strength to suck. Oh yes, he's a fox child all right, with a pointed chin and a wrinkled face. And whining all day long. Shall I bring him to you? We'll endure even so . . . and persevere hoping for your victory.

"But, that's too much for you and your—" Then the air raid sirens went off, and explosions soon followed. There was the thump of bombs and the whooshing of bullets in the air. The sliding screens burst into flames, and the captain jumped up shouting, "They're here! Finally they're here!"

He staggered about, the brandy evidently too much for him. The serving lady flew downstairs, nimble as a bird, and returned in a moment with the child on her back.

"C'mon, let's get out of here. Quick! Look out! It's dangerous. But pull yourself together. He may be a bungler, but even the last remaining soldier is here for the country's sake."

The soldier's limp body seemed devoid of bones, but she held him up from behind, walked him to the stairs and down. There she got his boots on and fled to the grounds of a nearby shrine, holding his hand the entire time. Immediately the soldier sprawled onto the ground, his legs far apart and hurled violent curses at the explosions overhead. A rain of fire splattered down and the shrine itself began to burn.

"Soldier, I'm begging you. Let's flee a little farther. I don't want to die here like a dog. Let's go as far as we can."

This thin woman with pale dark skin, her occupation said to be the most degraded of all, performed the noblest, most shinning deed I have ever seen in my dark life. Begone greed and vanity too. Japan has been beaten by both of you. The serving woman, free of greed and vanity, strove to rescue the customer still drunk in front of her. Exerting all her strength, she pulled him to his feet. Then, holding him to her side, she staggered toward the paddy fields. Once she had escaped, the grounds of the shrine became a sea of flames. She dragged the drunk captain to a field of recently cut barley and settled him on a low embankment. He was already snoring loudly as she sat down exhausted beside him, her breath heaving.

That night the town burned from one end to the other. It was almost dawn when the captain opened his eyes, sat up and gazed at the still smoldering fire. When he suddenly noticed the lady dozing at his side, he instinctively jumped to his feet in confusion and made as if to flee. But, after five or six steps, he turned around and came back. From the inside pocket of his jacket he took five of my companion hundred- yen bills and from his pants pocket he took me. He folded the six of us into a single wad, shoved us beneath the innermost layer of the child's underwear, then bolted.

At that moment I felt a surge of joy. If only we bills were always so used, how happy we would be. The child's back against which we lay was bony, the skin dry and flaky. But I could say to my companions: "What a blessing! We couldn't have a finer place. I want to stay forever, warming this child's back and helping him put some flesh on those bones."

With a smile, the others nodded in accord.

WAITING

I come each day to this small train station to meet some-one—someone I don't even know.

I shop at the market, stop by the station on my way home and sit down on a cold bench. I rest the shopping bas-ket on my knees and stare idly at the ticket gate. Each time a train from either direction pulls up to the platform, droves of people pour out of the coach doors and make for the gates. Their faces look uniformly angry as they show their passes or hand over their tickets. Then, without a sideways glance, they pass before the bench where I'm sitting, reach the plaza out front and scatter in the direction each one chooses. I re-main sitting blankly. Someone all alone smiles and calls out to me—just thinking of it is frightening. Ah, it's troubling. My heart is pounding and I start to shudder as though cold wa-ter is running down my back. And I feel suffocated. But, I am waiting for someone after all. Indeed, I sit here each day wait-ing to find out who. What sort of person? No, the thing I am waiting for is probably not a person. I dislike human beings. No, I fear them. When I meet one of them face to face and come out with "How are you?" or "It's really cold today"—those perfunctory greetings that are best left unsaid—I get the excruciating sense that I'm the world's biggest liar. And so, I might as well die.

The other person too offers cautious compliments and pretentious thoughts. Listening to this, I get depressed at the stingy circumspection of it. Society as a whole becomes more and more unbearable. Are people going to spend their entire lives exchanging stiff, careful greetings and making themselves weary of one another? For me, meeting people is disagreeable. So, I do not pay visits to my friends except for important matters. Staying home with Mother and sewing in silence gives me the greatest relaxation. But when the World War finally began and everything became tense, I felt guilty staying home when others were out and about. I was anxious and could not relax at all. I felt like working myself to the bone and making a direct contribution. I lost confidence in the life I had led till then.

I could not remain sitting silently at home; but, when I tried going out, there was no place for me to go. So, I do the shopping and on the way back I stop by the station to sit idly on the cold bench. If someone should suddenly appear! The hope that someone will, the panic over how I will act if someone does, and the resolve to yield to my seeming fate all twist together with various rude fantasies and fill my breast to the point of suffocation. Somehow I feel absolutely helpless, as if I were watching a daytime dream of not knowing whether to live or to die; and the people coming and going seem far away and tiny, as if I am observing through the wrong end of a telescope, while silence falls around me. Ah, what is it I am waiting for? Perhaps I'm a totally lascivious woman. When the World War began, I came up with a splendid excuse, the lie that I was somehow anxious, that I wished to be of use and would work my fingers to the bone. Maybe I was searching somehow for the right opportunity to realize my own rash fantasies. I may sit here like this, with a blank look on my face, but I feel as though wicked schemes are flickering inside my breast.

What am I really waiting for? Nothing of a definite shape. It's mere haziness. But I am waiting. Since the World War began, I stop by the station day after day on the way back from shopping, sit on this cold bench, and wait. Someone all alone smiles and calls to me. Oh, how frightening. Ah, how troubling. It's not you I am waiting for. Then, who is the one I am waiting for? A husband? No. A lover. Not at all. A friend? Certainly not. Money then? Never. A ghost? Oh, least of all.

It's something calmer, something instantly bright and splendid. I don't know what. It's like spring, for instance. No, it's different. Green leaves. The month of May. Clear water flowing through a wheat field. It's different though. Ah, but I am waiting. I am waiting while my heart dances. People in droves pass before my eyes. It's not that one, it's not this one. Trembling slightly as I hold my basket, I wait, focused and intense. Please don't forget me. Please notice, without smiling at her, a twenty-year-old girl who goes day after day to the station only to return home in vain. I have deliberately kept the name of this small station to myself. Even if I don't tell, you will see me someday.

THE SOUND OF HAMMERING

Dear Sir,

Please advise me on a certain matter. I'm twenty-six years old and deeply troubled.

I was born in the Teramachi district of Aomori City. You probably don't know the little Tomoya flower shop right next to Seikaji Temple, but I'm the Tomoya's second son. I graduated from Aomori Higher School and went to work in the office of a munitions factory in Yokohama. I worked there three years and then spent four years in the army. When the war ended, I came back home. But our house had been burned down, and my father, my older brother and my older brother's wife were living in a shed that had been thrown together on the site. My mother had died during my fourth year of higher school.

I might have squeezed into the shed, but that would not have been fair to the others. After talking things over with my father and brother, I took a job at a village post office about five miles up the coast from Aomori City. My mother's family lives there, and her older brother is the postmaster. More than a year has gone by now, and I feel more trivial with each passing day. That's why I'm deeply troubled.

I started reading you when I worked at the munitions factory office in Yokohama. I first read a short story in the journal style, and then I got into the habit of looking around for your books. While reading them, I learned that you had gone to Aomori Higher School ahead of me and had lived in Mr. Toyota's house during your school days. When I realized that, I was so excited that my heart nearly burst. If that's Mr. To-yota the dry-goods dealer, why, he lives in the same neighborhood as my family, and I know him well. Actually there are two Toyotas. Old Mr. Toyota is chubby, and his given name is Tazaemon. That's just right for him, since the first syllable is written with the character for "chubby." His son is also named Tazaemon, except that he's thin and dapper. I'd rather see him named after some lithe Kabuki actor, Uzaemon for example. But all of the Toyotas are fine people, aren't they.

It's a shame that their house was one of those burned down in the last air raid. It seems that even their storehouse was destroyed. When I learned that you had lived in their home, I really thought of asking the younger Mr. Toyota for a letter of introduction. But I only dreamed of paying you a visit. That's because I'm a coward. When it comes to doing something, I lose my nerve.

And then, well, after they drafted me, I was sent off to Chiba Prefecture. We were put to work digging fortifications along the coast, and that's how I spent every day until the end of the war. It was only when I got a half day off now and then that I could go into town and look for your books. I took up my pen countless times to write you a letter. But once I wrote, "Dear Sir," I was at a loss. As far as you were concerned, I was an utter stranger. And besides, I didn't have anything particular to write about. I would simply hold the pen in my hand, totally befuddled.

Finally Japan agreed to an unconditional surrender, and I went back to work in the post office. When I was in Aomori

City the other day, I stopped by a bookstore and looked for your works. I found out that the war had uprooted you as well and you were back at your birthplace in Kanagi. When I read that, my heart seemed ready to burst again. All the same I still couldn't work up the courage to pay you a visit. After considering all sorts of things, I decided to send a letter. This time I'm not at a loss after writing, "Dear Sir." That's because this letter has a purpose, a crucial purpose, too.

I would appreciate your advice on a certain matter. To tell the truth, I'm deeply troubled. I'm not the only one, either. Other people seem troubled by the same thing. Advise me for their sake as well. I felt like writing to you over and over—when I worked at the munitions plant, as well as when I served in the army. After waiting all this time, I hardly expected to be writing a letter that sounds so dismal as this one.

We were ordered into formation before the barracks at noon on August 15, 1945, to hear the emperor himself make a statement over the radio. But the static was so bad that hardly a word got through. When the broadcast finally ended, a young lieutenant promptly mounted the reviewing stand.

"You heard it?" he barked. "You see now? Our nation has accepted the Potsdam Declaration and surrendered. But that's politics—it's not our business. We're soldiers, and we'll keep on fighting till the very end. Then we'll take our own lives, every one of us. That's how we'll make up to His Majesty for this defeat. I've been prepared from the beginning, so I want all of you to be ready too. Is that understood? All right, dismissed."

Removing his glasses, the lieutenant stepped down from the platform, tears streaming down his cheeks as he walked away. I wondered if "solemn" was the word to describe the mood of that moment. As I stood at attention, the surroundings grew dark and misty, and a cold wind blew in from somewhere or other. My body seemed to sink of its own weight into the depths of the earth.

Should I take my own life? To die—I thought that alone was real. A hush had fallen upon the woods opposite the grounds, and the trees seemed like dark lacquer. A flock of small birds rose silently from the treetops and flew off like sesame seeds cast into the sky.

Ah, that's when it happened. From the barracks behind me came the faint sound of someone driving a nail. Perhaps the biblical phrase describes what I felt then—the scales fell from my eyes. Both the pathos and glory of military life disappeared in an instant. I felt utterly listless and indifferent, as though I'd been released from a spell. I gazed across a sandy field in the summer noon without any feeling whatever. Then I stuffed my duffel bag to the seams and wandered back home.

That faint sound of hammering stripped me of every illusion as if by a miracle. It seemed that I would never again be intoxicated by the nightmare of militarism. But was it because of a faint sound piercing through my brain that I became thereafter like an accursed epileptic?

Not that I ever become violent. Quite the contrary. Whenever I get excited or inspired over something, that faint sound of hammering arises from nowhere in particular, and I grow quite placid. The scene before me suddenly changes, leaving only a blankness in place of whatever images were present. I simply stare straight ahead, with a feeling of utter stupidity and emptiness.

When I first came to the post office, I thought I'd have enough freedom to work at whatever took my fancy. I decided to write a narrative of some kind and send it to you. During my spare moments in the post office, I worked hard at recording my memories of life in the army. By autumn the manuscript totaled almost a hundred pages, and I promised myself one evening that I would finish it the next day. After my shift at the post office, I went to the public bathhouse and soaked myself in the warm water. I was trembling with anticipation over getting to the last chapter that very night. Should I write it up as a grand tragedy in the manner of *Eugene Onegin*? Or end in the pessimistic mode of Gogol's *The Quarrel*? While pondering this question, I looked up at the bare light bulb hanging from the high ceiling of the bathhouse and heard in the distance the faint sound of hammering. At that moment a ripple arose along the surface, and I became merely another bather splashing about in a corner of the dimly lit pool.

Disheartened, I crawled from the bath and washed the soles of my feet. As I listened to the other bathers talk about rationing, Pushkin and Gogol seemed more like the names of a couple of foreign-made toothbrushes. I left the bathhouse, crossed the bridge and went home. After eating my supper in silence, I went to my own room and thumbed through the nearly one hundred pages of manuscript on the desk. It was terrible. So absurd, in fact, that I didn't even have the strength to tear up the manuscript paper. I use it for tissue now. And, since that day, I haven't written a line.

My uncle has a small library, and sometimes I used to borrow a volume or two of collected stories from the Meiji or Taisho eras. Whether I liked a story or not, I read it mainly to pass the time. Many evenings I simply went to bed and slept. My attitude changed the day I found a set of books on world art. I was unmoved by the Impressionists I had once liked, but I gazed in wonder at the paintings of Ogata Korin and Ogata Kenzan, two Japanese artists of the Genroku period. To me, the azaleas of Korin seemed better than the work of any other painter, whether Cezanne, Monet or Gauguin.

Once again my interest in things revived. Of course, I didn't have any bold ambitions. I would simply be a village dilettante, not a master artist like Korin or Kenzan. As for a job that I could throw myself into, well, sitting from morning to evening at the post office window and counting people's money was the best I could hope for. And for someone like myself without training or intelligence, this line of work was not degrading. Humility might have its own crown, and devotion to everyday duty could be the noblest life of all.

I was gradually beginning to take pride in my life when the conversion of the yen currency took place. Even in a village post office in the country—indeed, especially in such a place— everyone had to rush about, since there were so few of us. We didn't have a moment's rest from early in the morning. No matter how tired we got, we had to receive deposits, stamp old currency and whatever else besides. Aware that now was the time to repay my uncle for taking me in, I worked especially hard. My hands became numb, as if they were encased in steel gloves; after a time they no longer felt like my own.

And then, after working like this, I would sleep through the night like a dead person. And the next morning I'd leap from bed the moment the alarm clock went off by my pillow, hurry to the office and begin the cleaning. This was something the women in the office usually did, but my own working pace had so picked up during the hurly-burly of the yen conversion that I rushed to do any sort of chore, no matter what. I kept increasing the pace too—more today than yesterday, more tomorrow than today—as though I were half mad.

On the day this uproar over the yen conversion was to end, I rose as usual in the dim, pre-dawn light, frantically cleaned the office and sat down at my assigned window. As the sun rose, casting its light on my face, I narrowed my sleepy eyes in a mood of utter contentment and recalled the dictum about work being sacred. Then, just as I breathed a sigh of relief, I seemed to hear in the distance the faint sound of hammering. That did it. In an instant everything appeared absurd. I stood up, went back to my room, crawled under the quilt and fell asleep. When someone called me for breakfast, I refused to get up. I wasn't feeling well—that's all I said.

Evidently the office was busier that day than ever. And, with their best worker lying in bed, the others were sorely tested. Nonetheless, I dozed right on through till evening, an act of self-indulgence that increased the debt to my uncle. I simply had no interest in working and slept late the next day too. After I finally got up and sat down absentmindedly at my place, I let out one yawn after another, leaving the work to the girl at the next window. The following day, too, and the day after as well, I was sluggish and morose. In other words, I had become your typical post office clerk.

"You're still not feeling well?" my uncle inquired, a faint smile on his face.

"Oh, it's nothing really," I replied. "Perhaps I'm a little worn out."

"Just what I thought!" he exclaimed. "It's because of those books you read. They're too hard for you. Dumb fellows like you and me shouldn't try to think about things. It's better not to."

He smiled, and I tried to grin back.

It was only a technical school from which my uncle supposedly graduated. He didn't seem interested in books of any kind.

And then . . . You know, I seem to use that phrase over and over. It's probably another indication of how dumb I am. And then—it just slips out, even though I'm bothered when it does. But I guess there's nothing I can do about it.

And then I fell in love. Now don't laugh about this. Well, laugh if you want, I can't stop you. Anyway, I was living in a trance, like an inert minnow at the bottom of a goldfish bowl. Then I felt quite awkward, as the minnow would if it were to find its belly suddenly full of eggs.

When you fall in love, music permeates the soul, doesn't it? I think that's the surest sign of this affliction. She didn't love me, but I was so crazy about her that I couldn't help myself.

To all appearances she was not yet twenty years old. She worked as a maid at a small inn, the only one in this coastal village. My uncle the postmaster was a real drinker, and, whenever this inn had a party, he would certainly be there. He seemed to get along well with the maid. When she showed up at the post office to take care of her savings or insurance, my uncle always teased her with some stale joke.

"Things must be going well," he would observe. "You're really stashing it away, aren't you? Capital! Capital! Haven't found yourself a nice man, have you?"

"Don't be silly!" she'd retort, looking as bored as a nobleman in a van Dyck painting.

Tokita Hanae—that was the name written in her savings book. She must have been from Miyagi Prefecture, for there was a Miyagi address in the book with a red line running through it. Her new address had been entered next to the old one. According to the talk among the girl workers at the post office, Hanae's home in Miyagi had been damaged during the war. Apparently she was a distant relative of the mistress of the inn, and that's why she came to this village just before the surrender. She was supposed to be clever beyond her years too, and her behavior was far from ideal.

Still, there wasn't a single refugee here with a good reputation among the local people. That's why I didn't believe a word about her so-called cleverness. On the other hand, her savings weren't all that meager. Postal workers aren't supposed to reveal this sort of thing, but about every week Hanae would deposit a sum, even as the postmaster teased her. The amount would be two or three hundred yen each time, and so her savings grew quite large. I didn't believe she was able to do this because of some nice man. Yet, every time I wrote down the sum of 200 yen or 300 yen and pressed my stamp onto the form, my heartbeat would quicken and my face would turn red.

Gradually I became more and more tormented over Hanae. It wasn't that she was clever. No, every man in the village was after her—that was it. Wouldn't they ruin the girl by giving her all that money? When this thought occurred to me in the middle of the night, I sat straight up in bed.

Hanae didn't seem concerned. She calmly continued making her deposits about once every week. As I said, my heartbeat used to quicken and my face turn red when she first started coming. On later occasions I got even more upset, my face turning deathly pale and my brow oozing sweat. Counting each of the soiled ten-yen notes pasted with stamps which Hanae smugly handed over, I would be assailed time and again by the urge to tear her money to shreds. I also wanted to quote for her the famous words from Kyoka's novel: "Even if you die, don't become his plaything!" But that would be going too far. A peasant like myself couldn't speak such words. Still, being so serious about the matter, I could not help wanting to blurt out, "Even if you die, don't become his plaything! What does wealth amount to? Or material goods?"

If you love someone, you will be loved in return. Isn't there some truth to that? The middle of May had gone by when Hanae came demurely as ever to the post office window and handed me her savings book and money. With a sigh I took them both and began counting the bills. I was feeling depressed as I entered the amount and silently handed back her book.

"Are you free around five o'clock?"

I couldn't believe my ears. She had spoken quickly and softly, and I first thought the spring breeze might have deceived me.

"If you're free then, meet me at the bridge." She smiled lightly and walked away, demure as ever.

I looked at the clock, but it was barely past two. I'm going to seem like a pushover in saying this, but I don't remember how I spent the next three hours. I might well have wandered about the office, barely managing to look serious, and blurted out to one of the girls about how beautiful the day was. I might have glared at her surprised look (the day was cloudy), then headed for the toilet. In short, I must have spent the afternoon like a fool; I left at seven or eight minutes before five. Along the way I noticed that my fingernails needed cutting. Even now I can remember how badly I wanted to cry.

Hanae was standing by the foot of the bridge in a skirt that seemed rather short. Catching a glimpse of her long bare legs, I lowered my eyes to the ground.

"Let's go toward the shore," she calmly suggested.

Hanae set out first, and I slowly followed five or six steps behind. Despite the distance between us, we presently fell into step with one another, much to my embarrassment.

It was a cloudy day with a breeze, and the sand swirled along the beach.

"This will do," Hanae exclaimed. She slipped between two large fishing boats that had been pulled up on the beach and sat down right on the sand. "Come, you'll be warm if you sit here. It's out of the wind."

I sat down some six feet or so from where Hanae had settled with her legs outstretched.

"I'm sorry to bother you, but I had to do this," she began. "There's something I've got to say. It's about my savings account. You're wondering about it, aren't you?"

Here's my chance, I told myself. My voice hoarse, I replied, "Yes, I am."

"That's only natural," she agreed. Then, letting her head fall, she scooped a handful of sand and poured it along her leg. "You see, it's not my money. If it were, I wouldn't put it into an account. It's too much trouble making a deposit every week."

That made sense and I silently nodded.

"Don't you see? The savings book belongs to the mistress at the inn. That's a secret, so don't tell anyone. I can imagine why she handles things this way, but it's so complicated that I don't want to explain right here. You realize how hard it is on me, don't you?" She smiled, and then her eyes glistened strangely. I realized that she was crying.

More than anything, I wanted to kiss her. With Hanae I could undergo any hardship.

"The people from here," she went on, "are all terrible, don't you agree? I thought you might be mistaken about me too, so I wanted to have this talk with you. Today I made up my mind to do it."

At that moment the sound of hammering came from nearby. I wasn't hearing things this time. Someone had indeed begun pounding a nail inside the seaside hut that belonged to Mr. Sasaki. The sound echoed over and over, and I stood up trembling. "I see. And I won't tell anyone about the account."

A stray dog had left a sizable pile of dung just behind the spot where Hanae was sitting. I debated some moments whether to tell her. The waves undulated slowly, and a boat with a bedraggled sail made its way through the shallows.

"Well, goodbye then," I uttered.

A vast emptiness lay before me. What did I care about her savings? To me she was a mere stranger. So, what difference did it make if she became a man's plaything or whatever. Stupid! Besides, I was hungry.

Hanae has kept up with her deposits. She makes one without fail every week or so. Her savings must amount to thousands of yen by now, but I'm not the least interested. Since it doesn't make any difference to me, I don't care whether it's the landlady's money, as Hanae claimed, or simply her own.

So, which one of us got jilted? I suspect it was me rather than Hanae, but I'm not particularly sad about that. It was a strange affair in any event, and, since then, I've gone back to being your typical, idle clerk.

This June I went to Aomori City on an errand and happened to see a workers' demonstration. Far from being interested in social and political movements, I had felt in them something akin to despair. Regardless of the cause, those in charge always seemed to be seeking power and glory for themselves. It's as if one boards a ship only to become the captain's lackey. A leader pompously voices his own views without the least hesitation. Do as I say, he proclaims. Then you, as well as your family and your village and your country and the whole world too will be secure. Gesturing grandly, he roars on about how disaster will come from ignoring him. But then, as has happened time after time, his favorite prostitute gives him the cold shoulder, and this makes him cry out desperately for the abolition of her kind. Sometimes, after attacking his better-looking colleagues in a fit of indignation and raising a general ruckus, he receives his medal of distinction and races home on cloud nine to tell his wife. Mommy! he exults, Look here! Then, he opens the little box and gives her a peek inside. She is not fooled, however. What! Only a Fifth Degree? A Second or nothing, she insists, leaving her husband crestfallen. It's half-crazed men of this kind, unable to tell one thing from another, who throw themselves into political and social movements.

And so, when the clamor arose over democracy and whatever else during the general election in April, I wasn't inclined to believe a word. The politicians of the Liberal and the Progressive parties made plenty of noise, but weren't they simply taking advantage of things? They gave one an indelible impression—of maggots feeding on the corpse of a defeated nation. On April 10, the day of the election, I was told by my uncle to vote for Kato of the Liberal Party. All right, I said, leaving the house. But I only went for a walk along the beach and then came back. I believed that the gloom of our daily lives could not be dispelled, no matter how much one declaimed about society and politics.

However, when I ran into the workers' demonstration that day in Aomori, I realized how wrong I had been. Lively and vibrant—doesn't that describe it? What a joyous event the parade was. I didn't see even a hint of gloom, not one frowning face. There was only bursting energy, with young girls holding flags and singing labor hymns. My breast overflowed with emotion and tears began to fall. How lucky, I mused, that Japan had lost the war. For the first time in my life, I saw the manifestation of true freedom. If social and political movements gave rise to this, then people should begin by studying the ideas behind such movements.

As I watched the parade, I felt a great joy. It was as if the shining path I should follow had been made unmistakably real to me. Tears flowed pleasantly down my cheeks, and the green surroundings became blurred, just as if I had plunged into a pool and were looking at things underwater. In the middle of this swaying twilight, I saw the flags with their blazing red color . . . Ah, I wept over that color. Even if I were to die, I would not forget this scene. And then, distant and faint, the sound of hammering arose. And that was it.

What does that sound mean? It can't be dismissed simply as nihilism or whatever, for the illusion of hammering obliterates even these things.

When summer arrives, the young fellows around here suddenly get excited about sports. I'm inclined toward the pragmatic view of things that comes with age. Maybe that's why I can't see stripping almost naked and then getting tossed about and badly bruised for no reason at all in a sumo wrestling match, or running a hundred meters with a contorted face just to find out who will win, especially when the sprinters all look as alike as a bunch of acorns. Sports are stupid, and I have never felt like getting involved.

This year there was a long-distance relay in August. The course made its way through every village along the coast, and many youngsters took part. One of the relay points, where the runners from Aomori City were supposed to be relieved by the next group, was right in front of our own post office.

Just before ten o'clock, when the runners were due to arrive, the postal workers all went outside to watch, leaving the postmaster and myself alone to clear up some insurance accounts. I heard the crowd shouting, "There they are! Over there!" So I got up and went to the window. This must have been that "final spurt" one hears about. I saw the lead runner staggering toward the relay point, clad only in a pair of shorts. His fingers spread out like the webbed foot of a frog, his arms flailing about as if to part the air, his chest thrown out and his head swaying, he collapsed before the post office with a grimace of pain. A companion of his ran up and shouted, "Hurrah! You've done it!" Then, he helped the runner up and brought him toward the window where I was watching. Even after the runner was splashed with a bucket of water, he seemed more dead than alive. But, as I observed him lying there, his body slack and his face terribly pale, I felt a strange thrill.

I would call his deed "touching," but that sounds conceited coming from someone only twenty-six years old like myself. Perhaps a word like "heartrending" would be better. In any event there was something marvelous about this great waste of energy. Even though no one really cared whether the runner took a first or a second, he nonetheless went all out on that final spurt. He didn't run for some high ideal, either. For example, he wasn't trying to help his country raise its standing among the civilized nations. And he wouldn't mouth any such ideals merely to win the favor of people.

He didn't care about becoming a great marathoner. After all, this was only a country race, and he wasn't going to set any record pace. Realizing that, he certainly wouldn't feel like discussing the event when he returned home. On the contrary, he'd worry that his father might scold him. Despite all this, he had wanted to run, to give the race his utmost without being praised for his effort. He just wanted to run—to do something for nothing. As a boy he had recklessly climbed up persimmon trees so that he could eat the fruit. But he wasn't out to get anything in this grueling marathon. I suppose his passion was almost for Nothing. And that seemed close to my own mood at the time.

After I'd been working at the post office a while, I got into the habit of tossing around a baseball with the other employees. I would keep playing until I was dead tired. And just when I felt as though I had shed something of myself, the sound of hammering would arise. That sound demolished even the passion for Nothing.

I've been hearing it more and more frequently of late— when I opened the newspaper to examine each article of the new constitution; when a brilliant solution came to me as my uncle discussed a personnel problem in the office; when I tried reading your novel; when a fire broke out the other night and I leaped from bed to have a look; when I feel like another cup of sake while drinking with my uncle before supper; when I seem to be losing my mind; and, finally, when I think of suicide.

Last evening, while my uncle and I were drinking, I turned to him and asked in jest, "Define life for me—in just a word or two."

"I don't know about life," he replied, "but the world's nothing but sex and greed."

I hadn't expected so sharp a reply. Should I act upon it and become a black marketeer? When I realized what a bundle I could make, however, the sound of hammering arose immediately.

Please tell me, what does that sound mean? I'm paralyzed by it at the moment, so how do I escape? Please, answer my letter.

If you'll allow me, I'd like to say one more thing. I began hearing the sound quite distinctly before this letter was half-written. Bored—that's how I felt. Still, I kept going and wrote this much. I wrote in such desperation, though, that I now feel everything was a lie. There wasn't a girl named Hanae and I never saw a demonstration. The rest of it seems to be mostly lies too.

Not the sound of hammering, though. That part alone doesn't seem a lie. I'm sending you exactly what I've written, without even reading it over.

Yours sincerely,

The writer who received this strange letter was pitifully ignorant. He didn't have a thought in his head either, but he still managed the following reply.

Dear Sir,

Agonizing, isn't it? Well, I don't have much sympathy for a hypocrite. You still seem to be avoiding an ugly situation that can't be explained away, a situation others see and point a finger at. Real thought takes courage more than intelligence. As Jesus said, "And fear not them that kill the body, but are not able to kill the soul; but rather fear him that is able to destroy both body and soul in hell." In this passage "fear" means something like "to hold in awe." If you can sense the thunder in these words, you will not be hearing things anymore.

UNDINE

I

In the far north of Honshu there's a row of low hills known as the Bonju Range. Only about a thousand feet high at best, these hills don't appear on an ordinary map.

Long ago the entire area was apparently under the sea, and people in the region still say that the famous warrior Yoshitsune once came here by boat. It happened after he had gone into hiding and was fleeing northward toward the shores of faraway Ezo. His boat ran aground—there's a square patch of red soil some thirty feet across on a low tree-covered hill midway along the range that shows where he landed.

They call this particular place Bald Horse Hill. That's because, from the village below, the patch of red soil is supposed to resemble a galloping horse. In fact it's more like an old man's profile.

Bald Horse Hill is also famous hereabouts for its scenery. A stream emerges from behind the hill and flows past the village and its twenty or thirty homes. Several miles up this stream a waterfall descends from a cliff. The waterfall is one hundred feet high and looks very white.

The trees covering this hill begin to change color at the end of summer. The leaves are beautiful in the autumn, and people come from the provincial towns to view them, enlivening even this remote place for a time. At the foot of the falls there is a small tea stand to serve visitors.

Just as the season was getting underway this year, a death occurred at the falls—an accidental death, though, and not a suicide. The victim was a student from the city with a pale complexion. He had come, as others occasionally do, to collect some of the rare ferns that grow here.

The pool below the falls is surrounded almost entirely by high cliffs. A narrow gap opens to the west, and here the water rushes against the rocks and pours out into the stream. The ferns grow in patches down the cliffs, moistened by the constant spray and quivering in the roar of the waters.

The student had been scaling one of the cliffs. It was afternoon, and the early autumn sun still shone overhead. When he was halfway up, a rock the size of a man's head suddenly gave way beneath his foot, and he fell as though he had been torn away from the cliff he was climbing. On the way down he got snared by the branch of an aging tree. But the branch snapped, and he was sent plummeting into the pool below with a horrible splash.

Several people nearby witnessed the fall. The girl who looked after the tea stand—she was going on fourteen—saw it best.

She watched him sink far into the pool and then float up until his body rose halfway above the surface. At that moment his eyes were shut, his mouth was slightly open. His blue shirt was torn in places while the collector's box still hung from his shoulder.

The next moment he was again sucked down—all the way to the bottom.

II

On clear days, from late spring until well into fall, columns of white smoke can be seen even from far away rising over Bald Horse Hill. The sap runs abundantly then, and the trees are just right for producing charcoal. So the charcoal-makers work hard at their kilns during this period.

There are ten or so huts on Bald Horse Hill, each with a kiln. One of the kilns is located near the waterfall, off by itself. The other charcoal-makers are from this area, while the man working this kiln comes from a distant part of the country. The girl who runs the tea stand is the man's daughter. Named Suwa, she lives alone with her father throughout the year.

Two years ago, when Suwa was twelve, her father set up the little stand with logs and a reed screen. He also arranged a number of things on the shelves for her to sell—lemonade and crackers, rice jelly and all sorts of sweet candies.

With summer approaching once again and people beginning to come around, Suwa's father would assemble the stand. He would then carry the provisions there every morning in a basket, his daughter skipping along behind him in her bare feet. Upon reaching the site, he would soon go back to the hut and his own kiln, leaving Suwa there all alone.

If she caught even a glimpse of any sightseers, Suwa would call out the greeting her father had taught her—"Hello! Please stop in for a while." But the roaring falls drowned out her sweet voice, and she could seldom catch anyone's attention. In a whole day she could not even take in fifty sen.

Her father would return at dusk, his entire body black as charcoal.

"How much did you get?" he'd ask.

"Nothing."

"Too bad," he would mutter, as if he didn't much care. After looking up at the falls, he would place the sweets back in the basket. And then they would go back to the hut. It went on like this day after day until the frost came.

Suwa's father could leave her alone at the tea stand without having to worry. Since she had grown up among these hills, she wasn't going to lose her footing on a rock and plunge into the waterfall pool. In fact, when the weather was good, she would take off her clothes, dive into the pool and swim up close to the falls. If she noticed someone while she was swimming, she would toss her short brown hair from her forehead with one hand and then cry out, "Hello! Please stop in for a while."

When it rained, Suwa would crawl under a straw mat in a corner of the tea stand and take a nap. A large oak grew out over the tea stand, its abundant leaves providing shelter from the rain.

Suwa would gaze up at the thundering falls and imagine that the water would eventually run out. She also wondered why the waterfall always took the same shape.

Lately her thoughts had deepened.

She could now tell that the waterfall didn't always keep the same shape. In fact the varying width and the changing pattern of the spray made one dizzy. Finally the billowing at the crest made her realize that the falls was more clouds of mist than streams of water. Besides, she knew that water itself could never be so white.

One day Suwa lingered dreamily beside the falls. As the sky became overcast and the early autumn wind reddened her cheeks and made them smart, she remembered the tale her father had told her some time ago. He had held her in his lap then, while keeping an eye on the kiln.

The story concerned two brothers, Saburo and Hachiro, both of whom worked as woodcutters. Hachiro, the younger brother, had caught some trout in a mountain stream and had brought them back home. Before Saburo returned from the mountains, Hachiro grilled one of the trout and ate it. The fish tasted good, so he ate two or three more of them. After that, he couldn't stop until he had eaten the entire catch. He was thirsty now—so thirsty that he drank all the water in the well. Then he ran to the river at the edge of the village and kept on drinking. Scales suddenly spread out over his body. By the time his brother came running back, Hachiro had become a great serpent and was swimming in the river.

"Hachiro! What is it?" Saburo called out.

Shedding tears, the serpent called back from out in the river. "Ah, Saburo!"

Weeping and wailing, the two brothers called back and forth, one from the bank and the other from the river—"Ah, Hachiro!" "Ah, Saburo!" Unfortunately there was nothing that could be done.

This tale had so moved Suwa that she had put her father's charcoal-blackened finger into her small mouth and wept.

Coming out of her reverie, she gazed at the falls in wonder. The water seemed to murmur—"Ah, Hachiro! Ah, Saburo! Ah, Hachiro!"

Her father, pushing the leaves aside, emerged from the red ivy that hung along the cliff.

"How much did you sell, Suwa?"

Her nose glistened with spray from the falls. She rubbed it without making any reply. Silently her father gathered up the things.

They headed home, pushing through the bamboo grass that had grown over the mountain road. Before they had covered the quarter mile back, Suwa's father said, "Maybe you should quit now." He shifted the basket from his right hand to his left, the lemonade bottles clinking against one another. "It's getting cold," he went on, "and no one's coming any more."

As the sunlight faded, the only sound was that of the wind. Once in a while the leaves falling from the oak or fir trees would strike against the father and daughter like sharp hailstones.

"Papa," Suwa called out from behind him, "what are you living for?"

The huge shoulders merely shrugged. Then Suwa's father looked closely into his daughter's determined face and muttered, "Nothing, I guess."

Suwa bit off part of the long grass leaf she was holding.

"You're better off dead, then."

His hand flew up—he would teach her some respect! Then, hesitantly, he lowered it. His daughter had been on edge for some time now. He realized that she was getting to be a woman and he must leave her be.

"All right," he conceded, "all right."

Stupid! That's what this listless reply was—stupid! Suwa spat out bits of the leaf. "Fool!" she screamed. "You're a fool!"

III

The Obon Festival of the Dead was over, and the tea stand had been taken down for the winter. For Suwa this was the worst time of the year.

Every fourth day or so her father would hoist a bag of charcoal onto his shoulders and set off for the market. There were men for hire who did this sort of work, but he could not afford the fifteen or twenty sen they would charge. Leaving Suwa all alone, he would carry the load himself to the village below the hill.

When the weather was good, Suwa would hunt for mushrooms while her father was gone. After all, the charcoal would not bring in enough for them to live on even when it sold for five or six sen a bag. So Suwa had to pick mushrooms for her father to sell too. The moist, pea-shaped *nameko* mushrooms fetched a good price. They grew in clusters on decaying logs among clumps of fern. Each time Suwa saw moss on the logs, she thought of the student who had drowned, the one person in her life who might have become a friend. She liked to sprinkle the moss on top of her mushroom-filled basket and head for home.

Whenever her father sold the charcoal or mushrooms for a good price, he would return with sake on his breath. Once in a while he would bring back a paper purse or some other gift for Suwa.

One day a raging wind blew about the hill from early morning, causing the straw mats that served as curtains to swing back and forth within the hut. Suwa's father had gone down to the village at dawn.

She decided to stay inside today and arrange her hair, an unusual thing for her to do. When she had finished tying up her curls in a paper ribbon patterned with waves, a present that her father had given her, Suwa stoked the fire and sat down to await his return. Now and then the call of a wild animal could be heard, along with the rustling of leaves.

After the sun went down, Suwa prepared her supper. It was fried miso over brown rice, and she ate it all alone. As the night deepened, the wind died down and the weather turned cold. An unearthly quiet settled upon the hill, the kind of quiet in which wondrous events are bound to happen. Suwa heard all sorts of things—*tengu* demons toppling the forest trees, someone right outside the hut swishing adzuki beans in fresh water. She even caught the clear echo of a hermit's laughter in the distance.

Tired of waiting for her father, Suwa wrapped herself in a straw quilt and lay down by the hearth. As she dozed, a creature occasionally lifted the straw mat hanging in the doorway and peeked in. Thinking that this was a hermit from the mountains, Suwa pretended to be fast asleep.

In the glow of the dying fire, something else could just be made out fluttering through the entrance onto the dirt floor. Snow—the first of the season! Suwa was elated, even as she appeared to dream.

Pain. The heavy body almost numbed her. Then she smelled the reeking breath.

"Fool!" she screamed. Blindly she fled outside.

Snow! Whirling this way and that, it struck her right in the face. She sat down, her hair and dress already covered with flakes. Then she got up and trudged ahead, her shoulders heaving as she gasped for breath. She walked on and on, her clothes whipping about in the gale.

The sound of the falls grew steadily louder. On she marched, wiping her nose over and over with the palm of her hand. Now the roar of the falls was almost at her feet.

There was a narrow gap among the wintry, moaning trees. She leapt through it, murmuring one word.

"Papa."

IV

When she came to, everything was dim and shadowy. She sensed the rumbling of the waterfall far above. Her body, vibrating with the sound, felt chilled to the bone.

Ah, the bottom of the waterfall pool. With that realization she felt refreshed and clean.

She stretched her legs, sliding ahead without a sound. Her nose nearly bumped against the edge of a rock.

Daija!

Yes, she had turned into a daija serpent. How fortunate that she could never again go back to the hut. Telling herself these things, she tried moving her chin whiskers in a circle.

In fact, she was only a small carp. Her tiny mouth nibbled at the water while the wart on her nose wiggled back and forth.

The carp then swam about in the pool, near the deep basin beneath the waterfall. Moving her pectoral fins, she rose close to the surface, then suddenly dove, her tail thrashing hard.

She chased after tiny shrimp in the water, hid in the reeds

along the bank and tugged at the moss growing upon the edge of a rock.

Then the carp lay still. Once in a while the pectoral fins twitched ever so slightly. It remained this way for a time, as if in contemplation.

Then, with a twisting motion, the carp headed straight toward the waterfall basin. In an instant the waters were swirling about, sucking it down like a leaf.

HEED MY PLEA

Listen to me! Listen! I'm telling you, master, the man's horrible. Just horrible. He's obnoxious. And wicked. Ah, I can't bear it! Away with him!

Yes, yes, I'll be calm. But you must put an end to him—he's against the people. Yes, I'll tell everything—the whole story from beginning to end. And I know where he is, so I'll take you there right away. Put him to the sword then, and don't show any mercy. It's true that he's my teacher and lord, but I'm thirty-three years old too; I was born just two months after him, so there's really not much difference between us. The arrogance of the man, the contempt . . . Imagine, ordering me about like that! Oh, I've had enough. I can't take it anymore—better to be dead than to hold in one's wrath. How many times have I covered up for him? But no one realizes that—not even him. I take that back, he does realize it. He's fully aware of it, and that makes him all the more contemptuous of me. He's proud too, so he resents any help I give him. He's so conceited that he ends up making a fool of himself. He's convinced that taking help from someone like me makes him look weak. That's because he's desperate to have others believe him omnipotent. Pure stupidity! The world's not like that. You've got to bow before someone to get on. That's the only way—struggle ahead one step at a time while keeping the others back. What can he do, really? Not a thing. He's like a lamb that's lost in the woods. Without me he'd have died long ago in some abandoned meadow, together with his good-for-nothing disciples. "Foxes have their holes, the birds their roosts, but the Son of Man has nowhere to lay his head." There's the evidence! You see it, don't you?

And what good does Peter do? Or James, John, Andrew and Thomas? Fools, the whole bunch of them! They only follow at his heels uttering their unctuous, spine-chilling compliments. They're completely taken in by this mad notion of a heaven, and every one of them will want to be some sort of royal minister as the day of the kingdom draws near. The fools can't even earn their daily bread here in this world. Wasn't it I who kept them from starving? I who had him preach his sermons and then coaxed a donation from the crowd? I who got the wealthy villagers to contribute as well? Besides that, I did our everyday shopping and looked after our lodging too. I did everything and didn't complain either. But not a word of gratitude did I get, either from him or from those foolish disciples. Day after day I slaved on my own, but instead of thanking me, he would pretend not to know. And always there were those impossible commands: "Feed the multitude!" he insisted, when all we had were five loaves and two fishes. I had to struggle behind the scenes then and fill the order. Oh yes, I admit that I helped him time and again with all those miracles and sleight-of-hand tricks.

Considering the sort of things I did, I might seem a stingy person. I'm a man of taste, though, and not stingy at all. I saw him as a lovely, innocent person without the slightest greed. That's why even though I scrimp and save to buy the daily bread, I don't hate him for squandering our every penny. He's a beautiful man of the spirit, and I appreciate him even though

I'm only a poor merchant. I don't even mind when he wastes every pittance I've scraped together. But if he only had a kind word for me now and then . . . instead of all this hostility.

He was kind to me just once. We were all strolling along the shore one spring when he suddenly called out to me and said, "I realize that you, so helpful to me always, feel pangs of loneliness. But you mustn't keep looking so depressed. It's the hypocrite, wishing others to know of his melancholy, who lets his feelings show. You may be lonely, but you can wash your face, smooth your hair with pomade and smile as though nothing is wrong. That's the way of the true believer. You don't quite understand? Let me put it this way, then. We may not be able to see our True Father, but He can see even into our hearts. Isn't that enough for you? No? It isn't? But everyone gets lonely."

At these words I felt like crying out, "I don't care whether the Heavenly Father knows about me or not. Or people either, for that matter. I'm satisfied so long as you know. I love you. The other disciples may love you, but not the way I do. I love you more than anyone else does. Peter and the two Jameses merely follow you in hopes of getting something, but I alone understand. And yet I know that nothing will come of following you, and that makes me wonder why I can't leave. Well, without you, I would simply perish. I could not go on living. Here's an idea that I've kept to myself until now. Why don't you just abandon those useless disciples and give up preaching the Heavenly Father's creed. Be an ordinary man and live the rest of your life with your mother Mary and with me. I still own a small house in my native village. The large peach orchard is still there, and so are my aging parents. In the spring, just about now, the blossoms are splendid. You could spend your entire life there in comfort. And I would always be near, anxious to help. Find a good woman and take her as your wife."

After I had spoken, he smiled wanly and murmured as if to

himself, "Peter and Simon are fishermen. They have no fine orchard. James and John are also poor fishermen. They have no land on which to spend their lives in comfort."

He resumed his quiet stroll along the beach, and thereafter we never spoke intimately to one another again. He simply would not confide in me.

I love him. If he dies, I shall die with him. He is mine—mine alone, and I will slay him rather than hand him over. I forsook my father, my mother and my land. I followed him until now. But I don't believe in heaven or in God, and I don't believe he will rise from the dead either. *Him* the King of Israel? Those foolish disciples believe he's the Son of God, and that's why they leap about each time he speaks the Good News of God's Kingdom. They'll be disappointed soon—I'm certain of that. The man even says that he who exalts himself shall be humbled and he who humbles himself shall be exalted. Does anyone in the real world get away with such cajolery? Deceiver! One thing after another—nonsense from beginning to end. Oh, I don't believe a word he says, but I do believe in his beauty. Such beauty is not of this world, and I love him for that—not for any reward. I'm not one of your minions who believes the Heavenly Kingdom is at hand and cries out, "Hurrah! Now I'll be a minister of some branch or other!" I simply don't want to leave him, that's all. I'm content to be near him, to hear his voice and to gaze upon his person. If only he would cease preaching and live a long life together with me. Ah, if only that were possible, how happy I'd be. I only believe in happiness in *this* world. I'm not afraid of any judgment hereafter.

Why doesn't he accept this pure and unselfish love of mine? Ah, slay him for me! I know where he is, master, and I'll take you there. He hates me, despises me. Scorned—that's what I am. But he and his disciples would have starved without me. How could he mistreat me when I kept all of them fed and clothed?

Listen to this! Six days ago a woman from the village stole into the room where he was dining at Simon of Bethany's house. It was Mary, the younger sister of Martha, and she was carrying an alabaster jar filled with oil of nard. Without a word she poured the oil over him from head to toe—and didn't beg his pardon afterward either. No, she merely crouched there, quite calm, and began gently wiping his feet with her own hair.

The whole thing appeared very strange as the room became filled with fragrance. Then I shouted angrily at the girl—she shouldn't be so rude! Look! I went on, wasn't his garment soaked through? And using such expensive oil—wasn't that almost a crime? What a foolish woman! Didn't she realize that such oil cost three hundred denarii? How pleased the poor would be if the oil were sold and the money given to them. Where waste occurs, want will follow.

After I had scolded her, he looked straight at me and said, "Why must you make trouble for the woman? It is a fine thing she has done for me. You have the poor among you always; but you will not always have me. When she poured this oil on my body it was her way of preparing me for burial. I tell you this: wherever in the world this gospel is proclaimed, what she has done will be told as her memorial." By the time he finished, his pale cheeks were slightly flushed.

I usually don't believe what he says, and I could easily have ignored this as more puffery on his part. But there was something different, a strangeness in the voice and in the look too, that had never been there before. For a moment I was taken aback; but then I looked again at the slightly flushed cheeks and faintly brimming eyes, and suddenly I knew. Oh, how horrible! How disgraceful even to mention it. A wretched farm girl—and him in love with . . . No, not quite that—surely not that. And yet, it was something perilously close to it. Wasn't that how he felt? How humiliating for him to be moved even slightly by an ignorant farm girl. A scandal beyond repair.

All my life I've had this vulgar, detestable ability to sniff out a shameful emotion. One look and I can spot a weakness. It might have been slight, but there was something special in his feeling for her. That's the truth, no question about it. My eyes cannot err.

No, it just couldn't be so! This was intolerable! He was caught in a trap. Never had he seemed so ridiculous. No matter how much a woman had loved him, he had always remained beautiful—and calm as the very waters. Never had he been the least bit ruffled. And then he gave in, like any slouch. He's still young, so perhaps this was natural. But I was born just two months after him, so we're almost the same age. We're young, both of us, but I'm the one who's held out. I gave my heart to him alone and refused to love any woman.

Martha the older sister has a sturdy build; indeed, she's big as a cow, and has a violent temper too. She works furiously at her chores—that's her one virtue. Otherwise she's just another farm girl. But Mary the younger sister is different. She has delicate limbs and almost transparent skin. Her hands and feet are tiny but plump, and her large eyes are deep and clear as a lake. There's a distant dreaminess about them too, and that's partly why the villagers all marvel at her gracefulness. Even I was so astonished that I thought of buying her something, maybe even some white silk, while I was in town. Oh, now I'm getting off the track. Let's see, what was I saying . . . Oh yes, I was bitter. It just didn't make sense. I could have stamped my feet in resentment. If he's young, well so am I. I've got talent too, and I'm a fine man with a house and orchard besides. I gave up everything for him only to realize that I'd been taken in. I discovered that he was a fraud.

Master, he took my woman. No! That's not it! She stole him from me. Ah, that's wrong too. I'm just blurting things out— don't believe a word. I'm confused, and you must pardon me. There's not a word of truth to my babbling. Mere ranting and

raving—nothing more. But I was ashamed, so ashamed that I
wanted to rend my breast. I couldn't understand why he felt
this way. Ah, jealousy is such an unbearable vice, but my longing for him was so great that I continued to renounce my own
life and kept following him till now. But instead of consoling
me with a kind word, he favored this wretched farm girl, blushing in her company even. Well, he's a slouch and he's done
for. There's no hope for him. He's mediocre—a nobody. So
what if he dies. Perhaps the devil had possessed me, but here
I suddenly had a frightening thought. He was going to be slain
anyway, I reasoned, so why shouldn't I do it? He sometimes
acted as though he wanted someone to slay him. I'd do it with
my own hand, then, because I don't want anyone else to. I'd
slay him, then die myself. Master, I'm ashamed of these tears.
Yes, all right, I won't weep anymore. Yes, yes, I'll speak calmly.

The next day we set out for Jerusalem, the city of our
dreams. As we drew near the temple, a large crowd of both
young and old followed after him. Presently he took note of a
lone, decrepit ass standing by the road, and, mounting the animal with a smile, he looked grandly at his disciples and spoke
of fulfilling the prophecy, "Tell the daughters of Zion, 'Here is
your King, who comes to you in gentleness, riding on an ass'."
I alone was depressed by the incident. What a pathetic figure.
Was *this* how the Son of David was to ride into the Temple of
Jerusalem for the long-awaited Passover? This the debut for
which he had always yearned? Making a spectacle of himself
astride this decrepit, tottering ass? I could only pity him for
taking part in this pathetic farce. Ah, the man was done for. If
he lived another day even, he would only humiliate himself further. A flower doesn't survive if it's wilting—better to cut it in
bloom. I love him best, and I don't care how much the others
despise me. I resolved ever more firmly to slay him right away.

The crowd swelled moment by moment, and garments of
red, blue and yellow were flung down all along the route. The

people welcomed him with their cries and lined the way with palm branches. Before and behind him, from the left and the right, the crowd swirled about like a great wave, jostling the man and the ass he was riding, while everyone sang, "Hosanna to the Son of David. Blessings on him who comes in the name of the Lord. Hosanna in the Heavens."

Peter, John, Bartholomew and the other disciples—fools to the man—embraced one another ecstatically and exchanged tearful kisses, as if they had been following a triumphant general or seen the Kingdom of Heaven with their own eyes. The stubborn Peter held onto John and broke into joyful weeping. As I watched, I recalled the days of poverty and hardship when we traveled about preaching the gospel. In fact, warm tears welled in my own eyes.

And so he entered the temple and descended from the ass. Who knows what it was that possessed him then, but he picked up a rope and began brandishing it, both driving out all the cattle and sheep that had been on sale, and knocking over the tables of the money-changers and the seats of the pigeon sellers. "My house shall be called a house of prayer," he thundered, "but you are making it a robber's cave."

Was he daft? How, I wondered, could this gentleman carry on like a drunkard? The astonished multitude asked what he was talking about, and, gasping for breath, he replied: "Destroy this temple, and in three days I will raise it again." Even those simple disciples, unable to accept this claim, could only stare.

But I saw what he was up to—he was showing off like a child might. Since he was constantly saying that all things were possible through faith in him, here was his chance to show his mettle. But flailing a rope about and chasing away helpless merchants? What a niggardly way to prove something! I almost smiled at him from pity. If defiance meant no more than kicking over the seats of the pigeon sellers, then he was finished. His self-respect was gone, he simply didn't care anymore. He knew that he had reached his limit. And so he would be seized during Passover and take leave of the world, before his weakness became too evident. When I realized what he was up to, I gave him up for good. How amusing to think that I had once loved this conceited pup so blindly.

Presently he faced the crowd gathered at the temple and spewed forth the most insolent abuse yet. I was right—surely the man was desperate. To my eye he even looked slightly bedraggled. He was just itching to be slain.

"Alas for you, lawyers and Pharisees, hypocrites! You clean the outside of your cup and dish, which you have filled inside by robbery and self-indulgence! Blind Pharisees! Clean the inside of the cup first; then the outside will be clean also.

"Alas for you, lawyers and Pharisees, hypocrites! You are like tombs covered with whitewash; they look well from outside, but inside they are full of dead men's bones and all kinds of filth. So it is with you: outside you look like honest men, but inside you are brimful of hypocrisy and crime.

"You snakes, you vipers' brood, how can you escape being condemned to hell?

"O Jerusalem, Jerusalem, the city that murders the prophets and stones the messengers sent to her! How often have I longed to gather your children as a hen gathers her brood under her wings; but you would not let me."

Silly and stupid—that's what I thought. It turns my stomach just to repeat his words here. Why, the man who says such things has got to be deranged. He's carried on about other nonsense too—famines, earthquakes, stars falling from the sky, the moon not giving its light, vultures gathering to peck the carcasses that fill the land, the weeping and the gnashing of teeth. He speaks in such a reckless manner, as if he's stuck on himself. It's madness—the man doesn't know his place. But he won't get away with it. It's the cross for him—that's for certain.

Yesterday I heard from a peddler in town how the elders and priests had met secretly in the latter's court and decided to execute him. I also learned they were fearful the people would rise up if he were seized in public, so thirty pieces of silver would be given to anyone who reported when he would be alone with his disciples. He was going to die then, so there was no time to lose. I had better hand him over, I thought, rather than let someone else do it. It was my duty to betray him, a last sign of my enduring love. But this would place me in a trap too—will anyone, I wondered, recognize the devotion behind this deed? It makes no difference, though, because mine is a pure love that doesn't seek recognition. And even if people despise me forever and I end up suffering in eternal hellfire, it will be like nothing alongside of my unquenchable love for him. So determined was I to fulfill my mission that a shudder ran over me as I thought the matter over. I quietly watched for an opportunity, and finally, on the day of the Feast, it came.

We had rented a second-floor room in an old eating place upon the hill. All thirteen of us, both Master and disciples, were seated in the dim chamber about to begin the supper when suddenly he rose and removed his tunic without a word. What could he be up to, we wondered. We watched as he took the pitcher from the table and carried it to a corner. There he emptied the water into a small basin. Then, having tied a clean, white towel about his waist, he began to wash our feet. While he was washing the feet of one disciple, the others would idle about in total bewilderment. I alone sensed what was lurking in the Master's mind.

He was lonely—and so frightened that he would now cling to these ignorant bigots. What a pity. He must have realized what fate held in store for him. Even as I watched, I felt a cry rising in my throat until suddenly I wanted to embrace him and weep. Oh, how sad. Who could ever accuse you? You were always kind and just, ever a friend to the poor, and always shimmering with beauty. I know that you are truly the Son of God. Please forgive me, for I have watched these two or three days for a chance to betray you. But not any more. How criminal to think of betraying you! Rest assured that, even if five hundred officials or a thousand soldiers should come, they won't lay a finger on you. But they are watching, so let's be wary. And let's be on our way too. Come, Peter. And you too, James. Come, John. Everyone, come! Let's live the rest of our lives protecting this gentle Master of ours.

I felt a profound love for him, but I couldn't express it. There was something sublime about it that I had never known before. The tears of contrition that flowed down my cheeks felt quite agreeable. Finally he washed my feet—ever so quietly and gently, and then he wiped them dry with the towel at his waist. Oh, how he touched me! Ah, at that moment I seemed to be in paradise.

Then he washed the feet of Philip and Andrew. Peter was next; the simple man couldn't hide his misgivings. Pursing his lips, he petulantly said, "Master, why do you wash my feet?"

"Ah, you do not understand what I am doing, but one day you will," the master gently admonished, crouching next to Peter. But Peter grew yet more stubborn. "No! Never! You must never wash my feet, for I am unworthy of it," he said, then drew back his feet.

Raising his voice ever so slightly, the Master gave notice: "If I do not wash you, you are not in fellowship with me." The startled Peter bowed low and implored, "Ah, forgive me. Not only my feet, Lord, wash my hands and head as well."

I couldn't help laughing. The other disciples grinned, and the whole room seemed to brighten up. He smiled too and then said to Peter, "A man who has bathed needs no further washing; he is altogether clean. And not only you. But James and John too. All of you are clean and without sin. All of you except . . ." Here he paused and sat up straight. For an instant his eyes took on a look of unbearable suffering. Then they shut tightly and did not open. "Except . . . if only all of you were clean . . ."

I instantly thought—me! That's who he meant! He had seen through my melancholy a moment ago and knew that I planned to betray him. But things were different now—I had changed completely. I was cleansed and my heart transformed. Ah, but he didn't realize it. He hadn't noticed. "No! You're mistaken!" I wanted to cry out, but the words lodged in my throat and I cravenly swallowed them like spit. For some reason I couldn't speak. I just couldn't.

After he had finished speaking, something perverse sprang up within me. Meekly I gave in to the feeling, whereupon the cowardly suspicion that perhaps I was unclean expanded into a dark, ugly cloud that swirled within my gut and exploded into a righteous indignation. What! Damned? Me damned? He despised me from the bottom of his heart. Betray him! I told myself. Yes, betray him! I would slay him—and myself too. My earlier determination was revived, and I became an utter demon of vengeance. Seemingly unaware of how turbulent my feelings had become, he presently took up his tunic, carefully put it on and sat down at the table. By the time he spoke, his face was pale.

"Do you understand what I have done for you?" he asked. "You call me 'Master' and 'Lord,' and rightly so, for that is what I am. Then if I, your Lord and Master, have washed your feet, you also ought to wash one another's feet. I shall probably not be always with you, and thus I have set an example for you to follow. In very truth I tell you, a servant is not greater than his master, nor is a messenger greater than the one who sent him. If you know this, happy are you if you act upon it." Wearily he spoke these words, then began to eat in silence. Bowing his head, he spoke once more: "In truth, in very truth I tell you, one of you is going to betray me." There was a deep sorrow in his voice, as if he were both weeping and moaning.

The disciples nearly recoiled in shock. They stood up, knocking the chairs over, and gathered about him. "Is it I, Lord? Master, can you mean me?" they cried. Like one already condemned, he barely moved his head. "It is the man to whom I give this piece of bread when I have dipped it in the dish. Alas for that man by whom the Son of Man is betrayed. It would be better for that man if he had never been born." For him, these were unusually specific words. After he had spoken them, he took a piece of bread and, stretching forth his hand, placed it unerringly in my mouth.

Instead of shame, I now felt hatred. My courage immediately came back, and I hated him for turning malicious once again—he was his old self, humiliating me before the others. He and I were like fire and water; we would always be separate. To place a piece of bread in my mouth as though feeding his dog or cat—was this all he could do in revenge? Ha! The fool! Master, he then told me to do the deed quickly, and so I ran from the place and fled along the dark road as fast as I could. I arrived here only moments ago, and I've made my plea in haste. You must punish him—punish him as you see fit. You can seize him and beat him with a rod, strip and crucify him even. I've had enough of him; he's terrible . . . obnoxious . . . Tormenting me even yet . . . Ah, damn him! He'll be in the Garden of Gethsemane, by the River Kidron. The meal is over, and it's the hour for prayer, so he'll be there with the disciples. No one else will be around. If you go right away, you can capture him easily. Oh, those birds are making such a ruckus, aren't they? I wonder why I hear them singing tonight? I remember how the birds were chirping even as I ran through the wood just now. It's an unusual bird that sings in the night. My childlike curiosity got the better of me, and I wanted a glimpse of the bird. So I stopped and, tilting my head, looked up at the trees . . . ah, forgive me, I'm boring you. Master, is everything ready? Ah, the sweetness—it makes me feel splendid. It's also the final night for me, isn't it? Master, you'll be so good as to observe both of us standing side by side after tonight. I'll show you the two of us, Master, standing side by side this evening. I don't fear him. We're the same age, and I won't lower myself. I'm a young man of quality, just like him. Ah, those birds are still making a ruckus. How annoying! Why do songbirds keep chirping all over the place? What's all the noise about? Oh yes, the money! You're handing it over? Thirty pieces of silver—for me? Ah yes, but I really don't want it. So take it back before I hit you. I didn't make this plea for money. Take it back! No, wait, I didn't mean that. Please forgive me. I accept your offer. Yes, I'm a merchant. That's why that lovely man always scorned me. But I am a merchant, so I'll take it. I'll betray him fully, just for the lucre. That'll be my best revenge. Betrayed for thirty pieces of silver—just what he deserves! And I won't shed a tear since I don't love him anyway. I never loved him at all. Master, everything I said was false; there's no question that I followed him around for the money. When I realized this evening that he wouldn't let me earn a penny, I quickly changed sides, like any merchant would. Money—that's the only thing. Thirty pieces of silver. Oh, how splendid! I accept. I'm just a penny-pinching merchant, and I can't help being greedy. Yes, thank you. Yes, yes, I forgot to mention it, but I'm Judas the Merchant. Yes, that's Judas Iscariot.

Run, Melos!

Quivering with rage, Melos decided that he must rid the land of this wicked and ruthless king.

He was only a village shepherd who tended his flock and played upon his flute. Yet, though ignorant of politics, he was more sensitive to evil than most other people.

He had left his village early that morning and traveled the ten leagues to Syracuse over mountains and fields. His younger sister was a shy girl of fifteen who had become engaged to an honest shepherd. Since Melos had neither father nor mother nor wife, he had to select the bride's gown and order food for the wedding feast himself. It was to perform these tasks that he had come to Syracuse.

Having taken care of this business, Melos strolled down the main street looking for Selinunteus, a boyhood friend of his who worked in the city as a stonemason. They had not seen each other for quite some time, and Melos looked forward to the meeting. As he walked along, however, he began to sense that something was wrong. Since dusk had fallen, it was only natural that the city was quiet. Despite that, the place seemed so desolate that even the carefree Melos began to feel uneasy.

He stopped a youngster and asked if anything had

happened. On a trip here two years ago, he had found the place lively, with people singing even at night. The boy merely shrugged and didn't say anything. Melos next questioned an old man, more insistently than he had the boy. The man didn't reply either until, seizing and shaking him with both hands, Melos again asked what the trouble was. In a whisper that couldn't be overheard, the old man replied: "The king's executing people."

"Why is that?"

"He says we're evil, but it's not true."

"Has he executed many?"

"Yes. First it was his own brother-in-law. And then his very son and heir. His sister and her children were next. And then the queen. The wise councillor Arekisus—"

"That's terrible," Melos interrupted. "Is the king mad?"

"No, he's not mad. He says he can't trust people. Recently his own vassals have come under suspicion. If one of them lives a little too grandly, the king demands a hostage. And if the vassal refuses, why then he's condemned to death. The king had six of them crucified today."

Melos quivered with rage as he listened. "That's terrible," he exclaimed. "The king has got to be stopped."

Melos, being a simple man, marched straight into the castle still carrying his purchases. When the guards seized him, they found a dagger inside his cloak. An uproar ensued, and Melos was dragged before King Dionysius. His face pale and his brow carved with wrinkles, the tyrant questioned Melos in a quiet but authoritative voice.

"What were you going to do with this dagger? Speak up!"

Without flinching, Melos responded, "Free this town from its wicked king."

"You?" The king's smile was condescending. "Impossible fool! How could someone like you realize how alone I am."

"Hold your tongue!" Filled with indignation, Melos came

right back at the king. "There's nothing worse than suspicion. And you suspect your own subjects."

"They made me suspicious. They're selfish and unreliable, and I can't trust them." The tyrant spoke these words calmly and then he sighed, "After all, I too want peace and quiet."

"What for," Melos sneered, "except to keep your power? Killing innocent people—that's peace for you."

Instantly the king looked up and retorted, "Silence, you wretch! You can prattle on about innocence, but I've got to see into people. I'll have you begging for mercy on the cross soon, but don't expect me to listen."

"Ah, the king is wise. Go ahead, flatter yourself. I've decided to die, anyway. I won't beg for mercy. Only . . . ," Melos hesitated, his eyes lowered. "If you pity me at all, delay the execution for three days while I see to my sister's wedding. I'll return from my village once the ceremony's over. I'll be here within three days, I promise that."

"Ridiculous!" The tyrant laughed softly, his voice hoarse. "Are you trying to tell me a captured bird will return after it's been let free? What a joke."

"I'll be back." Melos insisted. "I don't break my word. Give me three days. My sister's expecting me. If you don't trust me . . . well then, there's a stonemason named Selinunteus in this city. He's my best friend, and he'll be my hostage. If I'm not back by sunset, have him strangled. Give me a chance; I'll prove I can keep my word."

At these words the coldhearted tyrant grinned. He could tell that Melos was bluffing and that he would never return. He would play along, though, pretending to be taken in and letting Melos go free. It would be fun to have the hostage executed three days later. And while the execution was being carried out, he himself would wear a melancholy look to show how much he regretted that people could not be trusted. Yes, he would teach these so-called honest fools a thing or two.

"I grant your request. You may summon the hostage. But come back," he cautioned, "in three days. And by sunset. If you're late, I shall execute him. Well, on second thought, you might come back a bit late. I'll see that you're acquitted for good."

"What was that?" Melos declared. "I don't see what you're getting at."

"Oh, come now, anyone can see that you don't want to die. If it suits you, be late. I can tell what you're up to."

Melos stamped the ground in anger. He wouldn't utter another word.

Late that night Selinunteus was brought to the castle, and the friends met in the presence of the king. Though two years had passed since their last meeting, Melos had only to explain the situation to Selinunteus who nodded and firmly embraced his friend. Nothing more was required between them. After Selinunteus was bound with a rope, Melos set off under an early summer sky filled with stars.

He hurried along the road, never pausing to rest. By the time he reached home, the sun was high and the villagers were busy in the fields. His sister was there too, tending the flock. Seeing her weary brother approach with faltering steps, she began to ply him with questions.

"No," Melos replied, "nothing's wrong." Forcing a smile, he went on. "I've still got something to do in town, so I must go back soon. The wedding will take place tomorrow—the earlier the better."

His sister blushed.

"Are you pleased? Look, I bought a nice dress for you. Now go tell the villagers the ceremony will be tomorrow."

After staggering on home, Melos barely managed to decorate the family altar and arrange the banquet chairs before collapsing to the floor. There he slept the entire day, hardly seeming to breathe. When he awoke, he went to see the bridegroom. There was a problem, he said, and the wedding would take place tomorrow.

That was impossible, the amazed shepherd replied. He hadn't been able to prepare anything yet, and so he asked that the wedding wait until the grapes were harvested.

It couldn't wait, Melos insisted. The groom would simply have to arrange the wedding for tomorrow.

But the shepherd was stubborn, just like Melos, and he would not agree to the idea. They continued the dispute through the night until finally, after much soothing and cajoling, Melos prevailed. By then, it was already dawn.

At noon the bride and groom took their marital vows before the gods. However, even as the ceremony was taking place, dark clouds began to cover the sky. At first, just a few drops began to fall, but then the rain started coming down in torrents. The guests at the banquet felt something ominous, but they roused themselves and began clapping their hands and singing lively songs in spite of the warm, stifling air. For the time being, Melos could smile with delight, his promise to the king forgotten.

The banquet grew even livelier as dusk fell and the guests stopped worrying about the rain. They were good company, and Melos wished he could stay. But he was bound by a pledge and could not do as he wished. Although he had to leave the banquet, he could still have a nap before setting out. It was a long time until sunset tomorrow, and it would be best to leave only after the rain had let up. Even a hero such as Melos felt attached to his home, and that's why he lingered there as long as possible.

Melos went up to the bride, who seemed almost dazed with happiness, and offered his congratulations. "I'm very tired," he went on, "and so I'll sleep awhile and then leave for town to take care of that business I mentioned to you. You're married to a fine man, so you won't miss me when I'm gone. You know the two things I hate most, don't you? Being suspicious of someone and telling lies. All I have to say is that I hope you'll be honest with your husband. And be proud of your brother, too, for he may well achieve something."

After the bride nodded to him as if she were dreaming, Melos went up to the groom and clapped him on the shoulder.

"The wedding had to be performed all of a sudden," he explained, "and neither one of us could do anything about this. I've got only two things of value—my sister and the sheep. I don't have anything else to give you. There's just one more thing to say," he went on. "We're brothers now, and I want you to be proud of that."

Melos smiled as the embarrassed groom rubbed his palms. Then he bade farewell to the villagers too and left the banquet. When he reached his own sheep pen, Melos crawled inside and fell sound asleep.

He awoke in the pale light of dawn. Oh God, he thought, springing to his feet, have I overslept? No, there was still time. If he left at once, he could reach Syracuse by sunset. He would show the king that men kept their word. And then he would laugh as they fastened him to the cross.

The rain seemed to slacken as Melos calmly prepared for the journey. When he was ready to leave, he swung his arms in a circle and dashed out into the drizzle like a flying arrow.

Tonight I shall die, he told himself. I will be put to death for having run. But I will rescue my hostage friend and defeat the wicked king as well. I must run—run that I may be put to death. Melos, be faithful even in your youth. Farewell, my native village.

It was heartrending to leave, and young Melos almost halted several times. But each time he rebuked himself, crying "Faster! Faster!" until his village receded behind and he found himself cutting through fields and woods. By the time he reached the next village, the rain had stopped and the sun was well up in the sky. Melos wiped the sweat from his brow with his clenched fist.

Having come this far, he no longer yearned for home. The wedding had taken place, so he needn't worry any longer about his sister. He need only go straight to the castle—and, since there was plenty of time before sunset, he could walk the rest of the way. Lapsing into his usual nonchalant manner, Melos strolled along chanting his favorite ballads.

He covered two more leagues, then a third. When he was halfway to Syracuse, disaster suddenly confronted him. Melos stopped dead in his tracks. What a sight! The river before him had flooded from yesterday's downpour in the mountains. The muddy torrent had gathered strength and knocked the bridge out; now it roared past, smashing the fallen girders to pieces. Melos stood in amazement before looking around and calling for help as loudly as he could. But the ferryboats had been swept from their moorings without a trace, and there was no longer even a ferryman present.

The river kept rising until it spread out like the sea. Melos could only crouch on the bank and weep like a child in spite of his years. Lifting his arms, he prayed to Zeus: "I beseech you, hold back this surging current. Time is going by, and the sun is high already. If I cannot reach the castle before dusk, my faithful friend will die."

As if to mock his plea, the muddy torrent rose even further. Wave engulfed wave, whirling and spreading out as the moments slipped by. Melos decided there was only one way across, and that was to swim. Calling on the gods to witness that the love and fidelity within him were stronger than this swift current, Melos plunged in. It was a desperate struggle, for the churning waves coiled about him like a mass of serpents. But Melos plowed ahead, putting all of his strength into each stroke. What matter if the swirling waves pounded him and pulled at his body? Perhaps the powers that be helped the fiercely struggling youth out of pity. In any event he was being swept away when—bravo!—he grasped a tree trunk on the opposite bank and held on.

Praise be the gods! Melos shook the water from his body like a horse emerging from a stream. With the sun already going down, he could not waste a moment. And so he set off running again. Gasping for breath, he climbed a mountain pass. Having reached the top, he let out a sigh of relief only to have a gang of thieves leap forth and cry, "Don't move!"

"What's the meaning of this?" Melos responded. "Get away! I've got to reach the king's castle before sunset."

"Leave your goods. Then be off."

"All I've got is my life. And I'm taking that to the king."

"We'll take it to him for you."

"So the king sent you to ambush me, then?"

Without a word the thieves began swinging their clubs. Melos ducked quickly, then flew at the nearest assailant and wrenched away his weapon. "Sorry," he declared, "I wouldn't do this if my honor weren't at stake." A ferocious assault sent three of them sprawling. As the others cringed, Melos raced down the pass without even pausing for breath.

As he ran on, however, the sun beat down on him and he felt exhausted. One bout of dizziness succeeded another, but he would not give in. With each attack he summoned his strength and stumbled ahead a few steps. But finally his knees buckled, and he lay helpless. Gazing at the heavens, he wept in despair.

Ah, Melos, you swam a muddy torrent and knocked down three thieves. A mighty effort had brought him this far; he had run like the Indian god Skanda in pursuit of the fleeing culprit who made off with the ashes of the Buddha. But now he was exhausted and could not go on. How tragic that a dear friend would die for trusting him. The king had been right: Melos would be known as a notorious traitor.

Melos reproached himself, but his sagging body could not even maintain a snail's pace. He rolled into the grass by the roadside. When the flesh is weary, the spirit too gives up; and somewhere within the body a sense of indifference takes root. Melos simply gave up.

He had already struggled valiantly, never questioning his pledge, and the gods knew he had done his best. He had run until he could no longer move. He wasn't a traitor. Oh, if only he could rend his breast and reveal the heart within. Then Selinunteus would see that love and loyalty were in his very blood. But at this crucial moment his strength was gone, leaving him utterly wretched. Surely he would be mocked and his family name besmirched. He had deceived his friend. Better if he had not set out at all than to collapse along the way. But fate had taken over and he no longer cared what happened.

Forgive me, Selinunteus. You always trusted me, and I have been loyal. Our friendship has never once been darkened by clouds of suspicion. Even now you await me, confident of my arrival. I am so grateful for that, Selinunteus. Trust between friends is the world's finest treasure, and I can hardly endure what has happened. I ran, Selinunteus; I never intended to deceive you. Believe me! I ran faster and faster. I swam a muddy torrent and escaped a pack of thieves. I raced down the mountain pass in one breath. I did it because that's the sort of person I am. But don't expect anything more. Let me be. I don't care any longer. I've lost. I'm a good-for-nothing. Oh, go ahead and laugh at me.

The king whispered that I should return a little late. The hostage would be dead by then and I could go free, he promised. I hated the king for being so deceitful, but things are turning out his way. I'll probably be late, and he'll just assume he was right. He'll have a good laugh and then let me go. And that will be worse than death. I'll always be a traitor, the lowest of creatures. Selinunteus, I too shall die. Let me die with you. You alone trust me, that's certain. (Or, Melos suddenly wondered, am I merely taking you for granted too?)

Ah, perhaps I should just be a scoundrel. I've got a home in the village and the sheep too. If I live, my sister and her husband will surely welcome me back. Justice, love, fidelity—they're really worthless when you think about it. We kill others to save our own skin—that's the way of the world, isn't it? Oh, nonsense! I'm just a disgraceful traitor. It's all over for you, Melos, you're finished. Go ahead and do as you please.

Stretching his limbs, the hero dozed off.

Melos awoke to the sound of trickling water. Holding his breath, he slowly raised his head. The sound seemed to come from just beyond his outstretched legs. Struggling to his feet, Melos saw clear water bubbling from a rock. He bent over the spring as if drawn down into it. Then he scooped a handful of water and swallowed it. Melos breathed deeply, as though awakening from a dream. He could walk.

He must be off. Perhaps he could still fulfill his pledge and die with honor. The rays of the setting sun still shone on the branches and leaves of the trees. Dusk had not yet fallen, and his friend must be waiting—quietly, trustfully. Compared with that trust, Melos' life meant nothing. He could take his own life to make up for his suspicion, but that would be too simple. He must live up to his friend's trust—that alone mattered. Thereupon he cried out, "Run, Melos!"

Someone trusted him. The evil dream of moments before was a delusion and he must forget it. When exhausted, anyone might have such a dream. Melos' honor was still intact, and he was brave as ever. He figured that if he started running now, he could still arrive on time. How fortunate! He could die honorably, then. But he realized that the sun was going down fast, and soon it would be gone. Oh Zeus, he pleaded, please don't hurry things so much. I grew up loyal, so don't let me die a traitor.

He fled like the very wind, shoving aside or knocking down wayfarers in his path. There was group of revelers picnicking in a meadow too, and Melos ran right through them, leaving everyone bewildered.

He kicked away a dog and hurdled a stream, his pace far exceeding that of the sun. Racing by another group of travelers, he caught an ominous remark—"The fellow should be hanging from the cross about now." Ah, this was the friend for whom Melos ran, the friend who must not die. Hurry, Melos. You mustn't be late. Reveal the power of love and fidelity. Don't worry about your appearance.

Melos's garb had been ripped and torn as he raced along. Now he was almost naked. He could hardly breathe, and blood spurted now and again from his mouth. Then he saw it—the Tower of Syracuse. Small and far off, the tower glittered in the setting sun.

Then a voice seemed to groan in the wind, "Ah, Melos."

"Who is it?" Melos called even as he ran.

"Philostratus, apprentice to your good friend Selinunteus," cried the youth even as he hurried after Melos. "Stop, it's too late. He can't be saved."

"But the sun's not down yet."

"They're putting him to death this very moment. You're too late. What a shame. If you had only been a little faster . . ."

"But the sun's still up," cried Melos, his heart nearly bursting as he stared at the huge, red orb. He knew that he must persevere.

"Stop, please. Don't run any farther. Your life's at stake now. Selinunteus believed in you. He was calm when they led him to the gallows. Even as the king mocked him, he remained faithful. He simply replied, 'Melos will return.'"

"That's why I'm running," Melos retorted, "because he trusts me. It doesn't make any difference whether I'm on time. I'm running for more than a life. Follow me, Philostratus."

"Ah, you must have lost your senses," exclaimed Philostratus. Then he gave in and said, "Well, maybe you won't be late. So keep on running."

This was well said. The sun had not yet disappeared, and Melos ran with his last ounce of strength. His mind was blank; he didn't think of anything. Impelled by a mysterious force, he merely ran. Finally, as the quivering sun dipped beneath the horizon and the twilight began to fade, Melos raced like the wind onto the execution grounds. He was in time.

He tried to cry out, "Wait! Don't execute him! Melos has returned. Here I am, just as I promised." But with his throat so raw, he could barely whisper, and no one heard him. The cross had been raised, and Selinunteus, a rope wound about his body, was being slowly hoisted. Melos plunged into the crowd, struggling forward with all his remaining strength just as he had when he had swum the muddy torrent.

"Hangman, it's me." Though hoarse, Melos cried out as best he could. "I'm the condemned one—Melos. I left Selinunteus as a hostage. Now I'm back."

Finally Melos climbed the platform and caught hold of his friend's ascending feet. A stir ran through the crowd and everyone cried out together, "Hurrah! Let him down."

Selinunteus was freed of his bonds.

With tears in his eyes, Melos addressed his friend. "Strike me, Selinunteus. Strike me with all your might. I had an evil dream on the way back. If you don't strike me, I shall not be worthy to embrace you. Strike me."

Selinunteus nodded as though he understood everything. Then he slapped Melos forcefully on the right cheek, the blow resounding throughout the grounds. Thereupon Selinunteus smiled gently and said, "Strike me, Melos. Strike me on the cheek just as hard. Once during the three days you were away, I lost my trust in you—for the first time ever. If you don't strike me, I won't be able to embrace you."

His hand whizzing through the air, Melos slapped his friend on the cheek.

"Thank you, friend," they both said at the same time. Then they embraced each other firmly and wept with joy. In the crowd too weeping could be heard.

The tyrant Dionysius, who had been gazing from the rear, silently approached the two friends with a look of shame on his face. "You have won me over, and your hopes are fulfilled. Loyalty isn't just a hollow word," he said. "Will you both accept me as a friend? Please listen to this request. I wish to be your friend."

A cheer went up from the crowd. "Long live the King! Long live the King!"

A girl came forward, holding out a scarlet cloak. Melos was confused, so his friend stepped in and said, "Melos, don't you realize you're utterly naked? Hurry up and put the cloak on. This pretty girl doesn't want everyone here seeing you like that."

The hero blushed deeply.

(*From a traditional legend and the Schiller poem*)

OSAN

I

I was in the kitchen cleaning up after supper, but I knew in my very bones that something was amiss. He had tiptoed out the front door as quietly as a soul slipping away. I felt so lonely a plate almost slid from my hand, and a sigh escaped. I stretched slightly and looked out the lattice window to see my husband already in the alley with its border of twisting, intertwining squash vines, a plain narrow sash wrapped about his laundered *yukata* cotton kimono, his back turned unfeelingly this way as he floated off into the summer dusk like an otherworldly spirit.

"Where's Papa going?"

When she asked this innocent question, our oldest daughter of seven was washing her feet by the kitchen door after playing in the garden. She favored her father far more than her mother, and every night she spread her futon next to his in the six-mat room and slept under the same mosquito net as he did.

"To the temple." It was the first thing that came to mind; but once I had spoken, I realized how ominous the words were. I felt a sudden chill.

"The temple? For what?"

"For the Festival of the Dead. He's visiting the graves."

The lie came with incredible ease. Indeed it was the thirteenth, the day of the festival, and all the other neighborhood girls were dressed in pretty kimonos, long sleeves flapping as they romped about the front gate of their parents' homes. The best clothes of my children had gone up in flames during the war. Even for the festival they wore their everyday things.

"Really? Will he be back soon?"

"Hmm, I wonder about that . . . If you're a good girl, Masako, I suppose he will."

From the look of things, however, he was certain to stay out overnight. Masako came into the kitchen, then went to the three-mat room where she sat on the windowsill and gazed mournfully outside. She murmured, "Mama, there's a flower on my bean plant."

I was so touched that tears welled up in my eyes. "Where? Where? Oh, you're right. Soon we'll have lots of beans."

There was a garden plot about twenty yards square near our front door. I used to plant all sorts of vegetables, but I could no longer manage with three children. My husband, who occasionally helped in the past, had ceased to care about any household matter. The man next door carefully tended his garden and raised splendid vegetables of all kinds. Next to his, our garden seemed a shameful patch of weeds. Masako had planted a single bean from our ration and watered it until a sprout emerged. With no toys or anything else, she took pride in this one thing she owned. Even when playing in the neighborhood, she seems to have spread word of the "family bean" over and over without the slightest embarrassment.

Ruin . . . misery . . . Of course, we weren't the only ones affected. No matter where you looked, especially in Tokyo, you could feel the weariness and pain in people. They moved about listlessly, as though tired of life. Our possessions too had gone up in flames and we felt utterly ruined. But something far more threatening than poverty distressed me as the wife of a man engaged in society.

My husband had worked almost ten years for a well-known magazine in the Kanda district of the city. At the time of our ordinary arranged marriage eight years ago, rented housing was becoming scarce. Eventually, in an outlying area on the Chuo Line, we found a small place in the middle of a farm field. We were still living there when the war began.

Since his health was poor, my husband escaped being drafted for the military or for labor. Every day he commuted from our remote home to the magazine office. As the war grew more intense, the airplane factories hereabouts were repeatedly attacked. Late one night, a bomb struck the bamboo grove out back, destroying our three-mat room along with the kitchen and bath. With the birth of our first son, Yoshitaro, there were four of us, too many to continue living together in the partially ruined house. Taking along the two children, I returned to my home in Aomori City while my husband remained in the six-mat room and commuted to work.

In less than four months, however, Aomori itself was bombed to the ground, and the things we had struggled so hard to bring along were all destroyed. With nothing but the clothes we were wearing, the children and I sought refuge in the home of a friend which had escaped the air-raid fires. The next ten days were like hell; I was completely at a loss, a burden to my friend. Then the surrender was announced, and I longed for my husband in Tokyo. I returned to the city with my children, all of us in rags. Since housing was unavailable, we asked a carpenter to do some rough repair work, and the four or us eventually returned to our sequestered life of old.

I was beginning to feel slightly relieved when my husband's luck took a turn for the worse. I was told that the magazine had met with misfortune and that the directors were squabbling over financial matters. When the company was liquidated, my husband lost his job. But he had worked there a long time and had many influential friends. Together they raised enough capital to form a new company. However, after publishing two or three kinds of books, the company took a heavy loss buying paper. My husband wandered off each morning hoping to clear the debt, and returned worn out in the evening. He had always been taciturn, but he now became silent as a stone. He managed to pay off the debt, yet lost thereby the will to go on working. All the same he remained home only for part of the day. For a time he would stand perfectly still on the veranda. There he would puff on his cigarette, ponder things over and ceaselessly stare toward the distant horizon.

"Ah, he's at it again," I would think. And it was always just as I feared. He would let out a sigh as if overcome by his thoughts and toss his half-smoked cigarette into the garden. He then took a purse from the desk drawer and slid it inside his kimono. Next he tiptoed out the front door as quietly as a soul slipping away. This usually meant he would not return that evening.

He was a good husband, a gentle husband. He would drink a half pint of sake or a bottle of beer at the most. He did smoke, but never more than his government ration of cigarettes. During the nearly ten years of our marriage, he never once beat me or reviled me. Yes, there was that one time a guest was visiting, and Masako—she was about two then—crawled over to the man's place and apparently upset his tea. My husband must have called to me, but I was fanning the charcoal fire so intently in the kitchen that I did not hear him. He came in carrying Masako and, with a scowl I have never seen before or since, put the girl down on the wooden floor. Then he stood straight up and for several minutes glared silently at me with murder in his eye. Finally he whirled around and left, slamming the sliding door shut with such violence that I felt the vibration in the marrow of my bones and shuddered to think how menacing a man can be. I don't recall any other time when my husband got angry. Like other people I underwent various hardships during he war; but mindful of my husband's kindness over the years, I consider myself among the fortunate.

When was it, I wondered, that he began turning into a different person? After I returned from four months in Aomori, my husband's smiling face seemed defeated, and he nervously avoided looking me in the eye. Living a hemmed-in life all alone had given him a haggard mien. I felt nothing but pity. Perhaps during these four months . . . but I mustn't dwell on that. The more I think, the deeper I fall into this slough of despair.

So now, with my husband away for the night, I merely laid out his futon next to Masako's and hung up the mosquito net.

II

Shortly before noon the following day, as I was crouching by the well near the front door to wash the diapers of our youngest girl, Toshiko, my husband came creeping along like a burglar anxious to escape detection. He noticed me and bowed slightly, then suddenly tripped and plunged headlong into the house. That he would instinctively bow to me, his own wife—yes, he too must be suffering. My heart filled with pity at the thought, and I could no longer attend to the washing. I stood up and followed him into the house.

"You must be hot. Why not take off your kimono . . . Two bottles of beer came this morning, and I put them on ice. They're rations for Obon, but perhaps you'd like some."

He grinned uncertainly. "How about that," he replied in a hoarse voice, then added, "Shall we have a bottle each?"

This awkward attempt at flattery was quite transparent.

"I'll join you," I said.

I could handle a drink better than my husband, maybe because my father used to drink heavily. Right after our marriage, my husband and I would walk about Shinjuku together and drop into the bars. His face would soon turn red, and he would be finished for the night. Except for a strange ringing in the ears, I didn't feel a thing.

The children joined us in the three-mat room for lunch. Having removed his kimono, my husband draped a wet towel around his neck and sat down with a beer. I drank a glass to keep him company, but refrained from wasting any more. When I gave my breast to Toshiko, who was still an infant, the picture of domestic bliss seemed complete. The tension, however, did not go away. My husband avoided my eyes, and I could not speak freely to him for fear of touching a raw nerve. Masako and Yoshitaro sensed there was something wrong between us, so they remained very quiet as they dipped their steamed buns into tea.

"A drink for lunch gets to you right away," my husband ventured.

"Yes, just look at you—red all over."

Then I saw it—a purple moth clinging to the skin beneath his throat. No, this was not a moth. A memory came back from the early days of my marriage, and I winced at the moth-like bruise. At that moment my husband too seemed to realize I was aware of the bite mark. He hurriedly covered it under the corner of the moist towel, a towel meant to hoodwink me from the very beginning. I tried my best to go along with him and I said, "Masako likes her bun better when she can eat with Papa, doesn't she?"

Even this jest sounded like a criticism. The tension inside me had reached breaking point when the radio next door began playing "The Marseillaise."

My husband listened attentively.

"Ah yes, it is Bastille Day." He spoke as if to himself and

quietly laughed. Then he resumed, partly for Masako and partly for me. "The fourteenth of July . . . today . . . the revolution . . ." He stopped, his mouth awry and tears in his eyes. He fought to keep from crying before proceeding in a voice choked with emotion.

"It was the Bastille they attacked . . . the prison. The people rose up from all over, and that was it for the party at Versailles. It was over and done, gone forever. They had to destroy it. They understood that a new ethic, a new order, could never be built. And yet they had to destroy the old one. Even as he died, Sun Yat-sen claimed the revolution in China was not over. A revolution never is, I suppose. But we've got to start them. They're sad and beautiful in their nature. That's what comes of a revolution—beauty, sadness, and . . . love . . ."

"The Marseillaise" played on and my husband wept even as he spoke. Finally, in his embarrassment, he tried to laugh away the tears. "Well, look at this. The old man's begun to cry in his cups." Turning away, he stood up and went into the kitchen. There he splashed water on his face. "Damn, I've drunk too much already—weeping over the French Revolution. I need a nap." He went into the six-mat room. The house fell quiet, but surely he continued his silent weeping.

He was not weeping over the revolution, not at all. But there seemed to be a close similarity between family love and the revolution. The elegant court and the peaceful home must be destroyed because both were sad and beautiful. I understood this man's pain perfectly. For I loved my husband, if not so intensely as the Osan of the famous old story loved hers.

> Does a demon reside in a woman's breast?
> Ah, does a viper there reside?

Revolution and nihilism have nothing to offer; they pass by oblivious to the lament of an abandoned wife. She can do nothing but sigh forlornly in her perennial place. What will come of this? Must I be submissive? Merely trust in heaven and pray my husband's affection will change direction with the wind? Having borne three children, I can hardly leave now.

After two nights out, even my husband would stay home. When supper ended, he played with the children on the veranda, trying to win their favor with servile compliments. "My, aren't we getting chubby," he cooed, awkwardly cradling our infant daughter. "And so pretty too."

"She is sweet, isn't she?" I responded casually. "When you're watching a child, don't you want to live a long time?"

Instantly he gave me an odd look and muttered something or other. I felt startled and ashamed.

As usual when he was home, my husband spread the futons for Masako and himself in the six-mat room and hung the mosquito net by eight o'clock. Although she still wanted to play with him, he dressed Masako in her pajamas and put her to bed. Then he too lay down and turned off the light. Everything was quiet after that.

I put our other children to bed in the four-and-a-half-mat room and sewed until eleven o'clock. After hanging up the mosquito net, I lay down between these two small ones. I could not sleep and neither could my husband in the next room. Hearing him sigh, I could not help sighing in return as I recalled Osan's words.

> Does a demon reside in a woman's breast?
> Ah, does a viper there reside?

When my husband came into the room, I turned rigid.
"What happened to the sleeping pills?" he asked.
"I took all of them last night. But they didn't do any good."
"They won't work if you take too many. Six is just right."
He seemed rather moody.

III

The heat continued day after day. What with that and my other worries, I could barely swallow my food. My cheekbones became prominent and the milk in my breasts turned thin. My husband too seemed to lose his appetite, and his sunken eyes had a terrible glitter to them.

Once he let out a snicker as if to mock himself. He added, "I'd rather go crazy and be done with it."

"I feel the same."

"But good people shouldn't have to suffer. I really admire people like you. How do you stay so upright and serious? Maybe there's a clear difference from the start between those who are born to make it in the world and those who are not."

"No, we're just dull, that's all. Only . . ."

"Only . . . ?"

He stared at me as if he were truly insane. I stuttered a moment, unable to speak of what actually frightened me. I managed to say, "Only when you suffer, I do too."

"What? That's all?" He smiled as though greatly relieved.

At long last I felt refreshed and happy. I knew I could be happy just by making him comfortable. Morality didn't count for a thing. One had to relax, that was enough.

Late that night I crawled under his mosquito net. "It's okay," I insisted, "I don't have anything in mind." I lay down next to him.

"*Excuse me*," he jested in English, his voice quite hoarse. He got up halfway and sat on the futon with his legs crossed. "Don't bother, don't bother," he went on, in a sort of English.

The summer moon was full that night. Four or five narrow rays came through the crevices of the shutters and filtered past the mosquito net onto my husband's thin, bare chest.

"You've lost some weight," I teased, sitting up on the futon.

"So have you. From worrying too much, I suppose."

"No. Didn't I just say I don't have anything in mind? It's

all right. Because I'm a clever one. Only, you gotta be nice to me now 'n' then."

His teeth glinted in the moonlight as he laughed along with me. I had told him soon after we married of my grandparents and their frequent quarrels. Though still a child when they died, I could remember how Grandmother invariably exclaimed during their fights, "You gotta be nice to me now 'n' then." The line had amused me as a child, and my husband and I would burst out laughing whenever I mimicked it.

This time he laughed a moment, then looked grave. "I try to do right by you, to keep the wind away. I do try to do right by you. You're a good person. Be proud and don't bother about trifles. Please take things easy. I always think only of you. You can be more confident of that than of anything else."

He spoke with such deadly seriousness that I was thrown off balance.

With my head bowed, I whispered, "But you've changed so much."

I would be relieved, I said to myself, if you didn't keep me in mind, if you disliked or even hated me. It's hell to imagine you're aware of me while embracing another woman. A man considers it noble to be ever mindful of his wife, but isn't he mistaken? Must he consider himself good and upright not to forget his wife even if he finds another woman to love? And, when he starts agonizing over a new love and the melancholic sighs emerge even in front of his wife, she too becomes infected by his mood and begins to sigh too. If the husband were merely blithe and casual about the affair, his wife would be spared this hell. If there's someone else, please forget about your wife and love the other woman— simply and innocently.

My husband laughed lightly, breaking into my reverie. "Me? Changed? I haven't changed at all. It's been so warm lately. I can't take it. This summer's . . . well, *excuse me please.*"

Again that English phrase. I could do nothing about it, so I too laughed a moment and said, "You're impossible."

I made as if to hit him, then slipped out from the mosquito net. I returned to my own room and lay down between the two children.

But having coaxed my husband to laugh and talk even a little, I felt content. The tension within me eased somewhat and, for the first time in a long while, I slept through to morning untroubled by any worries.

Thereafter I always took this light approach. I played up to my husband and joked with him, little caring that he was deceiving me. I didn't bother about right or wrong. I only hoped for a brief respite, an hour or so of contentment. We had reached the stage where I could occasionally pinch him and hear his laughter echoing through the house. Then one morning my husband suddenly announced that he wished to go to a hot spring.

"It's that place in Nagano," he said, "where one of my friends is living. He told me to come anytime and not to trouble about food. This heat is giving me a constant headache, and I need to rest for two or three weeks. I'll go crazy in Tokyo, I've got to escape."

Did he wish to escape from her? Is that why he's making this trip, I wondered.

"What should I do if a burglar comes in with a pistol while you're away?" I laughed about it, but wondered even as I spoke why sad people are said to laugh often.

"Tell him your husband's crazy. An armed burglar's no match for a lunatic."

There was no reason to oppose the trip, so I looked in the closet for my husband's summer suit. When I could not find it, I felt myself turning pale. "Your linen suit's not here. What happened to it? Did a prowler get in while we were away?"

"I sold it." My husband gave me a mournful smile.

I was taken aback, but still managed to appear calm. "Well, that was fast work."

"Better than any burglar."

I realized the woman was behind his surreptitious need for money. "What will you wear, then?"

"A sports shirt will do."

He was ready to leave by noon that very day. He seemed anxious to be off as soon as possible, but a shower—unusual during a Tokyo heat wave—delayed his departure. With his shoelaces tied and a rucksack over his shoulder, he sat in the doorway frowning impatiently. Then he mumbled all of a sudden, "Does a myrtle bloom every other year?"

The myrtle by our front entrance had not bloomed this summer.

"I guess so." That was the last thing I said to him.

When the shower ended, he virtually fled the house. Three days later a brief notice appeared in the newspaper: my husband and his mistress had drowned themselves in Lake Suwa. His final letter, posted from the inn by the lake, reached me in due time.

"I'm not dying with this woman for love," the letter began. "I'm a journalist, the sort of man who stirs up rebellion and slips away to wipe his brow once the devastation begins. A strange creature, the journalist, really the Satan of our time. I so detest myself that I've decided to take up the cross of a revolutionary. A journalist caught in a scandal—unheard of, isn't it? But if my death serves to shame Satan a bit and prompts him to look within, I shall be content."

And so it went, a stupid trivial letter. Must a man cling so proudly to his so-called values? Must he tell lies and strike poses to the very end?

From one of my husband's friends I learned that the woman was twenty-seven years old and a reporter for the magazine in Kanda. During my absence she had often stayed at our house.

Now that she was pregnant . . . Well, that's the whole story. Regardless of the fuss about dying a revolutionary death or whatever, the man was simply a loser.

Revolutions are supposed to make life easier, and I don't trust a revolutionary who pulls a long face. Why couldn't he love the woman joyfully and openly, so that I could be happy? When a husband's love for his mistress becomes a hell for him, the wife is the first bystander to be affected.

A nimble adjustment of feeling—that's a genuine revolution. There's nothing difficult if one can manage this. As I headed for Suwa with the children to claim the body, I was more appalled than I was sad or angry—appalled at the utter stupidity of a husband who, unable to adjust his feelings, thought revolution a terrible cross to be borne.

MONKEY ISLAND

I magine how bleak those early moments were. I had come all the way across the sea, and the island was shrouded in mist. Was it night? Or day? I couldn't even tell as I blinked my eyes and tried to look the place over. Finally I made out some large, bare rocks heaped upon one another to form a steep slope. Here and there, among the rocks, the dark mouth of a cave loomed. Could this really be a mountain? Without even one blade of grass?

I made my way along the beach at the foot of the slope. A strange cry reached my ears now and then—and not from far off, either. Was it a wolf? Or maybe a bear? I was exhausted after the long voyage, but that only stiffened my will. Ignoring the cries, I followed the path that ran along the beach.

I was amazed at the monotony of the place. No matter how far I walked, the path went on and on. The mountain was on my right, with a vertical wall of rough, pebbly stones on the left. Between them ran the path, six feet wide and utterly bare. As long as it continued, I would keep on going. I was too tired and confused for words, but that made me absolutely fearless.

I must have come about a mile when I found myself back where I had started. Only then did I realize that the path merely went around the foot of the mountain. But hadn't I passed by this very spot even after I started out? Of course. I must have gone around twice without realizing it. So the island was smaller than I had first imagined.

The mist was gradually lifting, and the mountaintop now seemed to press directly upon my brow. Irregular in shape, the mountain had three different ridges. The middle one was a mound, maybe thirty or forty feet high. This mound sloped gently on one side toward a ridge below; on the opposite side, it dropped off sharply until, about halfway down, it bulged out into another ridge. In the gap between the cliff and this ridge, a waterfall descended straight down. The rocks on this misty island were dark with moisture, especially those that were by the waterfall. There was a tree at the crest of the falls that looked like an evergreen oak. Another tree stood on top of the bulging ridge, but I had never seen anything like it before. Both of the trees were bare.

For a time I gazed at this desolate scene in utter amazement. The mist kept lifting until sunlight fell upon the high middle ridge, making its wet surface glisten. This was the morning sun, no doubt about it. I can tell morning from evening because of the difference in fragrance. Had the dawn finally arrived then?

Somewhat revived, I started to scramble up the mountain. The slope had looked steep from the bottom, but it was easy to climb. I found one foothold after another and soon reached the crest of the falls.

Here the morning sun came directly down, and a gentle breeze played upon my cheek. I went over to the tree that had seemed an evergreen oak and sat down. Was it really an evergreen oak? Or a Japanese oak instead? Maybe it was a fir? I looked up past the twigs to the treetop. Thin, dead branches stood out against the sky all along the trunk, with most of the lower ones roughly broken off. Should I climb up?

> The blowing snow
> Is calling me.

That sound was probably the wind. I found myself shinnying up the trunk.

> Calling me
> From captivity.

One hears all kinds of singing when exhausted. Reaching the tip, I swung back and forth on a withered-looking branch.

> Calling me
> From a wretched life.

Suddenly the branch snapped. Grabbing the trunk, I slid down recklessly.

"You busted it! Damn you!"

I definitely heard this, from somewhere above. Clinging to the tree trunk, I stood up and gazed in the direction of the voice. Instantly a shiver ran down my spine. From the gleaming, sunlit cliff a lone monkey was nimbly making his way down. At that moment the rage that I had kept down suddenly flared up.

"C'mon," I bellowed, "all the way down too! I broke it. If you want a fight, I'm ready."

He had reached the bottom of the cliff. "That's my tree," he said, coming toward the waterfall. I stood my ground, but he merely wrinkled his forehead. While gazing at me, he seemed dazzled by the sun. Finally he broke into a broad grin and laughed aloud. The laugh irked me.

"What's so funny?"

"You," he replied. "I'll bet you came here from across the sea, didn't you?"

"Yep," I remarked, nodding. My gaze remained on the crest of the falls where the water kept billowing wave upon wave. I was thinking of the long sea voyage in the small wooden crate.

"I mean the wide sea, whatever it's called."

"Yep." I nodded once more.

"Just like me, then."

After uttering these words, he scooped some water from the falls and drank it. In a few moments we were sitting side by side.

"We're from the same neck of the woods. One look and you can tell. It's the glossy ears. All the fellows from there have them."

He seized my ear and pinched it hard. Angrily I knocked his hand away. Then we looked at one another and broke out laughing. For some reason I felt relaxed.

Suddenly a shriek went up nearby. Startled, I looked around. A flock of hairy, thick-tailed monkeys were standing guard atop a mound and screaming at us. I leapt up.

"Hey, calm down! They're not looking for a fight. We call them howlers. They face the sun and howl like that every morning."

I kept standing, dumbfounded. Monkeys had gathered on each ridge, bending down to bask in the sun.

"Are they all monkeys?" I might have been dreaming.

"That's right. Not the same as us, though. They're from a different woods."

I looked closely at the monkeys, one by one: a mother nursing a baby, her fluffy, white fur ruffling in the wind; a crooner humming a tune, his large, red nose lifted toward the sky; a lover mounting his mate in the sun, his gorgeously striped tail wagging; a frowning malcontent busily striding about.

"Where could this be?" I whispered.

His eyes filled with compassion as he said, "I don't know, either. It doesn't seem like Japan, though."

"Hmm," I wondered, letting out a sigh. "But look at this tree—it's like the Kiso oak."

He turned around and rapped the trunk of the withered tree. Then he looked all the way to the tip.

"No, it isn't. The branches are different. And the bark on this one doesn't reflect the sun, does it? Of course, we can't really tell until the buds come out."

I stood there leaning against the withered tree. Then I asked, "Why aren't there any buds?"

"It's been withered all spring, ever since I got here. Let's see, April, May, June—that's three months now. It just gets more and more shriveled. Maybe it's a cutting; there certainly aren't any roots. The tree beyond is even worse—it's covered all over with their dung."

He pointed at the howlers as he said this. They had ceased their howling, and the island had become quiet.

"Why don't you sit down. Let's talk this over." I sat down right next to him. "It's not a bad spot—the best on this island, at least. Plenty of sunshine here, and the tree too. And there's the sound of water, besides."

He glanced contentedly toward the cascade at his feet and went on talking. "I'm from northern Japan, near the Tsugaru Strait. From my birthplace you can just hear the waves breaking in the night. Waves—ah, there's a sound that really grows on you. It's just unforgettable."

I wanted to speak about my home. "I was born in the mountains, right in the middle of Japan. For me, it's the woods rather than the sound of waves. I'll take the smell of fresh leaves anytime."

"That's right! We all yearn for the woods. That's why every fellow on this island wants to settle down near a tree—just one will do."

As he spoke, he parted the hair in his crotch, revealing a number of large, dark-red scars.

"It took some doing to make this place mine."

I thought I'd better be off. "Sorry, I didn't realize it was yours . . ."

"That's all right. I don't mind. You see, I'm all alone here. There's room for you, though. Just make sure you don't break any more branches, okay?"

The mist had disappeared entirely, and a fantastic scene lay before us. Fresh leaves—that's the first thing I noticed. I realized this was exactly the season when the oak leaves back home were at their peak. Nodding with pleasure, I gazed ecstatically upon a row of trees with their fresh leaves. But not for long. Another amazing sight opened up below the branches. There, on a gravel path sprinkled with fresh water, human beings were streaming past. They had blue eyes and were dressed in white. The women wore gaudy feathers in their bonnets while the men waved their heavy snakeskin canes and smiled hither and thither.

I was already trembling when my partner gave me a reassuring hug and quickly whispered, "Easy, now. It's like this every day."

"What's going to happen? They're all looking for us."

I remembered the whole ordeal—from my capture in the mountains to when I arrived on this island. I bit my underlip.

"They're putting on a show," he quickly remarked. "Just for us. Quiet down, now, and we'll have fun."

Once again he slipped his arm about me. Then, waving his other arm toward this person or that, he spoke to me in a whisper. "That one's a wife," he began, "and she knows only two ways to live—either she's the husband's boss or else his toy. I've heard this strange word belly button, and I often wonder if people use it with someone like her in mind. There's a scholar," he went on, "a creature who earns his bread by footnoting a dead genius or sniping at a living one. Just looking at the likes of him will make you drowsy." He pointed to an actress next, calling her an old hag. He told me how she played her own life more dramatically than any stage role. He groaned with exaggeration then, and he said, "Oh, how this back tooth of mine hurts! And there," he continued, "goes a landlord, a coward who always grumbles about how hard he works. Whenever you see him, you feel as though lice are crawling along the bridge of your nose. And over there, sitting on that bench and wearing white gloves—he's the worst one of all. Look at him! All I can say is, when he shows up, the air seems to smell like yellow shit."

I listened to his chatter half-heartedly, for something else had caught my attention. For some time now, two children had been peeping at the island, their faces just above the pebbly wall. They had a greedy look about them, and their clear blue eyes seemed on fire. Both must have been boys, with short blond hair that riffled in the breeze. One had dark freckles on his nose, while the other had cheeks fresh as peach blossoms.

Presently the boys cocked their heads, as if thinking something over. Then the freckled one pursed his lips and whispered excitedly into the ear of his friend. I seized my companion and shrieked, "What's he saying? Tell me! What're those kids talking about?"

The monkey seemed to be stunned. He stopped jabbering right away, then looked back and forth between the boys and me. Lost in thought, he twisted his mouth this way and that as though he was greatly troubled. Even after the boys spat out some words or other and disappeared behind the wall, he remained hesitant, his hand touching his forehead one moment and scratching his rump the next. At last, the corner of his mouth twisted in a cynical grin. "Those boys," he slowly drawled, "were grumbling how everything's the same whenever they come."

Finally, I caught on—everything's the same. My suspicions, which I had kept to myself until now, were right on target. If they were complaining, then we were putting on the show.

"I see. You lied to me before, didn't you." I could have thrashed him on the spot.

His arm tightened about my waist and he replied, "The truth is cruel."

I sprang upon his enormous breast, disgusted at his concern for me. I was even more ashamed of my own stupidity.

"Stop your whimpering. It won't do any good." Then, gently patting my back, he went on in a weary voice. "There's a long, narrow signboard over there. You see it, sticking above the stone wall? The back side is facing this way—just a piece of weatherbeaten wood. But the other side's got something written on it. Maybe it says, 'The Japanese monkey, known for its glossy ears.' Or else, something even more humiliating."

I didn't want to hear any more. I let go of him and raced over to the withered tree. Scrambling all the way up the trunk, I caught hold of a branch and looked out over the entire island. The sun was already high, and patches of haze were forming here and there. Beneath the blue sky, at least a hundred monkeys basked peacefully in the sun. He remained crouched near the waterfall, but I shouted down to him anyway, "None of them realize?"

Without looking up, he replied, "Them? Probably just you and me."

"Can't we make a run for it?"

"You want out?"

"I'm going," I insisted. The green leaves, the gravel path and the stream of people rushed before my eyes.

"You're not scared?"

He shouldn't have said that. I shut my eyes tight, trying to block out his words.

In the breeze caressing my ears, there echoed a low, melodic voice. Was he singing? My eyes grew warm. It was the very song that had brought me down from the tree before. I closed my eyes and listened.

"No, no. Come down. It's lovely here. There's sunshine and trees. You can hear the sound of water. Best of all, there's no worry about where your next meal's coming from."

I heard his voice as if from afar. And also the low laugh that followed.

Ah, how tempting it was. And close to the truth as well. Maybe it was the truth. Something almost collapsed within me. And yet, the stirring—the stirring of my mountain blood— would not be quelled.

I wouldn't stay!

A bulletin from London Zoo was issued in mid-June, 1896. A break had occurred at Monkey Island. Two Japanese monkeys, not merely one, had escaped. Both of them, the bulletin concluded, remain at large.

A POOR MAN'S
GOT HIS PRIDE

Long ago in Edo, in a thatched hovel near the Wisteria Teahouse at Shinagawa, there lived a huge, middle-aged man named Harada Naisuke. With his thick, fearsome beard and bloodshot eyes, Harada seemed quite menacing. But men of his type are sometimes so intimidated by their own grandeur that they turn into cowards. Despite a magnificent countenance—his eyebrows were bushy and his eyes glaring—Harada was utterly worthless. While fencing with an opponent, he would shut his eyes and let out a weird shriek. Then he'd charge in the wrong direction, shouting "Your match, I concede," as he slammed into the nearest wall. His reputation as "The Wall-banger" got a boost every time this happened.

On one occasion, a young peddler beguiled Harada with a hard-luck story. Harada started to blubber as the story unfolded, then bought up the fellow's entire batch of clams. Back home, he got a scolding from his wife, and for the next three days he ate clams—nothing but clams—for breakfast, lunch and supper. They gave him such painful cramps that he rolled about on the floor clutching his stomach. Opening his Confucian *Analects* for consolation, he started dozing after the first few words, "Learning is . . ."

Harada abhorred caterpillars. One look and he would let out a scream, his fingers spread apart as he backed away. Easily swayed by flattery, he seemed as if possessed by a fox whenever someone paid him a compliment. After fidgeting for a time, he would race to the pawnshop, trade something for cash and treat his flatterer to a meal.

Every New Year's Eve, Harada would drink from early in the morning and pretend that he was going to disembowel himself, all this just to keep the bill collectors at bay. His thatched hovel, incidentally, did not represent an aesthetic preference. No, the house was merely falling apart from age. Harada was indolent and penniless, his life unadorned by either flowers or fruit; he was a lone samurai, a ronin who merely embarrassed his relatives.

Luckily for Harada, two or three of these relatives were rich, and he could turn to them in a pinch. But, since he mostly squandered their largesse on drinking, Harada was always in trouble. What were the spring cherry blossoms and the autumn colors to him? Mired in poverty, he was oblivious to such things. After all, one might get by without cherry blossoms or fall foliage, but one surely could not pretend year after year to be unaware of New Year's Eve. Still, as the year's end drew near once more, Harada Naisuke imparted a mad look to his eyes and pretended to be crazy. Fumbling his long, unavailing sword, he let out that eerie chuckle—heh-heh—that made the bill collectors nervous.

It might be New Year's Day tomorrow, but Harada didn't bother to wipe the soot from the ceiling nor to trim his beard. He even left his wafer-thin futon lying unfolded on the floor. When he muttered pathetically, "If you want me, come and get me," to the bill collectors, he seemed feeble and delirious. And afterward, he again broke into that eerie chuckle.

Having witnessed this nightmare year after year, Harada's wife could bear it no longer. She went out the kitchen door and ran all the way to Kanda, where her older brother, a physician named Nakarai Seian, lived in a lane by the Myojin Shrine. Rushing into the house, she wept over her plight and begged for help. Though exasperated by these constant troubles, Seian still retained his sense of humor. "Every family has a fool," he jested. "Just to keep it in touch with reality." Then he wrapped up ten coins and wrote on the cover: Poverty Pills. To Be Taken As Often As Needed.

His unfortunate sister took the package and returned home. When she showed the Poverty Pills to Harada, he surprised her by frowning instead of rejoicing. Then, in a rasping voice, he came out with the most ridiculous statement ever—"I can't use this money."

His startled wife wondered whether her husband wasn't truly going mad. But that wasn't really the problem. It was merely that a ne'er-do-well such as Harada will bungle things whenever good fortune smiles upon him. People like him become fidgety and sheepish at the sudden appearance of fortune. They quibble over this and that, then get angry and drive off the luck that has befallen them.

"Good luck brings bad," Harada declared, a somber look on his face. "I might die if I spend this money." Then, glaring at his wife with bloodshot eyes, he asked, "Are you trying to kill me?" Finally he grinned and said, "No, you're not a she-devil, I guess. Well, maybe a drink will help. I'll die if I don't have a drink. Look, it's starting to snow outside. That reminds me—I haven't had my elegant friends in for a while. You go around right this minute and ask them to come over. There's Yamazaki, Kumai, Utsugi, Otake, Iso, Tsukimura—six of them in all. Oh, one more, Tankei the priest. That makes seven. Now hurry up and invite them—and stop at the sake shop on the way back. We'll take whatever snacks they've got."

So the earlier fuss didn't mean anything. Harada was so tickled that he wanted a drink, that was all.

Yamazaki, Kumai, Utsugi, Otake, Iso, Tsukimura, Tankei—all ex-samurai now living in poverty in nearby tenements. When the invitation to the snow-viewing party at Harada's arrived, they felt like sinners in hell blessed by the Buddha's mercy—now each one of them could escape the torment of staying home on New Year's Eve. After smoothing the wrinkles of a garment fashioned from paper, one of the men poked his head into his closet. Wasn't there an umbrella around? Or socks? Pulling together various odds and ends, he proceeded to outfit himself in a more presentable cotton kimono and a warrior's jacket. Another, with the excuse that he didn't want to catch cold, put on five unlined kimonos and wrapped his neck in an old cotton scarf. Yet another turned his wife's padded silk kimono inside out and rolled up the sleeves to change their shape. Still another donned a riding skirt over a short undergarment, then put on a formal summer jacket with an embroidered crest. Another hitched a quilted cloak about his waist, his hairy shins exposed and fluffy cotton sticking from the torn hem of the garment.

As it turned out, even though none of them were properly dressed, the fact that they were all ex-samurai gave a special touch to their camaraderie. Thus, when they gathered at Harada's home, there wasn't a single condescending smile to be seen. They greeted one another with dignity, and, after each had taken his proper place, old Yamazaki rose in his warrior's jacket and cotton kimono. Solemnly approaching Harada the host, Yamazaki dwelt at length on how grateful they all were to have been invited.

Though uneasy about the tear in the sleeve of his own paper-thin garment, Harada formally saluted his friends in return. "Welcome, each and every one of you. I thought you would like spending New Year's Eve away from home. Having neglected each of you for such a long time, I am especially pleased that you could all make it to this snow-viewing party even on such short notice. Please make yourselves at home," he added, urging them to eat and drink, humble though the fare might be.

One of the guests started trembling all over as he picked up his sake cup. Asked what the trouble was, he wiped his tears and said, "Oh, it's nothing really. I've been off sake for quite a while—couldn't afford it. I hate to admit it, but I've forgotten how to drink." Then he smiled rather lamely.

"It's the same with me," said the guest in the riding skirt and short undergarment, edging forward on his knees. "I've had just two or three cups in a row and already I'm feeling strange. What should I do next? I don't remember how to get drunk."

Everyone seemed to be thinking the same thing, for the men merely whispered to one another as they passed their cups back and forth. Things went on quietly for a time; but presently everyone seemed to remember how drinking was carried on. As the room grew lively with laughter, Harada Naisuke brought out the paper in which the ten coins were wrapped.

"I've got something unusual to show you," he began. "The rest of you swear off drinking and live a frugal life when your purse is empty. That's why even if you're in a bind on New Year's Eve, you're not likely to be tormented like old Harada. When I'm in a pinch, I want a drink even more. That's the way I am, and so the debts keep piling up. Every time the year comes to an end, I feel like I'm staring right into the Eight Hells. So I'm forced to set aside all this business about samurai honor and run weeping for help to my relatives. It's a disgrace. This year a relative came up with these ten coins—just in time for me to welcome in the New Year like other people. But good luck brings bad—I know that much. So I'd probably die if I kept this bounty for myself. That's why I decided to invite all of you here for some drinking." Harada was in a good mood, and the entire company breathed a sigh of relief. Several of the men expressed their feelings forthrightly.

"What the hell!" one of them exclaimed. "If I'd known from

the start, I wouldn't have held back. I thought Harada would ask for a donation. Wasn't much fun drinking with that on my mind."

"We know better now," another chimed in, "so let's drink up. Maybe Harada's luck will rub off on me. There could be a registered letter at my home—from somewhere unexpected."

Then another cohort spoke up. "You people with the right sort of relatives have it made," he began, "but with me it's the other way around. They all take aim at my purse. Humph!"

Eventually the company became lively and cheerful, much to Harada's delight. Wiping a drop of sake from the tip of his beard, he came out with a suggestion. "How about holding these coins in your hand for a while. They're quite heavy, but perhaps you'd like me to pass them around. Don't regard them as filthy lucre. Look, it says right here on the paper—Poverty Pills. To Be Taken As Often As Needed. He's quite a wit, that relative of mine. He wrote this and sent it over. Well, go ahead and hand the coins around."

Harada virtually forced the ten coins upon his guests. Each man was surprised by their weight and impressed by the clever inscription. As the money went around, one guest exclaimed that a verse had come to mind. Borrowing a brush and ink-stone, he wrote on the blank part of the wrapping: *He takes his Poverty Pills as the snow glistens*. This made the guests even more merry, and cups of sake were exchanged in a flurry.

When the coins finally came back to Harada, old Yamazaki sat up straight. A discerning look in his eye, he turned to the host and said, "Ah, thanks to you, I've forgotten my years and remained here longer than I expected." But Yamazaki did not stop with this expression of gratitude. Although he had wrapped his throat with an old cotton cloth for fear that he was catching a cold, he now threw out his chest and began singing a ballad entitled "A Thousand Autumns." Not to be left out, the other guests and the host too marked the rhythm by clapping their hands and tapping lightly upon their knees. When the song had ended, the company gathered the warming pans, the tier boxes, the pickle jars and whatever else happened to be there, took them to the kitchen, and handed everything over to Harada's wife. Whether in olden days or now, samurai breeding will tell; departing birds, as the saying goes, leave no trace.

At the urging of his guests, Harada was casually sweeping together the coins scattered on the floor where he sat when he suddenly turned pale. A coin was missing. Despite his fearsome looks, Harada remained a coward even when he drank. Fretting and fussing as ever about what his guests might think, he decided to act as though nothing had happened and to let even this truly startling discovery pass unnoticed.

"Just a moment," old Yamazaki mentioned, his hand raised. "Isn't there a coin missing?"

"Er . . . no. It's . . ." Harada looked flustered, like a criminal caught in the act. "It's . . . well . . . I spent one of the coins at the sake shop—before any of you arrived. When I passed them around earlier, there were only nine left. There's nothing wrong."

Yamazaki shook his head. "No, that's not true," he insisted, stubborn in his old age. "I held ten coins in my hand before. That's certain. The lamp may be dim, but there's nothing wrong with my eyes."

Once Yamazaki had spoken up, the other six guests all agreed with him. Yes, there certainly had been ten coins. The guests stood up together and, moving the lamp about, searched every corner of the room. The coin, however, did not turn up.

"There's only one thing left to do," Yamazaki said. "I'll strip to my bare skin and prove I'm innocent." He might be emaciated and shriveled, but a shred of samurai spirit still remained in Yamazaki, along with the obstinacy that comes with old age. A poor man's got his pride. To be falsely accused meant undying shame, and Yamazaki was incensed. So he removed his warrior's jacket and shook it out, then proceeded to take off his threadbare cloak. Wearing nothing but a loincloth, he waved the cloak grandly, as though he were casting a net.

"You see for yourselves, don't you?" His face was quite pale.

The other guests could hardly let the matter rest there. Otake stood up next and shook his summer jacket with its embroidered crest. After shaking out his undergarment as well, he removed his riding trousers. That left him without a stitch on, not even a loincloth. Without the least hint of a smile, he turned the trousers upside down and shook them.

The tension in the room was unbearable as Tankei the priest stood up, his kimono tucked about his hips and his hairy shins exposed. Suddenly an angry frown spread over his face, as though he were afflicted with severe stomach pains.

"Aware that my end had come," Tankei began, "I composed a trivial verse to leave behind: *He takes his Poverty Pills as snow glistens.* My friends, there's a coin in my breast pocket, no doubt about that. No need to even shake out the garment. I never dreamed such a disaster might happen. Only a coward would try to explain. This is it!" he cried, stripping to the waist and fingering the hilt of his sword.

With Harada leading the way, the other guests rushed forward and seized Tankei's hand.

"Nobody suspects you. Even though we're poor and live wretched lives, all of us have had a coin at some time or other. The poor are friends in their poverty. We understand how you feel—you'd take your own life to prove you're innocent. But isn't that foolish when no one suspects you?" They tried to calm Tankei, but he grew even more bitter over his misfortune. His grief mounted, and he gnashed his teeth.

"How kind of you to say that," he declared. "I'll cherish your generosity beyond the grave. It's so embarrassing to have a coin in my pocket just when this inquiry occurs. Even though you don't suspect me, the humiliation will remain. I'll be the laughing stock, a blunderer for life. As you all know, one can't live without honor. It doesn't matter that I earned this money yesterday when I sold my Tokujo blade to Juzaemon. He's a foreign-goods dealer in Sakashita, and he gave me a coin and two sen for it. A samurai would be humiliated to make such a foolish plea at this point. I won't say anything, just let me die. If you pity your unfortunate friend, go to Sakashita after I'm gone and discover the truth for yourselves. And see to my wretched corpse, I beg you."

Even as Tankei grasped his sword and struggled on once again, Harada suddenly exclaimed, "Look! There it is."

A coin lay glinting directly under the lamp.

"What the devil. How'd it get down there?"

"Well, it *is* dark right alongside the lampstand."

"Lost articles turn up in the most obvious places. But it's important to take the usual precautions." This last remark came from Yamazaki.

"Ah, what a fuss over one coin. Sobered me up completely. Let's have another round," Harada suggested.

The group was talking again and doubling over with laughter when Harada's wife cried out from the kitchen, "There it is!" In a moment she came bustling into the parlor. "The coin—it's right here," she exclaimed, holding out a tier-box lid. When they saw the glinting coin resting on the lid, the men looked at one another in utter astonishment. Harada's wife pushed a stray hair from her flushed brow and smiled sheepishly. Then she explained what must have happened. When she had brought in the boiled potatoes, her careless husband must have placed the steaming lid of the pot right on the floor mat. She herself had picked up the lid and placed it beneath the tier-box, without noticing the coin was stuck to the underside. After serving the meal, she had returned to the kitchen. Preparing to wash the pots and pans, she heard a tinkling sound—and there was the coin.

She finished her tale, already out of breath. Now that there were eleven coins, the host and the guests could only gaze in suspicion at one other.

After a moment's hesitation, Yamazaki let out a sigh and remarked somewhat pointlessly, "Ah, another stroke of luck. Congratulations. Sometimes ten coins turn into eleven. It happens often. Keep it."

The other guests were amazed at this absurd explanation. Nonetheless, they all realized that urging Harada to keep the coin was the wisest course. Several of them spoke up, endorsing Yamazaki's suggestion.

"You should hang on to it," one of them said. "Your relative must have sent eleven coins in the wrapping."

"That's right. Since he's supposed to be such a wit, he probably pretended it was ten coins, then played a joke by giving you eleven."

"Yes, of course. It might be an unusual trick, but it was clever of him. You should keep it." They spoke this drivel in an attempt to force the coin on Harada. Yet, for perhaps the only time in his life, this timid and worthless boozer, Harada Naisuke, revealed an obstinate streak.

"You won't persuade me, no matter what. So don't poke fun at me. You'll pardon me for pointing out that I'm as poor as the rest of you. I was lucky, though, and received the ten coins. I felt guilty before heaven because of that, and toward all of you as well. I couldn't relax—I just had to have a drink. It was so unbearable that I invited all of you here to get rid of this undeserved fortune. Now disaster has struck again. Don't force this extra coin on someone who has too much already. Harada Naisuke may be poor, but there's something of the old samurai in him still. I don't want money or anything. Take the ten coins and go on home, every one of you. And don't forget the extra coin, either."

Truly Harada expressed his anger in a strange manner.

When he stands to gain, even if it's only a trifle, the faint-hearted man becomes so perplexed that he cringes and sweats. But he seems transformed when threatened with a loss, mustering fine-sounding arguments and striving to deprive himself. He won't listen to reason, either; he just keeps on quibbling. As the saying goes, pull in your belly and your rump sticks out—and it works the same way with self-respect. Shaking his head, the desperate Harada stammered on about this and that, blindly sticking to his opinion.

"Don't make fun of me. Ten coins turning into eleven—a nasty joke if there ever was one. But it's not funny anymore. One of you couldn't bear to see Tankei in distress. Whoever it was happened to have a coin, so he slipped it under the lamp to solve this crisis. A cheap trick, really. My coin stuck to the lid of the tier-box. And the one under the lamp was put there out of compassion. It doesn't make sense to force the coin on me. Do you think I want it that much? A poor man's got his pride. I said it before, but just when I'm feeling guilty about the ten coins and disgusted with everything, you try to force another coin on me. Have the gods deserted me? When the battle fortunes of a samurai fall this far, he can't save his honor even by cutting open his belly. I may be a drunken fool, but I'm not a complacent dotard. You can't make me believe that coins produce children. Now, will whoever put the coin there please take it back."

With his generally fearsome look, Harada became truly awesome when he sat straight up and spoke in earnest. The whole company cowered and remained silent.

"Come, speak up," Harada declared. "A man of compassion did this, and I would be happy to serve under him my entire life. On New Year's Eve, when even a penny means so much, this man dropped a coin next to the lamp. He did it secretly, to save Tankei's skin. Poor men are brothers, and he couldn't bear to watch Tankei suffer. So he slipped this coin onto the floor.

One of you did this fine deed, and Harada Naisuke admires you for it. Come, speak up. Tell us who you are."

By this time, the mysterious benefactor was even less likely to reveal himself. In such a case, Harada Naisuke was no good at all. The seven guests were wide awake and sober, despite having drunk so much. They merely sighed and fidgeted at Harada's words, leaving the matter still unresolved. His blood-shot eyes turned on them, Harada urged time after time that the benefactor speak up. However, when the cock's crow announced the coming of dawn, he finally gave up.

"Excuse me for keeping you here so long," he said. "If the owner of the coin won't speak up, there's nothing we can do about it. I'll put the coin on the tier-box lid and leave it in a corner of the entryway. Then, you gentlemen will please leave, one after the other. The owner should quietly take the coin on his way out. Now, how does this idea strike you?"

Relief evident in their faces, the seven guests all looked up and agreed in unison. For the dim-witted Harada the scheme was brilliant—exactly what the fainthearted man will sometimes devise when working against his own interest.

Pleased with himself, Harada placed the coin squarely on the tier-box lid as everyone watched. Then he took the lid to the entryway. "It's on the far right side of the step," he explained upon his return. "That's the darkest part of the entryway, and no one can see if the coin's there or not. The owner should feel around with his hand and take the coin away without making any noise. The rest of you can just go out. Well then, let's begin—we can start with old Yamazaki. No, no, not like that—close the sliding door all the way, please. Now, after Yamazaki is outside and we can't hear his footsteps any more, the next person should leave."

The seven guests all did as they were told, quietly leaving in strict order. And, after they had gone, Harada's wife went to the entryway with a candle and confirmed that the coin had been removed.

"I wonder who it was?" she uttered, unable herself to understand why a shudder ran up her spine.

"Who knows," Harada replied, looking quite sleepy. "By the way, is the sake all gone?"

Even when fallen from his former glory, a samurai is still someone special. With this thought, Harada's wife went proudly to the kitchen and warmed the remaining sake.

(Based on "Tales from the Provinces," vol. 3, no. 1, "New Year's Eve with Debts Unmet.")

THE MONKEY'S MOUND

Shirasaka Tokuzaemon was the wealthiest man in Dazai Town, the capital of Chikuzen Province. Not only did he have a sake shop that his family had run for generations, he was also blessed with a daughter of unsurpassed beauty. Her name was Oran, and she astonished all who saw her from the time she was six or seven years old. Struck by her appearance, a man might well recall the sniveling countenance of his own daughter and take to drinking in despair.

In her mid-teens at the time of our story, Oran would drape her delicate figure in a long-sleeved kimono, bestowing her radiance upon the neighborhood. The spring sunlight so enhanced her beauty that the girl's mother merely gazed at her in wonder, forgetting what she was about to say to her own daughter. Oran's beauty lent a sweet fragrance to the region well beyond her own neighborhood. Indeed, many men fell in love without even seeing her.

Let's have a look now at our hero, Kuwamori Jiroemon. Heir to a thriving pawnshop run by his family in the district next to that of Tokuzaemon's business, Jiroemon wasn't terribly bad-looking. True, his face was somewhat plain, with his large nose, bushy beard and eyes that tailed downward at the corners. But he seemed honest, and he did have fine teeth and a charming smile. Perhaps that's all he needed. Anyway, something got started when he dropped into the sake shop during a rainstorm. Everyone knows that love is blind and foolish and that you don't judge a book by its cover. Nevertheless, Oran fell in love. That's where our story really begins, with Jiroemon winning the affections of this prized jewel.

While the parents on either side were still ignorant of the affair, Jiroemon confided his hopes to Denroku the fishmonger, a regular customer of his family's pawnshop. He urged Denroku to approach Tokuzaemon and propose a marriage between himself and Oran. Denroku was elated over the idea. Deeply in debt to the pawnshop for some time, he was now being asked to do something that Jiroemon could hardly manage by himself. The pawnshop was in this district, the sake shop in the neighboring one. If Denroku could adroitly negotiate the distance between them, he would end up drinking to his heart's content while postponing the interest payment on his debt too. With this in mind, he looked among the unredeemed clothes in the pawnshop for a fancy outfit. Then, all decked out, he marched into Tokuzaemon's place with such a discriminating air that those who saw him might wonder, Now who could *that* be?

"Heh-heh," Denroku chuckled as he snapped his fan open and shut. He then proceeded to praise the rocks in Tokuzaemon's garden. Watching him, Tokuzaemon felt his flesh crawl. But still he inquired, "Is there anything I can do for you, Sir?"

"Oh, nothing much," Denroku calmly replied. Eventually, however, he got around to speaking of Jiroemon's hopes. "Sir, you own a sake shop while the other party runs a pawnshop. They may be different businesses," he went on, "but they're connected all the same—make for the sake shop, but stop at the pawnshop first; leave a pawnshop and the sake shop's bound to be next." He babbled on in this insolent manner, claiming that the two businesses were related to one another like a doctor and a priest; that their strength was that of a demon armed with a club; that together they could lay the town low.

Denroku strained his wits as never before, and even Tokuzaemon felt tempted by his plea.

"If Mr. Kuwamori is the eldest son and heir, there's no objection on my part. By the way, his religion is . . . ?"

"Well . . . maybe it's . . ." replied Denroku hesitantly. Then he blurted out in desperation, "I'm not positive, but it must be Pure Land."

"Then I refuse," said Tokuzaemon spitefully, his mouth curling with malice. "My family's been in the Lotus sect for years. During my lifetime we've become especially devoted to St. Nichiren, and everyone recites the *Invocation to the Sutra* each morning and evening. I've brought up my daughter that way, so I can't have her marrying into another religion. Incidentally," he testily concluded, "if you're going to play the go-between, you shouldn't come around until you've investigated at least that much."

"But, uh . . . I . . ." Denroku felt the cold sweat on his back. "My people have been in the Lotus sect for years. We recite St. Nichiren's prayer both morning and night. 'All Hail to the Lotus Sutra'—that's how it goes."

"What're you prattling about?" Tokuzaemon retorted. "I'm not marrying my daughter to you. If Mr. Kuwamori is Pure Land, the answer is no. I don't care how much money he has or how good-looking and clever he is. Why, it would be an insult to St. Nichiren. Show me anything worthwhile in that gloomy Pure Land sect. The nerve—asking for my daughter when we've been in the Lotus sect all these years. Just looking at you makes my stomach turn. Off with you, now."

Having retreated from the fray, Denroku carried the sad news back to Jiroemon. Unperturbed, the latter merely remarked, "Oh, religion's nothing to fret about. My family can

switch easily enough. We've been more or less agnostic for generations, anyway. Lotus or Pure Land, it's all the same to us."

Without wasting any time, Jiroemon got hold of a tasseled
rosary and began reciting the Invocation both morning and
evening. When he suggested to his parents that they do exactly as he bade, neither one had the slightest idea what was
going on. And yet, being so indulgent toward their child, they
too began chanting, "All Hail to the Lotus Sutra," even as they
gawked about and yawned.

Shortly thereafter, Denroku again headed for Tokuzaemon's
place. Upon reaching the premises, he proclaimed that Mr.
Kuwamori, along with his entire family, had converted to St.
Nichiren's sect and had taken up the Invocation.

But Tokuzaemon was a difficult man and his response was
blunt. "No," he said, "a faith without root is shallow. Anyone
can see that the fellow has converted merely to win Oran."
He went on to remark that such conduct was shameful and
St. Nichiren himself would hardly approve of it. Why, anyone
could see through this scheme in a moment. No, his mind was
made up. He was going to marry his daughter into a family of
Lotus sect believers whom he knew.

Upon hearing this news from Denroku, Jiroemon was so
horrified that he wrote to Oran immediately. "So you're marrying into another Lotus sect family," his letter began, "and
Denroku hasn't accomplished a thing. Damn, I recited that
disagreeable prayer and blistered my hands pounding a drum
just for your sake. Maybe my name's at fault. Jiroemon is quite
close to Jirozaemon, and it's bothered me a long time now
that Sano no Jirozaemon, that fellow from Azuma Province,
got jilted right and left. If that happens to me, I'll brandish my
sword and take a hundred heads, just like he did. I'm a man,
so I can do it. Don't make a fool of me." Having finished the
letter, Jiroemon sent it off, tears streaming down his face.

Oran's reply came back by return mail. "I can't fathom your

letter at all," she began. "You mustn't do anything rash, like brandishing a sword or whatever. Before you take a single head, let alone a hundred, you'll be cut down yourself. And what will I do if something happens to you? Please, don't frighten me like that. This is the first time I've ever heard of another proposal. You're always so worried about your nose and your slanted eyes—that's why you lose confidence in yourself and start doubting me. It's terrible to hear the things you say. Who would I marry now? You needn't worry. If Father wants me to marry someone else, I'll run away. I've got a woman's determination, so I'll come to you. Keep that in mind, please."

Upon reading this, Jiroemon smiled a little. Still, he couldn't rest easy yet. Now he truly felt like clinging to St. Nichiren and the Invocation. And so, contorting his face into a scowl, he began shouting, "All Hail to the Lotus Sutra," and beating wildly upon the drum.

The next day Tokuzaemon summoned Oran to his room and solemnly informed her that, owing to St. Nichiren's providence, she was going to marry Hikosaku, a paper merchant from the Honmachi district. The bond would be forever, he declared, and she must enter into it gratefully.

Oran was horrified. But she kept her feelings hidden as she bowed circumspectly and took her leave. Once she was out of the room, however, she rushed up to the second floor and scribbled a note. "I must be brief," she wrote. "It's come, the day of decision is already here. I'm going to flee. So please, I beg you to meet me here this evening." Having finished the note, Oran had one of the clerks take it to the next district.

As soon as he had scanned the message, Jiroemon started to tremble. To calm himself, he went to the kitchen and drank some water. He must make a decision right away, so he returned to the parlor and sat down smack in the middle with his legs crossed. But he couldn't figure out what to do. Finally he got up and changed his garment. He then went to the accounting room and started ransacking the drawers. Confronted by the watchman, he mumbled, "Oh, just a trifle," whereupon he threw some coins into the sleeve of his gown and rushed blindly out of the shop.

Along the way he realized that his clogs didn't match. But he was afraid to return, so he went into a nearby shoe shop and bought a pair of straw sandals. The money in his pocket was all he had, so he chose the cheapest pair possible. The soles proved so thin that he felt as though he was barefoot. But he walked on to the next district, dejected and weeping. As he reached the back door of Tokuzaemon's house, Oran came rushing out and, without uttering a word, seized his hand and started off. Sobbing as his sandals slapped against the ground, Jiroemon let himself be led off like a blind man.

Well, this tale of a silly, thoughtless couple might seem trivial. It's not over yet, though, for genuine hardship seems to lie ahead.

That night they walked fifteen miles or more. The Sea of Hakata spread out on their left, and they gazed upon its pale gray waters as if in a dream. They had neither food nor drink; someone might be following after them as well, so their insides froze in fear whenever they heard a footstep behind them. Tottering on, more dead than alive, they reached a place called The Promontory of the Temple Bell, Where Riches are Revoked and Life Comes to an End. Crossing a field at the foot of a mountain, they finally reached the home of an acquaintance of Jiroemon's. The man was rather cold toward them, but Jiroemon realized that this was only to be expected. Wrapping some of his coins in paper, he handed them over while saying, "It's too much to ask, but . . ."

Lodged in a mere shed, Oran and Jiroemon began to suspect that a life of misery lay in store for them. Pale and haggard, they looked at one another and let out a sigh. Oran sniffled over and over, trying to hold back her tears. She also stroked the fur of Kichibei, the monkey she had raised from infancy.

And how did Kichibei get into the story? Well, Kichibei was Oran's pet—and so attached to her that he had instinctively followed along when he saw her hurrying off in the darkness with a man he had never seen. Oran, after noticing that Kichibei had followed them for several miles, scolded, shooed and even threw stones at the monkey. But Kichibei kept loping along behind until eventually Jiroemon took pity on the animal. Since he's come this far, Jiroemon said, let's take him along. Oran then beckoned, and the monkey scurried up to them. Once he was cradled in her arms, he blinked and gave them both a look of pity.

Eventually Kichibei became their faithful servant. He brought meals to the shed for them and kept the flies away. Wielding a comb, he would even put the stray curls of his mistress back in place. Though a mere animal, he also tried to console the couple, doing one thing after another, even when it wasn't necessary.

Though they had chosen a life of obscurity, one could not expect them to live forever in a cramped shed. Giving most of the leftover money to his coldhearted acquaintance, Jiroemon asked that a cottage be constructed nearby. When it was finished, the couple moved in with their monkey-servant and started a vegetable garden large enough to supply their table. When he had time, Jiroemon would go off to cut tobacco, leaving Oran at home to spin cotton into skeins. Having betrayed their parents and eloped, now they could hardly eke out a living. Certainly the dreams of youth, whether of love or hate, fade quickly.

So they had ended up as one more hubby and his missus, staring at one another in their poor household. When a clatter arose in the kitchen, each of them would stand up with an angry look. Had a mouse made the noise? They wouldn't tolerate having the beans soiled again. In circumstances such as these, even the autumn leaves and the spring violets failed to interest them.

Sensing that now was the time to repay his debt to Jiroemon, Kichibei would go into the nearby hills to gather decaying oak branches and fallen leaves. Back home, he would squat before the stove, his face turned away from the smoke, and kindle the fire with rapid strokes of his persimmon-dyed fan. After a few minutes had passed, he would serve them each a lukewarm cup of tea—in a manner so comic that the couple found something pathetic in it. Although Kichibei couldn't speak, he was visibly worried about the household's poverty. He would dawdle over his supper, eating just a little before rolling over to sleep as if he were full. Whenever Jiroemon finished his own meal, the monkey would run up to massage his master's back and rub his legs. Then he was off to the kitchen to help Oran clean up. Each time he broke a plate, a look of shame would appear on his face.

Consoled by the monkey, the couple gradually forgot about their wretched fate. After a year had passed and autumn had again come, Oran gave birth to a baby whom they named Kikunosuke. For the first time in months, the sound of laughter came from the simple cottage. Suddenly the couple found life worth living once more. They made a fuss over the child—Look! He's opened his eyes. There! He's yawning—and Kichibei pranced about with delight. The monkey would bring in nuts from the wild and place them in the infant's hand. Though Oran would scold him for this, Kichibei would not leave the baby alone. He seemed beside himself with curiosity. He would gaze in amazement at the sleeping face, only to be startled by the infant's sudden cry. Then he would run over to Oran and tug at her skirt, drawing her over to the cradle. The breast, the breast, he would motion to his mistress. As she proceeded to nurse the child, the monkey would crouch nearby, watching in fascination.

A splendid guardian—that's what Kichibei had become. Yet, no matter how pleased they were over the monkey's attentions, the couple still felt sorry for Kikunosuke. If the child had only been born last year in the Kuwamori house, he would have received heaps of swaddling clothes from the celebrating relatives and slept on silk too, with several nursemaids in attendance. Not a single flea could have come near him; his skin would have remained like a jewel. For being born a year later, however, the child had to sleep in a thatched cottage exposed to the wind and rain, with nuts and berries for his toys and a monkey as his guardian.

Oran and Jiroemon had themselves brought on Kikunosuke's plight by their rash love. But it was too late to blame themselves; they had to take care of the child. Despite their poverty, they were determined to put something aside for when Kikunosuke became aware of such things as wealth. If they could do that, they would return and set things right with their parents. Impelled by his love for the child, Jiroemon asked a neighbor how he could make money in business.

Kikunosuke laughed a lot even as he grew plump, imparting to the cottage a sense of life that had been missing a year ago. The child had dazzling looks, resembling his mother in this regard. Since the monkey Kichibei would bring grasses from the field and dangle them playfully over the child's face, husband and wife could go to the garden and dig radishes without having to worry about the child.

As autumn came near once more, the couple felt alive with anticipation. It happened that the neighboring farmer did have some encouraging news for them. So one fine day Oran and Jiroemon went excitedly to see him and inquire more precisely into the matter.

After they had been gone awhile, the monkey Kichibei stood up inside the cottage. From the look on his face, it was evident that he knew it was time for the child's bath. He did exactly what he remembered having seen Oran do. First, he lit a wood fire under the stove and brought the water to a boil. Then, seeing the bubbles rise, he poured the scalding water into the basin up to the rim. Removing the infant's clothes, Kichibei looked into the baby's face just as Oran would do, nodded several times, and then—without testing the temperature—plunged him right into the water.

"Waa!" That very moment the infant Kikunosuke ceased to breathe.

Having heard this shrill cry, the alarmed parents looked at one another and hurried back. Kikunosuke lay submerged in the basin while Kichibei fidgeted.

Oran scooped up her child, but he already looked like a boiled lobster. Unable to bear the sight, she merely fell back and let out a wail. Like one gone mad, Oran said that she would give up her own life to see the child's sweet face one more time. Then she rose and seized this stunned monkey who had murdered her own baby. Though a mere woman, she brandished a piece of firewood over Kichibei's head, intent on clubbing the monkey to death.

Jiroemon too was overcome with grief, and his tears fell without pause. But in spite of his sorrow, he realized that forgiveness would be better than revenge. So he took the firewood from Oran and tried to reason with her. The child had died, he pointed out, because that was his fate. Her wish to kill the monkey was understandable, but vengeance now would only harm Kikunosuke's chances for salvation. The child could not return. Besides, he went on, Kichibei had only wanted to help them. Alas, he was only an animal and didn't know much. It was too late to do anything now. Even as Jiroemon wept and said these things, the monkey shed tears in a corner of the room and brought his palms together in gratitude. Seeing him, the couple became all the more distraught. What sin from an earlier life, they wondered, could have caused this tragedy?

Once Kikunosuke was buried, the couple's will to live on gradually faded, leaving both of them ill and confined to their beds. The monkey Kichibei diligently nursed them, without even sleeping at night. He didn't forget Kikunosuke either. He went to visit the grave every week without fail, sometimes adorning it with flowers plucked by his own hand. A hundred days later, when the couple were feeling somewhat better, Kichibei went dejectedly to the grave and quietly made a water offering. Then, thrusting the point of a bamboo spear into his throat, he took his own life.

Worried over Kichibei's disappearance, Jiroemon and Oran, each leaning on a cane, hobbled off to the grave. One glance at the pitiful corpse and they understood everything. Their grief was especially poignant, for they now realized how dependent upon the monkey they had become. So they gave him a proper burial in a mound that they built next to the grave of their own child.

So Oran and Jiroemon abandoned the world for good . . . But, having written that, I'm not sure whether to have them pray to Amida Buddha of the Pure Land or chant the *Invocation to the Lotus Sutra*. In the original tale, Saikaku says that they chanted "All hail to the Lotus Sutra" incessantly in their cottage and read the Lotus Sutra without end. Tokuzaemon was a stubborn advocate of the Sutra. But, if his bigotry breaks through now, this tale of woe might well collapse. A real bind, if ever there was one. And so, all I can say is that Oran and Jiroemon, depressed at the thought of staying on in the cottage, set out through the autumn grass, their destination uncertain once more.

TAKING THE WEN AWAY

Preface to *The Otogi Zoshi Fairy Tales*

"Ah! There they go again."

Setting aside his pen, the father stands up. He wouldn't bother to stop just for the sirens; but when the antiaircraft guns start firing, he lays his work aside and gets up from his desk. Fastening the air-raid hood on his four-year-old daughter, he picks up the girl and heads for the backyard shelter. His wife is already crouched inside, their one-year-old daughter clinging to her back.

"Sounds pretty near this time," he observes.

"Hmm," his wife replies. "It's still cramped in here too."

"Is it really?" He sounds rather irritated and adds, "If I dug it deeper, we could be buried alive some day. It's just right like it is."

"Couldn't you have made it a little bigger?"

"Well, I guess so. But the ground's frozen now and it's hard to dig. I'll get to it sometime." Having put off his wife with this evasive reply, he listens carefully to the radio for information on the air-raid.

Now that one complaint has been set aside for the time being, his four-year-old daughter starts insisting that they leave the air-raid shelter. There's only one way to calm her down, and that's to get out the illustrated book of fairy tales and read her such stories as "Momotaro," "Crackling Mountain," "The Split-Tongue Sparrow," "Taking the Wen Away" and "Urashima Taro."

Although his clothes are shabby and his looks quite oafish, this father isn't a nobody. He's an author who knows how to create a tale.

And so, as he starts reading in his strange, dissonant voice, "Long, long ago," he imagines to himself a quite different tale.

Once upon a time there was an old man with a large, cumbersome wen on his right cheek.

This old man lived at the foot of Sword Mountain, located in the Awa district of the island of Shikoku. That's how I remember it, but there's no way to check here in this air-raid shelter. Worst yet, I can't confirm whether this story was first told in *The Collection of Tales from Uji*, as seems to be the case. I'm a bit hazy about where the other stories got started, too—"Urashima Taro," for instance, which I plan to tell next. I am aware that the true story of Urashima is duly recorded in the *Chronicles of Japan* and that there's even a ballad on him in the *Man'yoshu*. And let's see, now—besides that, there's a similar tale in the *The Records of Tango Province* and one in the *Biographies of the Taoist Immortals* as well. Coming down to recent times, didn't Ogai write a play about Urashima Taro? And didn't Shoyo set the story to music for dancing? In any event, Urashima puts in countless appearances on the stage, whether in Noh, Kabuki or geisha dancing.

As soon as I've finished reading a book, I either give it away or sell it. Without a library of my own to check things, I'm in a fix right now. I'd have to go around looking for books that

I barely remember having read. And that's almost impossible at a time like this. Here I am, squatting in the air-raid shelter with just a picture book open in my lap. I'd better forget about these inquiries and tell the tale on my own. It will probably turn out more lively that way.

And so, in the corner of his air-raid shelter, this oddball of a father rambles on to himself, as if unwilling to admit defeat. While he reads from the picture book to his daughter, he ends up concocting his own version of the story.

Once upon a time . . .

. . . there was an old man who really liked to drink sake. Now such a drinker often feels lonely in his own home. Does he drink because he's lonely? Or is he lonely because his family despises him for drinking? That's merely a pedantic question, like trying to decide which hand makes the noise when clapping. Anyway, when the old man was at home, he always looked glum.

This wasn't because his family was malicious, either. Though almost seventy years old, his wife was in fine health, with such a straight back and clear eyes that people still remarked about how attractive she had been as a young woman. She had never talked much, but she did the housework diligently.

Hoping to enliven her, the old man would occasionally say something like, "Spring must be here, the cherry trees have bloomed."

"Is that so," she'd reply unconcernedly. "Move over a bit. I want to clean there." The old man would look glum.

His only son, almost forty years old at the time, conducted himself in an irreproachable manner. It wasn't merely that he didn't smoke or drink; he didn't even smile, he never got angry nor was he ever happy. He merely worked the fields in silence. Since the people hereabouts could not but revere him, his reputation as "The Saint of Awa" kept growing. He wouldn't take a wife or shave his beard, so one might have mistaken him for a stone or a piece of wood. With such a son and wife, it was no wonder that the old man's house was regarded as exemplary in local circles.

All the same, the old man remained glum. Though hesitant to take a drink at home, he couldn't resist indefinitely, regardless of the consequences. Yet, when he did have a drink, he merely felt worse. Not that his wife or his son, the Saint of Awa, would scold him. No, they merely ate their dinner in silence while the old man sat there sipping from his cup.

"By the way . . ." When he was tipsy, the old man wanted to talk so badly that he would usually come out with some banal remark. "Spring will soon be here," he'd say. "The swallows are back already." Such a remark was better left unsaid. Both his wife and his son remained silent.

Still, the old man couldn't resist adding, "One moment of spring. Ah, isn't that equal to a fortune in gold?"

He shouldn't have tried that one, either.

"I give thanks for this meal," the Saint of Awa intoned. "If you'll excuse me . . ." Having finished, he paid his respects and left.

"Guess I'll have my meal too." Wearily the old man turned his cup over.

When he drank at home, it usually came to this.

One beautiful morning he went to the mountain to gather firewood. He liked doing this in good weather, a gourd bottle on his hip. Weary after gathering wood, he would sit with his legs crossed upon a large rock and clear his throat loudly.

"What a view," he'd exclaim. Then, taking his time, he would drink from the gourd bottle, a look of perfect contentment on his face.

Away from home, he was a different person. Only one thing remained the same—the large wen on his right cheek. About twenty years ago, the old man passed a milestone in his life by turning fifty. In the autumn of that very year, he noticed that his right cheek was becoming unusually warm and itchy. At the same time, the cheek started to swell. The old man patted and rubbed the growth, and it got larger and larger. Finally, he laughed wistfully and declared, "Now I've got a fine grandchild."

"Children are not born from the cheek," his saintly son responded in a solemn tone.

His wife too, without the least hint of a smile, said to him, "It doesn't look dangerous." Aside from this, she showed no interest whatever in the wen.

The neighbors, on the other hand, were very sympathetic. How did the wen get started? they asked. Did it hurt? Wasn't it a nuisance? But the old man laughed and merely shook his head. A nuisance? Why, he regarded the wen as a darling grandchild, the one companion who would comfort him in his loneliness. Washing his face in the morning, he was especially careful to use clean water on the wen. And when, as happened to be the case now, he was alone on the mountain enjoying his sake, the wen became absolutely essential—it was the one companion he could talk to.

Sitting cross-legged on the rock, the old man drank from the gourd bottle and patted the wen on his cheek. "What the hell," he muttered, "there's nothing to be scared of. A man should get drunk and not worry about appearances. Even sobriety has its limits. I cringe at that name, Saint of Awa. I didn't realize how great my son really is."

Having confided this bit of invective to the wen, he cleared his throat with a loud cough.

Suddenly the sky grew dark, the wind arose, and the rain began to pour.
A sudden shower seldom comes along in the spring—except for high up on Sword Mountain. Here, one must be alert for changing weather at any time. As the slope turned hazy in

the rain, pheasants and quail started up from here and there, flying like arrows toward the shelter of the woods. The old man, however, remained calm. "A little rain might cool off this wen. Nothing wrong with that," he said, smiling.

He continued to sit cross-legged on the rock, gazing upon the scene. But the rain gradually became even heavier, until it seemed as though it would never let up.

"This isn't just cooling things off, it's making things downright chilly," the old man complained as he stood up. Sneezing loudly, he hoisted the firewood he had collected onto his shoulder and crept into the woods.

Here he found a great crowd of birds and animals, all of them seeking shelter. "Sorry . . . excuse me," the old man mumbled, picking his way among the animals. He saluted one and all—the wild doves, the rabbits, the monkeys—as he advanced into the woods. Eventually he found a large mountain cherry tree that was hollow at the base of its trunk. "Ah, what a fine parlor," he exclaimed as he crawled in. "How about it?" he called out to the rabbits. "Ain't no saint or grand old lady here. Don't be shy. C'mon in."

Even though your habitual drunkard might spout such nonsense when tipsy, he usually turns out to be quite harmless. The old man was in a merry mood, but within minutes he had fallen asleep and was snoring gently.

As he wearily waited for the evening shower to pass, the old man fell asleep. Eventually the clouds moved on, and the moon shone brightly over the mountain.

In its final quarter, this spring moon floated in the watery sky—perhaps, one might add, a watery sky of pale green. Moonlight filled the woods like a shower of pine needles, but the old man slept on peacefully. When bats started flitting out from the hollow of the trunk, the old man suddenly awoke, amazed to see that night had fallen.

"Now I'm in for it," he said, a vision of his somber wife and austere son floating before his very eyes. Ah, he had gone too far this time. They had never scolded him before, but coming home this late would be very awkward. "Hmm, any sake left?" he wondered, giving the gourd bottle a shake. There was a faint splashing at the bottom. "A little," he murmured, before quickly summoning his strength and swilling the sake to the last drop. Slightly drunk, he muttered another trite thing—"Ah, the moon is out. A spring evening moment . . ." he went on tentatively and then he crawled from the hollow.

Oh, what noisy voices! What a strange sight. Was he dreaming?

Look! On a grassy clearing in the woods, a marvelous scene from some other world was unfolding.

As the author of this story, I must confess here that I don't really know what a demon is. That's because I've never seen one. Granted, I've come across demons in picture books since my childhood—so often, in fact, that I'm bored by them. I've never been privileged to meet a demon in the flesh, though.

Demons come in a variety of types, with names like "bloodsuckers" or "cutthroats." Since they're supposed to have a mean nature, we use the word demon for creatures we despise. But then again, a phrase like "the masterpiece of Mr. So-and-So, a demonic talent among the literati," will show up in the daily newspaper column on recently published books, and that really confuses things. Surely the paper doesn't intend this shady term as a warning about what a mean talent Mr. So-and-So happens to be. In extreme cases, Mr. So-and-So gets crowned a "literary demon." That's such a crude term you begin to wonder just how indignant Mr. So-and-So might become. But he doesn't seem to mind, and nothing happens. In fact, I'll hear a rumor that he secretly endorses the odd term himself. All this is completely beyond a stupid person like me.

I can't figure out why a red-faced demon who wears a

tiger-skin loincloth and wields a misshapen club should be our God of the Fine Arts. Perhaps we should go slow in using such difficult terms as "mean talent" and "literary demon." That's what I've been thinking for some time now; but my experience is limited, and I can't help wondering whether I'm just being foolish.

Yes, even among demons there seem to be various types. At this point I might peek into the *Japan Encyclopedia*, which would quickly turn me into a scholar admired by young and old, by women and children. (So-called scholars usually operate in this way.) I'd put on a knowing look and expound in detail about all sorts of things. Unfortunately I'm crouched here in this air-raid shelter, and all I've got is the child's picture book lying open in my lap. I'll just have to take it from there.

Look! There where the woods opened out, ten or so deformed . . . "beings," would you call them? "Creatures?" Anyway, these were ten or so large red figures, and each of them was indeed wearing a loincloth. They were sitting in a circle having a party in the moonlight.

At first the old man was startled. When sober, he may be worthless and lacking in self-respect, just like most other drinkers. But, with a few drinks under the belt, he'll show more pluck than your ordinary fellow. That's why the old man was feeling happy now, even heroic. Why should he worry about his straight-laced old lady or his irreproachable son? While watching the grotesque scene before him, he didn't quail or seem frightened in any way. Crawling from the hollow, he gazed at the strange banquet with a feverish look.

Ah, he could tell they were pleasantly drunk. In fact, he too felt a pleasant glow within his breast, a symptom any drinker feels while watching others carouse. This feeling, by the way, springs from benevolence rather than selfishness, and prompts the drinker to raise a cup to his neighbor's happiness. Somebody wants to get drunk, and so much the better if a neighbor will join in. Even the old man knew this. He saw intuitively that these huge red beings weren't people, nor were they animals. They belonged to that frightful tribe known as demons. Just one look at the tiger-skin loincloths made that clear. The old man would get along with them, however. That's because they were pretty high at the moment, and so was he.

Still on his hands and knees, the old man watched the strange, moonlit banquet yet more closely. Demons they surely were, but not the sort with an awful temperament—not like those bloodsuckers or cutthroats. Although their red faces were actually quite fearsome, the demons seemed friendly and guileless to the old man. He was more or less right about this. These demons, in fact, had such a gentle temperament they might well have been called The Hermits of Sword Mountain. They were an utterly different tribe from the demons of Hell. For one thing none of them carried a menacing object such as a steel club. This, one might say, proved they were not bent on doing evil.

At the same time they weren't like the Seven Sages of the Bamboo Grove, either. Even though we might call them hermits, these demons were hardly akin to those erudite Chinese hermits who took refuge in their grove. No, these Hermits of Sword Mountain were foolish souls, really.

The kanji character for "sage" shows a man and a mountain. That's why, according to a simple theory I've heard, anyone who lives in the depths of a mountain might be called a sage. If we go along with this, then the Hermits of Sword Mountain too deserve the title of "sage," regardless of how foolish they are.

Anyway, I think we should use the right term when referring to these huge red beings now enjoying their moonlight banquet. They're hermits or sages, not demons. Earlier, I spoke of them as foolish souls, and anyone who observed their behavior during the banquet could see why. They let out senseless cries, slapped their knees and howled with laughter, jumped up and pranced about, bent their huge bodies, and rolled from one end of the circle to the other—all of this apparently meant to be some dance or other. Their level of intelligence was more than obvious, their lack of talent simply astonishing. This in itself would show that terms like "demonic talent" and "literary demon" are utterly meaningless. I can't imagine why an ignorant demon without any talent should be a God of All the Fine Arts.

The old man too was flabbergasted by the moronic dance. After snickering to himself, he muttered, "What a clumsy way to dance. Shall I show them one of my graceful turns?"

The old man immediately leaped out and began performing one of the dances he loved so much, and the wen on his cheek flopped back and forth in a strange and amusing manner.

The sake he had drunk gave the old man courage. Besides that, he was beginning to feel easy about the demons. And so, he broke into the circle, not the least afraid, and began the Awa-odori dance which he took pride in doing so well.

> Girls in Shimada coiffures
> And old women in wigs;
> How tempting are their red sashes.
> Won't you go, wife, in your straw hat?
> Come . . . come . . .

The words were in the Awa dialect, and the old man sang them beautifully. The demons were delighted! They gave forth a strange staccato shout, then rolled on the ground laughing, weeping and slobbering.

> Across the great valley filled with stones,
> Over the high mountain of bamboo grass . . .

The old man had lost all restraint. His voice ascending another octave, he danced on and on to his heart's content.

The demons were immensely pleased. "Come every moonlit night and dance for us. But we'll need something valuable as a pledge."

The demons began whispering to one another. Didn't the wen glimmering on the old man's cheek seem like some unusual jewel? If they kept it, he would surely return. And so, having made this silly conjecture, they immediately tore the wen off without any trouble. A stupid thing to do, but after living so long in the depths of the mountain, they probably took it for a magical charm.

The old man was horrified. "No! Not my grandchild!" he exclaimed.

The demons gave a joyful shout of triumph.

Morning. Listlessly stroking his cheek where the wen had been, the old man descended the mountain road which glistened with dew.

With his wen gone, the old man felt somewhat lonely. After all, there was no one else he could talk to. Still, the cheek felt lighter, and the morning breeze on his skin seemed quite agreeable. Both gain and loss, both good and bad had come from this episode then, and perhaps the two sides simply canceled out one another. It had been good for the old man to sing and dance to his heart's content after these many years, wasn't that so? As he was going down the mountainside musing on these questions, he nearly bumped into his saintly son who was heading for work in the field.

The saint removed his hood and intoned, "Good morning, Father."

"Oh," the old man replied, somewhat at a loss.

Nothing more was said as they passed by one another.

Realizing that the old man's wen had disappeared overnight, even the saint was slightly taken aback. But he believed that quibbling over the features of a parent went against the Saintly Way. So he pretended not to notice and went on in silence.

When the old man got home, his wife calmly said, "So you're back."

She didn't ask about what had happened the night before. "The soup's gotten cold," she grumbled as she set about preparing the old man's breakfast.

"Oh, that's all right. Don't bother warming it up," the old man countered. He felt small and sheepish as he sat down to eat. Yet, the urge to describe his wondrous adventure of last night was very strong, and he almost began to relate what had happened. The words stuck in his throat, though, so cowed was he by the old lady's stern manner. Bowing his head, he ate his meal dejectedly.

"The wen looks like it shriveled up," his wife remarked offhandedly.

"Hmm," the old man mumbled, the urge to talk having passed.

"It broke, then, and the water just squirted out from inside?" She did not seem particularly impressed.

"Hmm."

"It'll swell up again if more water collects, then."

"That's true."

In his own home, this business of the old man's wen didn't much matter. One of the neighbors, though, another old man with his own wen, was quite curious about what had happened. This man's wen was on the left cheek, and he found it quite annoying. Believing it had kept him from advancing in the world, he hated his wen with a passion. Every day he looked repeatedly in the mirror and sighed. How much scorn and derision, the old man wondered, had been heaped on him because of it? He had let his sideburns grow long, hoping to conceal the wen; but, alas, the tip glowed from his flowing white beard like the New Year's Day sun rising gloriously from the sea. Rather then hide the wen, the beard set it off like one of the wonders of the world.

With his sturdy physique, large nose and glaring eyes, this oldster looked every inch a man. He spoke and acted with dignity, too, and he dressed with a certain splendor. His learning was impressive, his mind discerning. Rumor had it that his wealth far surpassed that of the other old man, the drinker. All the neighbors knew this second old man was special, so they addressed him as "Master" or "Sir" without fail. He was a fine man, a perfect man—except for that annoyance on his left cheek. His wen depressed him day and night, and he never could relax.

Though just thirty-seven years old, the man's wife was not particularly attractive. She was fair and plump, however, and she laughed as merrily and as often as a coquette. Her daughter, who was thirteen or so, was very pretty. The girl could also be quite saucy, but this gave her something in common with her mother. The two of them were constantly in stitches over one thing or another, and this made the home lively in spite of the master's scowling face.

"Mother, I wonder why Father's wen is so red? It's like the head of an octopus." The saucy girl would come out unhesitatingly with such a remark. Her mother would laugh rather than scold her, and then she would reply, "Well, maybe you're right. But, to me, it's more like one of those wooden drums that hang from the eaves of a temple."

"Shut up!" the old man would thunder. Glaring at his wife and daughter, he would spring to his feet and head for one of the darker rooms well within the house. There he would peek into a mirror and give way to despair. "It's hopeless," he would mutter.

Should he apply the knife, even at the risk of killing himself? It had come to this when the old man heard the rumor that the other man's wen had suddenly disappeared. Under cover of night he slipped over to the old man's hut and heard from him the marvelous tale of the moonlit banquet.

*When he heard the story the old man was overjoyed. "Well, well, then
I too can surely have this wen removed."*

Fortunately the moon was out again that very night. Excited
by what he had heard, this esteemed man ventured forth like a
warrior heading into battle, his mouth set in a grimace and his
eyes glaring. Come what may, he would impress those demons
this very night by dancing with gusto. And, if by some slight
chance he didn't impress them, why then he'd lay them low
with his iron-ribbed fan. He figured that a bunch of foolish,
drunken demons couldn't amount to much.

And so, to dance for the demons or else to quell them, he
marched into the depths of Sword Mountain, his shoulders
thrown back and his right hand grasping the iron-ribbed fan.
But a performance meant to impress the audience will often
turn out poorly. In his very eagerness the old man was almost
bound to fail.

He began with a stately move right into the circle of revel-
ing demons. "Your humble servant," he proclaimed, flipping
open his fan and gazing at the moon overhead. After pausing
momentarily as if he were a giant tree, he shuffled his feet
lightly and began a slow, groaning chant.

> A priest am I
> Performing my late spring meditation
> By the Straits of Naruto.
> It pains me to realize
> That in this locale
> The entire Heike clan met its end,
> And every evening
> I come to this shore
> To read the holy sutra.
> As I wait among the rocks of the dune,
> As I wait among the rocks,
> A boat—whose I do not know—

> Goes rowing with a splash of oars
> Amid the white-capped waves.
> How still the inlet this evening!
> How still the inlet this evening!
> But yesterday has passed,
> Today draws to an end,
> And so too will tomorrow.

Moving ever so deliberately, he again looked up at the moon and struck a rigid pose.

The demons were dumbfounded. They rose one after another and fled into the depths of the mountain.

"No! Wait!" The old man cried out in a pathetic voice and ran after the demons. "You can't forsake me now."

"Run! Run! He must be Shoki, the demon-queller."

"No, I'm not Shoki!" the old man exclaimed. Then, catching hold of a demon, he pleaded in desperation, "Please, I want you to take off another wen."

"What's that?" replied the confused demon. "You won't stop until we stick another wen on you? Oh, but we're keeping that one for the old man. It's splendid, but if you want it so bad, you can have it. Just stop your dancing! We'd just gotten nice and drunk, and then you came butting in. We've had enough of you, so just let me go. We'll have to go somewhere else now and get drunk all over again—that's enough. Let me go, now. Hey! Somebody! Give this fool that wen we got the other night. He says he wants it."

So the demons attached the wen they had been keeping to his right cheek. There! The old man now had two flopping wens and they were heavy. He returned to his village in shame.

Truly a pathetic ending. In these old tales someone who does wrong usually ends up getting punished for it. However, in this case, the second old man didn't do anything especially wrong. It's true that he became overly tense at one point, and so the dance he performed got out of hand. But that hardly counts. Come to think of it, there weren't any bad people in his family, either. And the old tippler too, as well as his family, and even the demons on Sword Mountain, didn't do anything wrong, either. Even though there's not a single episode of wrongdoing in this tale, one of the characters comes to grief. Try drawing a moral from this story and you're in real trouble. So why did I bother telling the tale? If the anxious reader presses me on this question, I'd have to answer that there's always something both tragic and comic in people's very nature. It's a problem at the very core of our lives, and that's really all I can say.

CRACKLING MOUNTAIN

In spite of appearances, the rabbit in the well-known Japanese folktale *Kachi-Kachi Yama*, or "Crackling Mountain" is actually a teenage girl, while the badger who undergoes a heartrending defeat is an ugly man in love with her. That's how things look to me, no doubt about it.

The setting of the tale is supposed to have been around Lake Kawaguchi, close to Mount Fuji in the Koshu region. The exact spot is now called The Inner Mountain of Funazu. People in the Koshu region are—well, brusque is the word. Maybe that's why "Crackling Mountain" is rougher than the other fairy tales from Japan's medieval period. First of all, the story begins on a cruel note, with the old woman being turned into a stew. Now *that* was hardly a prank! No, it was downright wicked. The badger committed other atrocities too—like that terrible business of scattering the old woman's bones under the veranda. It's a shame, but the tale had to be banned for children.

In the illustrated version now on sale, the badger only wounds the old woman before running away. In my opinion no one should object to this change as a means of getting around the ban. But, in taking vengeance for this mischief, the rabbit goes much too far. A valiant avenger should dispatch the enemy with one blow. Not in this case, though. Our rabbit taunts her victim, mocks him and almost hounds him to death before luring him into the clay boat that, as it crumbles, leaves the poor creature gurgling helplessly in the water. Yes, a cunning scheme from beginning to end, but hardly in accord with the Way of the Japanese Warrior. If the badger had followed through on his vicious intention to serve up the old woman as stew, no one would think twice about the well-deserved punishment he receives. But in the new version that protects innocent children and circumvents the ban, the badger merely wounds the old woman and flees. In all fairness, the rabbit shouldn't be allowed to torture and humiliate the badger so relentlessly, drowning him at last in that disgraceful manner.

The badger was merely frolicking in the hills when he got caught by the old man. With his captor planning to make him into stew, the situation seemed hopeless. Desperate for a way to escape, he finally succeeded in tricking the old woman and saving his own skin. Now, the scheme to make her into stew was wrong. But the badger's only crime in the recent illustrated version is to claw the old woman while making his escape. One can hardly call reasonable self-defense a terrible deed, even if unintended injury is inflicted.

My five-year-old daughter is very homely—just like her father. Unfortunately she thinks in the same eccentric way. We were in the family air-raid shelter together, and I was reading the illustrated "Crackling Mountain" to her when she blurted out, "The badger . . . what a pity." "What a pity"—that's a phrase she's picked up recently, and she repeats it over and over regardless of what she sees. Since she's obviously trying to play up to her softhearted mother, her behavior is hardly surprising. Of course, in this case it could well be that she likes badgers. She once saw a group of them nervously trotting about in their cage when her father took her to the neighborhood zoo in Inokashira Park. Maybe that's why she's instinctively drawn to the badger in "Crackling Mountain." Whatever the grounds, though, this little tenderheart of mine is mistaken. Her notions are flimsy, the origins of her compassion obscure. Actually, I shouldn't be making this much fuss over her.

Still, that chance phrase—"What a pity"—seemed to have something suggestive about it, even when mumbled by a mere child. Reflecting on the matter, the girl's father began to realize that, yes, the avenging rabbit had indeed gone too far. With this toddler of his, he might gloss over the matter; but wouldn't older children, having been taught about the Way of the Warrior and the Law of Fair and Square, find the methods of the rabbit underhanded? Now that he had reached the heart of the matter, the dim-witted man started frowning.

When things happen, as in the recent illustrated books— the badger terribly mistreated by the rabbit for merely clawing the old woman; his back burned and then smeared with red pepper; and his death assured by the ride in the clay boat— well, then it's only natural that any child smart enough to attend our public schools might begin to wonder. Even if the badger had tried to make the old lady into stew, why couldn't the rabbit have acted like a true warrior by solemnly proclaiming its pedigree and dispatching the enemy with a single blow? A rabbit may be frail, but that's no excuse for deviousness. God favors the righteous, and revenge must be carried out openly. Even in the face of heavy odds the avenger must cry out, "Heaven wills it!" and leap directly upon the foe. When his skills aren't equal to the task, he must discipline himself like that vanquished Chinese King of Yueh who slept every night on a woodpile to remind himself of the bitter taste of defeat.

Or else he might wholly devote himself to practicing the martial arts at Mount Kurama. For ages the Japanese hero has generally acted in this manner—in fact, there don't seem to be any other vendetta tales in which the avenger, regardless of how extreme the provocation, uses wily tricks and torments his opponent to death. Only in "Crackling Mountain" is revenge accomplished by disgraceful means. Hardly the way a man would act, is it? Child or adult, anyone with even a slight concern for justice would feel something was wrong.

But don't worry, I've thought this problem over. And I've figured out why the rabbit took this unmanly approach to vengeance. The rabbit's not a man, but a pretty girl. No doubt about that. She's fifteen years old—not quite ready to flirt, and meaner than ever for just that reason.

Everyone knows that lovely goddesses often appear in the Greek myths. Even in their company, Artemis is alluring beyond compare—after Aphrodite at least. Artemis is well known as Goddess of the Moon, and her brow displays the pale glimmer of a new, crescent moon. Like Apollo, she is shrewd and determined, and all of the wild animals are subject to her. That doesn't mean she's a sturdy Amazon, though; she has a small, slender figure, and her limbs are delicate. Her face is so uncommonly beautiful as to give one a shudder. In spite of this, she lacks the femininity of Aphrodite. Her breasts are small, and she is callous toward those whom she dislikes. By splashing the hunter who peeked at her while she was bathing, Artemis instantly turned him into a stag. If that's what happened to someone who saw her bathing, I can't imagine how she would punish a man who tried holding her hand. Such a woman will humiliate any suitor. It's too bad that stupid men easily give into temptation and thereby seal their own fate.

Those who doubt what I say should observe our poor badger as he yearns for his Artemis-like teenager. If I'm correct, the malicious and unmanly chastisement of the badger is perfectly understandable. Whichever crime he committed, stewing the old woman or clawing her, makes no difference to the girl—this we must grant as fact, even as we sigh over it. Moreover, our so-called badger is just the sort who would woo an Artemis-like teenager. That is, he's a roly-poly glutton both stupid and uncouth who cuts a sorry figure even among his cohorts. One can surmise already the wretched end awaiting for him.

In the story itself, then, the old man had captured the badger and decided to make him into stew. But, desperate to see his rabbit-maid once more, the badger fretted and struggled until he finally escaped into the hills. Restlessly he searched all over for her, mumbling something or other all the while.

"Cheer up!" he exclaimed upon finding her. "I got away in the nick of time. I waited till the old man was gone; then I let out a shriek, went right for the old woman, gave her a mighty blow and escaped. Was luck ever with me." Thus did the badger speak of his brush with death, his face beaming and spit flying from his mouth.

As the rabbit listened, she sprang back to avoid the spray. Humbug!—that's what her look said. "What's there to cheer about?" she retorted. "You're a filthy . . . Imagine, spitting like that. And besides, the old man and lady are friends of mine. Didn't you realize that?"

"Oh?" the badger exclaimed, taken aback. "No, I didn't. I'm so sorry, if only I had known . . . Even if they were going to make stew of me or whatever . . ." He was obviously disheartened.

"It's too late for excuses now! You must have known about their garden, and how I'd help myself to their luscious beans ever so often. If *only* you'd known . . . Liar! You've got a grudge against me."

Even while she berated him, the rabbit was already thinking ahead to his revenge. A maiden's ire can be scathing and merciless, especially when her victim is both ugly and dumb.

"C'mon, forgive me—I didn't realize. I'm no liar. Honest, I'm not." Even as he entreated her in his sweetest manner, the badger stretched his neck and gave the rabbit a bow. He also noticed a fallen berry and instantly gobbled it up, his eyes darting hither and thither in search of more. "I'd rather die than see you so angry," he said. "Really, I mean it."

"Nonsense! All you think of is eating." She turned away primly as though she felt nothing but contempt for him. "Besides being a lecher, you're the filthiest glutton I can imagine."

"Please, don't make a fuss about it. I'm so hungry . . ." Having confessed to this weakness, the badger anxiously scoured the nearby area even as he lamented, "If you only knew how I suffer . . ."

"Didn't I tell you to keep away from me? Phew! Move over there. You want to know what I heard? I heard you eat lizard, that's what. And animal droppings, too!"

"Oh, surely . . ." The badger smiled lamely, but he didn't seem able to deny the charge. His mouth twisting as he smiled once again, the badger meekly repeated, "Oh surely . . ."

"You needn't bother pretending. I can tell because you smell even worse than usual."

Even as she dismissed him, the rabbit seemed taken with a brilliant scheme. Suddenly her eyes glittered and she turned to the badger. Suppressing the cruel smile that seemed ready to cross her face, she said, "Well, I'll forgive you this once. Hey! I told you to keep your distance. You need watching every moment. And how about wiping that slobber from your face. You're dripping under the chin. Now listen closely. I'll forgive you just this once, but there's a catch. The old man's feeling dejected now, so he won't be up to gathering firewood in the hills. Let's go ahead and do it for him."

"Together? Both you and me?" The badger's small, turbid eyes lit up with pleasure.

"That doesn't suit you?"

"What do you mean—doesn't suit me? C'mon, let's go right now." The badger was so happy that his voice turned hoarse.

"Let's go tomorrow instead," the rabbit countered. "Is early in the morning okay? You're probably worn out today—and hungry too," she added, her generosity beyond belief.

"How good of you!" the badger responded. "I'll gather plenty of things for a meal. When we get to the hill, I'll work with all my might and cut a whole cord of firewood. I'll deliver it to the old man's place, and then you'll forgive me, won't you? And we'll be friends again?"

"You do carry on, don't you? Really, it depends on how well you do. I guess we'll be friends."

"Heh-heh," the badger snickered. "What a provocative tongue. So you're putting me on the spot. Damn! I'm already . . ." The badger paused, then snatched a spider crawling nearby and devoured it. "I'm so happy I could cry."

He sniffled and pretended to weep.

The summer morning was cool, and a white mist enveloped Lake Kawaguchi. Though drenched in dew, the badger and the rabbit busily gathered brushwood on the mountaintop.

To all appearances the badger was utterly absorbed in the task. He had worked himself into a near frenzy—flailing his sickle about, groaning excessively and making his travail known by crying "Ouch!" now and then. He rushed about without pause, anxious that the rabbit notice how hard he was working. This rampage had gone on awhile when he suddenly flung away his sickle, his look proclaiming that he was through.

"There!" he exclaimed. "You see these blisters? Ah, my hands really sting. I'm thirsty too—and hungry. Well, hard work'll do that to you. Shall we have a break? And get to the lunch, maybe. Heh-heh."

Having let out this sheepish chuckle, the badger opened the lunchbox. It was as huge as a utility gasoline can, and he stuck his nose right in. Thereupon the box echoed with sounds of snatching, munching and swallowing, the badger losing himself in the task of eating. The rabbit stopped cutting brushwood, a stunned look on her face, then peeked into the lunchbox. Whatever was inside must have been awful, for a tiny squeal escaped her lips and she immediately covered her face with both hands.

All that morning the rabbit had refrained from abusing the badger as she usually did. Perhaps she already had another scheme in mind; for, even as she ignored the capering rascal and concentrated on quickly cutting the brushwood, an artful smile had played about her lips. Though astonished by the inside of the great lunchbox, she went on cutting the brushwood in silence.

So lenient was the rabbit that the badger almost hugged himself with glee. Even this impudent girl had finally given in. Hadn't his brushwood-cutting act done the trick? Well, this masculinity of his—what woman could resist it?

Ah, he had eaten his fill. And was he ever weary. Yes, he'd have just a quick nap. Putting on his carefree manner, the badger became so relaxed that he was soon fast asleep and snoring heavily. Even as he dreamed, he mumbled about love potions— they weren't worth a damn, they didn't do any good . . . And when he awoke from his lewd dreams, it was almost noon.

"You really had a good sleep," the rabbit said, still indulgent. "I've got my wood bundled up too," she went on, "so let's hoist the load on our backs and take it to the old man."

"Oh," the badger answered, "let's be off then." He yawned prodigiously and scratched his arms. "Am I ever hungry. How could anyone sleep on an empty stomach like this? Too sensitive—that's my problem." Having said these things— without the least hint of a smile, either—he went on. "Well, I'll hurry up and collect my brushwood, and then we'll head down, I guess. Since the lunch is gone, I'll have to finish this chore quickly so I can look for more food."

They set off, each one carrying a load of brushwood.

"You go first," the rabbit urged. "There are snakes around here and I'm scared of them."

"Snakes? Who's afraid of snakes? When I spot one, I'll grab him and . . ." About to say "eat him," the badger caught himself just in time. "I'll grab him and kill him," he said. "You just stay behind me."

"At times like this you can really depend upon a man."

"Oh, please, no flattery," the badger answered sweetly. "You're certainly nice today, aren't you? It almost makes me edgy. Surely you're not taking me along so the old man can make badger stew? Hah hah, you can count me out of that."

"Well! That's an odd thing to suspect. If that's how you feel, maybe we should part company right here. I'm perfectly capable of going alone."

"No, no, I didn't mean it that way. We'll go together, all right? I'm not afraid of snakes or anything else in this world— except for that old man. He talked about making badger stew, and I didn't like that. Downright disgusting, isn't it? And hardly in good taste, if you ask me. Anyway, I'll take the brushwood to the hackberry tree in the old man's garden, but no further. I'm turning back there, so you'll have to carry it the rest of the way. All I can say is, a queasy feeling comes over me when I see the old man's face . . . Hey! What's that? That strange noise—what could it be? Don't you hear it too? It's sort of a crackling noise . . ."

"What did you expect?" said the rabbit. "That's why they call this place Crackling Mountain."

"Crackling Mountain? Here?"

"Sure. You didn't know that?"

"No, I didn't. It's the first time I've heard this mountain even had a name. It's such a strange name too—you're not making it up, are you?"

"Oh, really! But every mountain's got a name. There's Mount Fuji and Mount Nagao and Mount Omuro . . . They all have names, don't they? So this one's called Crackling Mountain. Listen, don't you hear that crackling sound?"

"Yeah, I hear it. Strange, though. I've never heard that sound before on this mountain. I was born here, and for thirty-some years this—"

"Wha-a-at! You don't mean to say you're *that* old? Why, just the other day you told me you were seventeen. Oh, this is too much. Your face is all wrinkled and you stoop a bit too, so I didn't take you for seventeen. But I hardly thought you'd hide your age by twenty years. So you're almost forty—the nerve!"

"No, seventeen, I'm only seventeen. Seventeen, I tell you. The stoop comes from hunger, and it doesn't have anything to do with age. My older brother—he's the one in his thirties. You see, he's always talking about it, and I mimicked him, that's all. It's only a habit I've picked up, my dear." Calling her "my dear!"—*that* certainly showed how flustered the badger was.

"Only a habit?" the rabbit replied curtly. "This is the first I've heard of an older brother. You once told me how lonely you were—no parents, no brothers or sisters. How did you put it then? I didn't know how forsaken you felt—wasn't that what you said? Now what did you mean by that?"

"Yes, yes . . ." the badger replied, losing track of what he wanted to say. "Things are certainly involved, you know, and it's not so simple. I've got an older brother, and yet I don't—"

"Nonsense!" interjected the rabbit, now totally fed up. "You're talking through your hat!"

"Well, to tell the truth, yes, I've got an older brother. It hurts to say this, but he's just a drunken scoundrel. I'm ashamed, embarrassed really, because for thirty-some years— no, that's my brother—you see, for thirty-some years he's been giving me trouble . . ."

"That's odd. A seventeen year old . . . trouble . . . for thirty-some years?"

The badger ignored this remark.

"There are plenty of things you can't sum up in a word. Right now, he doesn't exist, not for me, anyway. I disowned him and . . . Hey, that's odd. Smells like smoke . . . Don't you notice it?"

"Not at all."

"Hmm." The badger was always eating smelly food, so he couldn't trust his own nose. Twisting about with a suspicious look on his face, he said, "Could I be imagining this? There! There! That noise—isn't that roaring and snapping like something on fire?"

"Well, what did you expect? That's why this place is called Mount Roaring-and-Snapping."

"Liar! You just said it was called Crackling Mountain!"

"That's right. The same mountain's got different names, depending on the spot. Halfway up Mount Fuji there's Smaller Fuji, and Omuro and Nagao are lesser peaks of Mount Fuji too. Didn't you know that?"

"I'm afraid I didn't. So that's it—we're on Mount Roaring-and-Snapping, are we? Well, for thirty-some years I've been—not me, my brother, I mean—he's been calling it The Mountain Out Back. Oh, is it ever getting warm. Is there an earthquake brewing? Something's really wrong today. Yaa! Oh, is it ever hot! I can't stand it! Help! Help! My brushwood's on fire! Ouch! . . ."

The next day the badger remained secluded in his lair. "Oh," he moaned, "how painful. Too much even for me. I'm done for. Come to think of it, I've got the worst luck. The women shy away just because I was born good-looking—a respectable man always loses out. They all take me for a woman-hater. Hell, I'm no saint. I like women. They must think I'm noble-minded, so they never play up to me. But, when it comes right down to it, I want to run around screaming, I'M CRAZY

ABOUT WOMEN! Ouch! Ouch! Oh, why can't I do anything about this nasty burn? It just keeps throbbing. After I'd barely escaped becoming badger stew, I had to stumble onto this unheard-of place—Roaring Mountain, wasn't that it? And did my luck ever run out there. What a good-for-nothing mountain! Brushwood going up in flames—was it ever horrible. In thirty-odd years . . ."

The badger paused, his eyes darting about.

"So why hide it?" he went on. "I'm thirty-seven. Heh-heh, what's wrong with that? Be forty in three more years. It's so obvious anyone could figure it out. All it takes is one look. Ooh, that hurts! I've been playing on The Mountain Out Back ever since I was born, and not once in my thirty-seven years did I run into anything so weird. Crackling Mountain, or Roaring Mountain—even the names are odd. How strange," the badger concluded, knocking himself on the head and then lapsing into a reverie.

Presently a peddler called out at the front entrance, "Magic Ointment for sale. Anyone here suffering from burns, cuts or a dark complexion?"

Dark complexion—that really woke up the badger. "Hey, ointment peddler!" he called out.

"Oh, where are you, sir?"

"Here! In this hole! So it'll really cure a dark complexion?"

"In one day."

"Ho-ho." Elated, the badger crawled from his lair. "Whaa! You're a rabbit."

"Yes, I'm certainly a rabbit—and a medicine man, besides. Been peddling in this area for thirty-odd years."

"Whew," the badger wheezed, tilting his head. "There's another rabbit just like you. Thirty-odd years . . . Ah yes, so you must be the same . . . Look here, let's just forget about my age. Damned silly, anyway. Enough is enough. Well, that's that." Having confused the issue, the badger went on. "Anyway, could you spare a bit of that medicine? To tell the truth, I've got a little affliction."

"Oh dear, you've got a terrible burn! This will never do. Ignore it, and you're dead."

"Damn, I'd rather be dead—I don't care about the burn. Right now, it's my looks that—"

"What are you saying! This burn could be fatal—don't you realize that? Oh, your back's even worse . . . How did this happen?"

"Well, you see . . ." The badger twisted his mouth about. "You see, I'd just gotten to this place with the fancy name— Mount Roaring, Snapping or whatever, and the craziest thing . . . It was amazing."

The badger looked puzzled as the rabbit began snickering helplessly. But then he too started laughing. "Absolutely," he went on. "It was the craziest thing ever. I'm telling you, don't go near that mountain. First it's Crackling, then it's Snapping and then it's Roaring—and that's the worst kind ever. Things are bound to go wrong. When you get to Crackling Mountain, you'd better just beg off. If you stray onto Mount Roaring, you'll end up like me. Ooh, the pain! You follow me? I'm telling you for your own good, now. You're still young, so when an old-timer like myself says—well, I'm not *that* old. Anyway, just take what I say as friendly advice and don't poke fun at me. You see, I speak from experience. Ooh, that hurts . . . ouch!"

"Thank you, sir, I'll certainly be careful. Now, what about the ointment? In return for your kind advice, I won't charge anything. Shall I put some on your back? Lucky I came just now, otherwise you'd be good as dead. Something must have brought me here. I guess it was fate, wouldn't you agree?"

"I suppose so," the badger moaned. "If the ointment's free, rub it on. I'm pretty broke nowadays—fall in love and it's bound to cost you. By the way, would you mind putting some of that medicine on my palm?"

With an anxious look, the rabbit asked, "And what will you do with it?"

"Oh, nothing at all. I just want a look—so I can tell the color."

"It's the same color as any ointment. Here, have a little." The rabbit dabbed a speck on the badger's outstretched hand.

When the badger suddenly tried to rub it on his face, the startled rabbit seized his hand—the badger mustn't learn about this ointment just yet. "Aa! Don't do that!" the rabbit cautioned. "This medicine's slightly strong for your face. It won't do."

"No, let go!" the badger pleaded desperately. "I beg you, let go of my hand. You don't know how I feel! Or how wretched I've been for thirty-odd years—and all because of this dark complexion. Let go. Just let go of my hand so I can use this ointment. I'm begging you, just let me rub it on."

Finally the badger lifted his foot and kicked the rabbit away. Then, quicker than the eye could see, he smeared the medicine on his face.

"I'm ashamed of my face," he exclaimed. "The features are fine, but this dark complexion—well, this'll fix it. Wow! That's awful. Does it ever sting. If the medicine wasn't strong, though, it wouldn't cure my complexion. Ah, this is terrible. I'll bear it, though. Damn! Next time we meet, she'll really be taken with this face of mine. Heh-heh, so what if she hankers for me. Won't be my fault. Ah, does that ever sting. This medicine'll do the trick for sure. Well, I've come this far, so you might as well smear it all over—on my back or wherever. I don't care if I die, not if it lightens my complexion. Go ahead, smear the stuff on. Don't hesitate, just start splashing."

Already the badger was a pathetic sight. But a proud, beautiful teen is a virtual demon who is utterly ruthless. The rabbit calmly picked herself up and applied a thick layer of the pepper paste to the badger's burnt back.

The badger writhed in pain. "Oh, nothing to it. This medicine'll work for sure. Wow! That's awful. Gimme water! Where am I! In hell! Hey, you've got to forgive me—I don't remember falling into hell! I didn't want to become badger stew, that's why I went after the old woman. I haven't done anything wrong. In my thirty-odd years—and all because of this dark complexion—not one lady friend! Then, there's that appetite of mine—ah, what an embarrassment! But nobody's concerned about me, I'm entirely on my own. Yet I'm a good man and not so bad-looking, either." Racked with pain, the badger kept on with his pathetic ranting before fainting to the ground in a heap.

Even so, the badger's ordeal wasn't over yet. So terrible was his plight that your author, even as he writes these words, can feel a sigh welling up inside. In all of Japanese history, there are scarcely any instances of so depressing an end. No sooner had he rejoiced over escaping the ordeal with the badger stew than he sustained that strange burn on Mount Roaring and barely escaped alive once again. He just managed to crawl back to his lair where he lay groaning through twisted lips—only to have so much hot pepper smeared over his burn that he fainted in agony. Next he'll launch his clay boat on Lake Kawaguchi and sink to the bottom. What an utter mess! Yes, there's something to be said for a broken affair. Unfortunately, a sleazy instance like this one hasn't got any romance to it.

Hardly able to breathe, the badger remained in his lair for three days, his spirit wandering forth, but only along that dim border between life and death. When the hunger pangs started up on the fourth day, he was more miserable than words can describe. Nevertheless, he hobbled forth on his cane, mumbling to himself as he searched here and there for food.

Thereafter he quickly recovered, thanks to the large, sturdy body with which he was endowed. Within ten days he was back to normal, his appetite flourishing as of old, his lust also beginning to stir. He should have known better by now, but eventually he found himself heading once more toward the rabbit's nest.

"Here I am," the badger sheepishly announced. "Just thought I'd drop by for a visit, heh-heh."

"Oh!" the rabbit exclaimed, the malice in her look conveying more than mere astonishment. "So it's you?" Or something even stronger, like, "What's the big idea? Here? Again? The nerve . . ." No, it was even stronger than that. "Oh, I can't stand it! The plague's arrived!" Or even worse. "Filthy! Stinking! Rot in hell!" Yes, her look was one of utter hatred. But our uninvited guest doesn't seem to notice the host's mood—a strange phenomenon which the reader should take note of. You set out grudgingly for a boring, irksome visit and end up being most heartily welcomed. On the other hand, you fondly imagine, ah, what a comfortable place . . . it's almost like my own . . . no, more cozy than home even . . . a refuge . . . Yet, in spite of your high spirits, the host is usually upset, frightened, repelled—and the broom behind the sliding door is turned upside down to bring about your early departure. One who looks for refuge in the home of another proves himself a fool. A mere visit can lead to amazing blunders, so one should keep away even from close relatives unless there's a special reason for the visit. If you doubt my advice, observe the badger as he becomes entangled in this very folly.

The rabbit exclaimed, "Oh!" and gave the badger a malicious look, but he did not catch on. To him that "Oh!" seemed a maiden's impulsive cry of surprise and delight—and her look conveyed sympathy because of his recent accident on Mount Roaring. The badger shuddered with pleasure and said, "I'm fine, thank you," even though he had not been asked how he felt.

"Don't worry," he continued. "I've already recovered. The gods were with me. And I'm lucky. Mount Roaring wasn't much—just a farting *kappa* goblin. A kappa's supposed to be tasty, too. I've thought about getting hold of one and having myself a meal. Well, that's another matter. That was some surprise the other day. A real blaze. How'd you make out? Don't seem to have any burns. You got away quick, then, did you?"

"Got away quick, my foot!" the rabbit objected, looking quite peeved. "You're the one. You ran away and left me alone with that fire. The smoke was so stifling I almost choked to death. I was incensed. I realized then how little I meant to you. Now I can see what you're really like."

"I'm sorry, please forgive me. I got a bad burn too. Maybe the gods weren't with me. I ran up against it there. It's not that I forgot about you. You see, my back got scorched right away and I didn't have time for a rescue. Can't you see that? I'm no traitor—anyone would be helpless with a burn like that. And then there's that elementary—I mean, alimentary—salve or whatever it was. The worst thing—just terrible stuff. Doesn't help a dark complexion at all."

"A dark complexion?"

"No . . . I meant to say a dark, syrupy concoction. That was really strong. There was this odd runt—he looked a lot like you—and he said he wouldn't charge, either. Nothing ventured, nothing gained. And so I asked him to put some of it on. Good Lord! I tell you, be careful when the medicine's free. You can't be too cautious. I felt this whirlwind swirl right through my head and then I toppled over."

"Hmm," the rabbit murmured disdainfully. "Serves you right. That's the price for being stingy. Trying out a medicine because it was free—and not the least ashamed to tell about it, either."

"Damn your tongue," the badger muttered, although he didn't appear upset. Indeed, he seemed to bask in the warm presence of his sweetheart. He plopped down, his turbid, dead-fish eyes roaming about for something he could snatch up.

"Guess I'm just lucky," he uttered, gobbling an insect. "I keep ticking no matter what happens. The gods must be with me. You made it through, and this burn of mine got better without any trouble. So now we can just take it easy and have a chat. Ah, this is just like a dream."

The rabbit had been hoping he would leave, and now she could tolerate him no longer. He was so awful, she felt like dying. Desperate to be rid of him, she again came up with a devilish scheme.

"By the way," she asked, "have you heard that Lake Kawagu-chi is swarming with carp? They're supposed to be delicious."

"Nope, I haven't heard that," the badger replied, his eyes now sparkling. "When I was three years old, my old lady caught me a carp. That was some meal. But I can't even catch any sort of fish, let alone a carp. Not that I'm clumsy—no, not at all. I know how delicious carp is, but for some thirty-odd years now—hah-hah, there I go again, mimicking my older brother. He likes carp, too."

"Is that so?" the rabbit remarked offhandedly. "I don't care for it myself. But if you like it that much, I can take you fishing."

"Yeah?!" The badger was elated. "Those carp are slippery fellows, though. I tried catching one and almost went under for good." Having confessed to his own ineptitude, the bad-ger came right out and asked, "But how do you catch them?"

"It's easy with a net. Some really big carp have been coming near the shore at Ugashima. Well? Shall we give it a try? How about a boat? Do you know how to row?"

The badger sighed. "I wouldn't say I can't row. Not," he anxiously insisted, "if I put my mind to it."

"Then you do row?" The rabbit knew the badger was only putting on, but she pretended to believe him. "Ah, that's per-fect. I've got a boat, but it's so small we can't get in it together. It's not well made, and the flimsy boards always leak. I don't care about myself, but nothing must happen to you. Why don't we both pitch in and build you a boat? A wooden one's dangerous, so let's build something sturdy out of clay."

"Sorry to be such trouble. I'm about to weep—you won't mind if I have myself a good cry. Oh, why do I break down so easily?" But even as he pretended to weep, the badger came out with a brazen proposal. "Could you go ahead and build a sturdy boat, then? Huh, would you do that? I'll do something for you in return. Maybe I could put together a small meal while you're working. I do think I'd make a fine chef."

"Oh yes," the rabbit nodded, as if she agreed with this conceited opinion. The badger, musing about how indulgent people were, smiled gleefully—and thereby sealed his fate right then and there. The rabbit was nurturing a horrible scheme even as she pretended to indulge his silliness. But the simpering badger didn't notice. He merely thought that all was well.

When they arrived at Lake Kawaguchi, the surface was clear and utterly calm. The rabbit went quickly to work, kneading the clay for a fine, sturdy boat. For his part the badger scampered about diligently gathering a meal and mumbling over and over, 'Sorry to be such trouble." Eventually an evening breeze came up, and tiny waves rose all over the lake. In due course the small clay boat, gleaming like a piece of steel, slid into the water.

"Yep, not bad," the badger jested as he placed on board the large gasoline utility can that held the lunch. "You're good with your hands too—building such a nice boat in a twinkling. Now that's real talent," he concluded, a piece of flattery so transparent as to set your teeth on edge.

Greed, as well as lust, now held the badger in thrall. He imagined himself taking this clever, industrious girl for his wife, then living a life of ease and luxury on her labor. Regardless of what happened, he would cling to her forever. And, with this thought in mind, he clambered aboard.

"I guess you're pretty good at rowing too, then? When it

comes to rowing a boat, even I . . . certainly . . . Well, it's not that I don't know how. But just for today I'd like to observe my wife's skill." It was utter impudence, and it didn't stop there. "I used to row in the old days," he went on. "They called me an expert, a champ and all that. But I'll just lie here today and watch. Since it's all right with me, you go ahead and fasten my boat to yours. If our boats hug one another, we can only perish together. Don't abandon me now." After this odious and affected speech, the badger sprawled out on the bottom of his clay boat.

Did the fool suspect? Fasten my boat to yours—that remark had caught the rabbit off guard. One glimpse, though, and she knew that nothing was amiss. The badger was already dreaming, blissful love written all over his smiling face. The rabbit grinned scornfully as the badger began to mumble in his sleep—"Wake me up when the carp's ready. I can taste it now. Thirty-seven, that's me." Presently the rabbit tied the clay boat to her own and dipped her oar in the water. With a splash, the two boats slid away from the shore.

The Ugashima pines seemed to flare up, bathed as they were in the light of the setting sun. Now this next part will make me seem a know-it-all, but that's the pine grove pictured on a Shikishima cigarette pack. I've checked this out with a dependable person, and readers won't be any worse off taking my word for it. But then again, Shikishimas aren't around any longer, so younger readers won't care anyway. To them, I'll just be showing off about nothing. Pretend to know something, and you end up with this sort of foolishness. Oh, *those* pines! Perhaps readers thirty years or older—no one else—will faintly remember the pines, along with their geisha friends and parties. Maybe such readers can't do anything other than look bored.

"Ah, how lovely," the rabbit murmured, entranced by the sunset over Ugashima.

This is strange indeed. It seems that not even the worst

villain could be taken with natural beauty the moment before carrying out some cruel deed. Yet, our fifteen-year-old charmer squints her eyes and contemplates the scenery, an indication that innocence is truly a hairbreadth from villainy. Certain men will sigh—Ah, the Innocence of Youth—and drool over the nauseating affectations of a selfish, carefree teen. They had better watch out, though. She remains as composed as this rabbit, even while Murder and Intoxication dwell together in her breast. A wild and sensuous dance goes on, and no one notices. It's like the foam on beer—nothing more perilous.

Idiotic, demonic—such words come to mind when mere skin-deep feeling takes precedence over ethics. Some time ago, popular American movies portrayed boys and girls who were full of innocence. Highly endowed with this skin-deep feeling, they fidgeted around and darted about as if on springs. I don't mean to stretch things, but this "Innocence of Youth" I'm talking of might well be traced to America or thereabouts. It's just a Merrily-We-Ski-Along sort of thing.

On the other hand these innocents commit silly crimes without the least concern. That's the demonic, rather than idiotic, side of this. Or, maybe sometime in the past, the demonic was idiotic. Once comparable to Artemis the Moon Goddess—she of the graceful limbs and small, delicate figure—our fifteen-year-old rabbit has suddenly become dull and dreary. Idiotic, you say? Well, that's the way things go.

"Hyaa!" cries a strange voice from down below. It's that dear badger of mine, a thirty-seven-year-old male who's not the least bit innocent. "Water!" he cried, "it's water! This is awful!"

"What a nuisance you are! A clay boat's bound to sink. You didn't know that?"

"I don't get it. This is much too much. And not proper at all. Unreasonable—that's the word for it. Surely you wouldn't— not to me, anyway—surely not such a dastardly thing as . . . No, I don't get it at all. Aren't you my wife? Ya! I'm sinking!

That's all I can tell—I'm sinking! The joke's gone too far—it's almost a crime. Ya! I'm sinking! Hey, what're you doing to me? Won't the meal go to waste? There's earthworm macaroni and skunk droppings in the box. Isn't that a shame? Gulp! Ah, I just swallowed water. Look here, this bad joke's gone far enough. I'm begging you. Hey there, don't cut that rope! If we perish, it'll be together. Husband and wife for two lives—that's a bond you can't sever. No! Don't! Oh, now you've done it. Help! I can't swim! I'll be honest with you. In the old days I could swim a little, but the muscles stiffen here and there on a thirty-seven-year-old badger. I can't swim at all. I'll be honest. I'm thirty-seven—too old for you, really. But you mustn't forget the old maxims—Respect Your Elders! Help the Aged! Gulp! Ah, you're a nice girl. So act like you should now and stretch your oar over here. I'll get a grip on . . . Ouch! What're you doing? Don't you know that hurts—banging an oar on someone's head really hurts! So *that's* it. I get it. You mean to kill me. Now I know." Faced with his own death, the badger finally saw into the rabbit's scheme. But it was too late.

The oar banged mercilessly against his skull time after time. The water glistened in the sunset as the badger sank into the lake and rose to the surface over and over again.

"Ouch! Ouch! Aren't you going too far? What did I do to you? What's wrong with falling in love?" he exclaimed before going under for good.

Wiping her brow, the rabbit declared, "Whew, I'm drenched with sweat."

So, what have we here? A cautionary tale on lust? A comedy scented with advice on avoiding pretty teenagers? Or perhaps an ethics lesson that bids the suitor to moderate his delight in the beloved? After all, persistent visits provoke such contempt that one's life is endangered.

But maybe the tale is mostly humorous, merely hinting

that people don't revile and chastise one another because of morality. (Actually, they do these things simply out of hatred, just as they praise others or submit to them out of affection.)

But no, let's not fret over what conclusions a social critic might reach. Sighing, we allow instead the last word to our badger—"What's wrong with falling in love?"

That sums up, briefly and without any exaggeration, all of the world's woeful tales from the days of old. In every woman dwells this cruel rabbit, while in every man a good badger always struggles against drowning. In the mere thirty-odd years of your author's life, uneventful though they be, this has been made utterly clear. And probably, dear reader, it's the same with you. I'll just skip the rest of it, however.

Published by Tuttle Publishing, an imprint of Periplus Editions (HK) Ltd.

www.tuttlepublishing.com

English translation copyright © 2024 James O'Brien

Library of Congress Catalog-in-Publication Data in progress

ISBN 978-4-8053-1834-8

27 26 25 24
10 9 8 7 6 5 4 3 2 1   2405VP

Printed in Malaysia

TUTTLE PUBLISHING® is a registered trademark of Tuttle Publishing, a division of Periplus Editions (HK) Ltd.

Distributed by:

North America, Latin America & Europe
Tuttle Publishing
364 Innovation Drive
North Clarendon
VT 05759 9436, USA
Tel: 1(802) 773 8930
Fax: 1(802) 773 6993
info@tuttlepublishing.com
www.tuttlepublishing.com

Asia Pacific
Berkeley Books Pte Ltd
3 Kallang Sector #04-01
Singapore 349278
Tel: (65) 6741-2178
Fax: (65) 6741-2179
inquiries@periplus.com.sg
www.tuttlepublishing.com

Japan
Tuttle Publishing
Yaekari Building, 3rd Floor
5-4-12 Osaki Shinagawa-ku
Tokyo 141 0032 Japan
Tel: 81 (3) 5437 0171
Fax: 81 (3) 5437 0755
sales@tuttle.co.jp
www.tuttle.co.jp